PENGUIN

THE ANGEL OF EDEN

D.J. MCINTOSH's *The Witch of Babylon* has been sold in twenty countries, was shortlisted for the Crime Writers' Association Debut Dagger Award, and won a Crime Writers of Canada Arthur Ellis Award for best unpublished novel. It was a national bestseller, an Amazon.ca Best Book, and was named one of CNN's Most Enduring Historical Thrillers. McIntosh is a member of the Canadian Society for Mesopotamian Studies. She is a strong supporter of Reporters Without Borders and the Committee to Protect Journalists. She lives in Toronto.

D1224652

Also by D.J. McIntosh

The Witch of Babylon
The Book of Stolen Tales

THE **ANGEL** OF **EDEN**

D.J.McIntosh

PENGUIN

an imprint of Penguin Canada Books Inc., a Penguin Random House Company

Published by the Penguin Group

Penguin Canada Books Inc., 90 Eglinton Avenue East, Suite 700, Toronto, Ontario, Canada M4P 2Y3

Penguin Group (USA) LLC, 375 Hudson Street, New York, New York 10014, U.S.A.
Penguin Books Ltd, 80 Strand, London WC2R 0RL, England
Penguin Ireland, 25 St Stephen's Green, Dublin 2, Ireland (a division of Penguin Books Ltd)
Penguin Group (Australia), 707 Collins Street, Melbourne, Victoria 3008, Australia
(a division of Pearson Australia Group Pty Ltd)
Penguin Books India Pvt Ltd, 11 Community Centre, Panchsheel Park, New Delhi – 110 017, India
Penguin Group (NZ), 67 Apollo Drive, Rosedale, Auckland 0632, New Zealand
(a division of Pearson New Zealand Ltd)
Penguin Books (South Africa) (Pty) Ltd, 24 Sturdee Avenue, Rosebank, Johannesburg 2196, South
Africa

Penguin Books Ltd, Registered Offices: 80 Strand, London WC2R 0RL, England

First published 2015

1 2 3 4 5 6 7 8 9 10 (RRD)

*Publisher's note: This book is a work of fiction. Names, characters, places and incidents either are the product of
the author's imagination or are used fictitiously, and any resemblance to actual persons living or dead, events,
or locales is entirely coincidental.*

Manufactured in the U.S.A.

LIBRARY AND ARCHIVES CANADA CATALOGUING IN PUBLICATION

McIntosh, D. J. (Dorothy J.), author
The angel of Eden / D.J. McIntosh.

ISBN 978-0-14-317576-6 (pbk.)

I. Title.

PS8625.I53A75 2015   C813'.6   C2015-900012-2

eBook ISBN 978-0-14-319456-9

Visit the Penguin Canada website at **www.penguin.ca**

Special and corporate bulk purchase rates available; please see
www.penguin.ca/corporatesales or call 1-800-810-3104.

For my sister Ellen and daughter Kenlyn
who always make sure the wind is at my back

The Angel of Eden is Book Three of the Mesopotamian Trilogy, symbolized by Enki, the Sumerian god of wisdom and magic, associated with the serpent. The story begins in February, the month of evil spirits.

The real Faust lived in fifteenth-century Germany. Some branded him a charlatan; others regarded him as a gifted magician. His death was never verified.

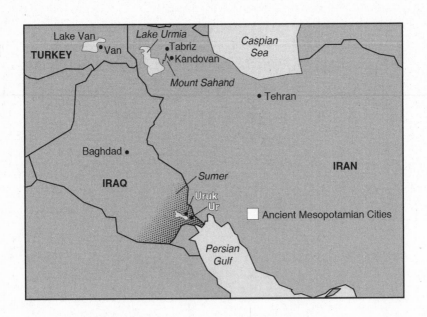

December 1970

Kandovan, Northwestern Iran

Yeva fed and watered the sheep and herded the brown hens into their coops for the night. When only soft rustlings and clucks could be heard she breathed deeply and closed the latch. Sweat slipped down her back and gathered in the curve at her tailbone. Damp spots showed on her dress underneath her arms and around her waist. She fumbled with the dusty serape wrapped around the infant in an effort to conceal the mark near his jaw. The baby's rosy cheeks puffed as he let out a breath. She touched his forehead lightly and he smiled in his sleep.

He is a good boy, no matter what they say.

To the east, the cloudless sky grew dark on the horizon. A pale sphere of moon hung like an ancient coin suspended between heaven and earth. A chorus of crickets sang from the high cliffs. The waning sun turned the tops of the sparse cedars to copper. All spoke of a peace she did not feel.

With the animals tended, she'd run out of excuses to stay outside. She had to go in now and face her father. Surely the whispers she'd heard earlier were false. Had the village men not already exacted a terrible price? Did they want even more vengeance?

Yeva thought of the strange book and shuddered. She'd chosen the hiding place carefully. Prayed it would stay concealed.

A blast of hot air met her as she pushed open the wooden door to the old stone building. The house had sheltered her family for generations, just how far back no one knew. Its very walls were a part of her. Despite the sweltering day, fire roared in the old iron stove; its metal casing glowed amber in the darkened room. The home's few windows were closed, turning the space into a hot, dry cavern.

Candles illuminated her father standing by the stove. His shoulders were hunched, his arthritic hands crooked from years of outdoor work, his skin the color of old leather. "You're late," he said, without turning to her.

She replied softly in the flickering gloom. "The baby slows me down, Papa. It takes longer to finish my tasks."

Her father cast a furtive glance at the bundle she held close. *He's afraid of his own blood,* Yeva thought.

He looked away and put an old enamel kettle on the stove. It hissed and sputtered. "They are coming tonight, Yeva. You must leave. You should have gone already."

"I can't part with you, Papa!"

He shook his head sadly and brushed his hand over his brow. "You will go tonight, Yeva. They killed that man in front of my eyes. Do you need any more proof?"

He picked up a small cloth bag from the table and held it out. He did not take a step toward her and still refused to meet her gaze. "Your brother is waiting with the horse behind the house; Alaz is impatient to leave. And your sister packed a few things. Food, enough for several days. She will take the mountain trail and meet with you as agreed. There is money in here to last you a while. It isn't much, but it will have to do. My cousin will receive you both in Tabriz. You remember how to reach his house?"

She nodded and took the bag. The child stirred in his slumber as if he felt her apprehension. She whispered, "My life is here, Papa. How can I leave it behind?"

"Only think of the pain in an old man's heart if he is forced to watch his family die."

She wanted to embrace him but a slight shake of his head stopped her. *He does not want to touch his grandson,* she realized.

When he spoke next, his voice was stronger. "Give me the book. When the village men come, I will throw it in the stove and they can see it burn. That may appease them. Where is it?"

Yeva gestured toward a wooden cabinet, the only fine piece of furniture in the small dwelling. "I put it in the space behind the middle drawer."

Her father walked over to the cabinet, pulled open the drawer, and reached in. He felt in the space and then grasped the old volume, its leather covers battered with wear, its papers tissue-thin and browned.

He raised his anxious eyes to hers. "Who would think that simple words inked out on a page could cause so much trouble, words in a language that is not ours, from a country we've never seen." He touched his hand to his lips and held it up to her. The boiling kettle began to squeal. "May God keep you safe, daughter. Now go."

Yeva rode behind her brother on her father's Kurdish horse, one arm supporting the baby wrapped in the serape and pressed to her stomach. With her other, she gripped a short plaited rope fixed to the saddle. Alaz kicked the horse's flanks to hurry it up the hill behind the house. She could smell the musky odor of sheep and grass on her brother's rough shirt, feel every rise and drop of the mare's fat rump. The night wind brought with it pungent fragrances of thyme and cedar.

Once they approached the river, Yeva chanced a sidelong glance at the ancient cypress tree. Gnarled and misshapen like her father's hands, hard as iron, it was said to be over a thousand years old. The ground beneath it appeared undisturbed and she uttered a silent prayer. It was a safe hiding place for the real book and well chosen.

Far above her the moon sailed high in the heavens and one bright star shone in the sky.

Part One

THE MAGICIAN

The only magic is really that of words.

—DR. THOMAS ERNST

One

February 14, 2005
New York

The box of sweets arrived by courier on Valentine's Day morning while I read the *Times* over black coffee and toast. I'd thought about running out for a proper breakfast, but the driving rain deterred me. To be honest, I was wallowing a little, feeling somewhat adrift, which explains why I was still in my robe when the courier knocked. At the kitchen table I unwrapped the package he brought. Bittersweet chocolate truffles from Black Hounds in a heart-shaped wooden box. They were a guilty pleasure to be sure and one of my favorites. Someone had done their research.

A card accompanied the box, nothing fussy, no valentine hearts and flowers, just a white card with "Have a Good Day" stenciled in gold. Inside, in a fine hand, was a simple message:

> *I'd love to meet you to discuss a project I'm working on.*
> *Please give me a call.*
> *Margaux Elizabeth Bennet, Ghostwriter*
> *(555) 671-2349*

Never take candy from a stranger. I smiled to myself as I bit into a truffle and looked again at the card. I didn't know anyone named Margaux. That alone might have tempted me to call and any woman with such superb taste in chocolates was worth meeting. After a few rings her voice mail came on. I left a message to say that although I was extremely busy, I might be able to squeeze her in around four P.M. The extremely busy part wasn't true, but it's never a good move for a guy to appear too eager. Margaux. The name conjured up a statuesque, high-heeled platinum blonde with scarlet lipstick and great legs. My day was looking up.

A quick glance around the apartment convinced me I'd been spending too much time alone. Clothes hung over the backs of chairs, dirty coffee cups were stacked in the sink. I spent the next hour tidying up.

The apartment was a stone's throw away from Madison Square Park. Unfortunately it wasn't mine; I'd moved here from my cramped unit in Queens thanks to a friend on a European sabbatical willing to sublet for less than a king's ransom. The park makeover in 2000 had spurred a frenzy of building renovations in the area and this place, too, was slated for an overhaul into luxury digs. It was a temporary home, but it felt good to be back in Manhattan.

Despite a dubious talent for landing myself in situations of high peril, I'd actually enjoyed the uneventful pace of my life for the last year or so. I'd been dividing my time between my new interest in hunting for rare books on behalf of clients and the steadier occupation of dealing in art and antiquities. So far, business was going well.

Like me, many residents in the building ran commercial ventures out of their apartments. As I had next to no walk-in trade, it never caused a problem. Still, we had nothing as fancy as a doorman, just a security guard who came on duty in the late afternoon. At precisely one minute after four, the guard rang up to announce my visitor. I spruced up my hair and threw on a jacket.

After a tentative tap on the door I opened it to find a gray-eyed waif, auburn hair wringing wet from the rain, wearing no lipstick I could discern, scarlet or otherwise. Her well-scuffed flats would have been sensible if they hadn't been soaked and her beige belted trench coat was much too thin for February. Petite and very pretty, she clutched a battered leather briefcase to her chest as if it held her life savings.

She extended her damp hand. "Mr. Madison? I must look a sight." She gave me an uncertain smile. "I forgot my umbrella. I considered going back for it but didn't want to be late." Then she grinned widely and warmly, showing a confidence that seemed at odds with her apologetic words.

I took her arm and ushered her inside. "Margaux Bennet, it's nice to meet you, wet or not."

She freed one hand from her briefcase and shook mine. Hers was cold and damp. "Please call me Bennet. Everybody does. Thanks for agreeing to see me on such short notice."

"Well, thank you for the chocolates." I helped her off with her coat. The cream-colored pullover she wore over a miniskirt was damp around the neck. "Would you like to dry off?" I gestured to the hallway. "The bathroom's just to the right down the hall. Help yourself to a towel. And while you're doing that, why don't I make us a coffee?"

"Any chance of something a little … stronger?" A mischievous smile lit up her eyes.

A lady after my own heart. "Would brandy do?"

"Perfect. It's cold out there!" She gave a little shiver as if to prove her point. She set down her briefcase, slipped off her shoes, and padded down the hall in her nylon feet, leaving wet footprints on the hardwood.

When she came back, her cheeks were pink and her hair had been tidied so it cascaded in curly ringlets to her shoulders. I detected a delicate hint of perfume. She looked around the apartment like an insurance appraiser. "Very nice place, Mr. Madison."

The main living area was one large room; with the judicious placement of a high credenza, I'd managed to screen off a section of it for my office. I handed her the brandy snifter. "Please call me John, and have a seat." I plumped myself down in my desk armchair. She sat on the sofa, curled up her legs, and made an unsuccessful attempt to pull her skirt down to cover her knees. A nice view. I'd had the "great legs" part right, anyway.

She took a staggeringly large gulp, enough brandy to paralyze a horse, and smiled. "That's better," she said, tipping her glass toward me. "Much appreciated. I saw a photo of you taken a couple of years ago. You haven't changed much. Don't see a lot of guys with beards, although—" She caught herself. "What I mean to say is, they're coming back in fashion again."

"A photo of me?"

"Yes. Where was it? I can't remember. Newspaper, maybe? You were born in Turkey but raised here—right? I can see that in your face." She bubbled on, "Kind of dark and exotic looking."

She was certainly forthright. "Well, I'm relieved you approve."

Bennet laughed and looked around the room with what seemed to be another admiring glance. Her eyes lingered on the paintings that had once belonged to my brother Samuel and then shifted to the precious Mesopotamian artifacts displayed on glass shelves that he'd brought back from his research trips. "You have great taste." She noticed the box of chocolates on the side table beside my chair, half empty. Her cheeks dimpled. "You've eaten an awful lot of those already."

"Well, yes. I assumed that's what they were meant for. How did you know I like that brand?"

"Claire Talbot told me."

An art world diva who loved to gossip, Claire had a rep for being as rapacious as a hyena. But she did know me pretty well. I could just imagine the rundown of foibles she'd given Bennet. "Claire a friend of yours?"

"No. I found an article online that said you two had once collaborated on a charity art show, so I contacted her. I wasn't sure how best to approach you and wanted to get some background."

"Background for what, precisely?"

"The article I'm writing about you."

Two

I set my glass down carefully on the desk top. In recent years my life had been more interesting than most—including some scrapes with the law—but someone going to the trouble of writing about it caught me off guard. "An article about me. To be published? For what reason?"

It occurred to me that I was in the hands of a scammer. A woman who preyed upon people's egos to dash off some digital masterpiece, throw it up online, and charge the subject a hefty fee for the pleasure of seeing his life story in print. "Let's cut to the chase. You're expecting me to pay for this *project*—correct?"

"Oh, no. I've given you the wrong impression. I've been hired to do it." I stared at her. She blushed and went into damage-control mode. "I'm sorry to have put that so clumsily. People say I have a habit of being too blunt."

"Hired by whom?" I imagined a hatchet job orchestrated by a disgruntled client, angry heirs challenging established provenances.

A headache started to form behind my right eye.

"Lucas Strauss."

I frowned. "Never heard of him. What's his interest?"

"I'm not sure exactly. He had me pitch the idea to *American Archaeology* magazine. A profile of you and your recent trips to the Middle East. I understand your brother was quite an expert in ancient Assyrian culture. And of course there's tremendous interest in Mesopotamia with the war going on and all ..."

She paused, catching the puzzled look on my face. "It will definitely be published—with your cooperation or without it. Strauss is very determined and he has a lot of media contacts."

I threw back some brandy and tried to stem my rising annoyance. Freelancers often pitched ideas to magazines, but a third party hiring them to do it seemed odd. "Who is this Lucas Strauss and why would he have any interest in me?"

"I can answer the first question for you." She picked up her briefcase, snapped the locks, and fumbled with the papers inside. "Here," she said, handing over a single page.

The photograph looked as if it had been printed off the internet: an imposing man dressed in a tux, his longish white hair swept off his face. The arresting blue eyes framed by dark brows contrasted oddly with the hair. He had slim, elegant fingers and the formidable scowl of someone used to having others do his bidding. A dead ringer for Christopher Lee. The short biographical text underneath indicated that he was unmarried, born in 1929, and educated at Harvard.

"Is he a collector? Did he know my brother?"

"He's an illusionist. A famous one. He only takes on private sessions as a spiritualist now but was once one of the foremost magicians in the world."

"A magician. As in 'hocus pocus'?"

She carried on as if she hadn't heard me. "I'm afraid that's all I can tell you. He didn't explain why he wanted me to take on the job. I know this must sound bizarre."

"Oh, just a little," I laughed. It creeped me out that a complete stranger was taking such an interest in my life. I didn't care for that kind of scrutiny, especially by some hack trickster. "Look, Bennet, I don't know what kind of game is going on but I'm not interested in playing it. I don't even know if you're who you say you are. I think we should end this conversation."

She made no move to get up. "There is no game. Not on my part anyway. I'm entirely legitimate. I make my living ghostwriting for celebrities." She rattled off some names, including a former baseball commissioner and a film actor in her early twenties who'd barely had enough life experience to warrant a paragraph. "You're welcome to verify all that," she said, handing me a business card. "This is my editor. I do a lot of work for her publishing house. Feel free to check me out."

When this didn't generate the response Bennet wanted, she persisted: "I've been hired to write this piece and it's going to happen. I'm not in a position to turn down paying jobs. Anyway, wouldn't you want to be involved so you'll be cast in the best light?" She dangled that last remark with a sympathetic turn of her lips that seemed sincere. "As to Lucas Strauss's motive, I'm as much in the dark as you." She pulled out her phone and looked at the time. "I'm starving. Any chance you'd be interested in dinner? There's a neat little place not far away. The chef does Loire Valley cuisine."

"It's Valentine's Day. I have a prior engagement."

Her lips now flirted with a pout. "Oh. It's just. Claire Talbot told me you weren't dating anyone at the moment."

I cursed Claire under my breath. "There's much about my life I don't share with Claire." I walked over to the closet in the vestibule.

Her coat was still damp. "I'm afraid I've run out of time. I hope you've warmed up by now." I saw out the window that the rain hadn't let up. "You're welcome to borrow an umbrella."

She rose reluctantly, stepped into her shoes. I helped her on with her coat. She took the umbrella and, putting on a suitably humble expression, made another plea.

"Please at least consider it. Times are difficult for writers, you know. I haven't had any real work in months and Strauss promised a generous fee. Are you sure you can't help me out?"

"I'm sorry," I said with a stony-faced shake of my head.

She had one more pitch in her repertoire. Her face lit up as if she'd just thought of the idea. "How about I arrange for you to meet Strauss?"

"And why would I want to do that?"

"Aren't you even the least bit curious?"

"No. And now I'll thank you for your time." Her shoulders slumped. I handed her the briefcase, held the door open politely, and watched her walk down the corridor.

Once she'd gone, I poured myself another healthy measure of brandy, put on Coldplay, sank back in the armchair, and stared at nothing. Life had been good throughout the last year except in one important respect. The physical and emotional punishment I'd endured on my last visit to Iraq had left me weakened. I suffered from sleep paralysis and the episodes had grown longer and more frequent. I'd wake up and find myself unable to move a muscle, unable to speak. It terrified me and I'd begun to fear falling asleep. A specialist had reassured me it was a common enough experience and said my anxiety likely made the syndrome worse. I'd taken to drugging myself with sleeping pills. On top of that, the blood disorder I'd been diagnosed with last year, a genetic anomaly that medicine couldn't put a name to, still worried me.

Until the accident that claimed Samuel's life and nearly killed me, I'd taken my strength and endurance for granted, looking forward to the future. Lately, though, I'd grown afraid for my well-being.

The only remedy I'd found for those night terrors was to indulge in punishing physical exercise. Mostly that took the form of rock climbing and extreme trekking. If I pushed myself to the limit, the experience seemed to stabilize me. In January, with a client who'd become a friend, I'd tackled the Devil's Path in the Catskills. Three days were recommended to cover the entire route, considered the riskiest and most challenging on the East Coast. We accomplished it in two, climbing the treacherous route up six mountain peaks, the highest almost four thousand feet. On our second night out a downpour turned into freezing rain, lashing our faces—and nothing focuses the mind like trying to gain a handhold in a rock crevice smaller than your baby finger when you can't open your eyes to see. My more cerebral fears and worries fled in the face of such immediate physical danger.

But the relief was always temporary, typically lasting only a few weeks. And now I had another worry. Bennet's peculiar proposition unnerved me. More than I'd let on.

Three

Despite the rain I was obliged to go out. I'd found a rare street-parking spot on East Twenty-first at Gramercy Park but needed to move my car before six P.M. I welcomed the brisk, fresh air and hoped a change of scene would dispel the gloom that had settled over me after my conversation with Bennet.

I reached my car with ten minutes to spare, a silver Porsche I was able to afford only because I got it for a steal off a bankrupt stock trader. I went to unlock my door when a sound caught my ear. A low whine came from somewhere near the trunk. I edged around to the rear of the car. The whine came again, more of a whimper this time. I stooped to check the undercarriage. Beneath the bumper, wedged in behind the right wheel, a black dog lay motionless on the pavement. Had it run out from the park into the street, been hit, and crawled to what it thought was a place of safety? I would have backed over it when I moved the car out.

I got an old towel from the trunk, spread it on the passenger seat, and gently picked up the dog. It was a little larger than a beagle and surprisingly light. Its head hung loosely, its mouth slack. Streaks of blood and white spittle mottled its pale tongue.

The dog didn't stir from where I'd laid it on the seat. I pressed my hand against its side to comfort it and felt the ridges of its rib bones sticking out under the layer of skin. It had no collar.

It looked like some kind of cross, with a long tail and upright ears like a German shepherd, its black fur matted and unkempt. If it lived I'd have to figure out how to return it to the owner, if it had one, and who in any case didn't deserve to get it back.

After checking on my phone, I found an emergency veterinary clinic wedged beside the Bentley Hotel on a bleak corner that saw a constant stampede of traffic heading for the FDR. When I walked in with the dog in my arms, the receptionist took one look and picked up the receiver, pointing me up the ramp to the second floor. Upstairs, a tall, thin, white-coated man came out and motioned for me to follow him into an examining room. As he snapped on latex gloves he asked me to place the dog on a waist-high stainless steel table. "I'm Dr. Jefferson," he said. "Tell me what happened here."

After I explained, he grunted something in response and began a preliminary examination, lifting the eyelids, listening for a heartbeat with a stethoscope, palpating the dog's chest, checking its neck, limbs, and pelvis.

When he finished he leveled his gaze at me. "Did you hit the animal with your car, sir? It's had a bad battering. The left hind leg is broken, and there are likely acute internal injuries."

"No. As I said, I found it under my car. The dog must have crawled there after someone else hit it."

"This is no dog," Jefferson said in a grim voice.

"What?"

"It's probably a coyote, or more likely a hybrid, a feral mix with a domestic canine. I won't be able to tell without further examination." He indicated the paws. "These are larger than you'd see on most dogs." He lifted an eyelid. "And the irises are yellowish—wolflike."

"A coyote? Are you serious? Wow. How could it get into the city?"

"Where exactly did you find it?"

"Right outside Gramercy Park."

Jefferson fiddled with the stethoscope around his neck. "Probably came straight across the Williamsburg Bridge at night. They'll hide during the day and hunt nocturnally. Pigeons, rats, garbage, pet food that people leave out for stray cats—it's a gourmet feast out there. They caught one in Central Park a couple of years ago."

I touched its back. "I didn't think coyotes had black fur."

"That's one reason I believe it's a cross with a domestic dog." He studied me. "Are you all right yourself? You seem upset. Not your fault if it darted into traffic. Just a simple accident, that's all."

Just a simple accident. For an instant the picture of my brother crumpled in the wreckage of my car flashed in front of me. If only that sin of mine could be absolved as graciously.

"The animal was already in very poor condition before it was hit," Jefferson continued. "I doubt it will make it through the night. Even if it does survive, the leg break won't heal properly. And if it's a dog–coyote hybrid as I assume, wildlife centers won't take it. The kindest course of action would be to euthanize it."

"Hell." I looked down at the broken coyote, its breath shallow and ragged. Pain pulsed behind my eye. The lights were so bright in here. With injuries that severe, I couldn't argue with the vet. Still, I felt torn about the thought of putting it down.

As if it understood, the dog emitted something between a whimper and a moan. It tried to open its eyes but could only raise the lids halfway when they drooped again. Jefferson's tone remained solemn. "You see how much effort that took. It can't even open its eyes. It will just go to sleep. The procedure is absolutely painless."

It took a few more moments for me to come to my senses. There was no point wasting any more time. "Go ahead then. You can send me an invoice for whatever it costs."

The vet's expression softened. "There's no need for that. You've made the humane decision."

The dog let out a tortured breath as I left the examination room. I tried to shut the sound out of my brain, embarrassed I even cared.

Four

I sat in the car with the key in the ignition, staring blindly through the windshield as if some invisible hand had locked on to me, forcing me to keep vigil for the injured creature. Why did I feel so bad? I hadn't done anything but offer it help and yet it seemed as if I'd shirked some duty. After a few minutes I rushed back to the clinic. The reception room was deserted. My stomach lurched. Had Jefferson ended its life in this short time?

When I barged through the door of the treatment room, the vet jerked his head up in surprise. He'd shaved a square of fur off the front leg. Beside it on the table lay two large syringes, one containing a blue liquid and the other a toxic-looking pink.

My heart pounded. "Have you done it yet?"

"No."

"I've changed my mind. Don't, please."

"Why not?"

I looked from his eyes to the dog on the table. "I just want it to live."

Jefferson shook his head. "It has very little chance of surviving, Mr. Madison. Do you know anything about wild animals?"

"Not really."

"Nine times out of ten they'll die out of fright, even with milder injuries. Merely the shock of being confined can kill them. I can treat this little one if that's what you want, but I'll have to charge you for its care. It'll be quite expensive and you'd be spending your money for nothing."

"That's okay. I'll pay for him. Whatever it takes."

"And you're prepared to take full responsibility for it?" I nodded. I had friends with country property; maybe they could be persuaded to look after it.

He waited a minute or so to see how resolute I was, then gave in with a shake of his head. "All right. It's quiet so far tonight. I'm on duty till seven A.M. I'll do what I can, but if an emergency comes through the door it takes precedence. Understood?"

I nodded, feeling a strange sense of elation. He promised to call me before he finished his shift.

"Oh, and one other thing," he said as I turned to go.

"What's that?"

"It's not a *him*."

"Pardon me?"

He pointed to the animal. "*She* is female."

When I arrived back home and checked my email, I found a message from Bennet.

Her high, exuberant tones echoed in every word. *"Great news! I spoke with Lucas Strauss and he's agreed to meet you. The appointment's for eight tomorrow night. I'll stop by your place at seven-thirty to pick you up. Looking forward to seeing you again!"*

She'd completely ignored my brush-off. What was her deal? Tenacious or just oblivious? Probably the former, given her desire to secure the job. Her pushiness bothered me all over again and I got set to tap out a rapid reply telling her to forget it. Then I had second thoughts. I should at least figure out who I was dealing with.

I Googled her profile and found she'd indeed been telling the truth, about her work at least. She'd ghosted a couple of memoirs posing as autobiographies; one of them had even hit the *New York Times* bestseller list. That probably had more to do with the publicity-seeking celebrity she was writing about than the quality of her prose, but still. I also found a smattering of magazine articles, mostly star-struck interviews under her byline. Glossy, frivolous pieces. Certainly not hard-hitting investigative journalism. She was pretty active on Facebook. I started to relax a little. Her bio was brief. She'd grown up in Connecticut, her father a banker, her mother a homemaker. She'd been educated at Bryn Mawr, on Daddy's money I assumed. The picture of a classic New England colonial complete with floppy-eared dog on the portico appeared in my mind's eye. No mention of siblings. Only child, then? Probably spoiled, her tenacity presumably a raging case of entitlement. I was likely the first person who'd ever said no to her. Her age was the only surprise. Thirty-one. I'd guessed younger.

Despite my misgivings about the whole thing, I emailed her to say I'd accept her invitation. I wanted to size up Strauss, to learn more about the man. His interest did not sit well with me.

February 15, 2005

Dr. Jefferson called the next morning to say the dog had pulled through and her injuries weren't as bad as he'd first thought. If she continued to improve at this rate, I could pick her up the following day.

I spent the next hours on my computer tracking down an item for a client, a 1536 volume of nineteen sermons about the peril of untruthful teachers, authored by the fiery Savonarola. The history behind the piece was fascinating but I had to fight to keep my attention on the job. I was keyed up and restless. I gave up mid-afternoon, made some coffee, and called the friends who had a large acreage near Kingston. I explained the situation with the coyote hybrid. Startled to hear that a wild animal that big could end up in Manhattan, they sympathized with her condition but said their two mastiffs would likely maul her. They suggested I call a relative of theirs with a farm upstate; he declined as well. He didn't give a reason and his gruff tone suggested he wasn't interested in prolonging the conversation. I gave up, got a quick steak and salad at a nearby restaurant, and then picked up some dog food, a leash, and bowls at a Gristedes. Would a coyote walk on a leash? I'd soon find out.

I showered, clipped my beard, and dried my hair. I chose a smart shirt, a Rick Owens leather jacket, and black trousers for my appointment with Strauss.

Bennet's call came at seven-fifteen. "I'm ten minutes away."

A yellow cab was idling by the curb by the time I made it downstairs. Bennet looked less disheveled than the day before, her red hair smoothed and held back on one side with a black barrette. She wore the same trench but had added a silk scarf and put diamond studs in her ears. Fake, no doubt, but they looked attractive.

"You look nice," I said when I slid in beside her.

"Thanks. You too."

"Where are we headed?"

"A townhouse in Carroll Gardens. It should be an *interesting* evening." She smiled at me, her eyes sparkling with mischief.

"Why do you say that?"

"You'll see soon enough." She turned her head and gazed out the window at the buildings lining the street as if to dissuade any further questions. "I love that church," she said, indicating a Romanesque Revival structure of gray stone. "When I used to come to Manhattan during school breaks as a teenager, it felt so free being here. My friend's parents were always traveling, so I'd stay at her place—it was just a couple of blocks away. The two of us had the apartment to ourselves. We'd often pass by this church when we went out."

I glanced out the window. "The Swedish Lutheran. I love the bright red doors. It's an elegant building."

"Yes. Not gaudy at all."

I realized I had no idea where she lived. "Did you move here eventually?"

"Oh yeah. I have a nice place on the eight hundred block, Fifth Avenue."

"Overlooking the park?"

She nodded. "Great location, close to the shops."

Close to the shops. As in Saks, Bergdorf's, Bulgari. "Ghostwriting must be lucrative."

"Oh, it is. The advance for my last memoir just about covered my car insurance. I was kidding. I couldn't afford to rent a closet on Canal Street let alone a Fifth Avenue apartment. Sure wish it were otherwise. How about you?"

"Grew up here and feel the same way you do. Best place on earth."

"You don't by any chance need a live-in domestic, do you?"

"Room and board only?"

"Deal." Bennet laughed, but I had the sudden sense that she might be half serious. She kept up a running chatter as we drove, remarking on everything but the subject of our meeting tonight. I tried to pry the information out of her, with no success. If you ignored her in-your-face style she could actually be quite witty. Despite my frustration, I found myself enjoying her company.

Five

The cab pulled up in front of a stately townhouse set well back from the street. It was one of those places with a large front garden that the district was famous for. Bennet hopped out when we came to a stop, leaving me to fork over the tab.

"I'll need a ten from you to share the bill," I said when I got out.

"Of course." She rooted around in her leather purse. "Oh, I'm sorry. I forgot to go to the bank and I'm low on change. Pay you back later?" Ignoring my frown, she grinned and reached for my hand as we went down the front walk. Bennet tapped the old-fashioned knocker on the imposing front door.

A tall woman with dusty blond hair opened the door. Her eyes were puffy and swollen and had the distant, strained look of bereavement. Bennet introduced us.

The woman, Gina, said, "Welcome. Mr. Strauss said to expect you." She showed us where to stow our coats and then led us into a luxuriously appointed salon. Three damask couches had been placed around a gleaming mahogany coffee table. I was surprised to find three other people already seated when we entered the room. "Isn't this Lucas Strauss's house?" I whispered to Bennet. "I thought it was supposed to be a private meeting."

"Shush." Bennet put her finger to her lips. "He isn't here yet. And no, it's Gina's house." She smiled brightly at the other guests, one young man and a couple around my age. The young guy resembled Gina so much I figured he must be her son. He didn't bother to hide the bored expression on his face, clearly wishing he wasn't here. I sympathized. After we took a seat on the vacant couch, Gina made the introductions. The younger man was indeed her son, the other two her daughter and son-in-law. She offered each of us a glass of claret from a silver tray. I swirled the wine in my glass, gave Bennet a dark look, then lowered my voice. "Tell me what the hell's going on or I'm leaving."

"Gina lost her husband a few months ago. Lucas will conduct a spiritualist demonstration. He wanted you to see it before you talk."

"Are you saying this is some kind of *séance*?"

Bennet smiled sweetly at the couple across from us before turning and whispering fiercely in my ear, "They're not called that anymore. It's termed channeling. Wait and see."

I considered making my excuses but Gina already seemed close to tears. Disrupting the event by leaving might upset her even more.

I glanced around the room for want of anything better to do. Two floor-to-ceiling windows overlooked a back garden; the bare tree branches outside still glistened from yesterday's rain. An elaborate cornice of pale gray–painted wood ran around the perimeter of the twelve-foot ceiling. A stately Italianate chandelier hung from a decorative plaster base. Facing us and set against the east wall was a piece of furniture oddly out of keeping with the elegant room: a coffin-shaped box of finished pine, about six feet high and three feet wide, standing upright on its base, completely open in front. Inside, someone had placed a chair. As I wondered what purpose this would serve, Gina dimmed the chandelier. She turned on a floor lamp beside the coffin that cast a reddish glow and sat down beside her son.

The salon doors opened. Lucas Strauss towered in the entrance. The couple who'd been quietly chatting clammed up the minute they saw him. "Good evening," he said, without a smile cracking his lips. He wore a white shirt and black tux for the performance— for surely that was what we were about to witness. He looked around at the assembled mourners until his eyes rested on Gina and he gave her a sympathetic nod.

As he walked past us his gaze fastened on me, so intensely it made me want to avert my eyes. Surprisingly, he took the seat inside the box. He pulled out a small white towel, reached into his pocket again, and withdrew a short knife with a cruel hooked blade. He spoke in a low baritone. A voice that commanded attention. "As you may know, I like to start my sessions with a feat of magic. It sets the tone, if you will, for what is to come. Let us begin."

Strauss removed his tuxedo jacket, hung it carefully on a peg inside the coffin, then rolled up his left sleeve to expose the pale skin of his forearm, roped with blue veins. He beckoned to Gina. She stood up and walked over to him, rather haltingly. He grasped her forearm and slashed the knife downward.

Gina gasped. For a second I feared she'd been cut. Her son jumped to his feet but stopped when he saw that Strauss hadn't sliced her flesh, only the button fastening her cuff. Strauss held the button up between two long fingers for everyone to see and nodded at Gina.

Without a word the illusionist waited until all eyes were upon him. To our astonishment, he put the button in his mouth and swallowed it. He didn't bat an eyelash, just sat for a moment or two, coughed, and pressed his hand to his chest. Then he draped the towel on his left thigh and with his right hand drew the knife's edge across the skin above his wrist.

Gina's daughter shrieked. Her husband put his arm around her and hugged her. The knife clattered to the floor as Strauss clamped his hand onto the sizable cut. Blood welled out through the spaces between his fingers. I'd been expecting some silly trick. This seemed only too real.

Finally he wrapped the towel around his wrist and applied pressure to the cut. He smiled. You could have heard a pin drop.

After a minute or so Strauss unwrapped the bloodstained towel and began probing the cut with his fingers. I'm not squeamish but I could barely stand to watch. The others covered their mouths with their hands and turned their eyes away. He manipulated the edges of the wound, eased something out, and then held it up, dark with blood in the lamplight.

The button from Gina's shirt.

Six

Blood drained from Bennet's face and I felt her body grow slack against mine. I put my arm around her. The whole thing had to be fake, yet I couldn't figure out how he'd pulled it off. The blood certainly looked convincing. Strauss was no run-of-the-mill magician pulling doves out of hats. Presumably his spectacular feat was engineered to soften up the patrons, make them more inclined to believe in the spirit that would no doubt put in an appearance.

Gina brought Strauss a bandage and a glass of water, holding them out to him with trembling hands. He wrapped his wrist thoroughly, rolled his sleeve down, and put his jacket back on. He took a quick sip and thanked her.

It seemed to be a cue. Gina placed a tape recorder on the coffee table, turned it on, then flipped another switch on a CD player. One of those trance-inducing Gregorian chants—although it sounded more Eastern in flavor—filled the room. Strauss rested both arms on his thighs, sat back in the chair, and closed his eyes.

Nothing happened for a few minutes. The chanting had an odd, unnerving effect. Much as I knew it was all a hoax, the sound made me uneasy, as if the music had actually invaded my body, shaking up the natural order of things.

A slight tremor passed through Strauss's frame. The chanting grew softer then stopped completely. He lifted one hand off his leg; his fingers quivered. A hazy, whitish light seemed to coalesce around his head. Gina let out a short, sharp sob.

This wasn't the hokey séance of B movies—patrons gathered around a table, hands hovering over an Ouija board—but the basic elements were the same, complete with grieving widow in such a vulnerable state that she'd believe anything. I wondered how much she'd paid for tonight's charade.

The white light appeared to solidify and migrate to Strauss's neck. It had the repugnant look of a bodily organ, a larynx, as if the medium's throat had opened to reveal his interior anatomy. Over the drone of the music, which had started again imperceptibly, I heard sounds of static and something else—a plaintive murmuring coming from the apparition. Strauss's eyes fluttered open. His gaze was vacant.

Gina began to moan. This went on for about two minutes until, abruptly, the light vanished. The son comforted his mother who was crying softly now. The daughter looked shell shocked while the son-in-law rolled his eyes and grimaced. Strauss remained with his eyes closed for another minute or so, shuddered, and came out of his "trance." He'd put on a good show. He looked pale and weakened, as if producing the spirit had drained all his reserves.

He rose and sat on the divan beside Gina, bending to fiddle with some of the buttons on the recorder.

"Let's see what your husband wants, Gina." Strauss rewound the tape to the beginning and pressed play. We all leaned in closer.

At first we could hear only static over the background chanting. Strauss played with the buttons again. The murmurings now sounded like real words, although they were still too fuzzy to make out. A sentence seemed to be repeated over and over again.

Gina cast a worried glance at Strauss. "What's Frank trying to tell me?"

Strauss raised his eyes to her. "Your husband says, 'I will return to the house from which I came.'" Gina covered her face with her hands.

"This is sheer foolishness," her son-in-law barked.

Strauss put his hand up to silence him. "'I will return to the house from which I came.' Do you know where that quote comes from?" He looked at each of us in turn. No one responded.

"Luke 11:24–26." He recited the complete passage:

> When the unclean spirit has gone out of a person, it passes through waterless places seeking rest, and finding none it says, 'I will return to the house from which I came.' And when it comes, it finds the house swept and put in order. Then it goes and brings seven other spirits more evil than itself, and they enter and dwell there. And the last state of that person is worse than the first.

Strauss's eyes came to rest on mine, as if the words should have some special meaning for me alone. Then his gaze returned to Gina. "Your husband is warning you. His soul is in torment. Release him. Let him go so he may battle his demons and find peace. Otherwise his spirit will bring injury and untold evil to your household."

Seven

The family asked for some privacy and we were glad to oblige. Bennet and I retreated to a small sitting room, a book-lined study with a cheery fire burning in the grate. Hot coffee had been set out. "What do you take in it?" she asked. "No, let me guess—just black, right?"

"You hardly need to interview me. You seem to know all my deepest secrets already."

"How'd your date go last night?" She fluttered her eyelashes and crossed her legs. She was wearing another miniskirt, this one a flouncy affair in plaid, its hem startlingly edged in lace. Bennet did have shapely legs.

"Splendid, thanks."

"What did you think of the channeling?"

"I hate to see susceptible people taken advantage of by a charlatan. Although he may have done Gina a favor with what he claims the husband said." Strauss's words had seemed harsh, but perhaps they'd help Gina let go of a destructive grief that was probably affecting her whole family.

"A charlatan?" Strauss's voice sailed into the room somewhere behind me. I turned around to see him coming through the doorway.

I shrugged. "I'm a skeptic. Nice to finally meet you."

He helped himself to a coffee and fixed me with his blue-eyed stare. "Perhaps when we're finished talking, Mr. Madison, you'll allow that human perception just skims the surface. There is much in this world unknown to us by any rational measure."

"It'll be a waste of your time trying to persuade me."

"We'll see."

"Well, you'll have to allow that I've been patient. Now, I want to know what this article Bennet's supposed to be writing is all about."

"It would be easier for me to show you." He set his coffee down and walked to the far end of the couch, picked up an aluminum case from the floor, pushed aside the cups and set the case on the coffee table. He punched in a code. Inside, nestled in a soft black mold, were three bubble-wrapped objects. He unpeeled the wrap on two of them and placed them carefully on the table.

"Have a close look. I'm sure they'll appear familiar to you."

He'd revealed two Mesopotamian seals, small stone cylinders that, when rolled onto clay, would produce images to denote ownership. In some cases they were also used as magic amulets worn about the neck, which may have explained why Strauss had them. At first glance they appeared to be originals, but without an expert opinion it was impossible to tell. I asked if I could pick one of them up.

"By all means," Strauss said.

I got a tissue from a box on the mantel and held the first seal gingerly, revolving it to see the complete image.

Adam and Eve Temptation Seal

It depicted what some believed to be the Sumerian Adam and Eve seated before the tree of knowledge. "This is a famous seal," I said. "But it must be a reproduction."

Strauss smiled. "It's no reproduction. And it was fashioned at least 5500 years ago, possibly more."

I raised my eyebrows and picked up the second seal. It showed a hybrid bird–human figure before a stylized plant, an image similar to one I knew belonged in the British Museum. "And this?"

"It's been authenticated too."

I shook my head. "I'm afraid you've been duped, Mr. Strauss. These are both well-known seals from a much later period. If memory serves correctly, dating to between 2100 and 2200 B.C. The originals are priceless artifacts presently held in museums. Who authenticated them?"

He named Tricia Ross, a University of Pennsylvania professor and one of the foremost experts in the field. Hearing her name surprised me; she'd been a good friend of Samuel's. I didn't know what to think. I suppose it was possible for more than one seal of a similar design to exist.

Strauss waved his hand. "Don't worry about authenticity for now." He bent over, unwrapped the larger object, and set it down on the coffee table.

Ubaid-Era Statue

I had to stifle a gasp. The terra-cotta figure stood about six inches high; its style, decoration, and posture, along with its elongated head, suggested it came from the Ubaid period in preliterate Mesopotamia. That could place it anywhere from 3500 to 6500 B.C. Actual elongated human skulls had been found all over the world, some dating back forty-five thousand years. The process was called cranial deformation—the deliberate wrapping of an infant's skull to create a permanently lengthened head in adulthood. Experts presumed the skulls were from high-status individuals—royalty or priests. I'd never heard of any elongated skulls being found among Mesopotamian ruins, but the statue Strauss had placed before me suggested that ancient Mesopotamians may have carried out this practice as well.

"Where did these come from? Were they all found together? And when?"

Strauss crossed his legs and settled in his chair. "Well, that's quite a tale."

"Seeing as you're claiming these seals vastly predate any other cylinder seals held in the British Museum—or anywhere else on the globe—yes, I'd say that *was* quite a tale."

I'd assumed Bennet had already heard Strauss's story, yet she listened eagerly when he spoke.

"When I was in my thirties," he began, flexing his long, slim fingers, "these old hands were much more dextrous and I was considered one of the greatest magicians on the continent. A young man approached me, begging to be taken on as my apprentice. He was badly dressed, a poor farm boy from a rural area near Batavia, upstate. His parents, he told me, were German immigrants; he was fluent in the language. His name was George Helmstetter. Naturally, I refused him. The magical crafts are highly secret and one risks having them revealed, or worse, stolen, by trusting the wrong people. Not dissuaded, Helmstetter then asked if he could at least demonstrate some of his own magical effects.

"I acquiesced and recognized his astonishing talent right away. Of course I know all the tricks of the trade. But Helmstetter had an ability to make birds and other objects vanish in such a way that I had no idea how he'd pulled it off. I thought I might even learn from him, although of course I didn't tell him that. I was perplexed. How could someone so young with no professional profile manage those illusions? He astounded me. I should have known he was no rube.

"It made sense for him to seek me out. Alone, even with such spectacular talent, he'd have a long, arduous journey to prove himself. Working with me would vault him into the limelight. At the time, I thought only of my own interests: that he'd prove a great addition to my show as the opening act. I agreed to take him on. In short, we made a deal. I would promote him, make him famous, provided he rewarded my trust by agreeing to stay with my show exclusively. We worked together for several years. He fell in love with my assistant and they married."

Strauss paused. His dark brows drew down and when he looked at me again his expression had changed. "Helmstetter had an engaging personality; he was a born entertainer. But he'd fall into black moods, mistreat his wife when he thought he hadn't achieved enough. He had an outsized ambition and wanted to be wealthy. Under my tutelage, he delved into the esoteric world. As you saw tonight, my practice leans heavily on mentalism and spiritual endeavors. I began to realize it was this specialty that had attracted him to me. But the more he learned about that world, the more unpredictable and temperamental he became. One day, thirty-five years ago, he simply vanished. I never heard from him again."

I stretched my legs out and drained my coffee cup. "An interesting story, but I can't imagine how it relates to those artifacts."

"Patience. I'm coming to that. George did not leave empty handed. He raided my safe, taking ten thousand dollars in cash along with a precious book, a 1792 German edition of *The Steganographia,* by a Renaissance scholar named Trithemius." Strauss's eyes blazed. "He betrayed me."

"I'm sorry to hear it." I knew of Trithemius and though I'd never seen a copy, or known one to come up for auction, I was familiar with *The Steganographia,* one of the first texts of cryptography disguised as a book of angel magic—the title came from Greek and Latin roots and meant "hidden writing."

Strauss leaned forward, his hands curled into fists. "I want you to find Helmstetter and retrieve my book."

Eight

That was the last thing I expected to hear. "Are you serious? Your assistant disappeared thirty-five years ago. I'm sure his trail has gone cold. And anyway, missing persons are hardly my forte."

"Yes, but ancient Near East artifacts *are* your specialty. And if you trace the origin of these objects, you'll pick up Helmstetter's trail." He glared at me so forcefully it felt like a blow. "Does my former assistant's name not ring a bell?"

"Not at all. Why should it?"

"But you've heard of Faust, no doubt."

"Of course," I said, puzzled about what all this was leading to.

"Helmstetter was one of Faust's names. Faust was a real person, you know, not just a character made famous by Marlowe and Goethe. The actual historical individual took up an assumed name: Georgios Faustus Helmstetter. He was a scholar, alchemist, and magician who lived in fifteenth-century Germany. My Helmstetter claimed to be a direct descendant. After he fled I traced his family history. He'd told the truth about his genealogy. He *was* descended from the real Faust's family."

"Since he disappeared so long ago, what makes you think he's still alive?"

"I have no proof, only instinct, and my instincts have never failed me."

Except those instincts didn't warn you about trusting your apprentice.

Strauss leaned back and crossed his legs. "Naturally I searched for him high and low—in North America and Europe. I hired private investigators, checked in with his parents and associates, ran newspaper ads. Yet I failed to pick up even a scent."

"You said he had a wife. What about her?"

"I was coming to that. She ceased working for me shortly after their marriage. When Helmstetter took off, he left her behind. Broken-hearted, she grew bitter. Refused to even speak his name. She remarried. She passed away last October."

He motioned toward the case. "Her will instructed her executor to send me those objects as a way of paying me back for Helmstetter's theft. It was most generous of her."

"Well, if they do turn out to be authentic, which I doubt, they're worth vastly more than the money and book combined. Consider yourself compensated."

A flash of irritation crossed Strauss's face. "Their financial value is of no interest to me," he snapped.

"Did you learn how they came into her possession?"

"All I know is that almost a year after he disappeared she received a package from Helmstetter containing the objects. It included a short, undated letter in which he begged her forgiveness and hoped the valuables would provide her with some financial security. She kept them all those years, unsure of their authenticity or provenance but unwilling to give them up. In the letter to her, underneath his signature, Helmstetter wrote some kind of code expressed in a series of numbers."

Strauss took out a sheet from his tuxedo jacket and handed it over.

20 8 9 18 20 25	6 15 18 20 25
5 9 7 8 20.	44 34 49.
30 34 32 33 45	20 23 15
19 9 24	76 55 68 65
26 5 18 15	19 5 22 5 14
6 9 22 5	31 34 47 30
14 9 14 5	101 80 93 90
51 30 43 40	55 59 57 58 70

"What do these mean?"

"I have no idea. But now I know why I couldn't find him."

"Why?"

"He'd journeyed to a remote location. A village named Kandovan near Lake Urmia in northwest Iran, close to the Turkish border. The package addressed to his wife was sent from there."

With another tissue in hand, I got up and bent over the case to examine the statue, turning it so the light shone fully on it. I could see tiny crystals lodged in the pits and crevices.

"You're thinking along the right lines," Strauss said, observing me. "Those are salt crystals. They're present on the cylinder seals as well. And I've had the microscopic molds and soil deposits on all these objects analyzed. They're consistent with samples from the Lake Urmia district near Kandovan."

"That doesn't make sense. Assuming they're authentic, the seals are clearly Sumerian. They would have come from southern

Iraq—over five hundred miles away from Lake Urmia. Helmstetter couldn't have unearthed them near Kandovan."

"Are you intrigued, Mr. Madison? I *thought* you would be."

"Yes, but only about the origin of these artifacts."

"Trace their origin and you'll pick up Helmstetter's scent."

"Why not just approach me about this directly? Why the excuse about Bennet writing that article? I'm assuming the article is a joke, just not a particularly funny one." Bennet's cheeks flushed.

"It's no joke at all. If you do agree to take on the task, I'd like her to be your chronicler. What could be more flattering than to have an account of your investigation?"

"You're saying you want me to travel to this Iranian village and try to track down Helmstetter and the book with Bennet as my sidekick?"

"As I said, if you find one, you'll discover the other. I'm convinced of it. *The Steganographia* never turned up, whether at a legitimate rare book sale or on the black market. I've employed the best people in the business to verify that."

"Two wars are being waged on Iran's borders right now. Even if I somehow managed to get into the country, I'm an American. I'd never make it out again."

Strauss got up slowly and leaned against the mantelpiece, an amused look on his face. He nodded to Bennet. "From what Ms. Bennet has been able to unearth, you've escaped even more dangerous conditions in Iraq, twice, in 2003."

"And nearly got killed doing so."

"Quite correct. I'll compensate you handsomely."

"Tell me."

Strauss swept his hand toward the case. "I have no interest in these objects. If you conclude the mission to my satisfaction, they're yours."

This appeared to surprise Bennet as much as me.

"Worthless reproductions aren't much of an inducement," I said.

"Talk to Tricia Ross. She knows they're real."

Bennet put her hand on my knee. "John. You must be aware how valuable they are. How could you turn it down?"

"If that isn't enough," Strauss said evenly, "I can offer you something else. Worth more than money."

"What do you mean?"

"The truth about your birth. Who your real parents were."

Nine

A clock chimed in another room. I was conscious of my heart thumping. "How would you know anything about that?" I said, feigning a calm I didn't feel.

"Our friend here is awfully good at digging out information," Strauss said.

When I turned to look at Bennet she blushed again.

"Bennet was able to learn that your birthright is a matter of concern to you. As to what I discovered about you when I started inquiring, I prefer not to say, until, that is, you carry out my request." Strauss smiled.

Who knew about the questions concerning my birth parents? Just my former housekeeper, Evelyn, who was like a mother to me—that was it. I couldn't see her talking to Bennet.

Evelyn and Samuel had always claimed that he and I were half-brothers, sharing a father. Samuel, much older than I, searched for me in Turkey after he heard about my parents' death in a mining disaster. He adopted me at the age of three, brought me home to New York, and one year later Evelyn arrived to be our full-time housekeeper. But I'd come to wonder about this story in a serious way ever since I'd been diagnosed with that genetic blood disorder—one of my parents must have had it and I had no way of knowing. Other things had since surfaced in my mind: not one photo existed of me with either of my parents. I had no idea what they looked like. When I'd asked my brother about it he'd change the subject or find some other way to avoid answering me. Samuel was dead—I couldn't get the truth from him. And when I tried with Evelyn she'd resisted; the whole issue seemed to upset her.

I stood up, fuming, gave Strauss a curt nod, ignored Bennet, and walked out.

I'd barely made it down half the block when Bennet flew after me, her coat undone and flapping in the wind. "John, please don't be angry."

"Lady, you've got a hell of a nerve. What was it? Did you hack into my medical records or something? I could report you."

She had to run to keep up with me; her breath came in gasps. "What are you talking about? That's not where I found out."

"Then how?" I stopped in my tracks.

"Evelyn Farhad told me. Or rather I should say, she let it slip. I told her I was writing an article about you for a prestigious archaeological magazine." Bennet hung her head at that point, suggesting she possessed at least a fragment of a conscience. "She was so thrilled and kept saying how happy your brother would have been to see you recognized. I'm afraid it made her talkative."

"So you squeezed out private information about me by manipulating a vulnerable woman?"

"You're putting the worst face on it."

I put both hands gently on her shoulders. "I'm heading to the subway. If that's the direction you're going in too, you're welcome to walk with me. After we say goodbye, I would appreciate not hearing from you again. Is that clear?" I paused to see whether I'd finally gotten through. She looked defeated.

"I'll go back to the house. Gina's son offered me a ride home." She stuck her hands in her coat pockets and trudged back down the sidewalk.

A pang of regret hit me as I watched her retreating figure. After what she'd done, I couldn't imagine why.

Ten

February 16, 2005

Sleep didn't come easily that night. I couldn't shake the memory of that strange chorus of chants—the ghost voices accompanying Strauss's channeling. The sounds reverberated through my brain like an earworm. I tossed and turned. Nor could I stop thinking about Strauss's biblical quote and the seven evil spirits haunting Gina's husband and home. *I will return to the house from which I came.*

Around four in the morning another episode of sleep paralysis hit me, one of the worst I'd ever had. It seemed to go on forever. Before, I'd always been aware of my own consciousness trying to fight off the dead weight of my limbs. But this time it seemed as if another presence was in the room, someone who wanted to harm me. When I finally awoke with a jerk and heaved myself out of bed, I was trembling and soaked in sweat.

By then it was late morning. I took a long shower, got some orange juice and food into my system, and finally felt human again. On my way to pick up the dog I dropped in to check on Evelyn.

She lived in a brown-brick high-rise complex on Ninth Avenue. When I tapped on her door and she opened it, I could see she was all set to go out, her coat on and her purse lying on her lap. She lifted her arms from the wheelchair pads and stretched them out for a hug.

"You're surprising me, John. I am so happy to see you. But it is Layla's birthday. I promised to take her to lunch."

I bent down to kiss her cheek, glad to see that today she looked well. She suffered miserably from arthritis and the pain became particularly bad in the depths of winter. "Don't worry. I just wanted to pop in for a few minutes."

"Let me make you tea. Let me call Layla and say for her to wait." She patted my hands and made to turn her wheelchair.

"No need, really—actually I just stopped by to ask you something." She gave me a questioning look. I had to be careful how I phrased this; I didn't want to upset her. "You chatted with Margaux Bennet the other day? She's been in touch with me."

Evelyn's eyes lit up. "Yes. A very nice girl. Much better manners than many you see now. So rude some of them are with their phones out all the time, hardly looking at you. I'm glad about the story in the magazine! I will show it to all my friends here when it comes out."

"It's pretty exciting all right. What did she want to know about?"

"Mostly about when you were younger. Your childhood and student days." Evelyn put a finger to her lips. "I forget what she called it. Background, I think she said."

"Listen, dear. It's great you had a chance to talk with her, but if she calls again just pass it on to me—all right? I'm really enthusiastic about the article but I want to make sure everything's accurate. These writers sometimes like to stretch the truth, you know."

Evelyn always read me well; I couldn't get away with anything when I was a kid that her sharp eyes wouldn't pick up. Her expression darkened. "Did I say something wrong to her, John? You're happy about the story, yes?"

"Not at all, it's fine. Nothing to worry about. Can I hang here for a few minutes? I need to make a couple of calls and it's too noisy out on the street. I'll lock up when I'm done."

"Of course. Baklava is made fresh today. Sitting on the counter. Take some home with you."

I gave her a hug and made sure her top coat button was done up and that she had her warm gloves. Layla was already waiting at her apartment door down the hall. I waved to them as they headed for the elevator.

I felt guilty lying to Evelyn about the phone calls. But the question of my parentage, raised all over again in my conversation with Strauss, made me determined this time to find out anything I could.

Evelyn's studio apartment was small, so if she'd kept any evidence of my origins, it wouldn't take long to find it. I searched through every drawer, putting everything back carefully. Bad enough that I was betraying her trust this way; I didn't want to risk her discovering what I'd done. She had no desk, just a bookcase. The bottom two shelves held a pile of assorted files and photo albums. Almost all the pictures in the albums were of Samuel and me or of each of us alone. One of them showed Samuel on his knees at an unnamed archaeological site, intent on brushing gray-brown dirt from an object in a marked-out trough. I remember poring over photos like that as a kid, cross-examining Evelyn about what Samuel had found. Of course she had no idea. In those times, I so badly wanted to be there with him, to make what I thought would be legendary discoveries, and yet I never got the chance.

Another photo was of me around eight years old, larking around at the Natural History Museum, pretending to scare the dinosaurs.

I saw nothing more of interest in the albums and turned to the files. They held old bills, tax letters and so on, newspaper clippings about Samuel's career, nothing personal. Then, in a Kraft envelope secured with a rubber band, I discovered that Evelyn had kept every greeting card I ever gave her. I looked through them just to be sure, smiling at my early childish scrawls and the earnest notes I'd written from boarding school.

Halfway through the pile of cards, I found something: a brittle piece of paper wrapped around a photograph and lodged between two larger cards, almost as though she'd tried to hide it. The page was an official-looking government document in Arabic text, complete with a stamp. The photo, an old black-and-white image, yellow with age, showed a settlement of unusual stone houses with conical roofs, seemingly carved from an immense rock face. I snapped a photo of both document and image, wrapped the page around the photo again, and put the items back in the envelope.

On my phone I sent the two pictures I'd taken to a colleague of Samuel's along with a request to translate the document. He was a man I liked, and more important, an archaeologist who'd spent a lot of time in the Near East. A last look around the apartment turned up nothing else. Remembering Evelyn's baklava, before I left I cut a slice, wrapped it in wax paper, and tucked it in my pocket. I let myself out.

On the way to the veterinary clinic I thought about names for the coyote. I considered calling her Wiley after the daredevil cartoon character. That name suited my penchant for taking huge risks only to find the bottom dropping out from under my feet. But I settled instead on Loki, after the Norse trickster god. She'd come to me in such an unusual way that, had I been of a superstitious turn of mind, I'd have taken it as a sign. Not that I'd be keeping her; it would be a temporary arrangement at best.

I waited in the reception room until Dr. Jefferson came down the ramp carrying Loki.

Her entire hind leg was encased in a pink cast with only the tip of her paw sticking out. He'd shaved her stomach. Her yellow eyes were open. Her black fur looked cleaner, although she was still rail thin. When she saw me she gave a little whimper, which I took, optimistically, to be a friendly greeting.

Jefferson set her down carefully. "As I said, there's not as much damage as I'd thought. She's recovering well so far. And she's definitely not pure *Canis latrans*." He looked at me over the top of his glasses. "That's Latin for coyote. It means 'barking dog.' She's indeed a hybrid—and young, probably around one year old. More important, we don't think she's feral. It's apparent she's been domesticated. If anything, she's timid."

"How do you know?"

"She's been spayed, for one thing. And she's shown a comfort level with our staff that a wild animal wouldn't display. Here's my best guess. It's become popular to sell these hybrids for a lot of money. Drug dealers will buy them for watchdogs, or they're used as bait in dog fights."

"They actually breed them?"

"They'll take a domestic female dog that's in heat out to a farm where it's known there are a lot of coyotes, muzzle her, and chain her up overnight. That isn't guaranteed to succeed if local farm dogs get there first. But often enough, a male coyote will breed with her."

"How do you think she ended up a stray?"

"She was probably dumped by someone who bought her and later decided she wasn't aggressive enough." He gave me a long look. "Are you sure you're up to looking after her? If she's been foraging in the city on her own for some time it will require a lot of patience to train her."

"I don't see it as a long-term thing. So far I haven't found anyone willing to take her, but I'll look after her until I do."

Jefferson grunted in response. "She's mildly sedated right now and it's best to keep her that way over the next few days. But once she's perked up, she's likely to run. You'll have to keep an eye on her."

He gave me enough pills to knock out an elephant. I thanked him and paid the bill, then took her in my arms. She struggled a bit when she got her first whiff of fresh air as we walked to the car, but seemed content once I'd settled her on the passenger seat. As I reached over to start the ignition, she gave my hand a quick lick. I took that as her seal of friendship and broke off a small piece of baklava for her.

At the parking garage near my place, my phone buzzed with an incoming text from Samuel's colleague. He'd gotten back to me with lightning speed.

John:
Confirming the script is Arabic. The document is an Iranian birth certificate in the name of Yeva Nemat, born January 21, 1946.

Then, an even greater surprise:

I'm 100% sure the photo is of Kandovan, a village in northwest Iran.

Eleven

My mind spun with possibilities as I got into the elevator to my apartment with Loki in my arms. Kandovan: the name of the town where Strauss's apprentice had mailed the package. Strauss's puzzle had suddenly become much more personal. The birth certificate—Yeva Nemat? That must be Evelyn herself. I knew she'd grown up somewhere in the Middle East, but she never spoke about it. She'd kept the birth certificate and photo together, so I guessed that Kandovan was her family home. "Evelyn" was likely an anglicized version of "Yeva," and she must have changed her name from Nemat to Farhad when she came to America. Or had she been married at some point before she came over here? Was there a husband somewhere in her past?

I made up my mind right then to accept Strauss's offer, if only as a way to find out what he knew about my parentage. Getting paid to do it would be a bonus. I shot him off a text suggesting we talk about terms.

Loki lay down on a fresh bath towel I folded for her on the
kitchen floor and lapped some water from her bowl. I gave her a
treat. She pushed it around with her wet, black nose disinterestedly
and finally put her head down on her front paws. I looked in the
fridge for something more enticing, found some precooked shrimp
and a piece of T-bone steak left over from the other night. I warmed
them up in the microwave and set them in front of her. She pushed
the shrimp away with her nose but seized on the beef—it was the
bone she savored. I left her to it.

My phone rang. Strauss was on the other end. "Pleased you've
reconsidered, Madison."

"Once I'm satisfied this is more than just a wild goose chase, we
can talk about whether to carry it any further."

He heaved a quick sigh of relief. "That's splendid. Can you start
right away?"

I was tempted to tell him I couldn't see the need to hurry when
the trail had gone cold thirty-five years ago. "I'll need some money
up front," I said instead, and named a generous figure. He surprised
me by agreeing to it readily. I told him to transfer the money to an
account I kept for client deposits. Strauss promised to send the
funds the next day.

"One more thing," he said. "I want to ensure Ms. Bennet is kept
informed of your progress every step of the way."

"Is that really necessary? I'd rather deal with you directly."

He chuckled. "Her bark is worse than her bite. She'll grow on
you, I'm sure."

"I'll need to speak to Professor Ross about the artifacts. Can
you pave the way for me?"

"Consider it done. I'll tell her she can provide you with any
information you need."

"Fine then," I said. "I'll be in touch."

I got a couple of Samuel's academic books down from the shelf and leafed through them looking for anything I could find about Kandovan. I glanced up when I heard something dragging across the floor. Loki, the bath towel clenched between her very white canines, was making her way across the living room, her pink cast bumping along the hardwood. She stood in front of me and whined. I'd never had a pet, dog or otherwise, and wasn't sure what she wanted. I picked her up and right away she curled beside my hip and closed her eyes. Definitely not fearsome watchdog material.

Hours passed while I immersed myself in learning about the region. A majestic defunct volcano called Mount Sahand towered over the village. Kandovan was also close to Lake Urmia, a salt lake four times more saline than the ocean. A major river, the Ajay Chay, emptied into the lake. Culturally, the area had been home to the Mandeans and the Medes, the latter fierce fighters who'd joined the Babylonians to vanquish the Assyrian empire. What I found most exciting was Kandovan's proximity to the Silk Road. I put my finger on the dotted line in the graphic indicating the great east–west trading route and traced an important branch that forked northwesterly, running close to Lake Urmia and Kandovan and then passing through Tabriz en route to Turkey. The Silk Road, famously associated with Marco Polo, was much older than that, likely stretching into prehistory. Fascinating though all this was, I couldn't imagine what had drawn Helmstetter, an aspiring magician from upstate New York, to the area.

My cell rang again.

"John Madison? It's Tricia Ross. Lucas Strauss asked me to give you a call."

"Thanks for getting in touch. Great to hear from you."

"I understand Strauss has hired you to look into the origin of the artifacts he'd asked me to validate."

"That's right."

"You're an antiquities dealer—aren't you?" I noted a suspicious edge to her tone.

"I deal with a range of art objects and rare books. We've never met, but you'll remember my brother, Samuel Diakos?"

"Oh my goodness, of course. I'm so sorry." The tightness in her voice vanished. "Samuel always talked about you, but usually just used your first name. How could I have forgotten?" She paused. "May I ask? Is Strauss planning to put those objects on the market?"

"I'm not privy to his plans, but I don't think so. You're satisfied they're authentic?"

"As best as I can be. They're at least 5500 years old. Not finding them on-site hampers my conclusions considerably."

"Of course," I said. "One of Strauss's seals is identical to the greenstone Temptation Seal in the British Museum. I can't believe it could be genuine—"

Ross cut in. "Strauss's seal is not only a lot older than the Temptation Seal, it isn't identical. There are small differences. It's not unknown for several copies to have originally been made of Mesopotamian seals. The real mystery is where it came from, not what it depicts."

"You're referring to its source, where it was found in Iran?"

I could almost see her shaking her head. "It's astounding. Was it transported there from the Euphrates delta for some reason? That's pure speculation on my part. Doesn't make sense at all, does it?"

"No, you're right. I've been wondering the same thing myself. Let me know if you think of anything."

"Will do." She was silent for a moment. "There's something else that might be helpful. As part of my research I put out a query on a listserv used by academics, museums, and dealers. I also ran a broader check to see whether the artifacts had been declared stolen."

"And?"

"Couldn't find anything. But I remain very suspicious and haven't given up checking."

"Lucas Strauss may have acquired them quite innocently. That's happened to other clients of mine."

"Yes, but …" Now she sounded wary and I could tell she was genuinely worried.

"What?"

"I got a phone call from a man named Yersan a couple of days ago. He wanted to see the objects and became so persistent I had to ask him not to contact me again. He claims to own the seals and the statue. At first he was pleasant enough, and I had the sense he was just fishing, but when I refused to disclose the owner he got belligerent. I told him to talk to the FBI. He just laughed."

"Do you have a number for him?"

"I think so—yes. Just a minute." She came back on the line. "No, I don't. I'm sorry. He must have blocked his number. But I did jot down a website address."

After she provided it, I thanked her and hung up, then checked out the site on my laptop. It sold religious emblems and articles used for the ancient religion of Zoroastrianism. Fire worshipers. From the same region in Iran where Strauss's artifacts had been found.

Twelve

Loki's head jerked up when the security buzzer sounded. I pressed the intercom. "Yes?"

"Lady here to see you," the security guard said. "Says she has an appointment."

I didn't have to ask her name. I considered telling the guard not to let her up, but reasoned that part of keeping Strauss sweet would be to cooperate with Bennet.

"I brought a peace offering," she said as she shrugged off her coat and handed me a big brown bag and the umbrella I'd lent her. "Have you eaten yet? I got a feast from Peking Duck House."

She was wearing another miniskirt. Perilously short, but this time she wore black tights, so I had the feeling of being cheated. On her feet were pert little ankle boots.

"There are chopsticks and paper plates inside." As she turned to set the packages on the coffee table, she spotted Loki. "Oh! I didn't know you had a dog."

"Why? Are you allergic?" I said hopefully.

She laughed. "No." She cocked her head to one side. "What happened to her? She's kind of different looking. What strange eyes."

"We think she was hit by a car. And I'm fostering her until I can find her a permanent home."

"Can I pet her?" She squatted down and Loki's tail flopped when Bennet scratched under her chin.

"Why don't you come with me while I take her out? I won't be long. We can keep the food warm in the oven."

It was a boon to have Madison Square so close by. Jemmy's Dog Run near Twenty-fourth was considered one of the best in the city although I didn't dare let Loki in to mingle with the Portuguese water dogs and boxers yet. Still sedated, she was too dozy to fight the leash very hard, but she clearly hated it. Bennet sensibly suggested I carry her until she was stronger and had a chance to get used to the idea. When we reached the park, I set her down with the leash attached until she did her business. Then I carried her home again, garnering more than a few titters from other dog walkers.

When we returned, the aroma of steaming Chinese food filled the apartment. I opened a bottle of chilled chardonnay and scrounged a candle from the kitchen, set it on a saucer, and dimmed the lights. Bennet knelt to pull the takeout from the oven. "We've got Szechuan scallops with bean curd, Grand Marnier prawns, veggie spring rolls, string beans with minced pork, and of course, Peking duck. We're all set," she said.

My stomach almost clapped in approval. We took our seats. Bennet placed her phone beside her plate. "The audio recorder's on," she said when she saw me glance at it. "I never got a chance to interview you before and I should get started." She cocked an eye at me. "That's okay with you, isn't it? Strauss said you'd agreed."

"As long as you can understand me with my mouth full—go ahead."

When she grinned, I noticed what full, shapely lips she had. "You've been to Iraq twice, in 2003, in search of ancient treasures looted by thieves. Tell me about that."

The shrimp I'd just swallowed set my throat on fire. I downed some wine and tried to get my voice back. "The first time I was hunting for a clay tablet created by an Old Testament prophet named Nahum. My brother had tried to protect it, to stop it from being looted during the catastrophe at the Iraq Museum. It led to a fabulous find associated with a king I'd always thought was more of a legend than a reality."

"That sounds fascinating!" Bennet exclaimed. "One of the Mesopotamian kings?"

"That has to remain my secret for the time being. Others were involved and they'd be in danger if I revealed too much."

Bennet sighed. "Can't tell you how many times I've heard a version of that. Someone hires you to tell their life story and then all you get from them is the vanilla, not the juicy stuff."

"Except I didn't hire you—let's not forget that."

Bennet had brought a bottle of Semper Fi Marine Corps Hot Sauce. "They named it that because it's so hot it'll make you stand to attention." She chuckled as she shook some onto her plate, heaped so full the food almost spilled over the edge. I gestured with my chopsticks. "No need to hoard, you know. I'm good at sharing."

"Sorry, I'm starving."

"The second time I was after a seventeenth-century anthology of fairy tales that I'd bought at auction for a client. It was stolen from me."

"Neat. Written by the Grimm brothers?"

"Almost two hundred years before them, penned by a poet and courtier from Naples. He included a number of the fairy tales we're familiar with, except the originals were darker and more sensual. Some were based on real life. Any idea who Snow White's prince actually was?"

Bennet looked up. "Seriously?"

"Phillip II of Spain before he was made king. Amazing, isn't it?"

"Did you keep a record of your experiences?"

"Only on my second trip, a journal, of sorts."

Her face lit up. "Could I have a look at it?"

"I'd have to go through it first. Other people were involved. An Italian woman and an American soldier. I'd want to keep their side of the story private."

"You could ask them. I've found people are usually flattered when I tell them I'll be writing about them."

A shudder ran through me, thinking of those two. Dina, her raven cloud of hair and pale, beautiful face. And Nick Shaheen, the man who'd fended for himself on the streets of Baghdad as a child and ended up as a respected U.S. military intelligence officer. Dead now.

"What was it like in Iraq, trying to cope in the middle of a war?"

"The military was everywhere of course, but when I was there, in the late summer and fall of 2003, the insurgency hadn't really got off the ground yet. Hellish in another way, though. The worst part was the toll on ordinary citizens, going months without clean water or electricity. On the streets you'd see people with horrible injuries. They looked shell shocked. Parts of the city lay in ruins. It would have broken my brother's heart to see it.

"I remember a fellow I came across outside my hotel. Noticing I was a Westerner, he came up to me. He intended me no harm. He said he'd once been a university professor. His home had been leveled by a bomb and he no longer had a job. He asked me, politely, why the war had happened. I had no answer for him."

Over the rest of dinner, I sketched out some of the more dangerous episodes I'd faced. Bennet gave me all her attention. Eventually I leaned back and checked the time. "First class food. Thanks. But it's late. Need to think about getting you home. I can drive you if you want."

"Oh, it's okay thanks. I have a car. No nightcap, then?" She got to her feet reluctantly.

I stood up. "Early start for me tomorrow. What about you? Do you have a long drive ahead? You never did say where you live."

Her cheeks colored slightly. "New Jersey."

I put Loki back on her towel bed in the kitchen and threw together a makeshift barrier. There wasn't much she could chew on in the kitchen.

"Full disclosure," Bennet said as we walked toward the underground lot on Sixth where she'd parked her car. "My family is acquainted with Strauss. That's why I got the job. Just didn't want you to think I'd been hiding anything from you."

"Well, that's the way things usually work. People prefer to hire someone who's a known quantity. But I appreciate your letting me know."

As we reached the lot's entrance Bennet turned to me. "Thanks for seeing me this far. I can manage from here."

"I'll come down with you. There aren't many people around at this time of night." She was nervous about something and I wondered why.

"Where's your car?" I asked when we arrived at her floor.

"Just over there." She pointed vaguely to the northeast corner, blew me a kiss, and then hastened away. I caught up with her just as she was unlocking a battered Chevrolet hatchback. Through the windows I could see that the back seat had been folded down to accommodate a makeshift bed with two plump white pillows and a pink blanket thrown over a creased white sheet. A couple of satchels had clothes spilling out of them. Empty fast-food containers sat on the dash.

"You're living in your car?" I tried to cover my surprise.

Bennet's cheeks flamed red. "It's just temporary. Until I find a new place to rent."

"How long is temporary?"

She looked away, avoiding my eyes. "A month or so."

"And where do you park when you're sleeping?"

"An RV campground in New Jersey. As soon as Strauss pays me for this job I'll find a place."

I took her arm. "Get one of those bags and pack some overnight things. You're coming back with me."

"Oh no. Really, it isn't necessary."

"It's dangerous for you to stay alone like that. No arguments. At least for tonight. When is Strauss paying you?"

"He won't give me anything until he's seen the first draft."

"Okay. We'll just have to work something out. But you're not sleeping in this car."

It was an impetuous decision on my part, but I was genuinely concerned for her safety. I wondered why her family hadn't helped her with money; maybe there'd been a falling out? I still didn't trust her, though. After all, she was working for Strauss—who knew if she wasn't part of some undisclosed agenda? And she'd manipulated Evelyn, however sweetly. I wasn't concerned about the valuable artworks I had in the apartment—they'd all been photographed, documented, and insured. She wouldn't get very far if she took anything. And if she did turn out to be more enemy than friend, I figured I'd be better off keeping a close eye on her.

After Bennet threw some things in a satchel and relocked the car, I marched her back to my place. I gave her some sheets and blankets and she fixed up a bed on my sectional sofa.

"I'm going to hit the sack," I said. "Make yourself comfortable."

She looked up at me as if I'd just saved her life. "This is really decent of you, John. I'm totally grateful."

"No worries." I gave Loki her medication with some small pieces of beef I'd cut up and she gobbled them down.

Normally I didn't wear anything to bed, but on this occasion I put on some lounging pants and a silk robe I'd bought in London.

The bedroom door cracked open and Bennet peeked in. "Thanks again. I owe you one."

"Don't mention it. Sleep well."

After falling into a deep slumber I woke sometime around three in the morning with the light still on and Bennet snuggled up to my back. She had one arm thrown around my waist and was snoring softly. Was it too cold in the living room?

I responded quite predictably to having a woman in bed with me, but Loki, even with her cast on, had somehow managed to clamber up on my other side and now lay curled up with her wet nose pressed against my abs. She whimpered and stiffened her legs when I tried to move her onto the floor, so, reluctantly, I gave up.

My two stray girls. Funny, I mused, how in the space of a day I'd gone from strict bachelorhood to a strange form of domestic bliss.

Thirteen

February 17, 2005

I rose early, and had already made coffee and toast by the time Bennet sashayed into the kitchen, rubbing her eyes. No mini-skirt today; she'd thrown on jeans and a long-sleeved sweater. Her hair was tied back in a ponytail. Loki wagged her tail in greeting.

"Loki saved your virtue last night because she insisted on sleeping with me too," I joked.

"Sorry—I was freezing on that couch. The covers kept falling off." Perhaps to hide her embarrassment, she quickly changed the subject. "What's on the agenda for today?"

"I want to visit Yersan, a man Tricia Ross told me harassed her about Strauss's artifacts. He sells antiquities and religious items. There's no phone number listed on his website, just an address and his store hours, so we'll have to take a chance and drop in on him."

"How did this Yersan find out about Ross in the first place?"

I told Bennet about the query Tricia had put out on the listserv. "Have a bite to eat while I take Loki out and then let's vamoose.

After we see Yersan, I made an appointment to visit the Conjuring Arts Research Center. I want to get some background on both Strauss and Helmstetter."

Bennet and I found Yersan's place on Pacific Street in Flatbush, wedged between a boarded-up movie theater and a grimy smoke shop. On the sidewalk we negotiated a jumble of cigarette butts, Styrofoam coffee cups, and assorted flotsam and jetsam. The last film advertised on the theater marquee was *The Matrix,* so it must have been closed since 1999. Bennet grabbed my arm and delicately stepped over a putrid-smelling green garbage bag. The place didn't have any windows, only a battered steel door, the street number, and a buzzer, with no sign to indicate what might lie inside. Not much of a shop at all, it seemed; Yersan must conduct most of his business online. I hoped the trip hadn't been in vain as I leaned on the buzzer and stood back.

We heard a rustling behind the door. A minute or so went by. I guessed someone was taking a good look at us through the eyehole. The person fumbled with the lock and the door opened. An old man wearing a belted white robe and a small white turban faced us.

"We'd like to see Mr. Yersan, if he's in?"

The man didn't speak, just gestured for us to wait after he ushered us into a tiny foyer. Other than an old wooden wardrobe for coats and a floor mat on which sat several pairs of men's shoes, the room was bare. The old man went through a second door, shutting it firmly behind him. When he returned he carried a patterned scarf that he held out for Bennet. I could sense her getting ready to protest. "I doubt they'll let you in otherwise," I pointed out.

She draped it around her head reluctantly. "I hate giving in to this," she said under her breath. The old man pointed to his stocking feet. I dutifully removed my shoes; Bennet took off her ankle boots. The man gave us a broad smile, glad, I guess, he'd been understood. My stomach turned over. Behind his broken brown teeth, he had no tongue.

The *Matrix* marquee turned out to be fitting—as we followed the elderly man out of the foyer it felt as though we'd stepped into an alternate universe. Rich, brightly colored cloth hangings draped the white walls. A deep plum carpet of lush pile covered most of the tile floor. A faint, spicy scent hung in the air. The short hall we entered ended in a T; directly ahead, two elaborately carved, open wooden doors revealed a room finished in white marble. On either side of the doors little fountains bubbled in stone containers. A bell dangled from a rope hanging from the ceiling, and centered on a podium was a huge brass vessel shaped like a goblet, its mirror surface polished to perfection. It was almost as tall as Bennet. A flame leapt up from what I concluded was fragrant burning oil. This, I guessed, was a Zoroaster fire temple. My readings yesterday had served me well.

Our mute guide turned left down the hallway and let us into a chamber. A man dressed in a business suit, dark eyed and olive skinned like me, looked up from his desk as we entered. He was small and wiry with a receding hairline, maybe in his mid-forties. He seemed tightly sprung, a hint of suspicion in his eyes as they swept over me and lingered on Bennet. A glance passed between him and the old man, who quietly went out again.

"Please have a seat," our host said, indicating a divan in ivory brocade with a carved wooden frame. "My name is Yersan. I understand you wish to see me?"

He made no move to shake hands, so we sat down as he'd directed. The room housed a collection of goods, some of which I'd seen on his website: books, enameled medallions embossed with various esoteric designs, silver bowls and collection plates, wall hangings, small triptych screens, sculptures of the famous Persian insignia featuring outspread wings superimposed on a male figure.

I handed him my business card, introduced Bennet and myself, and thanked him for agreeing to see us. "Like you, I have a professional interest in Near East artifacts. I'm trying to trace the origin of certain Mesopotamian cylinder seals, one with figures referred to as the Sumerian Adam and Eve, and also a terra-cotta statue depicting an elongated skull. I believe you questioned Professor Ross about these items?"

His expression hardened. "Are you colleagues of hers?"

"My brother was … at one time."

"And what's your interest in the matter now?"

"As my card indicates, I'm an antiquities dealer, like you. I've been hired to help trace the objects' source."

He clasped his hands together. "Well, you have a simple task then. They were stolen from my family. These items have great cultural value. My family has searched for them for decades."

"Did you file a police report? There's no record of theft. Professor Ross confirmed that and I checked it myself."

Yersan gritted his teeth. "My parents are simple people. They kept no accounts, so I lack any official proof of ownership."

"Are your parents here, in America?" Bennet put in.

He shook his head. "In Iran. As you can imagine, I am quite anxious to recover the articles. If you know of their whereabouts, or who is in possession of them, I would be grateful." His attempt at a smile didn't reach his dark eyes.

"Your parents are from the town of Kandovan, or nearby—is that right?" I asked nonchalantly. That got a reaction. His chair almost toppled when he leapt up and marched toward me. I didn't like the thought of him looming over us, so I stood too. I was heavier set than he was and taller by a good couple of inches. Bennet moved out of our way.

"How did you know that?"

"I'd be glad to tell you if you give me some information," I continued. "Where did the objects come from originally? Who found them and when?"

He searched my face, trying to determine whether to trust me. "Very well. The story is well known in my community. My father was a sheep herder. He often stayed out overnight with the animals, sometimes for a week if he traveled far enough away. He herded his flock onto higher ground one spring, a series of rocky hills and cliffs. A lamb became separated from the other sheep and my father went in search of it. He spied the animal near a crevasse high up on a cliff and realized that it was an entrance to a cave. Curious about what might be in the cave, he picked up a rock and threw it in. He was surprised to hear it shatter something. When he crept inside he found large clay pots. Most held nothing, but in one of them he found the artifacts." Yersan glared at me. "Now tell me how you knew about Kandovan."

The story he'd just told was a carbon copy of the famous Dead Sea scrolls discovery. I pretended to believe him. "A very interesting find. Material embedded in the statue and seals point to their having been found in the Kandovan area. The objects were sent to North America by a man named Helmstetter—does that name mean anything to you?"

"You know perfectly well it does. He stole the objects from my father in the first place."

"He just showed up thirty-five years ago in your hometown and managed to walk out with those valuables? Hard to believe. How long did he stay in Kandovan? When your family realized he'd stolen them, didn't they try to trace him after he left the village?"

Yersan made an impatient gesture with his hand. "You

appreciate I was only a child when this happened, so I must rely on what my father told me. Helmstetter came to the village because, according to him, it was close to a powerful place, full of magic. He stayed for many months, ingratiated himself with the villagers, hired a local boy as a guide, and set about exploring the surrounding area. He didn't divulge to my father exactly what he was seeking."

I'd learned from Samuel that isolated communities in the Middle East were highly suspicious of strangers, let alone Westerners. "I understand Kandovan's a small settlement and perhaps not too trusting of people they don't know. Kind of hard to believe they'd be taken in by Helmstetter."

"Then you're not very familiar with the man, obviously. He had an aura about him. He amused people with demonstrations of magic. Some admired him. Others feared him enough to stay out of his way. And he had money. He used it to burrow his way into my family's trust like a beautiful lizard with a poisonous bite."

"What became of him?"

"I don't know. One night he simply vanished. The next day my father discovered that his prized objects were gone. As I said, my father was a simple sheep herder who in his entire life had journeyed no further than Tabriz. It was well beyond his means and ability to search for him. Now it's your turn. Who owns the objects?"

"That information is not mine to share."

Yersan straightened his jacket. "Then I must ask you to go. I'm very busy. I'm sorry I agreed to see you at all." Bennet tugged my arm. Before I followed her out of the room, I turned to Yersan. "I wish I could have been more help. But the confidentiality of my clients is very important, I'm sure you understand."

He gave me a cold look.

Our elderly greeter was nowhere to be seen, so we let ourselves out.

Fourteen

"Men." Bennet swore as we headed down the sidewalk. "You should have let me do the talking. I would have gotten more out of him. At least I recorded it all."

I glanced quickly at her. I hadn't thought to tape the conversation. "His touching story about his father braving dark caves was a complete fabrication. Nor did he strike me as the kind of guy to go around volunteering such information to complete strangers. I'm pretty sure Yersan has no legitimate claim to the objects. But it's nice to have a record of exactly what he said. Good thinking."

"What's his motivation then, if not to retrieve a family treasure?" Bennet said.

"Getting his hands on a fortune. I bet he first heard about the objects when Tricia Ross sent out the theft inquiry and made up his mind to make a pitch for them. The story about his being from the area is no doubt factual. Northwest Iran is known to be a primary seat for Zoroastrianism. And by the look of that flaming urn we passed on our way in, Yersan must be a practitioner. But I still think he's a fraud. It's a common scam in the antiquities world. Make a claim on objects whose provenance can't be accurately determined then threaten to tie the rightful owner up in the courts. Stall any potential sales for years. The owner decides the best course of action is to settle and part with some of the value."

"I'm not so sure. I was watching him closely, and it seemed to me his anger was genuine. Under different circumstances I had the feeling he could be dangerous. What are you going to do about him?"

"Nothing I can do—except stay on my guard. Maybe sic Strauss on him." I laughed. "I'd love to see those two go head to head."

Bennet and I hopped onto the 2 train, got off at Thirty-fourth, and headed down to West Thirtieth and the Conjuring Arts Center. The arched doorway and carved lintel seemed appropriately medieval for a library about the history of magic. "I'm not sure what to expect here," I said as we took the elevator to the fifth floor.

"As long as we don't disappear into thin air before we get out again," Bennet laughed.

We stepped into a charming room that looked anything but esoteric—comfortable antique furniture, a polished hardwood floor covered with Turkish carpets, and a multitude of books arranged neatly on the tall shelves. An old black-and-white banner stretching above one shelf announced HOUDINI AT THE HIPPODROME. Just the kind of place that made you want to settle in for an afternoon and search through the treasure trove.

"John Madison and Margaux Bennet." I extended my hand to a tall woman with long gray hair who greeted us. "Thanks for arranging our appointment so quickly."

"Julia Morrow. Glad to help. If you don't mind my asking, is Helmstetter the subject of an article or a book you're working on? We've had a few inquiries about him lately."

"Yes, I'm writing about him," Bennet jumped in. "Who else was interested?"

Morrow's lips turned down in a slight frown. "That's private information."

"Of course. I understand," Bennet said quickly.

Morrow showed us where to stow our coats and then led us into another room with a long rectangular table.

After we'd signed the register I took a closer look around. "It must be fascinating to work here." Many of the books were old tomes in gilt, rich burgundy leather, and weathered green cloth with titles like *Valuable Secrets, Discoverie of Witchcraft,* and *The Expert at the Card Table.*

Morrow smiled proudly and pulled a book from a nearby shelf. "Watch this." The pages changed color as she thumbed through them.

"That's amazing," Bennet cooed.

"We own a page from Caxton's *Canterbury Tales* printed in 1496, a pilgrim's description of a magician. And we have a collection of personal papers from some of the most famous magicians in history, documents that escaped being burned through the ages over fears of witchcraft. You wanted to know about Helmstetter but I'm afraid there's very little about him. He disappeared before he could develop much of a reputation as a practicing conjurer. On the other hand, a lot is known about Strauss."

"We'd like to know more about Strauss too," I said. "I've only just met him."

Morrow folded her arms and leaned against a bookcase. "I've never met him myself, but the stories are legion. He came from a New Orleans family who ran a drama troupe; they traveled all over the country. Strauss was pressed into acting at an early age."

"New Orleans? He has no trace of that accent," Bennet said.

"No. He was ashamed of his family—they weren't much more than burlesque performers. Strauss was actually quite brilliant; he was accepted into Harvard on scholarship to study psychology, and that's when he managed to drop his accent. Nowadays you'd think he was a Boston Brahmin." Morrow pointed to the Houdini banner. "But he never lost his dramatic flair. He was a born showman, like Houdini. He chose to become primarily a mentalist, using traditional magic mostly to warm his audience up. His reputation for psychic powers grew to the point where people would shower him with money for private sessions."

"Strauss claims his assistant betrayed him," Bennet interjected. "Do you know anything about Helmstetter's apprenticeship?"

"People say Strauss grew jealous of his talent. And ultimately, Helmstetter was the only person to get the better of Lucas Strauss. I can't tell you much more. Why don't you take a seat and I'll bring you what I've found in our archives."

Once Morrow was out of the room Bennet glanced at me, put a finger to her lips, then hurried over to the register we'd signed and quickly flipped through it. She ran her finger down a page and let out a breath, shut the register, and returned to her seat at the table. She leaned over and whispered, "Interesting!"

"What?"

"Yersan paid a visit here two days ago. Clearly he knows more about Helmstetter than he let on. Pretty suspicious."

Morrow returned just then with a large folio, a file of letters, and a poster encased in a double sheet of clear plastic. The poster advertised a show at Milwaukee's famous Oriental Theatre. Morrow spread it on the table in front of us. It showed the theater's interior, a baroque banquet of soaring pillars, luxuriant draperies, stained-glass chandeliers, porcelain lions, and elaborate frescoes. It looked more like a maharaja's palace than a Milwaukee entertainment hall. Pictured center stage was a much younger Lucas Strauss wearing a black bowler and tux, releasing a pack of cards that appeared to float in the air. Morrow pointed to the image of a man standing stage left behind Strauss. "George Helmstetter," she said.

He had dark, slicked-back hair, a goatee, an aquiline nose, and a trim figure. Like an old-fashioned dandy, I thought. Assuming an exaggerated pose, he held a curved, bejeweled dagger, no doubt to advertise Strauss's next act. It was hard to say why, but as Yersan had remarked, I sensed an aura about Helmstetter, a menacing presence. Perhaps it was the way he carried the dagger, as if he were at ease with it, as if he'd enjoy using it for real.

Bennet sat very still beside me, her eyes transfixed by the image. I suspected she found Helmstetter as troubling a figure as I did.

I looked up at Morrow. "May I take a photo of this?"

We positioned the poster under the strongest light and I snapped a few pictures on my phone, then set it aside and opened the folio. It turned out to contain bound copies of *The Conjurer* magazine.

"There were only eight issues," Morrow said. "The first was published in 1975." She flipped through one of them until she got to an article entitled "The Lost Magicians." It discussed what had become of young illusionists who'd never achieved the success predicted for them. Several paragraphs were devoted to Helmstetter, brimming with phrases like "a soaring talent," "a singular magician," "one whom accomplished conjurers heralded."

"This piece was written by Veronica Sills, an entertainment reporter. She was in love with Helmstetter," Morrow said.

Bennet's head jerked up. "But he was married."

I couldn't hold back a laugh. "That isn't much of a barrier."

Morrow closed the book and patted the file. "Last year, Sills donated her personal papers associated with Helmstetter to the library. I'll leave you to peruse them. Look for the years 1968 and '69. This was no ardent fan whose feelings got out of control. Some of the letters will leave you in no doubt that he encouraged her romantic notions in every possible way."

"Last year? Is she still alive?" I asked.

"Far as I know. She lives in Harlem."

"Do you think she'd agree to meet with us?"

Morrow seemed to have warmed to us. "I'll call her if you like, and see."

We looked through the letters and notes, the exchanges between Sills and Helmstetter. I was surprised that Veronica Sills had included them; some contained intimate, explicit descriptions of their lovemaking. Hardly fare for public consumption. Had she done this as a kind of payback?

Bennet read alongside me. "What a cheating pig he was," she muttered. "I wonder how many other women he was stringing along?"

But it was the last letter that stood out explosively, like a lit match cast into an oil slick. A short note in Helmstetter's hand:

Darling Veronica,

The flight to Istanbul was turbulent and unpleasant, made all the worse by the knowledge that you and I will be parted for some time to come. I write to you from my hotel room overlooking Pergamon. Will I meet the angel of the underworld tomorrow when I venture into those ancient caves? For that is what my studies lead me to believe is possible.

It's been a lonely enterprise, the years of work I've poured into esoteric pursuits. Impossible to share with any colleagues who would simply laugh at my endeavors. It is for that reason, especially, that your loyalty has sustained me.

If I am to be disappointed in my quest tomorrow I will depart Pergamon.

After that it is on to Eden.

I leave the softest kiss on your lips until I see you again,

George

Fifteen

Was the reference to Eden meaningful at all? Could Helmstetter be using it as a form of code to hide his real destination? Or was it an in-joke between the two of them, a mistake to read anything more into it? I took the letter over to Morrow and pointed to the Eden remark. "Do you have any idea what he means here?"

Morrow read the sentence and shook her head. "No. Strange thing to say."

Perhaps Helmstetter *had* meant it seriously. The Adam and Eve cylinder seal he sent to his wife was, according to myth, set in Eden. Maybe he thought he knew the original garden's location. There are all kinds of odd personalities gullible enough to believe they can find the path to immortality, I reasoned, or that the Garden of Eden, Noah's Ark, and the Holy Grail actually existed. But the clever, ambitious man Lucas Strauss described sounded too cagey to get caught up in fanciful ideas. And yet he'd claimed a direct connection with Faust. I hoped his former lover could shed more light on all this.

After another half hour leafing through the files, we found nothing more relating to Helmstetter. Morrow said she'd connected with Veronica Sills, who agreed to talk with me. I gave Morrow my card, thanked her and we left the library. Bennet was uncharacteristically silent on the way to the subway. She trudged along with an angry expression, hands stuck into her pockets, her bag swinging from her shoulder. "What's bothering you?" I asked.

"The man was evil. You can see it on his face—those cruel lips. The poor wife probably suffered horribly when she found out he was in love with another woman."

"You don't know that. Why are you so sensitive about it?"

She sighed. "I'm going to spend the rest of the afternoon at the library putting an outline together and then go to see Strauss this evening and try to persuade him to give me an advance. Then I can get out of your hair."

I nodded, appreciating her efforts to get back on her own feet. "Where does he live?"

"On the Erie Canal, west of the Adirondack Forest Preserve. He bought an old industrial property there when he retired from show business."

"That's a long drive, Bennet."

"I know. Can I stay with you tonight? I won't be back until really late. If I can pry some money out of Strauss, I should be able to find somewhere else in a couple of days."

Without waiting for a response, she waved goodbye and headed uptown.

✵

On my walk home, questions swirled through my mind. Why had cylinder seals and a Ubaid-era statue ended up in northern Iran, so far away from the archaeological sites in southern Iraq? How had Helmstetter come to possess them? I didn't believe he'd stolen them from Yersan's family. Not in the manner described, anyway. And what did the allusion to Eden in Helmstetter's last letter to Veronica Sills mean? Was it a lovers' code or a real location? How did Trithemius's book of angel magic fit into it all? I needed to talk it all over with someone, and Tricia Ross seemed the logical choice.

When I called, she said I'd be welcome to come by that evening at seven. In her seventies but still energetic, she'd substantially reduced her teaching load and worked now primarily as a graduate adviser; she spent only a few days a month at U of Pennsylvania. She lived on Long Island, an easy drive after rush hour.

Meanwhile, I stopped by Barnes & Noble to see if I could find anything about the search for the Garden of Eden. One title looked promising: *Legend: The Genesis of Civilization* by historian David Rohl. Leafing through it, I could see it contained fascinating observations about the early Mesopotamians.

I arrived back at the apartment to find Loki's bowl upended and water spilled all over the kitchen floor. My makeshift barrier was in pieces; somehow she'd managed to breach it. A suspicious puddle stained the living room carpet and spots of blood were on the hardwood. The vet had stitched up a couple of cuts on her rump; I feared they may have broken open in her struggle to get out of the kitchen. Loki couldn't possibly have escaped the apartment—but where was she? After a frantic ten minutes I found her cowering under my bed. I coaxed her out with some tidbits of meat and held her until she stopped trembling, cursing myself for having left her alone.

Only then did I notice my desk. My laptop was missing. I set Loki down and opened the file drawers. They'd been searched, and hastily from the look of it. My papers were askew. No effort had been made to straighten them. I made it a practice to keep all my important documents on a flash drive. Ever since my old apartment had been vandalized, I'd stowed my flash drive and passport in a hollowed-out book—a photographic journey of Italy. It sat on one of my lower bookshelves. I pulled it out, thankful to see both were still there. My really precious items—the contents of my childhood treasure chest, along with the rare book I'd rescued featuring precious illustrations by de Ribera—were in the wall safe. I let out a sigh of relief when I saw the safe was intact. As far as I could tell, nothing else had been touched. The thief was after information.

And I had a pretty good idea who it was.

I grabbed my phone and called Bennet. "It's John. Keep an eye out for Yersan. I think he's just broken into my place and lifted my laptop. I'm worried he might try to threaten you."

I heard her suck in a breath. "He's upping the ante pretty fast then."

"If it's him—yeah. This is going beyond some scam; I think you may have been right about him. He's got another agenda."

Next I called down to the security guard. He said the only non-resident allowed upstairs in the last several hours was a florist's delivery man with a bouquet for someone on the third floor. The man had provided ID. I asked him to check whether the flowers had been delivered. A few minutes later he phoned back to say that no one had received flowers.

I considered calling the police and then rejected the thought. They wouldn't bother with a simple break-in and the deductible on my insurance was more than the cost of a new laptop. I imagined Yersan was searching for evidence as to who owned the artifacts.

By the time I'd straightened the place up, cleaned the kitchen, fed Loki and taken her out, it was time to leave for my appointment with Tricia Ross. Loki was still on edge, in no state to stay alone again. I got some treats, wrapped her in a warm blanket, and carried her to the car.

A chicken snack wrap and a large coffee from the McDonald's drive-through at Tenth and Thirty-fourth satisfied my hunger pains. Not my top choice of meal, but I was starving. I offered Loki the last bite but she wouldn't take it. Clearly she had better taste than I did.

Samuel and I had always chuckled at the name of the Long Island town where I was heading—Babylon. A more different landscape from ancient Iraq's ornate seat of power couldn't be imagined. The flat coastal terrain and relatively few trees made everything look stripped down and stark in the fist of winter. Now, in the early evening dark and with no wind, the ocean lay flat and gray; the water lent a salty sweetness to the air. I passed marine yards dotted with the skeletons of old sailing boats, iron hauls and winches, yachts covered with canvas and put to bed for the season, their keels like giant fish fins. It occurred to me how ironic it was that Tricia Ross, a specialist in Near East culture, would choose to live surrounded by water. Perhaps the years she'd spent working in dry, dusty areas had driven her to move here.

Tricia's house on Virginia Road was a cute, folksy, two-story clapboard. It had a stone walk and a garden that I imagined brimmed with flowers and shrubs in the summer but was now only brittle brown stalks. I arrived a little early and was glad to see her lights on and a car in the drive. Before we left I'd given Loki her medication; the sedative had kept her snoozing throughout the car ride. I opened the window a little to make sure she had air. She didn't even lift her head when I got out and shut the door.

Tricia didn't answer the bell. I waited a few minutes and tried again. I remembered she was punctual to the point of absurdity, known for refusing to let students enter the lecture hall if her class had already started. After another wait, I thumped my fist on the door. Still nothing. It was now almost fifteen minutes past the time of our appointment. I pulled out my phone. When the call connected, I got voice mail.

Samuel once told me that Tricia had fallen and broken her hip in Kuwait a few years before, and that she'd had mobility problems ever since. The accident put an end to her working trips to the Middle East. I worried she may have fallen again.

The lights were on next door. I forded the bushes through to the pathway and rang the neighbor's bell. A tough-looking man in his forties opened the door, glowering, probably because I'd just interrupted his favorite TV program. A heavyset woman I assumed was his wife hovered behind him.

"Hate bothering you but I have an appointment with Tricia next door and even though she appears to be home, she's not answering the bell. I tried calling her too. I'm concerned something may have happened and I'm not sure what to do."

He looked across the way to Tricia's front porch and squinted. "She's home. I saw her drive in around six."

"That's not like Tricia, Jack," his wife said. "We've got her spare key. Why don't I just run over and stick my head in the front—"

"Nope," he growled. "I'll go. Wait here a sec," he said to me.

When he returned he grabbed his jacket off a wall hook and motioned for me to follow him. "We'll check the back door first," he said. "Sometimes she leaves it open. Not much ever happens around here."

Jack led the way down a narrow flagstone walk running beside the house. I almost collided with him when he stopped abruptly. "That's weird." He jerked his head toward a small side window. "She's never had curtains on that kitchen window."

It wasn't a curtain. The window looked to be covered with a bath towel. Jack tried the back door but it was locked. He pulled the key out of his pocket. "Guess it's the front entrance for us after all."

We'd made enough noise tromping down the walk and fiddling with the back door that she should have heard us—but the house remained still as a tomb. Jack stuck the key in the front door lock. "Tricia will have my hide for doing this. She's very private." He twisted the knob and opened the front door. We stepped into the living room. Jack called out. Tricia didn't answer. He went through another doorway into what I assumed was the kitchen. I couldn't see ahead because his bulky figure filled the door frame, but I heard him readily enough.

"Mother of God."

Sixteen

Tricia was slumped against the kitchen table. Her head drooped on her chest, her ankles were trussed to the table legs, and her arms were bound by a thin cable to the spindles of the chair she sat on. The cable had been tied so tightly her hands were blue. Her mouth was a mass of blood—blood that had spattered onto her white sweater and now dripped from the tablecloth onto the floor. Her glassy eyes stared at nothing. I heard cursing and was barely aware it came from me. My stomach heaved.

"You got a phone?" Jack yelled. "Use it." He stood over Tricia protectively, part of him desperate to help her, another part seeming to realize she was already gone.

I called 911. I don't know exactly what I said. When my wits returned, I took a quick look around the room. The kitchen hadn't been updated for some time. It had old white appliances, a scuffed linoleum floor. Canisters and an open box of chai tea stood on the marbled Arborite counter. A teacup upturned in its saucer, crumpled napkins, and something small and round, all blood spattered, were strewn on the table.

I insisted we go outside to wait for the police. Jack agreed reluctantly. When we did, his wife peeked around their front door. "Everything okay, Jack?"

"Stay inside, Mandy."

Mandy shrugged on a pink duffel coat and rushed over, wide eyed. "What's wrong?" she said, staring at Tricia's front door.

Jack took a deep breath. "Tricia's dead."

Mandy stared at him in disbelief and burst into tears. Jack held her in an awkward bear hug until we heard sirens approaching.

A cruiser soon appeared around the bend; in its wake, an ambulance sped down the gloomy, empty street. Jack waved to the cops, who parked in front of the house, jumped out of their cruiser, and hurried over. The ambulance braked behind them.

"What's up, Jack?" one of the cops asked. His eyes flicked over me.

"Tricia's in there. Murdered. Some evil fuck beat the shit outta her."

"Stay with them, Kent," the cop said to his younger partner. He followed the ambulance attendants inside and returned about ten minutes later. He nodded toward me. "Friend of yours, Jack?"

Jack stepped away as if to disown his acquaintance with me. "Nope. He's how come I found Tricia. Knocked on our door. I let us into her place with the spare key she gave us for emergencies."

The cop glanced at me again, an appraising look. "Detective Shea," he introduced himself. "What's your name?"

"John Madison. I made the 911 call. I was supposed to meet Tricia here at seven. When she didn't answer, I got worried and went next door."

"That your Porsche over there?"

"Yes."

"Need to see some ID."

I pulled out my wallet and handed it to him with a sinking feeling. This was not going to go well.

"Jack, why don't you and Mandy get back home. I'll be over as soon as I can."

Jack nodded and put his arm around Mandy, who shuddered and pulled her coat tighter around her. They walked to their front door and Jack ushered her inside.

More sirens wailed. Two more Suffolk County police cruisers pulled up. Neighbors ventured out of their houses and stood at the top of their drives, gawking with that mixture of fascination and horror that always seems to accompany a tragedy.

A heavyset cop got out of the first cruiser and hustled over.

"Babysit Mr. Madison for me, Jeff," Shea said, handing him my wallet. "Check him out." He gave me a quick look. "I'll be back for a talk in a minute."

"My dog's in my car," I said. "I can't leave her for too long."

"She'll keep."

Jeff's babysitting consisted of frisking me for weapons, taking my cellphone and key fob, and stowing me in the back seat of his vehicle. He got into the driver's seat and thumbed through my wallet. He was parked right behind my car in Tricia's driveway. I could see two front paws, a black snout, and two bright eyes peeping over the front seat. Loki didn't bark. Her vocalizations were more like a yowl. When that didn't bring me running she moved over to the window and started scratching at it with her front paws. By the time this day was over, she'd be so frightened I'd never get her calmed down.

Almost an hour passed. The ambulance attendants left. A white SUV arrived, SUFFOLK COUNTY CRIME SCENE printed on its side. A man in a black windbreaker and pants climbed out, nodded toward the cruiser. He took a bag out of the trunk and went in.

Tricia's murder was such a shock that I hadn't yet wondered who might have done it. Now the implications of Yersan's threatening behavior came home to me. Had he caught Tricia unaware, forced her to reveal that Strauss owned the artifacts, tortured her to extract the information? No one could withstand a beating like that. How long had she held out? My mind raced with terrible images. It suddenly struck me that Strauss, and Bennet if she was still at his place, might be in danger too. I knocked on the Plexiglas partition to get the cop's attention. He shook his head without turning around. "Hey!" I pounded the glass. "Hey!" Still he ignored me.

Shea returned and tapped on Jeff's window. Jeff rolled it down and they exchanged a few words, but I couldn't catch what was said. Jeff handed my key fob to Shea, who used it to pop the trunk of my Porsche. He looked inside, shut it, then opened the back door and slid in beside me. "Let's hear it from your point of view," he said.

"Before I tell you, someone else is in danger from the man I suspect killed Tricia. I need to call my friend right now to warn him. His number's on my phone." I expected an argument but Shea handed my phone over straightaway. I called Strauss. His line switched to voice mail so I left a message. I couldn't reach Bennet either but left a message for her too. I prayed I hadn't been too late.

I filled Shea in on what had happened since Bennet first walked through my door, including Yersan's harassment of Tricia, and gave him the shop address in Flatbush. I told him about my place being broken into and my laptop stolen soon after my visit to the shop. Shea listened closely, interrupting only to clarify a point, then jotted down a few lines in his notebook. When he finished, he sat back and sighed. "What time did you get here?"

"Couple of minutes before seven."

"Anyone see you drive up?"

"Not that I know of, but hold on." The long wait in the cruiser had given me time to think. I'd anticipated his question and realized I did have proof. I dug into my pocket and pulled out a receipt. "Here. I bought some food and coffee at McDonald's in New York just after six P.M."

He reached for the receipt, read it, and handed it back. "Okay. That's good. Did you see any signs of forced entry when you first knocked on her door?"

I shook my head. "No. And that's when I got Jack next door. He had a key."

"Okay. How do I contact you?"

I handed over my card, and then he returned my things. "That's it?" I said.

"Yes, for now. You can go. I'll be in touch."

Loki yelped and leapt into my arms when I opened my car door. I snapped on her leash and let her take a leak before we left. As I backed out of Tricia's driveway, I waved toward Shea. He didn't seem to notice.

Seventeen

February 18, 2005

It was after midnight by the time I made it back to my place to find Bennet sleeping on the sofa, one arm thrown around a plump pillow. The eiderdown had slipped away from her shoulders and the tiny T she wore had ridden up, exposing her naked breast. Even in my troubled state of mind, I found that enticing.

She woke with a start, gaped at me, then hastily yanked her top down.

"You're back so late. I was worried about you," she murmured, still half asleep.

"I called you a bunch of times. Don't you listen to your messages?"

"The battery died. Have to get a new one tomorrow. Why? What happened?"

"It's been one hell of a night. Tricia Ross was killed."

"What?" She sat up straight.

"I went to see her this evening out on Long Island. She was beaten to death in her own kitchen." The scene ran through my mind once more. I sat on the edge of the sofa and related how the rest of the evening had played out.

"You're not saying they suspect you?"

"Sure felt like it while I was stuck in the back of that cruiser, but no, I don't think so." I slumped back on the sofa beside her. "I can't believe Tricia Ross is dead. I didn't know her but my brother did and he really respected her. Samuel said she was fearless, and braved some pretty narrow scrapes on-site in Iraq. Not this time."

Bennet placed a slender arm around my shoulders. "God, that's terrible. Who could have done it, do you think?"

"Did our visit to Yersan get him so fired up that he went out to threaten her?"

"Well, he was disagreeable, but I doubt he'd be capable of something that violent."

"I gave his name to the police. Just in case. What happened with Strauss? Did he give you any money?"

"I didn't end up going after all. I called him before I set out. He said he didn't want me to come up but agreed to send me the advance through an email transfer. So I'm rich now." She laughed sarcastically, her fingers brushing my cheek. "What an awful experience for you."

"You said it. But much worse for Tricia. This whole thing is so fucked up."

I calmed down a little after talking more with Bennet. She went back to sleep and I stumbled into my bedroom, undressed, rolled into bed, and drifted off. At some point my body jerked violently. Another bout of sleep paralysis. This time I had an overwhelming sense of déjà vu. It felt as if my hands and legs were bound tightly. I was in great pain but unable to move. A throwback to the times

Alessio held me under his spell or a flashback to the terror at Kutha? Somehow this seemed different. As if it were an actual memory. Once again I put up a monumental struggle to shake myself out of it. Despite a couple of shots of scotch to calm my nerves I lay awake for at least an hour before falling into a restless sleep.

The aroma of fresh coffee and bacon crackling in the pan woke me. Hearing me stir, Loki padded into the bedroom. She still walked on her three good legs, gingerly lifting the injured one with the pink cast off the floor. She licked my shoulder and I eased myself out of bed.

Bennet gave me a smile when I walked into the kitchen. She stood in her bare feet, wearing the same T-shirt over mint-green nylon panties fringed with lace. Quite the tasty treat. "Always did love a barefoot cook in the kitchen," I said.

"Bacon and tomato sandwiches—my specialty. Help yourself to a coffee and take a seat while I wait on you hand and foot. After what you went through last night, you deserve it."

I sat down and sipped at the coffee, taking surreptitious glances at Bennet's comely figure. The coffee wasn't my blend. Something stronger with a hint of chocolate. Bennet set the plates down, pulled a chair closer to me, and sat. "I took Loki out."

"In your underwear?" I laughed.

Bennet blushed. "Of course not. It's raining. My jeans got soaked."

"You could probably get away with it. All kinds of fashion statements in Madison Square." I took a bite of the sandwich. Perfectly done, juicy Canadian back bacon, thickly sliced tomato— where had she bought such sweet tomatoes this time of year?—and lightly toasted brown bread. "You're hired," I said, "but I can't afford as much as Strauss."

She smiled between enormous bites, finishing before me. We wiped our hands on paper napkins and sat with our coffees. After breakfast and its idyllic mood of domesticity, the world seemed to have come to rights again. The sense of doom from my sleep-paralysis episode had all but disappeared. Bennet's next words spoiled that brief interlude in an instant.

Eighteen

Bennet glanced at me as if afraid of my reaction to what she was about to say.

"What?"

"I don't know whether I should tell you."

"Now you have to."

"It's probably nothing. I mean, how could he possibly know?"

"Now you *really* have to tell me."

"It's Strauss. When I spoke to him last night he said a *very* strange thing. I don't want to ruin your day or anything. The article about you I'm working on? He said it would end up being your obituary."

I choked a little on my coffee. "Seriously? That's crazy. He likes to play with people, mind-fuck them. It's what he does for a living." Still, Strauss's remark bothered me. Especially coming so soon after Tricia's murder.

Bennet reached across the kitchen table and gave my shoulder a squeeze. "I know. I shouldn't have said anything but it freaked me out and I didn't want to hide it from you. Not after what happened yesterday. We've got to be really careful." She stood up and refilled my coffee. "So, tell me. What's the mystery about your background Strauss is so intrigued with?"

"It's not for the record—I don't want it in the article. Okay?"

"Agreed."

"And no talking to Evelyn behind my back."

"Fine," she said, a little exasperated.

"My half brother, Samuel—he was much older than me— brought me to New York from Turkey when I was three. Our father, who was Greek, fled after World War II and went to Turkey where he married my mother. They both died in a mining accident caused by an earthquake. That's what I was told, but less and less of the story adds up. I don't believe it anymore."

Bennet played with a curl of her red hair. "And at Gina's, Strauss hinted he has some information about that."

"Yes, but I don't see how he could. Really, I think he's just bluffing." I took a last swig of my coffee and got up. "I'm going to hit the books for a while."

"I'll set up my laptop in here then," Bennet said. "Watching you will be too distracting." She punctuated that with a flirty laugh. "Can I have your notes on those trips you took to Iraq?"

"Yeah, uh, hold on. Let me find them." After scanning them quickly, I gave her my rough copies, enough material to keep her busy for a couple of hours. That done, it was time to source my own reading materials. I'd donated Samuel's library to his university, except for some of the more important volumes, and kept all his journals. I looked through a couple of them now.

But I found it hard to concentrate at first. Loki noisily batted her makeshift toys around with her nose on the hardwood floor and Strauss's obituary line still disturbed me. The illusionist had a certain compelling draw, as a master hypnotist would, but I told myself it was simply an art he'd learned. No one could foretell the future. Nevertheless, his prediction, coupled with the previous night's sleep paralysis, pushed me to make an appointment to see my doctor later that afternoon.

As I leafed through Samuel's journals I finally left my fears behind to focus on another mystery—an ancient one. The Sumerian artifacts Strauss had shown us, and his claim that they'd been found near Kandovan rather than southern Iraq, intrigued me. For scholars, the Sumerians posed a giant enigma. Evidence of their presence showed up in southern Iraq between 3500 and 3100 B.C., a period associated with the onset of large-scale agriculture and the development of the first cities. But no one could prove their origins. Their language had no known affiliates, modern or ancient. Strauss's artifacts had been dated to around that time but from a place hundreds of miles to the northeast. Had the ancient Sumerians in southern Iraq simply grown out of the indigenous Ubaid culture that preceded them or were they especially gifted migrants from a different region?

The various theories—they came by boat from the Ganges river basin or they were a displaced Semitic people—were nothing more than guesswork.

Although Samuel respected the efforts to trace ethnic origins through pottery, written language, and physical remains, he believed the answers lay in their mythology. "They have told us where they came from in their stories," Samuel wrote, "and we only need to listen." Based on a myth, he'd concluded that the Sumerians were originally mountain people, pushed out of their domain by some calamity, environmental perhaps. In the early third millennium B.C. they moved down to the southern fertile marshes near the delta of the Tigris and Euphrates, where their advanced culture allowed them to dominate the people already living there.

The myth described a legendary conflict between Enmerkar, the king of Uruk, an early Sumerian city state in southern Iraq, and the lord of Aratta, a mountain kingdom in northern Iran. The two regions had a similar language and culture along with a trading relationship—grain from Uruk traded for precious metals and wood from Aratta. Another myth gave a concise description of the mountain kingdom.

> Aratta's battlements are of green lapis lazuli, its
> walls and its towering brickwork are bright red,
> their brick clay is made of tinstone dug out in the
> mountains where the cypress grows.

Inanna, the principal goddess of Uruk, was originally a mountain deity from Aratta. As I read, it became clear to me that the people of the two regions had so many similarities they were essentially part of the same Sumerian culture. But more important, insofar as my quest was concerned, Strauss's artifacts came from the same area in northwestern Iran that the myth called Aratta. The last line in Samuel's journal surprised me.

He'd pointed out that the word for the mountain plain where Aratta was located was *Edin*.

According to the Sumerians, who carefully recorded their history, Edin was a real place. Could this have anything to do with Helmstetter's reference to Eden in his last letter to Veronica Sills? I wished once more that my brother was alive so I could discuss the idea with him. I had only his writings left to try to decipher. In the margin beside this entry he'd written *Reginald Arthur Walker*. I didn't recognize the name and wondered why Samuel had put it there.

I glanced at my watch and reluctantly shut the journal, realizing that if I didn't leave now, I'd be late for my doctor's appointment.

Bennet was still immersed in my notes, and when I stuck my head in to let her know I was going out, she mumbled what sounded like "'Kay."

"Can Loki stay with you?"

She nodded without looking up. Leaving her alone in my apartment seemed incautious, but I reasoned that if she wanted to look through anything, or worse, steal, she'd had ample opportunity the evening before. I shut the door quietly on my way out.

As I stepped onto the sidewalk a figure detached itself from the shadows at the side of my building. Yersan. He headed directly for me.

"You told the police I killed that professor," he snapped.

"What makes you think that?"

"You're the one who asked me about her."

"You'd been harassing her. She probably complained about it to the police herself."

He shook his head slowly. "No. It was you. After your visit to my shop I pondered, why are you involving yourself in my affairs at all? You're a dealer like me and I've been checking. Your record's not so clean. You want those artifacts to sell yourself! For a fat commission. It's what I think."

"I did tell the police you broke into my apartment and stole my laptop. I'll find a way to make you pay for that."

"I know nothing of this." Yersan shrugged.

"I'm late for an appointment. Don't come back here." I pushed a finger into his chest to emphasize my words. But he wasn't finished and knocked my hand away.

"Leave this whole thing behind you, Madison, or I will make sure you don't get another chance to smear me."

I waved him off and carried on. After a minute I checked to make sure he wasn't still following. Then I whipped out my phone and called Bennet, warning her to slide the inside bolt on the apartment door. Yersan's threats made him only more suspicious. And it was clear I'd made an enemy, probably a lethal one.

I tried to put the confrontation with Yersan out of my mind as I sat on the 1 train up Broadway. I'd been seeing the same doctor since my days at Columbia; his office was on West 112th, not far from the enormous Cathedral of St. John the Divine. The route traversed an old Indian pathway once called the Hollow Trail. As the train clattered its way north, I thought about the cathedral's life-sized statue of St. Michael, the winged archangel I'd always regarded as a profoundly pagan work, surrounded as it was by sculptures of wild, mystical beings and symbols. Fascinating and quite at odds with traditional Christianity.

"Well, John, haven't seen you for ages," my doctor said when he ushered me into his office. "I've received the reports from your specialists, though—glad to see you're still breathing." He punctuated this with a barking laugh. He always found a way to lighten the mood. A pint-sized man in his fifties, Dr. Cass had a booming voice quite at odds with his height. He looked at me over his glasses. "What can I do for you today?"

"The injuries have all healed, the blood disorder seems unsolvable, but the sleep paralysis is getting really bad. Last night was the worst I've ever experienced." I indicated the fat file on his desk. "I even went to a sleep disorders clinic. Nothing's worked and it's driving me crazy. I'm hoping you can think of something." Cass had always seemed practical and possessed of good common sense. I shouldn't have bothered with specialists and come to see him sooner.

He pursed his lips. "Atonia. It's common enough, you know. I've had it myself on night shifts at the hospital when I'm dead tired. You experience that momentary terror—it seems as if you're paralyzed—but after all, that's what sleep is. The body is immobile while we sleep. With the atonia syndrome, your brain just wakes up before your body does."

"Why does that happen?"

"Well, for one, it's much healthier to be immobilized during REM sleep so you won't act out your dreams. Otherwise homicide would definitely be on the rise." His laugh boomed again in the small office. "How often do you have these episodes?"

"More and more. Lately, at least on a weekly basis. And last night it was almost as if I was hallucinating along with it too."

Cass frowned. "How so?"

"It felt like my hands and feet were tied up. That I was bound."

"You were having a nightmare. And transiting out of it. That's not a classical hallucination."

He flipped through my file until he found a sheet of notes. "You've had one hell of a time, John, starting with your car accident and Samuel's death. Your body took a lot of punishment in the Middle East because you got yourself into situations you weren't trained for. Or, I suspect, able to deal with psychologically. Emotional stress can be deadly if it's prolonged and severe enough." He sat down behind his desk and steepled his fingers. "I think you're suffering from PTSD. No doubt you've heard of it. There's no record in your file that you've seen a counselor, so I assume you haven't?"

"No."

"Well, let's check your vital signs and then we'll see about that."

After going through the usual procedures, he put the blood pressure monitor back and gestured for me to sit in the chair again. He sat at his desk and scribbled something out on a prescription pad, tore off the leaf, and handed it to me. "You're not taking any drugs right now?"

I hesitated.

He smiled. "I mean of the prescription variety."

I shook my head.

"I'm recommending you take prazosin. In layman's terms it's called Minipress. You may notice some dizziness and tiredness at first. Let me know if that happens." His voice lowered, taking on a stern, doctorly tone. "And you need to talk to someone, John. See a counselor. I can recommend a good one who's helped a lot of soldiers. After what you've experienced she'll have a cornucopia of bad memories to sift through."

"I'll think about it, thanks." I left his office with the prescription clutched in my hand. I wished I'd told him everything. I'd tried to convince myself that the sensation of being bound could be my body's way of interpreting my inability to move, the same way dreams can be simply a reflection of emotions. What I didn't tell Cass was that along with the terrifying immobility had come an unbidden image of conical houses fashioned from red rock.

A sight I'd only ever seen before in a photograph.

Nineteen

I called Bennet once I was out on the street. "Just checking on how my girls are doing."

She chuckled at that. "Took Loki to the dog park. She fell in love with a Boston terrier."

"She played with him? With her cast and all?"

"He was very considerate and didn't roughhouse." She paused. "I've finished reading your notes, and I've decided to write your biography—a simple article would never do you justice. How you came out of that in one piece I'll never know. You had to be stretching the truth in places—no?"

"Nope. All in a day's work."

"Sure. Is there an accounting of your first time in Iraq?"

"Afraid not. But if you promise to wear the same outfit to bed that you did last night, I'll whisper it all in your ear."

"Wouldn't you be too ... distracted to pay attention? How about over dinner?"

"Deal."

✳

Helmstetter's former lover, Veronica Sills, lived on the edge of Central Harlem, just east of Morningside Heights. I'd made a note of the address the Conjuring Arts Center gave me. It was close to four-thirty. I decided to stop by on the chance she'd be home.

Her place was an old five-story, red-brick walk-up. The buzzers had no names or numbers, but luckily a kid wearing a backpack who looked as if he was coming home from school held the door open for me. The small square of space serving as a lobby was clean but shabby. Marble steps leading to the upper floors dipped in the center, worn from decades of tenant footsteps, and the ornate iron railings had pieces missing. In the building's glory days, though, it must have been a splendid entry.

Although the original plates were missing, the number twelve was still faintly outlined in a lighter shade on the stout oak door. My knock echoed down the third-floor corridor. After a minute I heard the slow shuffle of feet. The footsteps stopped, then came the labored rattle of chains being undone and locks freed. The door opened a crack.

"Veronica Sills? My name's John Madison. I believe Julia Morrow at the Conjuring Arts Center let you know I wanted to talk with you. Might I come in? It's about George Helmstetter."

She let out her breath in a cross between a sigh and an exclamation. "Has he been found at last?"

"Not exactly. But I can add something to the information about his last known destination."

She opened the door. She was dressed smartly in a white silk shirt that revealed a curvaceous figure, tailored navy slacks, a jade and gold bangle. She looked me up and down and then stood aside to let me enter. "You may as well come in. George's name hasn't crossed my lips for a very long time, but his memory hasn't faded any." She carried herself well; Veronica Sills was hardly the feeble, elderly lady I'd imagined.

We entered a small living room with a wide, bright window facing the street. A sturdy table pushed up against the window that served as a desk for her computer held stacks of files and binders. White bookcases so full there didn't seem room to add another volume stood against the west wall. Framed prints hung on the other walls; I recognized a Calder and an Albers. Stems of dried white roses, their petals like faded tissue paper, sat in an exquisitely tiled fireplace. Such elegance stood in odd contrast to the high piles of files, newspapers, and cardboard boxes crowding the room. She was a pack rat, but a neat one.

"Can I offer you a glass of wine? It's almost cocktail hour."

"That would be great, thanks."

While she went into the kitchen, I beat a path through the narrow canyon between newspaper piles and took a seat on her honey-colored leather couch, obviously old but of such good quality that the leather had worn beautifully with age.

I jumped when a voice croaked, "Sorry for the mess you're late."

It seemed to come from a large palm beside the desk, the only plant in the room. Above it, the plush white plumage of a cockatoo with a yellow crest peeked out. The bird appeared to be perched on a stand hidden by the palm leaves. It tipped its head to one side and said, "Go home now."

Veronica came back into the room carrying two glasses of white wine. "Shush, Bandit," she said as she handed me one. "You have bad manners. Say something nice."

"You're pretty."

Veronica smiled rather awkwardly. I sensed she was of a serious turn and smiles didn't come easily to her. "Bandit's a sulphur-crested cockatoo, almost thirty-six years old. A gift from George."

"Helmstetter?"

"Yes. One of the few gifts he ever gave me." She sat beside me on the couch and leaned forward, holding her glass in both hands. "So what is it you have to say?"

"You'll remember Lucas Strauss? George's mentor? He's hired me to find Helmstetter and a stolen book by a Renaissance abbot named Trithemius."

If my words surprised her, she didn't let on. "*The Steganographia*. Are you some kind of private detective?"

"I'm an antiquities dealer, and sometimes I source rare books." I handed her my card.

"George vanished thirty-five years ago. Why is Lucas reviving all that old pain now?"

"Some items have come into his possession. After Helmstetter left America he sent them from Kandovan, a remote Iranian village, to his wife. She died recently and passed them along to Strauss."

Veronica's face blanched at the mention of Helmstetter's wife. That old wound ran deep.

I took a sip. The wine was crisp and cool. "Other than the fact that he may have been in the village and had a strange association with Faust, I know little about Helmstetter. Can you shed any light on him?"

She glanced at her desk. "You know I was an entertainment reporter? I still freelance. I've met loads of celebrities in my long career and have a good eye for hubris and outright shams. Actors, publicists, agents, writers, performers of all kinds. The entertainment world attracts those who are skilled at pulling the wool over people's eyes. But Lucas Strauss and George Helmstetter were the real deal. Both frightening and powerful individuals. I wish I'd never met either of them."

"Why do you call them frightening? And you don't seem surprised that Strauss thinks Helmstetter is still alive."

Her eyes darkened. "If you'd known George as I did you'd believe the same thing. He was fascinated by alchemy. Not the trick of turning metals into gold. The alchemists had a second great quest—the search for the elixir of life. George sought immortality through the practice of the black arts. He developed a thirst for profane knowledge, just as his beloved Faust had."

"How could a man who's supposed to be brilliant believe such foolishness?"

She took a long draft of her wine, her hand trembling slightly. It obviously cost her a lot just to discuss her former lover even after all these years. "I'm aware of how it must sound to you. And if we were talking about anyone else I'd agree. But we don't know everything in the universe, do we? And there was something about George. When he claimed triumphantly one day that he was close to finding the solution to immortality, I didn't doubt him."

"'Solution.' Did he mean a formula of some kind?"

"He kept it to himself. When I questioned him about it, he'd just say, 'You wouldn't approve.'"

I took a moment to let her remark register. "Well, after all, Faust regretted making his bargain."

Veronica toyed with her glass. "You're referring to the deal with the devil? If George thought he could achieve his aims that way he wouldn't have hesitated."

"Faust's biographers, Marlowe and Goethe, gave him a bad end. What about Helmstetter? Did he leave himself a way out if he changed his mind?"

"There's always a way out if you know the way in, I should think. George claimed he used Trithemius's book as his guide, that's all I know. I consider myself a sensible woman, Mr. Madison.

I was brought up by strict Catholics. They were not people given to fantasies. But George, he reached into my soul somehow. I loved him passionately. I suppose at my age I don't have to be embarrassed about such a confession. If anyone managed to achieve immortality, George could. I know that lies within the realm of the absurd. But practically speaking, he could easily still be alive. Why, he'd only be sixty-five."

"Don't be sad," Bandit squawked and ruffled its feathers.

We both laughed.

Veronica thought for a moment. "I don't have any photos of him. George destroyed all the photographs of himself, including those of the two of us. I discovered that shortly after he left. But they wouldn't have been much good to you; he would have aged a great deal by now. I can tell you one thing, though. Before he visited Kandovan, he wanted to see Pergamon in Turkey."

"What did he hope to achieve there?"

Veronica stood up and pressed her hand to the small of her back. "I can't sit for too long on this soft couch. My back kills me if I do—too many years spent in front of typewriters and computers. Anyway. Pergamon was considered by some to be Satan's dwelling place. George regarded it as a primary seat of power. He said he wanted to visit Satan's Throne."

"The letter I saw among the papers you gave to the Conjuring Arts Center mentioned that if what he found at Pergamon didn't satisfy him, he'd travel to Eden. Do you know what he meant by that?"

"He believed Eden existed. As a real place, not a biblical allegory. And that if he could find it, Eden would be the most potent place of power imaginable. I'm afraid there's nothing more I can tell you. Talking about him has awakened some bitter memories. I wonder if I might have some time to myself now?"

"Of course. You've been really helpful. Before I go, did you ever hear from him again—a letter or a note?"

She let out another sigh. "Not a word."

I stood up and shook hands with her. "Thank you."

She walked me over to the door and took my hand again. "May I give you some advice? You said Strauss hired you. I don't know what he's paying, but no amount of money is worth it. Have nothing to do with this quest of his. It won't—it can't—end well." She glanced over at Bandit. "Have you ever seen cockatoos in their natural environment?"

"Can't say I have."

"They're such exceptionally beautiful birds. In the wild they mostly eat fruit or seeds, but occasionally they'll prey on insects. In their natural environment I've seen those lovely birds tear the wings and heads off creatures to devour them. They have a savage side. If you're tempted to continue on with Strauss, think on that."

"Did he ever harm you?"

"Not me—personally, no. But others who were foolish enough to get in his way? He destroyed them."

Twenty

The rain had started up again. That evening Bennet and I went to Bocca, an Italian place with warm wood accents and varieties of fresh pasta laid out in bowls for the choosing. Back at our table, I told her all about my conversation with Veronica. But when I recounted what she'd said about their love affair, Bennet seemed to lose interest and quickly changed the subject. Odd, given that she was supposed to be documenting everything.

After dinner the rain obligingly stopped. Since it was mild out, we decided to pick up Loki from the apartment and take a slow stroll to Union Square. We got some sodas, spread newspaper on a bench and sat down to people watch, then browsed in the Strand, one of my favorite bookstores. I was still thinking about what Veronica had said about Pergamon, and so I picked up a book called *The Origin of Satan* by Elaine Pagels. For Bennet, I got a guidebook featuring that ancient city. Fortunately, no one objected to my carrying Loki around. Bennet seemed to enjoy herself equally and was delighted with the book. It surprised me how in sync I felt with her. Still, I needed to try something out.

"I've decided to go see Strauss," I announced on the way home. "I don't think I want to continue with his project."

Bennet stopped in her tracks. "Why not? I thought it was all settled." I could see how surprised she was.

"It's ridiculous, that's why. Helmstetter must have died in Iran long ago. After all this time, how could I find anything out? I can't even speak the language."

"You could hire a translator."

"I'd need an army for protection to get there."

"You just need someone who knows the territory." She paused. "If you change your mind, I want to go with you."

I put my arm around her. "That would just complicate matters. We're talking about Iran. A Western woman would stand out like a sore thumb. Both of us would."

"We'll take precautions, John. I want to see this through. Strauss insisted I record your journey, remember? Talk to him about your concerns; maybe he can come up with a solution."

Although everything I'd said was true, I'd raised the idea primarily to test her reaction. All along, Bennet had seemed unduly insistent on this venture and I'd begun to suspect there was more to it than just her commission. And I did want to see Strauss— I wanted to test him out, too. I could have just called him, but I sensed that a meeting would give me a better idea of where he was coming from.

The rain started up in earnest, heavy as a tropical downpour, just as we reached home. Bennet went right out again for drinks with a friend and I settled down with my book about Eden.

I read that, as nineteenth-century explorers began sending home the magnificent antiquities they'd unearthed, interest in Mesopotamia spread like wildfire through Europe and America. Then came the translation of cuneiform tablets, and interest reached a fever pitch. The tablets not only attested to the actual reign of kings like Nebuchadnezzar; they also recounted old Sumerian legends of a flood remaking the earth—legends that bore a marked resemblance to the Old Testament story. Here, people thought, was concrete proof of the Bible's historical accuracy. The Bible itself tantalized readers by appearing to give Eden an exact geographical location.

> A river flowed out of Eden to water the garden, and there it divided and became four rivers. The name of the first is the Pishon. It is the one that flowed around the whole land of Havilah, where there is gold. And the gold of that land is good; bdellium and onyx stone are there. The name of the second river is the Gihon. It is the one that flowed around the whole land of Cush. And the name of the third river is the Tigris, which flows east of Assyria. And the fourth river is the Euphrates.

Everyone knew the Tigris and Euphrates rivers. But what of the Pishon and Gihon? And where were the lands of Havilah and Cush? People tied themselves up in knots trying to come up with an answer. Serious scientists pointed to the once fertile, irrigated plains of southern Iraq at the confluence of the two great rivers, believing that the Pishon and Gihon might actually be ancient manmade canals feeding into these rivers. Even then, in a more religious age, others thought Eden to be allegorical, not a real place at all.

Personal agendas to prove the scientific accuracy of the Bible spawned hilarious results. One pastor placed the garden in the

Arctic. Another scholar declared it was a serpent mound in the Midwest. Some early Mormon leaders said Eden was in Jackson County, Missouri. Historians suggested the ancient site of Dilmun, an island in the Persian Gulf, or that Eden had been submerged beneath the Gulf waters. Not surprisingly, a lot of money was made off the lecture circuit by these Eden proponents.

I'd become so immersed in my reading that I barely heard the apartment door open. Bennet walked in, or rather tried to put one foot ahead of the other while keeping her toes pointed in the same direction. Tipsy from her night out. "Had a good time, did you?" I remarked. She gave me a salute while balancing her other hand on the armchair to avoid falling over, made it to the couch, and tumbled onto it. "Night," she said, and closed her eyes. I got the eiderdown from the bedroom and tucked it over her.

The break in my concentration proved fruitful. The name I'd seen annotated in Samuel's journal—Reginald Arthur Walker— popped into my mind, and I decided to look him up on the web, expecting more wild speculation that he'd found Eden near the Nile headwaters or in the Himalayas. Not so. I should have known as much; Samuel would never entertain such baseless theories. It turned out that Walker had written a paper, "The Land of Eden," and the brief summary I managed to find was enough to make me sit up and take notice: Walker's conclusions were ingenious. Apparently the New York Public Library had a copy. I resolved to look it up in the morning.

Twenty-One

February 19, 2005

"I've lost a few hours out of my life. I have no *idea* what I did last night," Bennet said as she struggled out from under the eiderdown.

"I can only hope it was legal."

"I'll never know. Shit. My head is one tremendous crucible of pain."

The rain continued to cascade down; Loki got soaked when I took her out. Back at the apartment I toweled her dry and fed her, then made extra-strong coffee for Bennet and poured some in a travel mug for myself. "It'll take me around five hours to get to Strauss's, and I'm stopping off at the library first. So I'm not likely to get home until late. You'll be okay with Loki?"

"No," she mumbled, sipping the coffee and holding her head. "I might not be alive when you get back."

I blew her a kiss and left.

I filled Dr. Cass's prescription at the local Duane Reade, but after reading all the cautionary notes, decided not to risk any dizziness before a long drive. I reached the library before it opened. By mid-morning I'd found Walker's essay, photocopied the fifty pages, and was back on the road. Rain misted the windshield but thankfully didn't slow traffic.

My Maserati had been totaled in the accident that took my brother's life. I used to love letting my car rip on country drives. Now I put on J-Kwon and pushed the Porsche up to seventy-five. It had been a while since I'd tasted the true freedom of the road. It felt good.

Heavy clouds turned the sky into a dense curtain of gray and the wind blew across the fields with a vengeance. An hour before Albany the rain hit again in earnest. Flat sheets of it whipped sideways at the cars. The pavement turned slippery, water sprayed out from wheels, and even with the wipers slapping away I could barely make out the cars in the southbound lanes. Traffic both ways slowed; it felt like driving through an endless waterfall. A red glow from the truck taillights ahead of me faded and disappeared.

I had to continually nudge the brakes, but the Porsche did its job and gripped well. A typical cloudburst would briefly drench the landscape and then lift as the tempest passed through. Not this time. The weathermen, predicting a major storm, had been right after all. The drenching kept up for almost an hour until it dropped to a steady rain and more than a few feet of highway became visible again. I'd planned to stop near Albany for a bite, but I'd lost so much time I decided to keep going.

Mistake. I tuned in to the forecast and heard that the deluge, on top of yesterday's rain, had caused the Mohawk River and Erie Canal to overflow their banks. Flooding in the railway bed had

forced Amtrak to halt all train traffic. Sure enough, about twenty
minutes outside Albany, when the highway turned west toward
Rotterdam Junction, traffic began to crawl. Up ahead I could just
make out yellow barriers and red lights slicing through the gloom.
As I inched up, the police, standing in front of emergency vehicles,
waved all the cars off to the ramp. Beyond the exit, a propane tanker
had flipped onto its side. It lay like a beached whale in a lake of
water that had gathered in a dip on the Thruway, a silver SUV
crumpled against its nose and a red Honda smashed against its tail.
They'd draped an orange blanket over what was left of the Honda
driver's side window, the car so wrecked it looked as if it had gone
through a compacter. One of those heart-sinking moments. You
knew the driver couldn't have made it out alive.

A hand-lettered sign propped up against a cruiser read
PORTIONS OF THRUWAY FLOODED. MUST DETOUR. Most of my fellow
travelers followed each other like a long line of ants, turning their
cars southbound on the Thruway to head back. I considered following suit. Under good conditions I'd be only an hour from Strauss's.
At this point it made more sense to carry on, so I got off the
highway altogether and tried to find another route. The 5 was
closed and the 5S too close to the river for my liking. I'd have to
climb north and pick out a lateral course to Herkimer, the village
closest to Strauss's place. The farmland and forest I now traversed,
with the odd house and barn in the distance, would have been
pleasant on a bright summer day, but the rain had turned gullies
into rushing torrents and creeks into raging rivers. Hollows in the
road became muddy ponds. On one bridge, the water level almost
spilled over the roadbed. And the rain, although no longer violent,
continued to fall with a steady drumbeat on the roof of the car. My
breath caught in my throat when a fox, its coat dripping wet, leapt
out of the wood in front of me. I missed it by inches.

The GPS kept sending me into flooded roads; again and again I had to turn back and look for alternative routes west. This led me to increasingly worse thoroughfares until I found myself on a one-lane stretch of sopping gravel. Only the power of the car kept me from getting mired in mud. I silently thanked the Porsche gods. Even aside from the risk of an accident, I felt tense and apprehensive. If the car got stuck there was no guarantee of finding shelter. While not cold enough to snow or produce freezing rain, it was chilly and I had no boots with me, just an overcoat. My stomach was turning somersaults from lack of food. At least I wouldn't run out of water, I thought grimly.

It was now well into the afternoon. I hadn't seen the sun all day and already the sky was growing darker. I reached a bridge. Made of bolted metal and anchored at both ends by stone bases, it looked as if it had been built out of rust. Heavy forest cloaked it on either side, restricting visibility so that an oncoming car would have no room to avoid me. I could see water rushing underneath the vertical gaps in the bridge's iron platform, the metal so worn and corroded I wasn't sure it would hold. The car crept forward and the metal sang and bent under its weight.

I made it across and carried on. When the road forked I slowed down and realized there was only one choice if I wanted to keep heading west, a secondary gravel road that would take me close to the point where I could find a route south to Herkimer. I cursed silently when a battered cargo van sprayed muddy water onto my car as it sped past, almost hitting me. Who the hell would pass in these conditions? After I'd mounted a crest in the road I started to follow it sharply down into a glen. To one side was an old trailer, so deteriorated I couldn't believe anyone still lived there. Bicycles, garden implements, and barrels lay scattered beside a dirt path leading to its door. On the other side the van that passed me had slid into the gully and was now acting as a kind of dam, forcing the gully water to form a shallow pond over the roadbed. The door to the van was open.

A man lay sprawled beside it on the ground, face down in the mud.

Was it a heart attack? I made it out of the Porsche in seconds and whipped out my phone to call 911. He pulled out a gun as he lurched up and fired at me.

Twenty-Two

The shot went wild. Before he had a chance to squeeze off a second shot, I scrambled behind the protection of the Porsche. I hadn't shut off the ignition. I leapt into the car and gunned it straight at the guy.

He tried to run but I hit him, a soft thud as he slammed up against my windshield, cracking the glass. The impact flung him into the air. His body hit the side of the van and fell to the ground. He lay still.

I glanced at the decrepit trailer, afraid someone might come out with guns blazing. All was silent, so I got out of my car again, shaking now, and went over to him. He was a slim, short man with a rough-looking, mud-streaked face. I pressed my fingers to his neck and found a pulse. A search through his pockets revealed some wet dollar bills, the key fob for the van, and a black plastic device that I guessed might be a chip tracker. A metal ornament with an image of flames burning in a vase dangled from the dash inside the cab. I cast around for his gun but couldn't see it and didn't want to waste time looking. Taking the chip tracker and his key fob with me, I got back into my car and tore down the road.

I couldn't believe what I'd done. But driving straight toward the guy had been my best option. If I'd just taken off he would have followed me in his truck and tried to run me off the road or shoot at me again.

I kept my speed up, hoping to find a place to turn in. I had the chip tracker, if that's what it was, so I could no longer be followed, but I didn't want to take any chances. Salvation came in the form of a garage and gas bar, two miles farther along. It sat at a bleak crossroads in the middle of nowhere, a tow truck and some combines parked on the asphalt in front. I pulled up, and ignoring the rain, got out and quickly scanned my car. The right front headlight was broken and the metalwork around it scratched and crumpled from where I'd hit the shooter. I got a tissue out of my pocket and ran it over the damaged light but couldn't spot any blood. The rain must have washed it away. After groping along the underside of my car, I located the tracer underneath the front bumper, pried it off, and stuck it in my pocket.

Just then the red neon WE'RE OPEN Coca-Cola sign blinked off to a green WE'RE CLOSED. A blond-haired guy who looked like he could hoist a truck with one hand walked out of the garage and shut the door.

"Any chance you can help me out?" I said.

He stopped under the overhang and looked me up and down, then checked out the Porsche splattered with mud. His gaze flicked to the crack in the windshield and the broken headlight. "Rough way to treat it," he said. "Car like that."

"I've been driving around for hours, got lost a thousand times. The freeway's closed. A rock hit my windshield and wrecked it.

Could I leave it here and have you fix it? Any chance you'd have a replacement car?"

"You can leave it here if you want till you git where you're goin'. I can tow her into the mechanic in Utica when the rain lets up. Can rent you some wheels for now—how's that?"

"Fantastic, I'd appreciate that very much."

He took me back inside where we did the paperwork. I paid him in cash and added a hundred for a tip to reward his discretion. He asked me to leave the loaner car at the mechanic's shop when I picked up the Porsche the next day. I bought a pop and a package of chips then got a spare pair of jeans out of my trunk. He gave me the keys to an older model Ford Taurus and I was on my way.

I kept a close eye out for anyone following me but chances were there'd been just the one guy. I hurled the chip, the tracker, and the van's key fob into a ditch rushing with water.

Turning south toward the village of Herkimer, I saw it was less than half an hour away. Being so close to the Erie Canal, the place had suffered badly from the downpour. The low-lying parts lay awash in water: houses and commercial buildings like tiny islands marooned in a lake, vehicles drowned, trees uprooted and submerged like wet logs. I had to ford a main street transformed into a fast-flowing stream. On the outskirts, away from the canal, an inn advertised vacancies. The place was a touch shabby, but, as I discovered, the sheets were clean and the water hot. I'd never been so glad to see a $65 room.

I changed into the dry jeans but kept on my shirt. It wasn't too wet. Nothing I could do about my shoes. The owner kindly threw my wet stuff in her dryer, and even better, sat me down in the lounge and fixed me a hot roast beef sandwich with farm mashed potatoes and a coffee. No one else was there. They were either helping the emergency workers or standing guard on the home front. "Rain's letting up now," she said as she brought over the coffeepot to refill my cup. "'Spect the worst is over."

"Sure hope so," I replied. "A lot of damage in the town."

Her eyes darkened. "People've died in this more than likely. Somewheres along the canal. State'll have to give us disaster relief. You from New York?"

"Yes." Not hard to guess with my accent.

She raised her eyebrows as if to suggest this wasn't a point in my favor. "Come to Herkimer for sightseeing? Bad choice in this weather I'd say."

"No. I'm on my way to see someone and I can't get there along the canal route or on the Thruway. Any chance you can explain how else I could reach it?" I told her the address and then mentioned Strauss's name, figuring someone that famous would be well known around here.

Her face dropped.

"Do you know him?"

"Not well. He keeps private. That's fine with us around here. People don't like him. He hardly ever comes into town, but when he does he has the sidewalk all to himself. People stop to let him pass."

"Why is that?"

"Some older ones think he can put spells on 'em. Believe he can call on the spirits. I don't have those fancies. But I know he keeps wild animals. My nephew saw one once when he and a couple of his friends tried to prowl around that place of his. Unless your business is pressing, I'd give the magician a miss." She gave me a motherly pat on the arm and sidled back to the kitchen.

I wolfed the meal down like it was filet mignon and went through almost a jug of coffee. I couldn't get anything but voice mail for Strauss, and left a message saying that I'd show up the next day, weather permitting. When I reached Bennet on her phone I gave her a snapshot of my trials, omitting the gunfire.

Back in my room, the events of the day crowded in on me. The innkeeper's warning resonated—only a veneer of gentility masked Strauss's mercurial personality and I believed him capable of trying to kill me. But he had no reason to. Quite the opposite: he wanted me very much alive to pursue Helmstetter and the book. Yersan, on the other hand, might want me out of the way to more easily obtain the cylinder seals and the statue. That little decorative item in the shooter's truck depicting the Zoroastrian symbol of a flaming vase pointed the arrow straight at him.

Reporting the assault to the police was out of the question. I couldn't prove I'd been shot at and risked getting charged with hit and run. Nor did I think the gunman, assuming he'd survived, would make any official complaints. If he died I'd probably end up in deep shit. It wouldn't take long for the cops to question the locals and a damaged Porsche would definitely pique their interest. Something else continued to eat away at me: I hadn't spared a second to think about the consequences of aiming my car at another human being. Yes, the fear of getting shot had put me on autopilot. But even after I knew I was safe, I hadn't cared about the man's condition at all. Atrocious sights were the norm in Iraq, and I'd been directly involved in a few of them. Cass was right. I had PTSD, and it had taken not only an emotional toll but a moral one as well. With no energy left, I crawled into bed and slept like the damned.

At breakfast the next morning the innkeeper shook her head and gave me directions to Strauss's place—another convoluted route but one that, for the most part, kept me away from the canal. The rain had finally stopped, although it was still cloudy and even colder. Pleasant enough territory at the right time of year, it now felt like a freezing, watery hell.

Strauss lived on an isolated stretch of land. I had to take such a roundabout route that I found myself retracing territory I'd come in on. Bennet had told me Strauss had fashioned his home by converting a once bustling mill where grain was processed and packaged, then sent down the canal to New York. The outbuildings and silos where farmers stored their grain were long gone but the original red-brick mill remained. The canal banks up and down the state were littered with these reminders of past prosperity, many of them now sad derelicts, rust-belt victims of jobs sent offshore.

In summers when he was home, Samuel would often take me to the Great Lakes—Erie and Ontario. I remember being fascinated by the canal, where we'd often stop for a picnic lunch before driving on again. In those days it seemed a semi-tropical paradise. I'd chase the monarchs and viceroys that fluttered among the wildflowers, lie on my stomach to scoop up water spiders spinning on the canal surface, watch for leopard frogs or the white bodies of slow-moving carp weaving through the water. And yet, in my child's mind, the canal always gave me an eerie feeling. There was something about the still, flat water; when the sun was at its strongest it took on a poisonous green hue. For some time I'd even thought that's why it was called the Eerie Canal until Samuel laughed and corrected me.

The last stretch having taken me through a small forest of spruce and cedar dappled with white birch, I arrived at Strauss's place around ten. High chain-link fencing encircled the densely wooded property. I could see no sign of a house. Nor was there another car in the little gravel parking area. I walked up to the gate. The buzzer had a street number and a single name—STRAUSS. When I pressed it I got no response. After punching it a second time, the gate slid open and nearly caught me as I went through. A narrow asphalt path littered with fallen leaves and spruce needles led straight forward. Mist hung in the air and moisture, almost like a fine rain, dripped off the trees. My shoes hadn't entirely dried overnight and I shivered from the cold, pulling my now very wrinkled overcoat closer around me. Low-hanging cedar branches rustled ahead. As I looked toward the sound, I thought I detected movement and stopped in my tracks.

Another twist of the branches startled me. And then out from the trees came a flash of brown and white. A fawn. It couldn't have been more than a week old; it was still unsteady on its feet. It stared at me with its huge chocolate-brown eyes, flicked its big ears, and dashed off again into the cover of the wood. I gave an inward sigh and relaxed, continuing up the walk until I heard another noise close by. A huffing sound, one I wasn't familiar with. Something large crashed its way through the bush. The branches parted ahead. A black shape emerged, a blond snout, claws, small ears flat to its skull and beady eyes. The bear turned toward me and reared on its hind legs.

I practically swallowed my heart and ran, despite knowing I could never outpace a bear. The gate was locked. I reached the fence, the chain link still so wet that I couldn't gain purchase. I chanced a look behind: no sign of the bear. I calmed down a little.

And then it came to me: fawns were born in spring, not in the depths of winter. I marched back to the spot where it had appeared. The little brown-and-white spotted body danced in front of me again before it vanished. A few yards on, the black bear stood on its hind legs once more. I walked toward it and pushed my hand into its fur, feeling only a spruce branch and thin air. Strauss must be employing the most recent special effects technology. Coupled with my natural fear, the trick worked well.

Another fifteen minutes down the path and the trees gave way. A weak sun peeked out from the cloud cover. A flat-roofed structure came into view; it looked like all the other abandoned factory buildings along the canal. It was three stories high with potted and worn brickwork. There was no door. All the windows on the first floor had been boarded up on the inside. Water, several inches deep, lay on the ground surrounding the building. The canal glimmered behind it. I gritted my teeth and slopped through the water, soaking my shoes all over again. The front facing the canal had no proper entrance either, just a wide opening about the size of a double garage door. A low concrete ramp, green with slime, extended from the opening to the canal, only ten yards away. I hoisted myself onto the ramp and went inside.

A couple of inches of water covered the floor. It smelled musty inside, almost putrid. The room's contours were barely visible. Old oil drums had been stacked along one wall, the fuel they once held presumably running the machinery. I yelled for Strauss, my voice echoing in the cavernous space. Close to the back wall something rectangular stood on a kind of platform; as I approached, I could see it was a square frame draped by fringed velvet curtains with the name STRAUSS embroidered in gold. An old prop from his glory days? My better sense told me not to look behind them, but I'd come this far and had no intention of leaving now. I reminded myself again that Strauss had no motive to do me harm. I pulled open the curtains and staggered back in horror.

Twenty-Three

February 20, 2005
Erie Canal

A huge vertical block of ice glimmered blue-white as if it were lit internally. Strauss was frozen inside, his intense blue eyes open, his wrinkled hands held up defensively in front of his chest as though protecting himself from an attack, his old man's skin, frozen pink. After a moment of shock I questioned what I was seeing. Another visual trick? It had to be. I ran my hand down the surface, expecting to find air, but instead I felt a rigid, cold surface. My fingers burned. I couldn't pull my hand away. It was glued to the ice, like a kid whose tongue had stuck to a freezing iron railing.

"Best to look and not touch, Mr. Madison. Although I must admit, it *is* tempting."

I wrenched myself around to see Strauss descending a staircase that seemed to be coming from a dark hole high up in one corner of the room. He carried some kind of implement.

"Get my hand off this fucking thing."

"Why of course," he said. "Child's play."

I shrank back when he climbed onto the platform and raised the implement. But when he flicked a button on its handle I could feel heat radiating from it. "My magic wand," he joked. "Ease your hand away; otherwise your skin will tear."

The ice melted rapidly around my palm. I pulled my hand free and shook it. "You bastard," I said.

"I'm sorry you weren't amused. This"—he waved his hand toward the ice block—"is pure entertainment. A well-known magician actually did encase himself in ice and almost died because of it. I lack that degree of commitment."

I glanced around the room. "Why the hell are you living in this decrepit cave?"

"I prefer my own company. I find it discourages visitors."

That was the understatement of the year.

Strauss put a hand on my shoulder. "Come, let me offer you more hospitable surroundings."

I followed him up the stairs, apprehensive but determined not to show it, and saw that the dark hole was actually a black door. It opened onto a luxurious, open-concept space with a grand-looking kitchen separated from the main area by a bar. A partitioned-off corridor, I figured, led to the bedrooms. An attendant was busy at the bar.

Crackling logs in a fireplace with a brass and black granite mantel pumped out welcome heat. Plush carpets covered a floor of wide blond planks. The original factory floor, I guessed, refurbished. Large framed posters—advertisements for Strauss's old magic acts—hung on the walls. The weak light on the canal cast rippling greenish reflections on the ceiling and pale cream walls. The effect was both beautiful and calming.

Strauss slipped out of his boots and I did the same. He looked at my soaking shoes. "I imagine your feet are pretty cold."

"You've got that right." I was still infuriated by his charade downstairs.

He took my overcoat, hung it in a closet, and reached for a pair of slippers.

"Sit there." He indicated an old-fashioned armchair, one of two placed near the fireplace. "Harrison will bring us some coffee."

As if on cue, Harrison began pouring our coffee from a carafe into steaming china mugs. He brought them over to us. "That's fine now, Harrison," Strauss said. The man nodded and went through to the room beyond, closing the door behind him with a soft click.

I waited until Strauss took a sip before I tasted mine. "You don't warn your guests about the perils of getting in here?"

"Now that wouldn't be any fun, would it?" He cocked his head and fixed his blue gaze on me, a flash of hostility quickly replaced with something more benign. That look echoed his attitude toward me at Gina's séance. As though he had some personal gripe with me and hated me because of it. It made no sense.

"I gather you found my sculpture convincing?" He had a way of chuckling with all the mirth stripped out of it. "Done by a talented young artist, Jude Luscombe. He got his start in movie special effects and makeup. Taking representative art to the extreme, you could say. Like the anatomist Gunther von Hagens's pieces, only without the gory internal details. Jude uses real human skin. Preserves it somehow."

My stomach turned.

"From cadavers of course. All legit. A good likeness, don't you think?"

"Yes. Especially encased in a block of ice with next to no visibility in the room." I took another swallow of coffee and welcomed the heat in my throat. Strauss had taken advantage of me twice. It was time to turn the tables and give him a run for it. "I've decided to decline your commission." I fixed my own gaze on him and saw his face grow pale. I liked putting him on the defensive for a change.

"May I ask why?"

"For one thing, being involved in your scheme is turning out to be hellishly dangerous. Tricia Ross was murdered two days ago and a guy tried to run me off the road yesterday. When that failed, he took a shot at me."

"Someone shot at you? Heavens, why?"

"I think he wants Helmstetter's artifacts. I presume Tricia told you about a man named Yersan?"

He gave me a measured look. "Yes. Very sad about Miss Ross. I understand the police believe it to be a robbery gone wrong."

"A *robbery*?"

"Her collection of Iraqi artifacts is missing. A small collection, but it included some valuable items."

"Surely she didn't keep them in her house."

"In her safe, in the bedroom upstairs. They must have pried the codes out of her before they killed her. Poor woman."

"I'd like to get back to the reason for my visit. Thanks for the opportunity and the generous payment, but I must decline. Even if Helmstetter is still alive somewhere, no one will ever find him if he doesn't want to be found. By all accounts, including yours, he's a talented illusionist. If he'd wanted to vanish, he'd be capable of disappearing forever."

Strauss couldn't keep the spark of excitement from his eyes. "You're right. He was as ingenious as his forebear, Faust. I've told you about the original Faust—and knowledge of him is relevant to understanding Helmstetter's character." Strauss noticed my impatience. "Bear with me for a moment. As I said before, many believe Goethe modeled Faust on George Sibelius, who later changed his name to Georgios Faustus Helmstetter. Heidelberg University records indicate that a man by that name was enrolled there for five years, beginning in 1483. Some believed Faustus to be a skilled fortune teller. But Trithemius, the author of my missing *Steganographia,* who was a contemporary and knew Faustus, loathed the man."

Strauss reached for a book on the low table beside him, licked his thumb, and combed through the pages. Despite his age, he didn't need glasses. "Ah. Here it is. The letter where Trithemius expresses this opinion of Helmstetter.

> "That man, about whom you wrote me ... who dared to call himself the foremost of necromancers, is an unstable character, a babbler and a vagabond ... continually asserting things in public that are abominable and contrary to the teachings of the Holy Church."

Strauss looked up. "Rather churlish of the abbot, considering that he too dabbled in alchemy." He snapped the book shut and laid it down. "Faust was last seen in Amsterdam when a group of Anabaptists took over the city and carried out a rampage of sexual orgies and killing. He disappeared in the melee. If he died there his body was never identified."

I waited. I wasn't going to make this easier on Strauss.

"Helmstetter, like his fifteenth-century forebear, was a fortune teller who sought to know more than the future. He wanted forbidden knowledge, and I don't doubt that he'd make an unholy bargain for it. He's alive, somewhere. I know it. And I believe you have the skills to find him."

"Well, why did Helmstetter want to disappear? Do you know what his motivation was? Surely not the measly ten thousand dollars he stole from you."

"He had the best of motivations. He knew I'd kill him if I ever found him again." Strauss blinked rapidly. I sensed he was genuinely upset at the thought of my abandoning his mission. "If you found Helmstetter, or at least were able to tell me what happened to him, I promised to reveal your true birth story. I gather you no longer care about that?"

"I can't imagine how you'd know anything about it."

"You were born in Kandovan—I know that and much more."

A sledgehammer slammed into my brain. That Evelyn had grown up there and concealed that fact from me, put together with the shaky story she and Samuel had given me about my own origins, had started to form a picture. Strauss had just confirmed my suspicions. "I'd like to hear the rest."

"That was promised only if you completed the commission."

"Who told you where I was born?"

"Tricia Ross. It's one of the reasons she recommended you for the job. Your brother let the information slip in an unguarded moment when they were in Baghdad together."

This did not ring true. Samuel never had unguarded moments. And Tricia couldn't have recommended me for the job—she hadn't even known my last name when we spoke on the phone the night before her death. I decided not to call him on it. He wouldn't be any more forthcoming if backed into a corner. "That's interesting but it doesn't change my mind."

"Perhaps this will convince you then. What if the FBI is told you stole those antiquities from Iraq I showed you?"

"That would be a little difficult, since they aren't in my possession."

"You happen to be right—for now. But you've witnessed my abilities with sleight of hand. Success in magic depends on manipulating perception. People see what they're expecting to see. You've been to Iraq—twice. You had a tablet, a stolen object, in your possession—as you call it. You're an antiquities dealer. When my objects are found on your premises, it wouldn't be a big jump for authorities to conclude you were tempted. And I can make those arrangements anytime I wish. The FBI might eventually conclude you're innocent of the charges. But not before the whole thing has cost you money for lawyers, given you a gigantic headache, and smeared your professional reputation. Because I'd make the accusation public."

I set my cup down, stood up, and paced over to the window. I took a minute to look out at the canal, the waters sluggish in the weak light, trying to keep a rein on my temper. "One question: Helmstetter mentioned an intention to travel to Eden. Do you have any idea what he was referring to?"

"My assistant was interested in loci of power, and like Buddhists and indigenous people, he believed transformations were possible only in certain geographic locations. He became convinced Eden not only once existed but could still be found. I think that's what took him to the Middle East."

"He thought he could find Eden in Kandovan?"

"That's two questions, Mr. Madison. I'll leave it for you to discover."

I didn't want to spend another minute in Strauss's company. "I'm leaving now. No thanks for your hospitality."

"By all means." He didn't bother to rise from his chair. "I look forward to your reports."

I steamed down the pathway back to the rental car. Neither the bear nor the fawn put in an appearance on the return route. Strauss's magic apparently didn't work in reverse.

When I reached the garage in Utica, I saw they'd done a great job replacing the windshield. "Expensive little toys," the mechanic said after handing me the bill.

The Thruway had mercifully reopened. I reached my apartment around six in the evening, angry and frustrated. It was a warm homecoming on the other side. Loki rubbed up against my leg, overjoyed to see me again. I asked Bennet why she hadn't warned me about Strauss's lair. She confessed she'd never visited his home but met with him only when he came to New York. She was appalled to hear about his threats and did her best to smooth me out. Strauss had trapped me; I felt like a fox twisting in his snare. I had no doubt he'd make good on his word if I didn't follow through with his plans.

And I couldn't get Tricia's sightless eyes out of my mind.

Twenty-Four

The next day I hatched a plan. The task Strauss had set me was impossible—and what would be the end point? How long would he persist in holding a so-called theft over my head? The solution was easy. Give him what he wanted: an account of Helmstetter's fate and, ideally, the book. Simple, really. I'd manufacture both.

Despite his wiles, Strauss had a big Achilles' heel: his passionate hatred for Helmstetter and the fervent desire to pay his former assistant back. He'd kept that animosity alive for thirty-five years. And when people let that kind of anger control them, their judgment lapsed. That gave me an opening. I took my cue from something he'd said: "Give people what they expect to see." Well—I would do just that.

First, I learned all I could about Trithemius, who was born Johann Heidenberg in 1462. Caught in a terrible blizzard one night, he sheltered in the Benedictine abbey of Sponheim, decided to stay, and eventually took monastic orders. Remarkably, one year later, Trithemius became its abbot at the age of twenty-one. A Renaissance man, he was highly regarded as a magician, man of letters, and adviser to nobles. He studied the occult, numerology, and the Kabbala and transformed the poor abbey into a center of learning, expanding its library by thousands of volumes. His most famous work, *The Steganographia,* purported to be a record of angel magic. A covert masterpiece, it was one of the first demonstrations of cryptology—and was banned for three hundred years. The code Trithemius devised was finally broken by Thomas Ernst, a German professor, five hundred years after the book was written.

It would be impossible to duplicate the entire book convincingly—Strauss would inevitably spot the ruse. But a few pages? That was feasible. I'd tell him it was all that remained of his book. No original copies were known to exist; Strauss had said his edition was published in 1792. The NSA's National Cryptologic Museum had some of Trithemius's works but not the right one. I eventually learned that a copy was available for viewing in the Library of Congress.

I called a friend in the antiquities business who enjoyed a passing acquaintance with Alice Jacobs, a rare-books authority who'd strayed, becoming one of the most skilled book forgers in America. After years of success, she'd been caught, not through any fault in her work but because her ex-husband reported her. A plea bargain landed her a short term in prison; afterward, she moved from New York to Pennsylvania. Rumor had it she still dabbled in forgeries. She was my choice to duplicate the pages—if I could talk her into it. I suspected dollar bills might do the trick. The beauty of it all was that I'd be using Strauss's own money to dupe him.

Inventing a credible story about what had happened to Helmstetter presented a greater challenge. For that, I'd have to go to both Pergamon and Kandovan. There was no other way I could gather enough convincing information. Traveling to Pergamon would be a breeze; Kandovan, next to impossible.

I also needed to find out more about Yersan. Since he was an antiquities dealer, one of my contacts would surely have heard of him. I emailed a query to a couple of colleagues.

Avery Mandel called me late that afternoon. "I've done business with the guy, John. What do you want to know?"

"Not sure exactly. I had a run-in with him. Is he on the level?"

"No. But he's cagey about it. Always looking for any edge he can use to jack up a price. Which is fair enough, I guess. We all do it. He makes a lot of money."

I filed that away. So far it confirmed my suspicions. "Anything else?"

"Not directly, but there's rumors."

"I'm listening."

"Yersan can be vicious if you get in his way. Word has it a former business partner died when he crossed him. Nothing they could ever prove and maybe I'm wrong. But still. And he subscribes to some esoteric clan. He's called a magi."

"Come again?"

"Traces back to the Medes. Fifth century B.C. Iranian. They're followers of Zoroaster. Fragments of that community live in Iranian Azerbaijan. They still practice it. He travels back and forth from there to America a lot. That's about it as far as I know."

Mandel had been very helpful. I thanked him and clicked off. What he'd told me made it all the more apparent that if I were to travel to Iran I'd need expert security—someone who knew the territory. Nick Shaheen, who'd grown up in Baghdad but was of Persian descent and spoke perfect Farsi, would have been my man of choice had he not died in the Iraq war. I still missed him. He'd been a good friend to me and a protector. All I could think of was to try contacting Nick's man, Ali, who at least might recommend someone else. I had Ali's cell number, but that was from over a year ago. Still, it was my only alternative, short of hiring some security firm blind, which I was loath to do. That night I texted Ali asking that he contact me.

Bennet and I would be away for a couple of weeks. What to do about Loki? Introducing her to a new family seemed harsh, although better than sticking her in some boarding kennel—if they'd even take her. Diane Chen was a good friend of mine, a theater actor when she could land a part, a sometime fortune teller, and a barista at my favorite watering hole—Kenny's Castaways. I remembered she loved dogs.

"I can't take a dog," Diane said when I called. "My landlord would throw us both out on the street. Wish I could. She sounds really cute."

I hadn't enlightened Diane on Loki's parentage—wasn't sure what she'd think of caring for half a coyote. "How about staying at my place? Luxury digs and all." I laughed. "And of course, I'd pay you."

"Seriously! You're near Madison Square now, right? That's awesome. Save me the bone-cracking commute. How long for?"

"Couple of weeks. I'm going to Turkey."

We arranged for her to stop by later in the evening to meet Loki and get the spare key. When she arrived and saw Bennet, her look of surprise was priceless. Bennet, meanwhile, eyed Diane's magenta hair and midnight-blue fingernails with suspicion.

Later, after Diane had left, came the inevitable question. "Are you *sure* she's trustworthy?"

I detected a bit of jealousy there, and couldn't help grinning. "That's funny. Pot calling the kettle black or anything? I've known her much longer than you."

She shrugged as if she didn't care.

Meanwhile, my antiquities friend had come through with an introduction to Alice Jacobs, and so the next day I drove to her home in Pennsylvania on the outskirts of Bethlehem. We chatted about what I had in mind, and I gave her all the information I had about Trithemius's tome. She was discreet enough not to ask why I wanted the pages reproduced.

"It'll take me at least three weeks," she said. "I'll have to find blank endpapers similar to the page leafs Trithemius would have used. That'll be expensive, of course, since I'll have to use material from the same time period." Duplicating the original inks would also take a while, Alice told me. And she'd have to choose pages that contained only text: illustrations would present too much difficulty. We talked for a long time, and by the end of it I felt satisfied that she'd do an excellent job.

I texted Ali again to say that I was traveling in the next few days to Pergamon, staying at the Hera Hotel, and needed his advice urgently.

February 22, 2005

That evening I took Evelyn out for dinner. She wasn't in the best of moods but she'd dressed up for the occasion and brightened considerably when she heard where we were going: Ilili, a place I relished too. It served some of the tastiest lamb and Lebanese sausage in the city.

She admired the light-filled space, the walls covered with copper-colored squares of cedar, the oval tables and red leatherette chairs.

We chatted about nothing in particular until our food was served. I felt a familiar pang of concern to see how badly her fingers were twisted from the arthritis; at times, she had difficulty using her fork.

"I'm going to Turkey for a couple weeks, dear," I said finally. "Can't hack any more dark winter days. Planning on doing some sightseeing at Pergamon."

"I know it, John."

I set my fork down. "How did you find out?"

"That girl came to visit. Yesterday. Bennet. The one who is writing the article about you. She is very sweet. She brought me a lovely scarf."

"Oh? She didn't mention that to me. What did she say?"

"She was very excited to be going with you to be her expert on the old ruins. 'Much better than taking one of those tours,' she told me. Samuel, he would have liked her."

I was far from an expert on Turkish antiquities. I cast around for some reply that sounded convincing. "She's taking her responsibilities as a writer very seriously by documenting everything firsthand."

Evelyn narrowed her eyes and gave me a long look. "It's time you had a companion. You are too much alone. And kids are better with younger fathers."

"Kids? Whoa. I barely know Bennet." I tried desperately to change the subject. "Did she say exactly where we're going?"

"Istanbul and Pergamon."

I let out a sigh of relief. The last thing I wanted was for Evelyn to know about Kandovan.

For the remainder of our dinner I managed to deflect any further forays into the question of matrimony. Before we left the restaurant I asked a waiter to snap a picture of us on my phone. Then I took Evelyn home, made sure she wouldn't need anything while I was gone, and gave her a long hug goodbye. She was only in her late fifties, but when her illness got the best of her she seemed more like a fragile eighty-year-old.

A weight settled on my shoulders as I walked out of her building into the gloomy February night. A feeling that I'd never see her again. No matter how hard I tried to shake it, that feeling followed me all the way home.

The next morning things rapidly got worse.

Twenty-Five

February 23, 2005

Bennet had gone out to do some errands for our trip and I was thumbing through source books deciding which I could take without overloading my luggage when I heard a not too subtle knock on the door. "Who is it?" I said, not recognizing the face peering through the eyehole.

"Detective Shea, Suffolk County police force. Madison. Need to talk to you."

He'd brought a small army. Two uniformed NYPD officers stood on either side and behind him were a man and a woman, both wearing navy blue jackets emblazoned with FBI in yellow block letters. Loki ran over, growling. I scooped her up before she had a chance to do any damage.

The two uniforms stepped in, followed by Shea and the others. "What's up?" I said.

"Need to take a look around. It's official," Shea said.

He thrust a paper at me. I scanned it, saw it was a search

warrant, and passed it back with my free hand. "I don't see why this is necessary. I'm a suspect now?"

He grinned. "More like I need to weed people out. It was a homicide. I like to be thorough." He nodded to the FBI officers. "They're helping me out here with some forensics. Which way's your bedroom?"

Odd that he'd ask for my bedroom first. I showed him where it was and the poker-faced FBI officers trooped into the room with their heavy bags.

"Have a seat," Shea said. He and the uniformed cops remained standing. I plopped myself down, Loki squirming in my arms. Ordering me around in my own place irritated me. It felt like a home invasion and I suppose that's what it was, although of a genteel variety—so far.

Shea's gaze lit on the glass cabinets where I kept some of Samuel's less valuable Iraqi artifacts. "Where'd those come from?"

For a second I worried that Strauss had made good on his threat and accused me of stealing his artifacts. But I dismissed the idea almost as quickly—Strauss had been pleased when I told him I was going to Turkey. "Most of them belonged to my brother. He was an archaeologist. Some are mine."

"Is that your whole collection?"

"I have more in secure storage."

"I'll need to see those too. 'Fraid we're going to have to take these with us. Get them checked out."

I couldn't keep the anger out of my voice. "No way. Surely you don't think I'd be dumb enough to keep stolen goods here. They're all completely legitimate. I have the documentation on them. You can have someone come and check all that out if you want. And you couldn't just throw them into bags anyway. They'd have to be packed by an expert."

Shea sat down opposite me, probably to lower the tension a bit. Perhaps sensing he'd gone too far, he said, "All right. I'll have the techs photograph everything today and send someone over to check out your storage. Do you have a safety deposit key for the ones you've stored?"

"It's a number code. I'll have to go to the vault with whoever you send. I gather this is all because items were stolen from Tricia Ross?"

"I can confirm that," Shea said, "but won't give you a description of the missing articles. You can see why there's an issue ... given your past history."

"I'd never set foot in her home before. Her neighbor can attest to that."

"Still got to check it out."

"And you're referring to my past history *saving* a stolen antiquity and restoring it to the authorities? Talk to Paul Gentile, he's a detective with the NYPD."

He gave me a lukewarm grin. "Already have. He speaks well of you."

Shea spent the next while asking for details on what had transpired during my two forays into Iraq. I had a feeling it was just to keep me talking.

On Shea's request, one of the techies snapped photos of the artifacts in the cabinet while I photocopied the provenance documents. I let Loki run around at that point—I was pissed off enough not to care whether she got in their way.

Shea insisted I stay in the living room while the techies did an extensive search of it and the rest of the apartment. I sat and watched them create an unholy mess, taking virtually everything out and leaving it on the floor. They missed my hollow book, though, throwing it in with the others scattered across the floor. I got some satisfaction from that.

But the male techie's eyes lit up as he ran his fingers along a center shelf of the cleared bookcase. My heart sank. Then came the click and one of the back wooden panels dropped down to reveal the wall safe hidden behind. The friend who'd sublet the apartment had it installed for his own stuff but it now contained the treasure chest my brother had given me when I was a child. I'd completely forgotten to tell Shea about it and now it would look as though that was deliberate.

Shea jerked his thumb toward the safe. "Open for us please and then stand back."

"I just forgot about it," I said, knowing how weak that sounded. "Sure."

I punched in the numbers and the door swung outward. The techie reached in and pulled out the chest. He crouched, opened it up, then spread a large clear plastic bag on the floor and laid out the contents: my seven gold coins, a copper medallion with an image of a vulture stamped on it, a cameo in its enameled box, a stone cylinder seal, a golden key.

Shea heaved a sigh. "You've got papers for these?"

"No. They were a gift from my brother. I've had them since I was a child. My former housekeeper can vouch for that."

"No papers. I'll have to take them in." He nodded to the techie, who put each object into a separate zip-locked bag.

"I'd like you to photograph them all right now, in case there's any damage done while they're in your possession," I said curtly.

"Okay, Jess." Shea nodded at the woman, who proceeded to snap pictures of every item.

I cursed myself silently for keeping the chest here rather than leaving it in the vault. I hated the thought of losing the pieces, even temporarily. Of all the possessions of my childhood, these were the most precious to me. "When will I get them back?"

"When I'm satisfied they aren't stolen."

They were packing up now. Before leaving they took a swab of my saliva. "We've got your fingerprints on file," Shea said, "but no DNA. Appreciate your cooperation. I'll send the antiquities expert over tomorrow. And I'll be in touch."

My place was an infernal mess: drawers left open, their contents strewn about haphazardly, cushions overturned, carpets rolled up, books heaped on the floor. The minute the door closed behind them, I marched into my bedroom. The bed had been completely stripped and some of my clothes laid out on it in a strange kind of tableau, as if they'd been photographing them. The rest of my jackets, shirts, and pants lay in a pile beside the bed on the floor but my sock and underwear drawers seemed untouched. How weird was that? I couldn't guess what their motive was.

Half an hour later Bennet walked in to find me slouched on the sofa amid the devastation. Her first instinct was to burst out laughing. Then I told her what had happened—and she spent the rest of the evening helping me straighten up.

The next day I accompanied Shea's antiquities expert to the storage vault. He was an older man, a professor at Yale who'd known Samuel, and he acted like a kid in a candy store when he saw the quality of objects my brother had collected. I was curious about what had been stolen from Tricia Ross and still confounded as to why they'd photographed my clothes, but didn't manage to pry anything new out of him. In the end, he seemed satisfied that everything was legit. I heard nothing further from Shea. All I wanted now was to escape the city.

Two days later, Bennet and I left JFK at noon on a Turkish Airlines flight bound for Istanbul.

Part Two

THE DEVIL'S
THRONE

I know your works and where you dwell … where Satan's Throne is.

—REVELATION 2:13

Twenty-Six

February 26, 2005
Istanbul, Turkey

During the flight Bennet confessed that, except for a gap year spent trekking around Europe, she'd never left the U.S. I'd wanted to go straight to Pergamon, but given her excitement about the trip it wouldn't be fair to deny her the chance to see Istanbul. We made it smoothly through customs, found our baggage, and hailed a taxi. When we entered the old city—the site of the original Constantinople—the streets were largely empty, the historic area a lonely place in February without its flocks of tourists. Bennet's lovely gray eyes grew wider as we passed narrow cobblestone streets, each one its own flamboyant bazaar of shops with rich kilims, oriental lamps in a rainbow of colors, copper and bronze vessels swinging from awnings. And dominating it all, like an aging monarch surveying her domain, were the spires and dome of the Hagia Sophia.

I'd once taken pride in the city, believing Turkey to be my original home. The history of my birthplace, its position at the intersection of Eastern and Western cultures, had become a legend in my mind, probably because I grew up so far away. As a child I'd imagined romantic spires, exotic mosques, the smell of spice, the muezzin's song at sunset. The real Istanbul did not disappoint, but my dreams now seemed a farce. I no longer believed I'd been born there at all.

I'd booked us in at the Four Seasons Sultanahmet, a five-star neo-classical hotel close to the city's main historic venues. We were on Strauss's dime; why not bask in a little luxury? The decor gave it a distinctive Eastern flavor—warm, mellow colors, dark wooden accents, metal grilles, and marble floors that shone like mirrors. Bennet couldn't hide the smile tugging at the corner of her lips as we entered the elegant lobby.

The next morning we headed straight for Topkapi Palace, an exotic fantasy of courtyards, fountains, and magnificent chambers numbering in the hundreds. The royal compound originally functioned as a small city, home to thousands of people. Through the Gate of Felicity we reached the Third Courtyard, its ancient hollow trees still sprouting green leafy canopies. The Harem Quarters entrance, almost hidden at one side of the gate, had itself once housed a multitude of wives, concubines, slaves, and guards, all living in a labyrinth of corridors and rooms. Struck by the beauty of the chambers, Bennet took wads of photos with her high-end Leica. "I couldn't bear to part with my camera," she'd said before we left the hotel. "I'd rather go without food than relegate it to the pawnshop. And photos are going to be as important as the prose." As we made our way through the rooms, she'd break off to make entries in her laptop while I consulted the fat guide-book I'd bought.

"'Muslim women could not be concubines; it was forbidden. Many in the harem were Christians from Armenia completely subject to the whims of the sultan and his mother, who behaved more like a queen than the sultan's first wife,'" I read out. "It says here that once, in a pique of temper, a sultan ordered 280 concubines forced into sacks, taken out in boats, and drowned in the Bosphorus."

Bennet tucked her laptop under her arm and shuddered. "The place is glorious. But imagine never being able to leave."

I flipped the guidebook page and sucked in a breath. "The eunuchs had it even worse."

"Glad we were born in this day and age, no?"

"Even if I'd lived back then I wouldn't have qualified. The Ottoman harem eunuchs were all black men, Abyssinian or Nubian. An Egyptian Coptic monastery supplied the new recruits. The priests would cut off the boys' testicles and penis and insert a bamboo stick as a gruesome replacement. After that, the boys commanded a very high price."

"Disgusting." Bennet gazed about her as though the walls could tell tales if only she listened hard enough. "Hard to believe all this beauty existed alongside such cruelty."

That afternoon we wandered through the rest of the palace. Every new room boasted decorations of magnificent Iznik tiles patterned in cobalt blues, violets, reds, and dusky greens. We gazed dumbstruck at buildings with intriguing names like the Fruit Kiosk and the Gilded Kiosk. High, arched stained-glass windows in the Twin Kiosk shone like the radiant blue of pure lapis lazuli.

The treasury was aptly named, brimming as it did with valuables—weapons encrusted with so many jewels it was hard to imagine their actually being used, an oriental throne wide as a piano and covered with gold and precious stones, a teardrop diamond called the Spoonmaker. Uncut precious stones spilled out of golden boxes. Brooches, pendants, headdresses—each must have been worth a small fortune. Silver tea services, gold urns, elaborate armor. So many splendors they made the English crown jewels seem pallid. If there was such a thing as sensory overload, we experienced it.

Later we found a quiet place for dinner, a tiny establishment run by an expat American who'd fallen in love with Istanbul on a trip and never left. The place was crowded with Turks; they must have found the frites and mouthwatering steaks exotic. Or maybe the appeal lay in the host himself, who greeted each customer as if they were a long-lost relative.

"What a fabulous day," Bennet said as we sat with our espressos. The stars hadn't left her eyes since we'd set out that morning. "Make something up. Tell Strauss we're hot on Helmstetter's trail but need to spend a few more weeks here."

I smiled to myself. What she'd said came close to the ruse I'd already planned. "You're fun to travel with," I said. I meant it genuinely. "Can't wait to see how much you're going to like Pergamon."

Bennet grinned, then ducked her head and busied herself with her notes. She looked up occasionally, read out a sentence or two, and asked whether she'd gotten it right. "The article is supposed to be about you, your impressions. I want to be true to that."

I couldn't help wondering whether the article would ever see the light of day. I'd sensed early on it was more of an excuse for Strauss to keep his eye on me than a real project. Still, Bennet clearly took it seriously.

The next day we visited the colossal Hagia Sophia. Built by Justinian in 537 A.D. as a Byzantine Christian church, it was converted to a mosque almost a thousand years later when Mehmet the Conqueror claimed Istanbul for the Ottomans. "The museum interior is surfaced with thirty million gold tesserae—tiny mosaic tiles," our tour guide explained. "They've recently been restored. See how they shine with such brilliance?" She pointed up to the dome. "Those two figures are seraphim. Strange, aren't they? They have six wings." Our little group gazed upward as she spoke. The figures were indeed unusual—odd, moonlike faces in a cluster of gray-feathered wings.

"Are those Islamic interpretations of angels?" Bennet asked.

"It is forbidden to portray the human form in Muslim art," the guide began, "although you will find some representations in their books. These figures are Christian seraphim—dating from the Byzantine era. They were hidden under seven layers of plaster and have only recently been uncovered. Several passages in the Old Testament associate seraphim with venomous desert snakes, suggesting a demonic quality. And yet Christians believed they were the highest form of angel, representing purity—burning hot and closest to God. It is another one of those biblical conundrums, no?" She laughed pleasantly and led us to the next venue.

That evening would be our last in the city, and to mark the occasion I'd made a reservation at the Matbah Ottoman Palace Cuisine, recommended by the hotel concierge for its traditional recipes. As I waited in Bennet's room for her to shower and change I leafed through a thick volume I'd bought at the museum. I admired the excellent reproductions of Islamic book arts, some dating as far back as 750 A.D. Caught up in the images, I barely heard Bennet step out of the bathroom.

"Earth to John," she chuckled. "Ready?"

I took one look at her and blinked. My waif had transformed into a glamour queen. I was used to seeing her in her usual getups—loud funky miniskirts, tights, mismatched tops. Tonight she wore patent-leather stilettos and a figure-hugging black dress that showed off her cleavage. She'd pulled back her auburn hair to reveal dangling gold earrings that matched the bracelet around her slim wrist, reproductions of an Ottoman design she'd bought at the museum store. Mascara and bright red lipstick made her look positively sultry.

I walked over and put my hands on her shoulders. "You look beautiful." I hesitated. We'd been flirting with each other almost since we met. I'd been careful to book us separate rooms—Strauss would eventually see the bills and I didn't want him prying into my personal affairs any more than he already had. Still. "Maybe we should stay in and order room service," I said. "Later."

"Not after I've gone to all this work." She laughed and wrapped a cashmere shawl around her shoulders. "Let's go."

The Matbah proved as elegant as I'd been led to expect. We were ushered through a stylish room to a banquet-style table covered with crisp white linen. The floor-to-ceiling windows gave us a fabulous view of the Hagia Sophia's lighted dome.

After the waiter took our order I opened the Islamic art book I'd brought with me. "You asked about the angel in the Hagia Sophia." I found the image I wanted and showed it to her.

Islamic Angel

"This is a very early example of an Islamic angel. The Quran considers angels to be messengers. They name very few of them. It's probably Israfel pictured here, who's similar to Raphael and is supposed to blow his trumpet twice to warn of the end times."

Bennet touched the page with a scarlet fingernail. "It looks so human—the wings seem almost incidental."

On my phone I brought up more pictures: the Hagia Sophia angel we'd seen earlier in the day and the Mesopotamian Apkallu guardian figure.

"There's no proof," I said, "but the Apkallu figures are what I think first gave rise to our idea of angels."

Byzantine Seraphim   Apkallu, Mesopotamian
                                      Guardian Figure

"Hard to argue with that when you look at them."

"Interesting that the three foundational religions all recognize the existence of angels. Makes you wonder how far back the idea of a celestial winged messenger goes."

Our food arrived, a veritable feast of Turkish delicacies: flatbread with an olive and walnut tapenade; peach stuffed with minced lamb, currants, and almonds; goose in pastry and pilaf. We dug in with gusto.

On our way back to the hotel, Bennet made a flimsy excuse for wanting to see my room. As soon as the door closed behind us I slipped off her shawl and bent my head toward the nape of her neck. She turned, put her arms around me, and pressed her lips to mine in a deep kiss. All the innuendos, the electricity that had only grown since we'd gotten to know each other, had whetted our appetites and we lost no time satisfying them. I unzipped her dress and released the clasp on her bra, brushing my fingers over her soft skin. "It's about time," Bennet whispered. "It seems like forever since I've wanted you."

"I thought you'd be worth the wait," I murmured into her hair. I shrugged off my clothes. I think we made it as far as the bed. The sun peeked through the window before either of us had any desire for sleep.

Twenty-Seven

March 1, 2005
Bergama, Turkey

We set out for Bergama, the city surrounding the Pergamon ruins, early the following morning. A ferry took us across the Sea of Marmara to Bursa, where I rented a car for the six-hour drive. By late afternoon we'd reached our destination: the Hera Hotel, deep in the twisting lanes of the old part of the city. It was a ten-room affair, an old Greek house built of local weathered stone, lovingly restored and so picturesque it seemed made to order for a travel magazine. Ornate iron grilles protected its tall blue wooden doors. Its art pieces and antique furniture reflected Anatolian themes—handmade throws and rugs in dazzling colors, vases, and fat, rustic urns. From the lounge you could look down a jaw-dropping plunge to the Acropolis in the distance. It had all the modern touches too, including free Wi-Fi and a wine bar to die for.

After dinner I asked the owner about Bergama's oldest hotels. He wrote down three names and gave me directions. "I'll go tomorrow,"

I said to Bennet. "There's a slim chance Helmstetter stayed at one of them. I've got to start looking somewhere."

She ran her hand through her hair, grown curly with the humidity now that we'd traveled south. "I was hoping we could sightsee around the old city. Get our bearings first."

"Why don't you start out without me? It's entirely safe, I'd think. I doubt I'll be long."

"Are you sure?"

"You'll have much more fun than poking around in old hotels."

That night brought another terrifying episode of sleep paralysis. Again I had the sense of being watched—I peered into the gloom of the hotel room and thought I saw a figure move. A winged creature, moon-faced like the Hagia Sophia seraphim. I tried to get up, but as before, it felt as if my hands and feet were bound. It was the first instance since I'd started taking the drugs Dr. Cass prescribed and it seemed even more of a nightmare.

Bennet tried her best, but even her consoling touch made me apprehensive. I couldn't explain it to myself or to her. Eventually, as my heart rate slowed, I put it down to a resurfacing anxiety about Yersan. After all, we were much closer to his home turf. Still, I had no reason to suspect he knew where we'd gone.

After breakfast the next morning, Bennet parted from me reluctantly. I gave her a kiss and she turned to her right, off to see the Red Basilica. The day was bright and unseasonably warm—a relief from New York's endless rain and perfect for a stroll.

Halfway up Soğan Dere Street I found the first hotel the owner had suggested. Inside, an officious-looking gray-haired clerk gaped at me blankly as I explained my mission. He snapped his fingers at another man who was on his way out and spoke to him in Turkish.

"Would you mind explaining again?" the second man asked politely. He motioned toward the clerk. "Not understanding too well."

"I'm looking for any record you might have of someone who may have stayed here thirty-five years ago."

When the man translated what I'd said the clerk's deadpan expression cracked. He broke into a peal of laughter and waved his hand back and forth: "Not possible!" I thanked him and left.

A similar reception awaited me at the next establishment.

I considered not bothering with the last place on my list but figured I'd better go through the motions. I reached it by climbing a precipitous set of stone steps toward a guest house that looked so old it seemed to have grown, like a sturdy plant, out of the same stone as the street. It had gaily painted shutters and caramel-colored flower pots from which sprang a few early flowers. An old man sitting on a wicker chair outside the entrance dozed in the morning sun. A little bell sounded as I pushed open the front door and stepped into a cool interior smelling pleasantly of herbs. The front room held several tables and chairs; a young woman sat at one of them, snipping strands of rosemary. She looked up and gave me a broad smile. I introduced myself and posed the same question I'd asked the other hotel clerks.

She stood. "My dede should be able to help you." She popped outside, returning after a few minutes with the old man shuffling behind her. He gave me a congenial nod and then smiled, showing me a mouthful of broken, stained teeth.

"Come with us," the woman said, pushing strands of brown hair off her face. "Dede has kept all the ledgers since he began the hotel." She spoke English very well, with what sounded like a Scottish accent. When I complimented her on it she explained she'd done her undergrad in Edinburgh.

A curtained doorway led into a larger room with a flagged floor, two burgundy overstuffed sofas, ashtrays and brass lamps on end tables, and a TV fixed to the west wall. An enormous rustic cupboard stood against the opposite wall. The old man lowered himself gingerly to his knees and pulled open the cupboard's bottom doors. They held dozens of musty, cloth-bound ledgers. He began to take out each dust-covered tome, glance inside the covers, close it again, and put it back. *This might take a while,* I thought.

The daughter suddenly spoke. "You said the man came to Bergama in July 1970? And his name was Helmstetter?"

"That's right. I don't know whether he stayed here or not. Really, I don't mean to put you to all this trouble." I was beginning to feel guilty.

Her face lit up with another smile. "Oh no. Dede is glad someone is interested. He's very proud of the business. He started it right after the Second World War."

The old man said something in Turkish. He put one shaky hand on the couch, eased himself up, and brought over a green ledger with the pages open in the middle. All the entries had been printed neatly in faded blue ink. He pointed to a name a couple of lines up from the bottom.

And there it was. *George Helmstetter, September 10–16,* along with a Park Avenue address. His U.S. passport number was recorded beside it. Following that, in a spidery script, his signature. I could hardly believe my eyes.

With their permission, I took out my phone and clicked some pictures of the page.

"Dede says he remembers him."

"Really—that long ago?"

"Dede says he remembers because that guest was special."

"How so?"

"He was a sorcerer. He came here to see the snake god."

Twenty-Eight

March 2, 2005

M y hands were practically shaking when I called Bennet. She
suggested we meet at a café and gave me the directions. I
spotted her, looking cool and collected, sitting at an outdoor table,
typing away at her laptop with a bottle of lemonade beside it.

"I've got something to show you. You won't believe it."

She looked up expectantly. "What?"

A waiter scurried over the minute he spied me.

Bennet blanched when she saw Helmstetter's scrawl. She put
her fingernail on the screen and ran it along the name as if she were
trying to erase his signature. She looked up at me sharply. "What
an amazing find. Email me the photo?"

"The guy at the guest house remembered Helmstetter and told
me he came to Pergamon to find the snake god."

"*Snake* god? My lord. Did he say where?"

"Pergamon. Either at Satan's Throne, the place Veronica Sills
said Helmstetter wanted to see, or the Asklepion, the site of the

ancient healing center. Veronica painted such a frightening picture of Helmstetter—and this suggests she was right. I think he wanted the knowledge to do evil."

"Let's go," Bennet said eagerly. We stopped only to buy bottles of spring water and pogaca, savory pastries filled with cheese and olives.

In the first century, Pergamon was the most important city in Asia Minor. Emperors rewarded its fierce loyalty to the Romans with sumptuous temples, palaces, and public buildings. Its library, reputed to hold two hundred thousand scrolls, was the second most important in the world next to Alexandria's. It took us an hour to make the arduous trek to the summit of Pergamon's Acropolis, grateful to be doing the climb now rather than in the summer's heat. We followed the blue dots marking the route, marveling at the majestic scenes unfolding around us, Bennet snapping photos all the way.

We encountered a few other travelers. A group of French teenagers, a couple taking pictures with their phones, and a solitary man who seemed somehow out of place. He was a thin guy with longish dark hair, wearing sunglasses and a hat with the brim pulled so low you couldn't see much of his face. He kept some distance behind us, yet never let us out of his sight. Despite the temperate weather he wore a dirty windbreaker.

When we reached the parking lot at the top he approached us, stopping about ten feet away. "You American, no?"

I nodded.

"Which way the Temple of Trajan?"

I pointed west to a series of columns gleaming white in the sun, recognizing it from a guidebook photo. I figured he'd started up the conversation with some other agenda in mind, like asking for money, but he surprised me by heading off toward the temple.

Although I kept my eye out, I saw nothing more of the mysterious man. We toured the landmarks for over an hour, gazing in awe at the amphitheater, a colossal affair that once held an audience of ten thousand, its crumbling tiers spilling down at a death-defying angle. Finally we reached the site of Satan's Throne, more properly known as the Altar of Zeus. According to the guidebook, in the 1930s German engineers cut the magnificent marble friezes and columns from the altar's base and transported the huge structure to Berlin, where it now sat in the Pergamon Museum. Constructed in the second century B.C., "Satan's Throne" was probably so named because early Christians proclaimed Pergamon a center of orgies and vice. Others believed the location was near an entrance to Hades. Today, little more remained than a square of stepped stone walls buttressing a platform of grass, shaded by one large pine tree. Pretty and peaceful though it was, we both felt discouraged. Hard to imagine the wild pagan rites this place once saw.

We unwrapped our pogaca. "Not much sign of *la dolce vita* here. It was hardly worth the climb," Bennet said glumly. She bit off a generous chunk of pastry and chewed it thoughtfully, her cheeks bulging. "I wonder why Helmstetter thought he'd find anything worthwhile."

"He must have concluded otherwise," I said, "or he wouldn't have gone to Kandovan afterward. I've seen the altar in Berlin's Pergamon Museum; there's nothing resembling a throne."

"The name was just a metaphor, then? It's so tranquil here. Maybe all the action took place in vaults underground." Bennet carefully studied the stone walls and the platform of grass.

"If so, they're filled in. What a travesty that Turkey lost one of its grandest works of art. The Germans making off with the entire altar was almost as bad as the Brits stealing the Elgin Marbles."

We'd left the Asklepion to the last. Now, in late afternoon, we entered it by means of a rickety slatted bridge joined to a structure of stone walls with arches keyed in vertical bricks. Its remarkably preserved hewn stone was as regular and well mortared as anything you'd find today. A vaulted tunnel of the same stone led to a sizable, perfectly round room.

We stood in the middle and let our eyes travel along the smooth circular wall. "This is where the saying 'doctors doing their rounds' came from. People traveled from all over Europe to be healed here. The doctors made sure that everyone who left the healing center survived."

"How could they do that?" Bennet asked.

"By refusing any terminally ill patients. A sign over the entrance gate said 'Death is not permitted here.'" Our laughter echoed in the room.

The muted patter of footsteps alerted me. I looked around to check whether the strange guy we'd talked to was anywhere in sight. The sound abruptly halted. I hoped the sentiment that once stood over the gate applied to us, too.

Other rooms held stone niches big enough for a small man to curl up in. "The place looks like a burial crypt," I remarked. I imagined Helmstetter practicing his incantations here, a place strange enough that he'd fit right in.

"Asklepion was famous as a health spa too," I added. "A mud bath would be okay, but I think I'd pass on the diagnosis."

Bennet gave me a quizzical look.

"These rooms were patients' dormitories, and at night the priests let snakes slither over them. In the morning, diagnosis would be based on their dreams."

As if to confirm that, we came into a clearing and saw a broken pillar with two snakes carved onto it.

"Helmstetter said he came here to find the snake god. Maybe he associated some form of Satan with the god Asclepius. The staff entwined with a serpent was the god's emblem."

"The caduceus?"

"Yes. The traditional insignia for medicine. It symbolizes wisdom."

Farther on, we found a stone basin in a small open-air plaza. "This must be the sacred pool," I said. "The waters are supposed to be curative." The square stone well looked about six feet deep, the water at its bottom lurid green with algae. It looked anything but therapeutic.

A water fountain, crystal clear this time, poured into a carved marble basin from a distinctly modern metal pipe fixed to a stone wall. I'd become fascinated with the mystique of the place—it was beautiful and unnerving at the same time. I emptied my water bottle and bent down to collect some from the fountain. Who knew? It might help counter my night terrors.

Once I'd filled the bottle and capped it, I straightened up. Bennet had disappeared.

I called out to her and got no response. Thinking she'd gone back to shoot more pictures of the round chamber, I retraced our steps and kept calling her. My voice echoed, ghostlike, through the corridor. The sun was fading fast now, so I returned to the plaza. Other than a few stragglers from the group of French teenagers, no one else was there.

I asked one of boys in my imperfect French if they'd seen Bennet. *"Avez-vous vu mon ami? La femme avec les cheveux rouges?"*

He thought for a second. *"Avec jean bleu et chemise blanche?"*

"Oui, la même," I said, elated he'd seen her.

He turned and pointed to the scrubby slope, a field lying outside the amphitheater. *"Elle y est allée."*

After thanking him I slipped through a gap in the wall to reach the field, inwardly cursing Bennet for taking off like that. I followed a rough footpath down the slope, but when I surveyed the rocky terrain below me, my heart sank. No sign of her. I cupped my hands around my mouth and yelled out her name again. Silence. A cluster of trees partially blocked my view so I continued along the path, aware of the waning light; we had less than an hour left before sundown.

Just past a grove of trees, where the land bordered a clutch of houses marking the perimeter of the ruins, a crumbling fence of small boulders circled a stone hut with a corrugated tin roof built into the side of the hill. There was no door, just an opening about five feet high. When I looked inside and my eyes became adjusted to the gloom, I saw it wasn't a hut at all but the entrance to some kind of tunnel dug into the side of the hill.

As I peered down the corridor, a square of light shone at its terminus. That gave me some hope: Bennet carried a Maglite in her knapsack to allow her to take better photos in dim interiors. When I stepped forward, something rolled away from my foot. A plastic water bottle of the same kind we'd bought earlier.

Twenty-Nine

The tunnel might have once run under ancient Pergamon. A food-storage facility, or a wine cellar? It was cold and damp and angled steeply downward, stretching for maybe a hundred and fifty feet.

The rectangle of light at the end of the corridor proved to be another opening. I ducked down, stepped through it into another room, and saw Bennet. Relief flooded through me. She was crouched on the ground with the Maglite on. Her camera, propped up with a stone, was aimed at one of the most bizarre objects I'd ever seen: a life-sized bull made entirely of brass, gray with tarnish.

Bennet jumped up when she saw me. "Look at this! What a strange sculpture. Who would have put it here?"

I kept my voice neutral. "It's not a sculpture. At least, that's not its real purpose." I ran my hand over the lifelike sinews in the bull's neck, rendered in precise detail. Its throat stretched to what would have been the full natural length; its nostrils flared and its mouth yawned open. A large vat had been placed on the flat, earthen floor beneath its belly and a crude door about two feet square was set into its flank. Inside the head would be a network of pipes. I touched the door in the bull's side. "It's a torture device called a 'brazen bull.' A man would be forced inside it and the door bolted, then a fire was kindled in the vat to roast the victim to death. His screams, channeled through pipes in the head, came out like a mad bull's bellow."

Bennet stepped back. "That's horrific!"

"Why did you just take off like that?" I burst out. "It's damn lucky I found you."

"I told you I was coming back and just to wait. Didn't you hear me?"

She may have said something when I was concentrating on filling the water bottle. "No. How did you end up here, anyway?"

"I returned to the room you said reminded you of a crypt to shoot more photos and ran into that weird guy who'd asked the way to the temple. He said if I really wanted to see something special, I should come here. I didn't think it would take so long."

At that moment, we both heard the sound of boots treading down the tunnel. Since Bennet had trained her Maglite on the room, I could see nothing through the doorway. I motioned for her to get down behind the vat and then snatched up her lamp, the only thing I could use as a weapon, and aimed it at the entrance.

The mystery man took a few steps into the room and stopped. He still wore his wide-brimmed hat and sunglasses. He gave me a crooked smile. "Well ... both birds in one net. You've made it too easy for me. Tell your friend to come out from behind the bull or she'll be the first one to roast."

He had the look of a street fighter, but I was a head taller and figured I could take him. The tone of his voice chilled me. I'd heard it somewhere before. At least I knew this wasn't Yersan.

He took a step toward me. "I just came to ask you a question. If you answer it, you get to leave in one piece."

"Ask away then." I tightened my fist around the Maglite.

"Which way the Temple of Trajan?" he mimicked—and doubled over with laughter. His hat tumbled to the ground. He straightened up and whipped off his sunglasses. I stared in shock at Nick Shaheen.

"What the hell? You're supposed to be dead!"

"Don't tell me you're disappointed."

I took two strides over and gave him a quick, hard hug. "God. I can't believe this. It's really you."

Bennet crawled out from behind the bull and stood next to me, demanding to know what was going on.

"This is a good friend of mine—with a very perverted sense of humor," I said as I let him go and stood back. Nick put out his hand to her. "Great to meet you. I'm Nick."

I saw new lines in his face; he was younger than me but now appeared older. He still looked more like an enforcer for the Genovese crime family than a decorated lieutenant in the U.S. Special Forces. Silver streaks peppered his lanky black hair and there was a new, grim determination to the set of his jaw. Even when he laughed, it was clear his eyes had lost their old sparkle.

"This place"—he waved nonchalantly at the bull—"was someone's crazy idea to make money. The property owner, knowing how close he was to hordes of tourists visiting the sites, commissioned the bull and stuck it into this old storage vault that had been on his land since forever. He figured to make a fortune charging admission to see it. The government shut him down in less than a week. They said it wasn't safe but the real reason lay with the site archaeologists, who claimed it wasn't in keeping with Pergamon's image."

Bennet narrowed her eyes. "How do you know all this?"

"Took the guided tour."

"Well then, your little drama is entirely within the spirit of this place, I would think," she said, feigning a sweet smile.

"Take it easy, Bennet," I said softly. "If we're very nice, Nick may just protect our asses in Iran."

She gave me a long look, then turned, picked up her camera, and went back to taking shots of the bull.

Nick grabbed my arm and steered me out into the tunnel. "Tell her you met me when I was a private contractor in Iraq and don't mention my surname," he whispered.

"It's too late. She's already read my notes—my account of what we did there. She's probably already put two and two together. Hard to put anything over on her anyway."

"Shit. You didn't mention her in your message to Ali."

"I know. The last thing I expected was to see you over here."

He grunted. "Let's talk about it later."

Nick had left his rental car in the Pergamon parking lot, so he drove us back to our hotel. I booked a room for him there. Later, I suggested we go out for a bite. Bennet said she was tired from the long day and just wanted to curl up and sort through her photos. Diplomacy wasn't her strong suit, but I sensed she was giving Nick and me some space to catch up.

We found a family-run restaurant, a hole in the wall really, just a few tables with faded tablecloths and vases of plastic flowers. The air had turned cold as soon as the sun went down, so we were glad of the warmth and cheerful atmosphere inside. A little fire burned brightly in a wood oven and the place smelled of delicious home cooking. The owner brought over a bottle of a heavy-bodied red wine called Papazkarasi. Roughly translated, that meant Black Priest.

"To your health," I said, clinking his glass. "Glad to see you in such fine shape, considering I thought you were six feet under."

Nick laughed and drank but then grew serious. "Tell me. Who's on your tail? Other than me, that is. I've been keeping an eye on you two since you arrived."

"What do you mean?"

"Two guys following you. Western dress. Don't look like locals. Driving a black SUV. Unfortunately they had some engine trouble so they missed your expedition to Pergamon. Their motor problems will keep them busy for a while." He grinned.

I filled him in on all the events in New York, and told him I suspected Yersan of murdering Tricia Ross and putting a hit out on me. Chances were high that the men Nick spotted belonged to him.

"Iranians?"

I nodded. "Ethnic minority. Not Muslim. They're followers of Zoroaster, fire worshipers."

"And knowing that you still want to walk into the lion's den? Kandovan is their territory. Must be worth a lot of money to you."

"More than that, Nick. I'm pretty sure I was born in Kandovan, and I'm close to finding out who my real parents are. I wouldn't have tried to enter Iran by myself, of course. With you here, it changes everything. Will you take us there?"

"I'm no miracle worker, Madison. I have my own problems. Why incur the risk?"

"Strauss threatened to accuse me of stealing the antiquities he'd shown me unless I finish the job. Of course what he wants is impossible. Bennet will be an effective witness and corroborator. I've already got a forger working on replicating pages of the book Strauss claims his assistant stole. To make it all believable, I really should go to Kandovan."

Nick swore. "If I was in the U.S., I'd screw the asshole over for you."

The owner brought our dinner—fried eggplant, zucchini patties with yogurt, grilled calamari, and homemade dumplings. We dug in as if we hadn't eaten for days.

I waited patiently for Nick to tell me his story. Finally I poured the last of the bottle into our glasses and prompted him gently. "What's the mystery?" I said. "You on a mission—under deep cover?"

He threw down a long draft of wine. Again I was struck by how haggard he looked. He bent his head and kept his eyes on the table. "Officially, I'm listed as Duty Status Whereabouts Unknown. That's army speak for 'We don't have any proof of what happened to him but we're pretty sure he's dead.' I engineered a rumor—that I'd been captured and tortured with my body dumped in an undisclosed location."

I sat back. "Are you telling me you're a *deserter*?"

He raised his eyes to mine and I could see a spark of anger. "I'd sooner cut my arm off than do that."

I felt awful about mistaking his words. "I drew the wrong conclusion, sorry."

"How much you keep up with the war? Did you see the news about Fallujah?"

"We wasted the place, didn't we?"

"Yeah, pretty much. Bombed the shit right out of it. One of the people they were after was a key man, a Jordanian Sunni. The guy hated the Shia and U.S. in equal measure. By last November he'd accumulated a lot of control and influence. Pretty much all of Fallujah went rogue. I was one of the few to get inside. We heard he might put in an appearance at a wedding. If we could take him out there, we might be able to avoid a bloodbath. But I guess romance trumps everything. Some locals saw it coming down the pipe and went ahead with the wedding anyway."

Nick sighed. "I'd been able to set up good surveillance. Don't know whether he got wind of our plans or what but the main man didn't show up. My message back to command got crossed somehow—not hard under those conditions. They went in with white phosphorus. Wasn't expecting that. Usually it's deployed for a fire screen before a troop advance. That stuff is worse than napalm. Skin melts right off of people. Fries them. Everyone died."

He was silent for a moment. "When I saw what happened … I felt like someone had just clawed my heart out of my chest."

"Lord. That's brutal."

"And on top of that, I was made. Marines saved my ass. It had to happen sometime. But you psyche yourself up pretending it won't. I couldn't go on after that. Beyond a couple of burns and a few slices on my arm I wasn't physically hurt but the doctors declared me emotionally unfit for my job. Just could not shake those bodies out of my mind. Still can't. That was four months ago. Off the record, I got extended leave and my commander let it be known I'd probably been killed in battle but they couldn't locate my remains. Enough time goes by, they're hoping I can get back in the race—but I don't think so. This horse can't run anymore."

"That sounds like hell, Nick."

He gave me a wan smile and picked up his glass again. "I'm currently hanging out in Istanbul under an assumed name. Nick Voss. Just call me Nick when we're around anyone so you don't make a slip. I'm thinking about getting into corporate counter-intelligence. Good money there and I can officially leave the army in another six months. You got a job for me? I need wads of cash to buy that New York penthouse."

I laughed, hoping it would ease the pain he was feeling. "I do have money; none of it mine, fortunately, so I can be generous." I paused. "So what do you think? Can you get us into Iran and babysit us while we're there?"

"Oh yeah, piece of cake." He grinned. "It will come as no surprise that Americans aren't exactly welcome there. But you're talking about the extreme northwestern end of the country—right? Close to the Turkish border?"

"Yes."

"We'll see. Getting you into Tehran, I wouldn't try it. That location might be doable—just. Ethnic minorities mostly live in the area; they keep to themselves as much as possible, so that would help us. They don't live easily with the government."

Nick glanced at the glowing embers in the oven fire, at the painted earthenware china atop the cupboard, at the owner humming to himself while he polished glasses. He saw nothing. You think you know someone, especially after what we'd been through. Still … people change. War changes them no matter what side they're on. It erodes your soul. At least that's what I believed.

After I'd paid the bill we stepped back into the narrow lane outside. "You carry on," Nick said. "I have to go back to my car for something. I'll head over to the hotel later. And keep your eyes sharp. Can't swear those guys I saw were after you but it's better to assume the worst."

I had to make my way along a network of short streets no wider than alleyways. After midnight, cold now, and lacking tourist traffic, the place was empty of people, many of the houses dark, shops long shuttered up. Whether it was Nick's warning or my sixth sense, something felt wrong. I kept looking over my shoulder, envisioning those two men behind me.

A young woman with bobbed black hair and bright lipstick emerged from a cross street about thirty feet ahead. It was a relief to see someone else out and I unconsciously slowed my pace. She looked at me nervously and hesitated as I approached, probably afraid to encounter a strange man. I nodded as I passed her and said "Good evening," hoping to reassure her.

"Yes it is—now," she said in perfect English.

Thirty

She came at me with a knife, gripping it close to the top of its shaft. The blade sliced through my jacket arm; I heard the sleeve rip, felt the sting of its tip. I managed to twist away and started to run. Then I saw a heavyset man step from a recessed doorway just ahead. I was boxed in. I heard the woman rush at my back and did the only thing I could think of. Went into a feint, dropped to the ground, and bashed into her below her knees.

She catapulted over me and fell heavily, her jaw striking the pavement. I dodged her and whipped around to face the man. He began to yell—and then his voice cut off abruptly. Nick had him by the throat. A lightning quick movement of Nick's hands, a sickening twist of his neck, and the guy went soft at the knees and collapsed. He was out cold. The woman tried to sit up, blood flowing from her lips where her teeth had cut into the soft pulp of her mouth. The knife had landed a few feet away from her. I wrapped my hand in a plastic bag that lay on the cobblestones, picked it up, and slipped it into my jacket pocket.

Nick felt in the guy's pockets, got his key fob, then grabbed him by the armpits and dragged him over to the side of the street. He shoved refuse containers away from the wall and wedged the body behind them. Then he jerked his head in my direction. "Put your arm around her. Pretend she's drunk or something." The woman whimpered as I raised her, holding one hand to her ruined jaw. "Where's the car?" Nick barked at her.

She had difficulty making her mouth work and so pointed to the cross street she'd come from. The SUV sat about halfway down, partly blocking the short street. "Did Yersan send you?" I asked her. She mumbled something unintelligible and I repeated the question. Again she tried to answer, but her mouth was so damaged I couldn't make out what she said. Finally she raised her head and nodded.

We got her to the vehicle and wedged her in between us in the front. The woman held her head in her hands and moaned.

As Nick drove the SUV back to the intersection he told me to take off my jacket and stay beside her. He jumped out and half-lifted, half-slid, the guy's still unconscious form into the back. Then he threw his jacket and mine on top to conceal him as best he could.

When he got back behind the wheel I turned to him. "You didn't really have to get something from your car, did you." It was more a statement than a question.

"Nope."

"I thought you said you'd seen two *guys*."

"She wasn't wearing lipstick at the time and she had on a hoodie." He cracked a smile. "Don't rat on me. I'd never live it down."

Minutes later he pulled up outside the stair leading to our hotel. "Get out, Madison. I'll take it from here." He took out his pistol and trained it on the woman.

"What are you going to do with them?"

"They'll be well looked after, I can guarantee that." The woman shrank away from him. "I'll be in touch," he said. "Wait for me."

I watched him rev the motor and drive away, praying I'd see him again and that we wouldn't end up in the hands of the Turkish police. I couldn't be sure that a window on the alley hadn't silently opened, that someone wasn't already talking to them. I threw the knife in a garbage bin. When I reached the hotel I took a few breaths to calm down as I rolled my sleeves back, trying to hide the mass of blood where the woman had cut me. The lobby was empty and I beat it upstairs.

Bennet was curled up in bed when I came in. "Hi—I remember you," she said. Then she sat bolt upright. "Is that *blood* on your sleeve?"

"Nick and me—just settling an old score." I feigned a laugh. "You should see him." I headed into the bathroom. "I'm going to take a shower."

Bennet marched in and stared at me as I unbuttoned my shirt and shrugged off my jeans and briefs.

"That's a horrible cut!"

"It'll heal."

"I thought you liked him."

"It was nothing serious. You didn't seem so hot on him, though."

"Who would, after he played that stupid game?"

"You'll get used to him. He grows on you."

"What do you mean 'get used to him'?"

"He'll be our security contingent in Iran—if we make it there." I turned the shower on full tilt and stepped in. The hot water washed the blood away but stung like hell. It wasn't a deep cut; more like a razor had shaved off a patch of skin on my upper arm. After I dried off, I got band-aids out of my kit. It took five of them to cover the wound. They looked pathetic but they were all I had. I threw on a pair of sweats and a T-shirt and went back into the bedroom.

Bennet put her laptop away, lay down, and pulled the cover over her. "Come here," she said. As I climbed under the blanket, she rolled closer and put her head on my chest. "Tell me what really happened."

I sighed. "A couple of guys tried to beat up Nick and me. Maybe some local hotheads or something worse. I don't know. It's over now." No sense alarming her if I could help it. I ran my hand along her arm, feeling her soft, warm skin that smelled of soap with a distant hint of the perfume she'd put on that morning.

"Are you going to keep on with it? Strauss could hardly expect you to give up your life for him."

"He's quite capable of that. We're here anyway. No point in wasting the trip. What do you think? *Should* I continue?"

She heaved a sigh. "You will, no matter what I say."

"Bennet. You need to go home for your own safety. If Nick can get us into Iran, I'll keep a complete record of the journey. I'll even email you as I go along if you want."

"If you're going, so am I." She rolled away from me, plumped up her pillow, and said nothing more.

It took quite a while before I nodded off too. For one, like an anxious parent, I kept waiting to hear Nick's door across the hall open. Something else kept me awake, too. In the heat of the fight I'd felt triumphant. Gloated over getting the best of the woman. That was only natural. Yet when she'd moaned and held her head in her hands, her agony hadn't touched me at all. And I couldn't have cared less what happened to her when Nick drove away, just like when I'd hit that guy in my car on the way to Strauss's. A coldness at the center of my heart had stolen over me. Now I feared I'd never get my old self back.

⚜

I heard nothing from Nick the following day. In the morning, Bennet and I made a return visit to Asklepion. I drank more of the water from the fountain; it did seem to revive my spirits. We saw a slate-colored snake slipping into a rock crevice and I wondered aloud whether it was a descendant of the healing snakes. Bennet disagreed, pointing out it had the triangular head of a viper.

We struck up a conversation with an Englishman, who turned out to be an Anglican priest. He'd noticed the snake too. "The poor maligned serpent," he chuckled. "Once a sign of wisdom. Our churches have much to answer for. Clever chaps though, the Roman prelates—blame it on them. In choosing an animal to associate with the devil, they opted for one that humans instinctively fear the most. Pagans revered the snake, as you can see among these ruins." He tipped his peaked cap to us and with a swing of his walking stick trundled away.

It left me wondering again—was it a sacred power Helmstetter sought here? Or had he tried to follow in Faust's footsteps by conjuring up the devil?

Thirty-One

March 3, 2005

That afternoon, the weather still being fine, we found a café and sat outside with our coffees. Bennet caught up with her writing while I buried myself in the material I'd brought with me and whatever I could find on the web. I'd been intrigued by what the Englishman told us about the Christian devil and his close tie with serpents.

There was now general agreement among scholars that many of the Genesis stories could be traced all the way back to early Mesopotamia. The Sumerian serpent god Ningishzida—called the Lord of the Good Tree, or, if one translated the Sumerian correctly, Lady of the Good Tree—was famously illustrated on the vase of Gudea, dating to 2100 B.C.

Ningishzida, Sumerian Serpent God

In the Mesopotamian legend *Adapa and the South Wind*, Ningishzida encourages Adapa, Adam's prototype, to eat the bread and water of life, promising that the food will grant him immortality. The god Enki, who gave Adapa wisdom, warns the mortal he's being tricked and that if he takes the food and water he'll die. Adapa listens to Enki and refuses Ningishzida. In this way Enki fools man into denying himself immortality, keeping it for the gods. In time, the story was retold in Genesis as Adam and Eve facing temptation in the Garden of Eden.

Ningishzida, like the devil, occupied the underworld and possessed great knowledge. There, it seemed to me, lay the original concept of the snake in Eden. Until now, I hadn't realized the Old Testament made no association between the serpent in the garden and Satan. Satan's name meant "adversary"; he'd started out as God's prosecutor. Nor was he particularly important—references to him could be found only three times in the Old Testament. It was Justin Martyr, an early Christian thinker living in the second century A.D., who connected Satan with the serpent in the garden. So it wasn't until many centuries after the Old Testament was written that Satan began to embody pure evil.

The plethora of serpent gods in antiquity interested me: Apep, an evil Egyptian snake god, opposed the light; Glycon, the Macedonian snake god, had magical powers; Naga, the Hindu god, represented freedom; and Ladon, the Greek god curled around the tree in the Garden of Hesperides, guarded the golden apples.

The texts I leafed through explained that *Lucifer* meant "the shining one," and that the passage in the Book of Isaiah, "How art thou fallen from heaven, O Lucifer!" came to be interpreted as a description of the rebellious Satan cast out from heaven. But the scribes who originally wrote this passage were referring to the King of Babylon, not Satan. Over time, the devil absorbed various pagan attributes and became the dark, fallen angel, the convenient whipping boy, the personification of evil that is a hallmark of Christian beliefs.

Bennet's eyes were still glued to her laptop, so I had time to take another look at the photocopy I'd made of Helmstetter's letter to his wife and the strange columns of numbers it contained. Presumably the numbers were some kind of cipher. I made the assumption that Helmstetter had used the modern alphabet. When I applied the simplest substitution code, assigning a number to each letter of the alphabet, commencing with 1 = A, the figures translated into words for numbers—20 8 9 18 20 25 became thirty, and so on. But not all of them: some numbers didn't translate into any word that made sense. I played around with the code for another half an hour until I threw down my pen.

✳

I'd become so caught up in trying to figure out the numbers that I barely noticed the sun setting. Bennet stretched, leaned over, and tapped me on the shoulder. As we made our way back to the hotel, we questioned Helmstetter's obsession again. Was his pursuit of knowledge sacred or profane? We got nowhere, talking in circles, postulating theories and rejecting them just as quickly.

Not long before midnight, Nick returned. He'd gone through another change—a haircut, a close shave, and a casual jacket with a clean blue shirt and trousers.

"What's the occasion?" Bennet asked.

"Better to look respectable if we're heading into Iran." He gave us an appraising glance. "Both of you will need to dress conservatively. No bare legs, no jeans, no miniskirts."

He beckoned for us to follow him across the hall. As we sat down in his room he pulled some documents out of his satchel and dropped them on the bed. "Your visas."

I whistled. "That was damn fast."

He grinned. "It helps to know a talented printer in Turkey."

"You must have great contacts," Bennet observed dryly.

"Contacts are nice, money is more persuasive."

He glanced at me. "Can you turn your rental in—here in Bergama?"

"Probably. Let me see." I scrolled through the rental car website and found an office in the city. "Looks good."

"Okay. We'll drive in my car to Izmir and get a flight out to Van the next day. That'll take us pretty close to where we want to be in Iran. You're going in under your own names, legitimately. We'll be joining a custom tour. It'll leave from Van in Turkey, cross over to Iran, and stop at Tabriz, Esfahan, and Shiraz."

I frowned. Esfahan and Shiraz would take us pretty far from our real destination. Nick knew what I was thinking. "In Tabriz," he continued, "one of you will fall ill from food poisoning, forcing us to drop out of the tour. When you've recovered, we'll substitute a sightseeing trip to Kandovan."

"Won't the authorities be alerted if we leave the tour?" Bennet asked.

"The tour leader has been in business for over twenty years. He runs contraband into Iran. He knows how to finesse these things. And of course he'll be well paid."

"Of course," I said.

March 5, 2005
Van, Turkey

As the landing gear clunked down, I looked out the window to see Lake Van sparkling blue in the winter sun. Nestled against a backdrop of high, snow-dusted mountain peaks was Van itself, a modern city with ancient roots. I knew it to be an ethnic melting pot—Kurdish territory that also belonged to Armenians, Yarsan, and Assyrians.

At the Royal Berk Hotel we met our tour leader, Helim Rosan, a genial guy with a round stomach and the kind of drooping black mustache favored by Turkish men. He wore three gold rings, one bearing a flashy diamond: a sure sign the contraband business was flourishing. I'd smiled to myself when Nick told me how much Rosan wanted for his discretion. We might well have paid for that diamond ring. But what did I care? Before we left Bergama I'd texted Strauss to tell him I'd been able to hire security and could therefore go to Iran. He refilled the coffers without protest.

Rosan introduced us to the other tour members—a young German couple who spoke very little English and an Italian history teacher. "You are lucky to choose this tour," Rosan proclaimed. "The United Kingdom is advising no one cross the Iranian border for any reason except in this northwest section. Yes. Very lucky." He looked each of us in the eye. "You are about to enter a fascinating country but one with very strict rules—never stray from our group."

He told Bennet and the German woman they had to wear head scarves, long sleeves, and long pants or skirts. Both rolled their eyes. Rosan noticed. "It is for your protection. Ladies of such loveliness will be noticed by many men. And it is not bikini weather anyway." His attempt to make light of things fell as flat as a burlesque joke at a church supper. Undaunted, Rosan added that since Bennet and I were sharing a room, we should make it look as if we were married.

"But we have different names on our passports," Bennet said.

Rosan waved his hand airily. "Iranian women may keep their own birth names. It will seem normal. Just pretend—not for real. Like a game. It is better for you in Iran if you are married."

We set out the next morning in a fifteen-passenger van driven by Rosan's young cousin. Nick had bought a fake gold ring somewhere and Bennet now wore it on her left hand. It was supposed to be a six-hour drive, but with the border crossing and tough road conditions, Rosan said we wouldn't reach Tabriz, the first stop on the tour, until dinnertime. As we drove he'd periodically light up a cigarette of sun-cured Turkish tobacco, roll down his window, and between drags hold it out in a vain attempt to avoid filling the van with smoke. Naturally, the breeze from the open window blew the smoke right into the back seats. We suffered in silence until Bennet asked him to butt out for the rest of the drive. Rosan apologized, but perhaps in keeping with his natural high spirits, he kept right on smoking.

In mid-afternoon we reached the border: a naked patch of land, just bare earth and low-lying scrub. On either side of a chain-link fence stood a long building like a trailer park home, one with a Turkish flag and the other an Iranian. Military men guarded both. Given the years of paranoia since Iran's revolution, not to mention two ongoing wars on its western and northern flanks, I'd expected an elaborate fortress.

We got through Turkish customs quickly and came to a grinding halt on the other side. A man in his thirties stepped out of the trailer with a scowl. Then, noticing whose vehicle it was, he put on a welcoming smile. Nick leaned closer to murmur to me. "Money always changes hands somehow."

Rohan hit the button to roll down his passenger window. The official leaned one elbow in and spoke in rapid Farsi. Rosan turned to us. "Hand over your passports, please."

The official took some time perusing the documents. He handed five of them back to Rosan and addressed him again. Rosan cranked his thick neck around to face us. "You Americans, they want you inside."

Rosan's cousin got out and opened the side door for us. *Here goes nothing,* I thought. *We'll be kicked out of the country before we even make it in.*

We filed into the trailer. Two armed military men flanked a desk where a third man sat, gray haired and dressed in civilian clothes. The soldiers' eyes followed Bennet, taking in her curves and the way her slacks clung to her bottom. She pulled her scarf, patterned with red roses, tighter around her neck as the two of us headed for a row of plastic chairs against one wall.

Nick approached the man at the desk and began speaking to him in fluent Farsi. The official's eyes lit up with a spark of surprise, quickly extinguished behind his poker face, the universal expression of border officers. He and Nick talked on, the man lobbing questions. Nick maintained a genial expression throughout. I mentally crossed my fingers. Bennet sat stock still, her eyes downcast, her hands in her lap, nervously twisting the gold wedding band. Just as I began to suspect we'd be marched into some windowless room in handcuffs, their conversation ended. The official laughed. All was well. He stamped our passports and said in English, "Please enjoy our beautiful Iran."

Thirty-Two

March 6, 2005
Tabriz, Iran

The drive to Tabriz through the Zagros mountain range was both stunningly scenic and damn hard on the ass. The van's shocks left something to be desired, particularly when the highway did a bump and grind along rough asphalt surfaces. We stopped at Khoy for refreshments and a bathroom break, drove south to Salmas, then turned east along Highway 14 to skirt the top of Lake Urmia. "There is a bridge across," Rohan remarked. "Never finished it. So now—a very long pier." He shook with laughter.

Just before Sharafkhaneh our route dropped closer to the lake, and Rohan's cousin made a little detour so we could see it. Like the Dead Sea, Urmia was a salt lake. The water, a deep blue green, glittered like liquid crystal. Sheets of salt turned its shores white; fabulous salt formations shaped like giant brain corals clustered on the beaches. A pillar of limestone sprouted like a mushroom from the water, its narrow base etched by the waves.

"Hey, look." Bennet pointed with excitement to a rosy cloud rising from the lake's surface. A flock of pink bodies and flapping pink wings. Flamingos, swarming the sky in such numbers they seemed an organic whole.

At one point we spotted what looked like an ancient ruin, until I realized that the row of columns were posts for a dock whose platform had long ago disintegrated. Beside it, the hulk of an old ship tilted on its keel—a fishing boat perhaps, with a long chain still fastened to its anchor, and so corroded its original color could only be guessed at.

I'd heard it was easy to drown in salt lakes, something Rosan confirmed when he spoke next. "Drinking too much of that water can poison—so salty. If too much is ingested it fails the organs." He held his hands up wide and then moved them closer together. "Urmia, once a vast lake, now shrinking, shrinking. Getting even more salty. Too dry and hot everywhere. But not in winter so much."

This corner of Iran was such a beautiful, alien land. I wondered what mysteries it held for us.

Less than an hour later we reached Tabriz, a sprawling industrial city, once a key location on the Silk Road. As Rosan promised, we arrived in time for dinner. Together at the hotel's restaurant we ordered a hearty dish of *koresht beh*—lamb cooked with quince and split peas, accompanied by Persian white rice and stone-baked naan. After the plates had been cleared, Rosan held up his index finger. "Tomorrow we will see the bazaar, famous even in the Middle Age, then the Blue Mosque. Also a factory where they make legendary Tabriz rugs. If you wish to buy items, we make all arrangements to send over to your homes."

Bennet had been careful to order last, choosing a chicken dish instead of the lamb the rest of us had. When we'd drawn lots to see who'd come down with acute food poisoning, the short straw fell to her. Now, as we sipped our tea, right on cue she got up and pressed her hand to her stomach. "Please excuse me," she said. "I may have eaten too much. I don't feel well."

The Italian murmured sympathetically. I noticed he'd taken quite a shine to her. "Rest, dear," Rosan said, scraping his chair back and rising politely. "You will feel much better in the morning."

I followed her out of the restaurant, explaining that I wanted to make sure she was okay. Nick stayed behind to talk. As he'd once told me, "You learn far more by socializing than at the point of a gun."

The next morning I told the group that Bennet still couldn't keep anything down, adding that the hotel had summoned a doctor. Rosan put on a good show of worry. When the group returned in the afternoon, I reported she was in no shape to travel.

"We are spending several days in Esfahan," Rosan said. "You may take a bus to join us after the lady has rested and can travel." I nodded solemnly and Nick said he'd stay with us.

In a strange case of life mimicking lies, Bennet really did come down with some kind of bug; she got into bed early that evening and stayed there. While Nick ventured out to rent a vehicle and collect some provisions, I arranged to meet Rosan in his hotel room.

He winked when I handed him a healthy wad of cash. "Discretion is the better velour," he said, getting the expression wrong but somehow retaining its meaning. "I have contacted the Kandovan hotel. They have a place for you."

"Thank you—you've been great."

He took a drag off his cigarette and waved away the compliment. "May you have a safe journey."

That night Rosan's words kept returning to me. The time spent in his company had been a pleasant interlude; the journey ahead, a troubling prospect. I thought about turning back but knew I wouldn't. The mystery surrounding Helmstetter had me in its grip.

❈

While Bennet slept, I sat in our room's most comfortable chair reading the photocopied paper by Reginald Arthur Walker, the man whose name my brother had noted in the margins of his journal. Walker's startling theory about the Garden of Eden's location made a lot of sense.

According to the Bible, the Garden of Eden could be found at the heads of four rivers. The Tigris and Euphrates were known, of course; their headwaters lay in the region encompassing Lake Van and Lake Urmia. But what about the Gihon and Pison? Those names didn't resemble any known watercourses today. Walker thought the former was the Araxes—which flowed southeast from the same region down to the Persian Gulf—because in the eighth century, large portions of the Araxes were called the "Gaihun." As for the Pison, Walker noted that in the Hebrew of the early Genesis text, a *P* had migrated to a *U*. The name of the fourth river, then, should be Uizhon, not Pison. The Uizhon had its source in the same area, flowing east to the Caspian Sea. It was an amazing feat of investigation. And it placed Eden firmly in the territory near Lake Urmia, centered around Tabriz: the same land my brother thought might be the earliest home of the Sumerians.

I'd brought David Rohl's book with me and consulted it now, running my finger down a passage I'd noted before.

> Genesis 2:13 describes the River Gihon as winding "all through the land of Cush." Are there any classical or modern topographical clues in the general vicinity of the River Aras (formerly Gaihun) which suggest that this region may once have been called the land of Cush?

... to the north of the modern city of Tabriz there is a high mountain pass through which the modern road winds its way up to the towns of Ahar and Meshginshahr. Several of the Aras tributaries have their headwaters near these Azeri towns. The modern Iranian name of Ahar is Kusheh Dagh—the Mountain of Kush.

Mesopotamian histories called the region Aratta, or Edin. That territory held abundant stores of gold and precious stones similar to the biblical description of "the land of Havilah." And Abraham was identified as having come from Ur, a Mesopotamian city. So the picture of Eden drawn by the authors of the Bible described what they believed to be the land of their ancestors. The ancient Persian word for enclosed garden was *pairi daza*—the stem word for paradise. Lush, walled gardens were a prominent feature of the Persian landscape even today.

And right at the heart of that Mesopotamian Eden lay Kandovan.

Part Three

THE SECRET GARDEN

Food of death they will set before thee,
Eat not. Water of death they will set before thee,
Drink not ... The counsel that I have given thee, forget not.
The words which I have spoken, hold fast.

— FROM THE MESOPOTAMIAN MYTH *ADAPA AND THE SOUTH
WIND*, PRECURSOR TO THE TEMPTATION IN GENESIS

Thirty-Three

March 8, 2005
Kandovan, Iran

The next morning, after eluding our tour group, we drove south out of Tabriz through a smoggy industrial corridor in the Chai River valley. Nick was at the wheel; he'd rented an older model Jeep Cherokee for the trip.

As we neared Kandovan, the towering silhouette of the long-extinct volcano Mount Sahand reared up in the distance. The cave city itself was a cluster of what resembled pink stone beehives, just like the photo I'd found in Evelyn's apartment. In the oldest part of the village the conical homes had been hollowed out from soft volcanic stone and fitted artfully with windows and wooden doors. High, wooden-slatted bridges connected walkways; in some houses, balconies jutted out from windows. Stone steps, cut in the center to provide rain sluices, rose steeply between dwellings. Power lines stretched between homes. Even Bennet, still feeling under the weather, brightened at the prospect of actually staying in one of these fairy-tale structures.

After leaving the Jeep in the lower town we made our way up to the stone hotel—and entered a surprisingly comfortable, even luxurious, interior. Whitewashed stucco walls and ceilings, mortared stone floors, beautiful wooden furniture with Persian motifs, and red-patterned carpets gave the place a rich, sensuous feel. Brass and copper wall sconces, along with the sunlight filtering in from the deep-welled windows, cast a gentle light.

When we reached our room, Bennet and I were greeted by more rich colors and Persian-inflected designs, including a desk and a banquette inlaid with delicate enamel tiles. The bed looked plump and inviting. Bennet flopped down on it. "This is heaven. There's even a Jacuzzi in the bathroom. I thought we'd be roughing it—nothing like this. Guess you could consider it our honeymoon suite." She laughed.

"Well, in that case, Mrs. Madison, don't you think we should follow tradition?" I pressed her down playfully on the bed and gave her a long kiss and one thing led to another.

Lazing in bed together afterward, I proposed that the three of us go on a recon mission. If there were any traces of Helmstetter left in this fantastical place, I was determined to find them. Nearer to the present, there was Yersan: he came from here; surely there was information to be gleaned. Most important to me, I wanted to waste no time in finding Evelyn's family. I had only one real lead—Nemat, Evelyn's family name. Rosan had told me of someone who might be able to help trace her relatives.

The weather was still temperate, apparently unusual at this elevation in March. We got away with our windbreakers instead of the heavier coats we'd bought in Tabriz. As we strode down the narrow laneways people would look at us with friendly interest; since the advent of the tourist trade, though, the novelty of Western visitors had faded.

A helpful shopkeeper directed us to where Rosan's contact lived. A grizzled fellow with brown, wind-roughened skin and a thick mustache greeted us. Nick spoke to him in Farsi and introduced us; the man grinned when he mentioned Rosan. After a bit more friendly-sounding talk, Nick turned to us to explain that the man ran mule rides for sightseeing excursions. Six mules munched hay in a large stall behind the man. They were quartered on the first floor of his house; the family lived upstairs. The reek of old hay and manure permeated the room.

Nick turned back to the man and began his questions. I tried to make out what he was asking. A few sentences on, I distinctly heard Nick say "George Helmstetter," and later, "Yersan." After more talk, Nick gestured toward me as he pronounced the name "Nemat."

At this, the donkey man, as I'd begun to think of him, spoke rapidly, gesturing with his hands. Finally, it seemed, we'd scored. Nick chatted with him a little longer and then bade the man goodbye. I smiled my thanks.

"He said the Nemats still live here," Nick told us once we'd gone a little way down the street.

"That's fantastic." Elated, my mind started spinning—I might learn something of Evelyn's mysterious past after all.

"Never heard of Helmstetter," Nick continued in a rush. "So he claims."

"Do you have any reason to doubt him?" Bennet asked.

"He hesitated before he told me that. Maybe it was just my imagination, but I sensed he was hiding something."

"And you asked about Yersan?" she prompted.

Nick turned to me. "I told him you were an antiquities dealer and that you'd done some business with him."

"That's one way of putting it."

"Apparently he's considered quite a success. Not many people venture far from the village, let alone immigrate to America and become rich enough to send money home. The guy was reluctant to say anything more, which suggests Yersan's still pretty influential around here."

Following the donkey man's directions to the Nemat home resulted in nearly an hour of wrong turns, with Nick continually checking in with locals and then redirecting our steps. Finally we found ourselves in front of one of the last conical cave houses to the east. We climbed yet another set of steeply angled stone stairs—a few more days here and I'd be in top physical form. I knocked on the stout, weathered wooden door. It opened a crack right away, as if someone had been waiting for us. Had the donkey man sent word? Through the open gap came a male voice. "Yes?"

I was surprised to hear him speak English. "My name's John Madison," I began. "I've traveled here to see Mr. Nemat about a relative of his who lives in America. May we come in? Do you know who Yeva Nemat is?"

At this the door swung open. A well-groomed man in a white shirt and dark trousers stood before me. I guessed him to be in his late forties. "Please come in," he said and stood aside. As we were about to enter, he glanced at Bennet and then at our feet. Nick tapped me on the arm and removed his shoes. Bennet and I followed suit.

Two other people looked up when we entered a hot, stuffy front room smelling of wood smoke. An elderly man with a snow-white beard and a white turban, his face a mass of wrinkles, had a blanket thrown around his shoulders. He sat on floor pillows next to an

iron stove. A woman sat beside him. Her age was hard to guess—
only her face, neck, and hands were visible—but she was perhaps in
her early fifties. She wore a scarf around her head patterned in
bright greens and pale yellow. Scars disfigured one side of her face.

An old wooden cabinet, a small green-tiled table with low legs,
more floor cushions, and two large Persian rugs were the only other
furnishings. Oil lamps had been placed in wall niches in addition
to an electric light overhead.

The man who'd opened the door spoke first. "I'm Alaz Nemat."
He tipped his hand toward the old man. "My father, Mernoush
Nemat. Please take a seat." He didn't introduce the woman.

"This is Margaux Bennet and Nick Voss," I said. Nick dipped
his head, first toward the old man and then toward Alaz, before the
three of us sat on floor cushions. Alaz walked over and stood next
to his father.

"May we offer you tea?"

"Thank you—no," Nick said quickly. "It's not necessary."

"But I insist. Have you just arrived in Kandovan?" He turned
to the woman and muttered a few words. She scurried through a
curtained doorway.

We told him this was our first day visiting the village and
chatted about our trip from Van. I complimented his English.

"I live in Tabriz," he said. "I own a tourist shop there. My father
is not well, so I visit often."

We exchanged more pleasantries. The woman bustled back in
carrying a tray with five red and gold glasses of steaming mint tea
and a bowl heaped with sugar cubes. She served them, we thanked
her, and she resumed her seat. Her silent gaze kept flitting to me.
She was evidently following our conversation with intense interest.

I introduced the reason for our visit, pulling the copy of
Evelyn's birth certificate out of my inner jacket pocket and

handing it to Alaz. "I'm wondering if you might know this woman—Yeva Nemat?"

He took one look at the birth certificate and his face went white. He raised his eyes to mine. The look was not friendly. "Where did you get this?"

I decided not to reveal too much. "It belongs to an acquaintance of mine in New York. Do you know her?"

The old man had so far said nothing. Now he spat out some words. Nick gave a very slight shake of his head as if to caution me not to speak. Alaz crouched down and showed the birth certificate to his father, who took it with a gnarled, trembling hand. The paper shook as he read it. The woman glanced over the old man's shoulder, peered at the paper, and let out a cry, covering her mouth with her hands. The old man's eyes were bleary and reddened but there was no mistaking the alarm in them. He blurted out more words.

Alaz gave the paper back to me. "I'm afraid I must ask you to leave. My father is upset, as you can see. He does not wish to speak of this person."

"But we've come all this way to talk to you," Bennet protested.

Nick darted a warning glance toward her and then addressed Alaz. "It's okay. We'll go now. Please accept our apologies. It wasn't our intention to upset anyone."

We took our leave quickly. I couldn't conceal my deep regret that this first meeting with the Nemats had turned sour so fast.

"Clearly they knew Evelyn," I said as we walked away, "and pretty well, too. What the hell do we do now?"

"We'll have to try to talk to Alaz another time," Nick said. "Maybe find a way to see him on his own. If I can learn where his shop is in Tabriz, we might have more luck when he's not on home ground with his father listening to every word he says."

Bennet pursed her lips. "He'll probably just clam up again."

"That remains to be seen," Nick said.

The sun was waning now and we hurried back along darkening pathways. With the cold night air and strange shadows cast by the conical structures, the village no longer felt quaint, but sinister. Nick stayed close and kept alert. This was Yersan's hometown. Another threat seemed almost inevitable. And it did come. Just not the way I expected.

Thirty-Four

The bright lights of our hotel were a welcome sight, and as we entered the lobby I began to relax. Then I stopped in my tracks. Yersan, slouched on a divan, stood up. He walked toward us, halted a few feet away, looked Nick and Bennet up and down. Finally he trained his gaze on me, the hatred in his small, intense eyes unmistakable. "What are you doing here? In my town? If you want artifacts to buy, you'll find it barren ground."

He'd just handed me an excuse for being in Iran. "Why? Because you've siphoned off anything worth having? I've already sourced some very nice pieces in Tabriz."

Yersan moved closer. Nick stepped in and blocked his way. Out of the corner of my eye I could see the hotel attendant throw a worried glance at us. Nick put his hand out, stopping just short of touching Yersan. "Give us some space," he said with quiet menace.

Yersan stepped back but his voice grew harsher. "You are after more of the treasures stolen from my family. There are none left."

He pulled his trench coat closer around him. "I will go now." He shot a pointed look at Nick. "I tell you politely to leave Kandovan. Or you will never leave at all."

"I'll go when my business here is finished," I said. "And be assured: I'll pay you back for Tricia Ross."

He seemed about to respond, thought better of it, swept past us like a malicious whirlwind and blew out the door.

Bennet folded her arms around her as if to ward off a chill. "He's afraid of you, Nick. That was plain."

"He must have heard about what happened in Pergamon," I said.

"Doubtless he did." Nick looked thoughtful. "But you need to wrap up here as soon as you can. Waging a battle on someone else's home turf is rarely a winning proposition—unless you have a load of firepower. And we don't."

We had the dining room practically to ourselves. Bennet was famished, having eaten little for the past twenty-four hours. We ordered a meal of local cuisine and wolfed it down; Nick, of Persian extraction, ate with particular relish. As we finished our tea the waiter came over, spoke a few words in Farsi to Nick, then silently retreated.

Nick patted his mouth with a napkin and smiled. "Well. Looks like you're a regular social butterfly here, Madison. Alaz Nemat's just arrived. Wants to talk with you outside."

I shot out of my seat, hurried through the lobby, and swung open the hotel door. Nick and Bennet rushed to catch up. In the dark I could just make out Nemat's form at the bottom of the stone stair. He peered anxiously up at me.

"I'm glad to see you again," I said, extending my hand as I walked down toward him. Alaz gave me a tentative smile and grasped my hand in return. "If you don't mind," he said, glancing at Bennet and Nick, "I'd prefer to speak in private."

I nodded to the other two. Nick sauntered across the pathway and leaned against a stone wall, out of earshot yet still within a safe distance. Bennet reluctantly joined him.

"I wish to apologize for this afternoon," Alaz began. "My father is quite ill and I didn't want to disturb him any further."

He gave me a searching look before he went on. "The birth certificate—it put us all in shock. We have not known anything of Yeva for decades. We thought she was long dead. My younger sister whom you met today is full of joy to hear of her but greatly aggrieved—Yeva never told us she went to America. My sister implored me to ask how we can get in touch with her."

"And who is Yeva to you?"

"My oldest sister," he said flatly. "Has she ... passed away? Is that why you've come?"

"She's fine. Living in New York. She goes by the name of Evelyn now, was our housekeeper for many years. I'll have to talk to her first before I can put you in contact. You can appreciate that she's kept herself hidden from you all this time. And she's in fragile health."

Alaz nodded solemnly. "We would be greatly indebted to you."

His expression grew more serious. "And what of the boy? What became of him?"

What of the boy. The words rang in my ears. I put my hand out to steady myself.

For the past year I'd been moving the jigsaw pieces around and ignoring the whole pattern, clinging to the story I'd been given of my birth until the holes became too obvious to ignore. Now everything fell into place.

I was Evelyn's son. That meant the man standing before me was my uncle; Mernoush Nemat, my grandfather. I looked Alaz in the face again. He had wide, soft brown eyes and a mouth I imagined laughed often in happy times. He was almost exactly my size and build. I resisted the temptation to throw my arms around him. I'd keep my thoughts to myself for now.

"I'm not sure about the boy," I said in a neutral-sounding way. "That's something I'll have to ask Evelyn about. Why do you think she didn't get in touch with you over all these years?"

He grimaced. "It's not like America over here. A woman with no husband …"

Alaz let the rest of his sentence drop, but the implication was plain. Yeva, the woman I knew as Evelyn, had given birth out of wedlock—likely considered a greater iniquity than killing someone. And it explained why she was so reluctant to tell me the truth: she was ashamed.

I swallowed hard. "Did you know the boy's father?"

Alaz gave me a long hard look as if he were trying to unravel my innermost thoughts. "Why do you ask that?"

"Evelyn may have mentioned his name."

"You must understand it's not something we like to speak of in our family. The father came from Tabriz. He was not of our people and my father denied them the right to marry. He won't speak of him to this day."

Alaz's lips tightened and he refused to say more. I did understand: it was a matter of family honor.

Nick cleared his throat in the shadows, recalling me to the other reason I'd traveled halfway around the world. "A man named George Helmstetter visited Kandovan thirty-five years ago. Is there any chance you'd remember him?"

He cast a quick, nervous look over his shoulder. "Yes."

"You knew him?"

"I was only fourteen. In those days tourists were not as common here. He had money—a lot. Even without that, no one could forget him." Alaz spoke quickly now, the words tumbling out. "The village people called him a magi—an enchanter. He could make you believe in what was not real. One evening, he asked people to gather around him in a square off one of the pathways. A very cold night; it was snowing. We had only kerosene lamps to see by. He wore a thick black cloak; the white flakes of snow dotted it like confetti. He murmured some words in a language we didn't understand—not English. He called them angel words. He bent low and swirled the cloak around his body, fast and then faster still. The cloak fell in a heap on the ground. He'd vanished beneath it. The next day he reappeared as if nothing had happened. From that time on, people regarded him with an equal measure of fear and awe. No one dared to cross him."

An hour ago, I couldn't have imagined I'd make this much progress. "Do you have any idea what became of him?"

Alaz glanced fearfully down the pathway again as if expecting an enemy. He kept his voice low. "No one knows for sure."

I pressed on. "He brought a rare book with him, very old and very valuable. Did you ever see it?"

"Why do you ask about that?"

"Because Helmstetter stole it from the rightful owner."

"That book was evil."

"Do you have any idea what happened to it?"

"My father burned it."

I tried one more question.

"Helmstetter sent three ancient artifacts back to his wife in North America: two stone seals and a little statue of a man with a long head. Do you know where he got them?"

Alaz gave me a long, appraising look and then seemed to make up his mind to trust me. "I was there when he found them."

Thirty-Five

For a second I was speechless. Alaz saw my surprise and hesitated, seeming to measure his words. "I said some people stood in awe of him. That included me. You can imagine the innocence of a fourteen-year-old boy, one who never ventured outside his village except to pasture his sheep. If lightning struck me, I could not have been more amazed than when I witnessed Helmstetter's magic. From then on, I followed him everywhere. He found me useful—to run errands, explain who the influential men in the village were, tell him about the natural features of the landscape. He paid me well. We were poor; my father welcomed the money. The old book you mentioned? Helmstetter carried it with him everywhere. Said it gave the names of many ranks of angels and showed how you could talk with them."

"Did he ever explain why he wanted to come here?"

"Some call our territory—the land surrounding Lake Urmia and Mount Sahand—sacred. Our people lived here long before men even knew of writing. We believe in reincarnation, that the divine being manifests himself in human form seven times. The first of those manifestations took the form of an angel.

"Helmstetter wanted to find the path to immortality. What he didn't understand until he came here was that reincarnation is a form of immortality. Of anywhere in the world, this was the most logical place for him to find it."

My mind traveled back to Strauss's strange séance and the message he'd delivered from Gina's dead husband: *"When the unclean spirit has gone out of a person, it passes through waterless places seeking rest, and finding none it says, 'I will return to the house from which I came.'"*

I shook myself mentally. "And how did he find the treasures?"

"He'd heard about a cave system not far from here and wanted to see it. I showed him through it and we reached a cliff, a very steep drop. He scaled down it. I was too afraid to follow. I waited for more than a day—it was my duty not to abandon him although I feared he might be dead. When he did finally return, I was overjoyed. He had the treasures in his pack—all he could carry. He said he'd found many more."

So much for Yersan's claim to family ownership. "Could you take us there?"

He hesitated. "It's dangerous terrain. I cannot promise you'll ever find anything."

"I'd be willing to pay you well for your time."

Alaz shrugged. "Then yes—why not? It's in the salt caves. An isolated area. Except for some scientific expeditions, no one ever goes there. I have to return to Tabriz soon. If you want me to show you, it will have to be tomorrow."

He told me we'd need climbing gear and threw another glance over his shoulder, anxious to be off.

"One more question. Do you know a man named Yersan? A local antiquities dealer?"

"Everyone does. Why do you ask?"

"He just threatened me."

"Don't cross him. You'll be the loser. He's a powerful man."

Back at our room, I filled Nick and Bennet in, omitting the part about Evelyn and the boy, still feeling too overwhelmed by what I'd learned.

"Incredible," Bennet burst out after I'd finished. "So now you have the information you wanted—far more than Strauss has any right to expect. Helmstetter's long gone. So is the book. Meanwhile we're supposed to be rejoining Rosan's tour, and every day we spend in Kandovan we risk the Iranian authorities finding out. I vote for leaving."

"People here have no love for the government," Nick put in. "There's been a long history of persecution. I don't think you need fear anyone going to the police."

Nick was right. But so was Bennet. My task here was finished. I could go home, tell Strauss the book had been destroyed, offer up Alaz to verify the story. Plus, I'd heard enough for a very direct talk with Evelyn. She'd have to tell me the truth now.

And yet as a child I'd always imagined being at my brother Samuel's side, like the explorers of old, making fabulous finds. In time, of course, I'd learned that most archaeological work was anything but romantic—an exacting science that proceeded at a snail's pace, the "finds" more likely to be pottery shards than golden jewels. Still, an opportunity to unearth objects from the beginning of civilization had just dropped in my lap.

"You've been quiet, John," Bennet said. "What do you want to do?"

"We have a one in a million chance to find some remarkable antiquities. I'd like to take Alaz up on his offer."

"He's been awfully accommodating," Nick said. "I wonder about that."

"I said I'd pay him something to guide us. I imagine that influenced him. He could probably use the money."

Nick was rarely temperamental, but this time his irritation showed. "I'm taking a risk to spend time with you here. I'd gone to ground in Turkey and that was working out well. You've got me for a couple more days—that's all."

"Understood. Alaz wants to go to the salt caves tomorrow—we can get supplies in the morning before we head out. So just one more day and then we're out of here."

Nick got up to go back to his room. "I'll hold you to that."

The next morning we drove into Tabriz to get the climbing gear. I took the wheel, relishing the chance to drive. It was almost noon by the time we piled into Alaz's car to set out for the caves.

Thirty-Six

March 9, 2005
Salt Caves, Lake Urmia Region

The highway west from Kandovan ran through mostly barren terrain—beautiful in its way, with the early spring light enhancing the ground's coppery hues. Red earth: the soil from which Adam sprang and the meaning of his name. At one point we passed a semicircular mound rising about forty feet off the plain. At its top sat a little square brick building with a domed roof and arches cut into its sides. Gas flames shot up from chimneys placed at the four corners of the roof; another flame burned inside the building itself.

"A fire altar," Alaz said. "A place of worship for us." He indicated a round building set between two tall rectangular pillars some distance away. "Those are *dakhmas*, towers of silence where the dead are taken."

We turned north just before Saray Deh. A village stood at the foot of farmers' fields, a V-shaped cleft of green amid the dusty scrub and red rocks.

Alaz kept his eye peeled for the road he wanted to take. "There," he said, gesturing to his left. "Road" was an exaggeration. A rough, furrowed track extended upward, climbing the low mountain that rose out of the plain.

We bounced and jostled over the bumpy surface, the Jeep's poor suspension making my teeth chatter. It required Alaz's full concentration just to stay on course. Before long the track ended and he pulled over to a lee under a rocky outcrop to park his car. The sun disappeared behind gathering clouds and the air grew chilly.

"It's going to be a long hike." Alaz pointed upward as we dug into the trunk for our climbing packs.

The track reappeared, this time as a footpath dipping and twisting among high limestone outcrops and gigantic boulders. For almost two hours we steadily ascended until we entered a narrow canyon. Cliffs shot up on either side of us. The rocks here took on fascinating shapes. Full of pits and spherical hollows, they looked like huge upright sea sponges.

"Almost there." Alaz motioned for us to hurry. "It's ahead."

We rounded a bend. Far below was a small valley, its flat rocky floor bisected by a curving river of white crystals. The ghost of a river: the water had evaporated, leaving only a trail of salt. Alaz stopped at a yawning, ellipsis-shaped hole to his right, about the width of a soccer pitch. He tilted his head, looking up at the somber blanket of clouds. "We've got to do this as fast as possible," he said. "The way ahead is not so hard at first."

He told us to leave our shoes behind a rock and put on our rubber boots. Before long, the entrance widened into a space the size of a ballroom. Bennet let out a gasp of surprise. The low-hanging rock roof amounted to a giant natural arch, striated with ribbons of gorgeous grays and reds, washed smooth by some long-lost underground river. Little white cones stood up from the floor like miniature stalagmites. Thick wedges of white salt coated the base of the rock walls. I bent down and picked up one of the thousands of small pebbles that covered the cave floor, polished by an ancient water flow.

"Amazing," Bennet breathed. We'd all fallen silent at the splendor of the place.

Alaz smiled. "Much more to behold ahead. This was once thought to be an old salt mine. That proved false—far easier for people to gather all the salt they wanted on the lakeshore." We switched on our headlamps and paced along a funnel-shaped corridor that tightened until it wasn't much more than five feet wide. Twenty minutes later we stepped into what looked like an underwater paradise. Salt encrusted the cave's entire ceiling in a multitude of forms: twisting crystalline pillars, frozen lace, cornices of dripping icing, branches of white coral—a fantasy of glittering, upside-down sculptures.

Bennet furiously snapped photos. Even Nick stretched his neck to gape. A shallow greenish pond extended over most of the cave floor. Bennet dipped her finger in. "Yech. Really salty."

"Never drink that," Nick cautioned. "Get enough salt in your system and it'll shut your kidneys down. Believe me, it doesn't take much." Rosan, I remembered, had said the same thing.

The pond turned out to be a stream that disappeared into a nearby cleft in the rock wall. Alaz motioned us forward. "We're taking the river route now," he said. "We have no other choice."

We waded slowly through the water, stepping carefully along the flat, slippery river bed. I began to feel claustrophobic. The place had a damp, ancient smell and you could hear the steady *plink, plink* of water without knowing where it came from. The farther we went, the more I could taste salt in the air. I was glad there were four of us with headlamps to banish the gloom.

The current flowed in our direction, making it easier to proceed. We now entered another wide underground space, our lights dancing off more magical shapes—icing sugar snowflakes, giant frosted icicles, salt heaped on rocky ledges like snowdrifts. Except for the dripping water, I hadn't realized how silent it was until a rush of sound came at us like the whoosh of wind. Above us bats swooped and spiraled in the air. Bennet laughed and took more pictures.

The current picked up and now a distant murmur reached our ears. The sound of rushing water.

Thirty-Seven

Frothy waves flushed up against the vertical wall on our right. On our left, the ground had widened to a ledge of pebble-strewn rock. Alaz scrambled onto it, lurched, and fell on his hands and knees. Then he stood, brushing off his pant legs as we clambered after him. "I'm sorry," he said. "It's been a long time since I was here. And this"—he waved his arm, seeming to take in the entire cave system—"is always shifting. In limestone caves, the stalagmites last thousands of years, perhaps grow larger—that's all. Here it is salt. In a few days the whole landscape can change if enough water goes through."

"What do you mean, 'if enough water goes through'?" Bennet sounded anxious.

"This area is arid. Dry most of the time, although occasionally it does rain. If so, the water finds its way through cracks and crevices. This stream can fill up, become a torrent."

"I didn't much like the look of the sky," Nick interjected. "Why didn't you tell us that earlier?"

Alaz shrugged. "You wanted to come here. It's probably better to go on. We've almost reached the cliff."

Another fifteen minutes and the ledge broadened to a wide platform that dropped off sharply in front of us. The salt formations were only thin white streaks now, like spittle on the rock. The stream, though, had become a little Niagara, plunging over the platform's lip. We looked down into a cavernous space. The water disappeared far below in a plume of white. I could make out nothing but blackness. "How far does it go, Alaz?"

"I don't know. I cannot remember what Helmstetter said. Maybe a couple of hundred feet."

We all had climbing experience. Nick was the most skilled but I wasn't far behind him; I'd climbed in the Catskills recently and in Iraq, crawled through underground passages dangerous enough to make your hair stand on end. Bennet had once done a story on free climbing in the Rockies and picked up the basics as a result. Despite our collective experience, I felt a jab of fear.

"Scared?" Bennet's eyes twinkled as she came up beside me. "I saw those guys in the Rockies scramble down something like that in twenty minutes—without ropes."

We decided to take a quick break. As we drank from our water bottles and chewed our energy bars, we began to work out how to negotiate the drop. Having been the one to persuade everyone to come here, I offered to go first. Alaz would follow—this at Nick's insistence; presumably he didn't trust a guy he barely knew with the anchors—and Bennet and Nick would bring up the tail. We slipped off our rubber boots and put on our climbing shoes.

The store in Tabriz sold 210-foot lengths of climbing rope—which meant a maximum 105 feet, since I'd have to double the rope and thread it through the anchor. I'd also have to hammer in new pitons every 100 feet. Descending would be a slow process.

With only one person at a time able to use the rope, the whole group would need to assemble at various points on the way down, after I banged in new pitons to begin the next leg.

Nick flaked out the rope, its tough nylon black-and-tan bands making it looked like snakeskin. We secured the webbing to a sturdy stump of rock shaped like one of the bollards you see on a wharf. For the second anchor, Alaz stuck a wedge into a narrow crevice. To be really bombproof we needed three anchors but there wasn't another decent crack in the rock for that. Once we'd fixed the rope, Alaz and I pulled hard on it to make sure the anchors held.

I got rigged up and ready to rappel. I threaded the rope into my belay device and clipped it with a locking carabiner onto the belay loop on my harness. Then I tied a prussic hitch around the rope as a safety and attached it to the harness strap around my leg. The hitch qualified as a precious piece of equipment: pretty much my only protection against a deadly fall.

It was time for me to launch. Heart pounding now, I stared down into the abyss. My headlamp illuminated the area immediately around me but little more. The rest was pitch black. I had no idea whether I'd encounter jutting shelves of rock or smooth sailing all the way.

I'd once seen that famous Colville painting of a dark horse galloping full tilt down railway tracks at night toward the single light of an oncoming train—as though the horse was unconscious of the threat and yet knowingly embraced it. I felt the same way now.

A wide, shallow crevice of bumpy rock that I thought might provide easier footholds lay close to the waterfall. I knotted both ends of the rope—fail-safes if my equipment cut out—and tossed them over the lip, hearing them slap the rock as they swiveled down. I turned around and half bent at the waist. The last thing I saw was Bennet's camera flash as I gingerly stepped over the edge.

The first section was bare limestone, pitched at a steep angle but offering enough purchase for an easy balance. No dramatic bungee-type jumps on this escapade—I'd be walking it down, and very slowly at that. Despite the spray, I didn't see any green algae or organic material on the rock, probably a result of the pervasive salt in the atmosphere. Just as I was getting into my stride, feeling that the rock and I were working together, it offered up another obstacle: about forty feet down, the crevice narrowed and then disappeared altogether. The spume now tumbled over straight vertical rock. Perhaps the limestone here was harder and less subject to erosion. I halted and repositioned myself.

I tried to keep my legs more or less perpendicular to the rock face. It was damn slippery; I cursed my decision to stay close to the waterfall and slipped repeatedly. At one point my legs windmilled. I began to think I'd have to slide rather than walk it down.

Shortly thereafter I hit the salt.

The cliff began to tip slightly outward—that must be why the salt remained on the surface. At first it was just a powdery overlay, no more than a light coating, like fresh snow when the temperature's very cold. I could easily sweep it away with my boot to expose the bare, thankfully drier rock underneath. I figured I'd made it close to seventy feet down, although in the darkness I couldn't see where the rope ended.

The salt grew denser, making it harder to uncover the under-lying rock. The crust was brittle, almost icy. I began to slip again. I tried using my boot to kick a toehold into it, thinking we should have worn crampons, but this had been the last thing I'd expected. I prayed it was just a dip in the rock face where salt had collected. But no. It seemed to stretch on. I looked below. For the short distance I could see, the cliff face was white. No sign of the bottom.

I continued to take it slowly—I had no idea how stable the salt crust was and didn't want to start a mini landslide. Moving at a snail's pace now, it took much longer to chip little footholds into the dense crust. The next time I slipped, I kicked out hard in frustration. The crust cracked and split. Beside me, a section the size of a small boulder calved like an ice floe and fell. Splinters of salt flew into my face. I took a worried look down. A long ledge was about ten feet below, not entirely horizontal but wide enough that the others could get a purchase on it when they rappeled down after me. Good thing, too: I could now see the rope ends lying in a coil there. Not much length left, but it was a perfect opportunity to bang in another piton for the next leg down. God only knew how far that was.

I reached the ledge and found I could stand on it easily. My heart was in my mouth. I didn't trust the salt; another break could happen anytime. No point in punching the piton into the crust; it would never hold. I had to find the rock surface that must surely lie beneath it. I braced myself and chipped away carefully. Then came a sound unlike anything I'd ever heard. As if the rock itself groaned. A fissure at the level of my chest split through the crust horizontally, widening fast. I grabbed the rope, dropped my pick, and summoned all my energy to haul myself over the spreading gap.

With a crack as hard as a rifle shot, salt crust the size of a small house broke off, sweeping me away. My knee hit something. Pain set it on fire. My eyes were blinded by salt spray. I breathed it in and choked. I was not aware of falling, of the time it took. Just naked terror as I dropped through a vast space.

My body slammed into something. The force punched all the breath out of me. I felt as if I'd been cut in half, my spine severed. Still in my harness, I dangled over a black void. I couldn't move my leg. It didn't matter—nothing was there to reach for. Pain eclipsed everything. I tried to suck in a breath but couldn't make my lungs work. The world turned gray.

Thirty-Eight

Nick would come. I was certain of it. He was invincible—all I had to do was wait. I tried to lift my head but felt too weak. I tasted a sour bitterness in my mouth mixed with the salt. I'd thrown up and couldn't remember doing it. How long had I been out? A band of pain sliced through my back. That was nothing compared to the agony of my leg. I tried to move it again and couldn't. I listened for the sounds of rescue—the scrape of boots digging into salt.

But the void was quiet except for the nearby rush of water. Had the salt shelf that split off been weakened by it? Water—now my enemy. How close was I to the bottom? Or had Alaz lied and there was nothing below me but a black hole stretching to the center of the earth? Had Alaz even *known* Helmstetter, or was that story of his going into the cave's depths thirty-five years ago a complete fabrication?

Had my real family tried to murder me?

I swung a little in the harness cradle, the light from my head-lamp bouncing off a rock wall. I brushed the salt from my eyes: the wall looked to be about ten feet away. Too far. Even the smallest movement ignited an incandescent pain.

And then I felt the slightest shift in the rope. A loosening. I dropped a few inches. It hurt badly when the harness jerked, eating the slack of the rope, but I didn't care. My heart soared. Nick *was* coming for me after all. Rescue was only minutes away. Someone above was deliberately adjusting my rope. They must be rappeling toward me. I raised both hands and waved them. Tried to yell but managed only a whisper. Nick would need to know I was still alive. I waited to feel his reassuring grasp.

Another jolt. Another blast of fire through my spine. This time the rope dropped almost a foot.

In the first instant, I couldn't understand why coils of rope fell on me. And then I ran out of time to think at all. I went into free fall. My body spiraled in the air. I braced for the end.

Thirty-Nine

The salt woke me. Mixed with my blood, it stung the torn flesh where my teeth had cut into the soft flesh of my mouth. I vomited again: this time a mercy; it cleared much of the salt from my throat. I was very dizzy. I tried once more to yell for Nick, managing a weak cry. It was pitch black wherever I'd landed. This second fall killed my light. I felt around on the ground—I seemed to be lying on a bed of hard, sharp chips, like a hill of broken glass. My hands were cut and they stung, too. My back and leg ached. At least I had sensation in my leg; it wasn't paralyzed. I managed to raise myself into a sitting position. I could be anywhere. Whatever lay beneath me might not hold and the slide and the fall could begin all over again.

I unclasped my pack, shrugged off a shoulder band, reached around, and pulled the zipper open. I groped inside and found the spare bulb. After feeling for the harness that attached the light to my helmet, I managed to unfasten it and bring the headgear close to my face. I unscrewed the cap, got the dead bulb out, and put in the new one, praying it would work. The beam shone out like a beacon, cutting through the night.

I'd come to rest on a hill of salt chards, the remains, perhaps, of the shelf that had broken off and taken me with it. I turned my head to swing the light around. I could just make out a protruding ledge of rock high above me: the salt crust that broke had probably formed over that ledge. Banging away at the crust had been enough to shear it off. Below the ledge the cliff sloped outward again—the chunk would have fallen briefly and then slid the rest of the way down rather than taking the entire drop vertically. Which explained why I was still alive. At least I was at the bottom with nowhere farther to fall.

My eyes watered constantly to rid themselves of the salt. Everything was blurry. I played the light around again, this time on the surrounding ground. And then I remembered the rope. It lay curled and twisted on the ground around me, its snakelike, black-banded coils stark against the white chips. I took a couple of deep breaths and drew it in hand over hand.

I could see the end of it slithering toward me as I pulled. When the last couple of feet came close I grabbed the end and held it up, brushing it with my fingers. Frayed. The pressure of the falling salt shelf had been so great as to weaken the rope enough that my weight finished the job, tearing it like a strand of thread.

Clearly an accident, then. Nothing like this could have been planned. But had Alaz known of the danger and not said anything, hoping for an accident to take our lives? After all, Kandovan was a small village. He probably knew Yersan well. Were they *working* together? Or was I just being paranoid?

I retrieved my phone from my inside jacket pocket and turned it on. Mercifully it hadn't broken in the fall. Close to midnight. I'd been unconscious for at least six hours. The battery was almost done. I shut it off quickly. If Nick was coming for me, he would have shown up long ago.

That last thought sucked dry whatever hope I had left. Fatigue overwhelmed me. Blood still leaked into my mouth; my leg and back hurt like hell. I fished in my pack again and found the bottom was soaked—the fall had crushed my extra water bottle. One left. I flipped off the top and took a long drink, nauseated by the coppery taste of my blood as it slipped down my throat. I pressed my hand along my leg to try to feel whether it had broken. When I reached my knee, a knob of bone seemed displaced. I got the knife out of a zippered pocket in the front of the pack, slit my pants along the seam, then bent my head to train the light on my knee. It was swollen to three times its size and hurt so much I could barely touch it. Dislocated or broken, I couldn't tell.

I unbuckled the harness to brace my knee and thigh. Then I wrapped the coils of rope around my shoulder and tried to get up. I fell three times; whenever I attempted to stand on my bad leg the pain made me almost faint.

If only I had something to use as a crutch. Then I thought of the aluminum frame on my pack. I pried the straps off it and managed to bend the metal bar almost straight. Now I was able to stand without toppling over. It felt like a miracle.

God knows where my pick had fallen. It was useless anyway. Even if I recovered it, climbing that treacherous cliff again with my damaged leg would be impossible. Harder than scaling Mount Everest.

I found that by balancing on the bar, taking a step with my good left leg and dragging my right, I could move. Every step was excruciating, made more so by the weight of my pack and the rope. Progress was agonizingly slow but eventually I reached the waterfall. The plume cascaded into a dark pool and ran off as the stream resumed its course. I thought of filling up my half-empty water bottle and then remembered Nick's warning about salty water. I positioned my head to shine the lamp on the stream. A wedge of bare rock ran beside it. I couldn't make out how far it extended but it seemed my only option.

This deep underground, I could expect to find no other entrance to the outside world. Still, the stream had to lead somewhere. I decided to follow it. It was either that or a slow death at the cliff base.

The cave roof grew lower and to follow the stream I had to stoop through a narrowing corridor. After a while the roof dropped to less than four feet. With my injured knee I needed to be upright to walk, so I had to get down on the rock floor and crawl along, using my left leg to propel myself. Soon I shifted the pack and the rope coils onto my chest and shunted along on my back—I couldn't stand the pain that flared up when I tried crawling frontward. Moving my body in this fashion took an age. I checked the time again. Over three hours had passed and I'd made little headway. I flipped back onto my chest. Ahead, my lamp revealed a fork in the tunnel. The stream continued to the left of the fork. The right branch of the tunnel opened up into a larger area with more salt formations.

I was bone tired, so exhausted I lacked the energy even to be afraid. I dragged my bad leg and could barely manage to move my good one. Shivering, I curled up with my back to the rock wall. The lamp battery would be good for six hours and I had only one more replacement. Without a light I'd be done for. I turned it off. An inky blackness swallowed me. As my thoughts began to drift, I wondered idly whether Helmstetter had taken this route. I'd never know.

I put my head down on my pack and sank into a dreamless sleep.

Forty

March 10, 2005

I awoke to a rushing sound coming from the tunnel I'd just traversed. I fumbled for the lamp and switched it on. A low, gray fog rolled toward me, pushing stream water ahead of it in small waves. In minutes I'd be engulfed. As it approached it started to sound like fine sand flowing through a sifter and carried with it a dank smell tinged with iodine. Alaz's words came back to me. *"In a few days the whole landscape can change if enough water goes through."* And Nick's nervousness about rain coming. Had there been a downpour above ground after all? Had water rushed into the cave system and absorbed tons of salt, turning the stream into a thick soup?

I shot up, ignoring how much I hurt, half dragging my pack and the rope toward the larger opening. My knee screamed in pain as I squeezed through the gap. I spotted a short rocky outcrop beneath some stalagmites, the only place that rose above the rock floor and offered any hope of safety. The mass of water swamped the fork in the tunnel. It had enough volume to flow into the larger area, slapping at my feet and lower legs. By craning my head I could see the main channel of the stream. The sluggish water now filled the tunnel. If I hadn't woken, I would have drowned. I kept my light on, not daring to remain in the dark.

I hugged the outcrop, expecting to be washed away any minute. Eventually the viscous water diminished. It must have been a flash flood, the kind that would sweep down desert arroyos and catch hikers off guard, submerging them in its wake.

My throat burned. I took another swig from my bottle. The water tasted as pure and sweet as a mountain spring.

Time for me to move. But where? Logic suggested venturing farther into the wide cavern where I could easily stand upright. And yet somehow my instincts pointed me toward the tunnel and the now quieter stream. I'd followed it before, believing it might lead to safety. There was no reason to change my mind now.

My light flickered. I replaced the battery and lay on my back again, put the pack and the ropes on my chest, and resumed my ungainly, ass-backward crawl along the thin ledge that served as a stream bank, slick with water from the flood. It was so slippery I nearly toppled into the stream.

Why not simply stop here? Accept the verdict fate had handed me. Just stop trying. Every cell in my body screamed for rest; continuing seemed utterly pointless. And yet I kept on. Like some warped perpetual-motion machine, it was as if my brain had shut down but my legs and arms still moved. As I crawled on, the stream level began to rise over the edges of the rock ledge. The ceiling lowered yet again to barely two feet high. I had to take the pack and rope off my stomach, push them ahead of me with my hands, then inch my body along behind them. Soon I was backing through a couple of inches of water. The salt in it stung my hands like crazy.

My hair, spine, rear, and hips were sopping wet. My skin burned but I felt chilled at the same time.

I was about to give up and return to the cavern when I became aware of an unearthly glow. A greenish light dancing across the rock over my head. I turned off the headlamp. The tunnel ceiling glimmered with phosphorescence.

Stretching my arms out, I gave the pack another push. My hands felt a vacuum. A crevice in the rock? It was a hole—I had no idea how deep. I turned my lamp on, bit my lip against the knee pain, and shifted onto my stomach. The cleft in the rock was about three feet wide. It bisected part of the tunnel floor and wall on my right side. When my light shone through the cleft, it revealed another enormous cavern. Water filled the cleft, but I could see that it stopped just inside.

I couldn't tolerate the thought of trying to squeeze through the tunnel anymore. I was exhausted and thirsty beyond measure. Somehow I twisted myself through the crevice and crawled onto the cavern floor. A huge space. Larger than anything I'd seen in the entire cave system. Its roof soared as high as a cathedral. Here were more massive salt formations like huge white statues. The space resembled a giant's warehouse, a storage yard for long-forgotten artworks fashioned by some mad sculptor. I crawled to a relatively dry space, took one more drink of water. I ate an energy bar. Only one left now. My face was hot; I must be developing a fever. I pulled some tissues out of my pack, wiped my face and hair with them, then lay my head down on my pack and slept.

I woke up shivering. My fever had worsened. I dragged myself over to the gap and unzipped my fly. Nothing more than a dribble came out. My lips tasted of salt but I was afraid to spit, not wanting to lose even that much liquid. I remembered Nick saying *"The salt will shut your kidneys down. It doesn't take much."* Along with every-thing else, dehydration was killing me.

I panicked then and stuffed down the last energy bar, hoping the moisture contained within it might help. Someone set adrift on the ocean could at least wait for rain. And I'd been so tired, I now realized I'd fallen asleep with my light on. I pulled out my phone. The battery was dead.

I forced myself to stand, even though I wobbled, woozy as a drunk. The cavern seemed endless. Its floor sloped upward like a very long natural ramp. With the pack and rope once again on my back, I took up my bent aluminum cane and staggered forward. I could make out a big mound in the gloom ahead. As I drew closer I could see it was white—a hill covered with salt crystals? A strange hill, though, as it rose from the cave floor almost at right angles.

Some of the salt had drifted away at the hillock's base, exposing a circle of rock. I touched it. Not rock—wood. Impossible. Was I hallucinating? Something, round as well, stuck out at its center. I dropped the rope and my pack and eased myself down to give it a closer look. It felt like wood too. Around this mound was a series of small hillocks, also covered in salt crystals. I bashed at one of them with my closed fist. The salt broke away. A man's face stared up at me.

Forty-One

My first thought was that I'd found Helmstetter.

I whipped off my windbreaker and used the sleeve to wipe away the salt crystals crusting his features. This wasn't the face of a modern man. Underneath the fine powder of salt his eyes were mere sockets; his corrupted, heavily pocked skin looked like leather. His hair and long beard were thickly braided, and plugs, faintly gold in color, were fixed to his pierced ears. Ragged strips of wool hung under his neck. He wore a metal helmet of some kind. I remembered seeing pictures in the National Geographic News of the Iranian salt men, well-preserved specimens who'd died in salt mines near Zanjan, southwest of Tabriz. The salt absorbed their bodily fluids, leaving them as desiccated as mummies. The same phenomenon had preserved this ancient man.

But the truly astonishing find was what he wore around his throat: a medallion in green tarnished copper, embossed with the figure of a bird with outstretched wings. A vulture. Very similar to the medallion in my treasure chest. I unfastened the chain link holding it and took the copper disc in my hand.

A new energy burst through me. This must be where Helmstetter found the artifacts he'd sent back to America. Elated, almost manic, I ignored my aching leg and scrabbled up the hillocks to chip away at the salt with my knife. One mound revealed the skull of a mule or donkey: *onangers* they were called in ancient times. Another mule lay beside it, its rough hairs and leather yokes and traces perfectly preserved.

The tallest mound must have been six feet high. I gritted my teeth against the pain in my knee and pulled myself up. Judging from the placement of the mules, I figured I was at the back of a primitive wooden cart. I dug into the salt and felt hard chunks beneath my fingers: blocks of something about the size of a brick but irregularly shaped. I pulled one out. It, too, was white with salt. Rubbing it against my shirt, I could see faint traces of a heavenly indigo color. Lapis lazuli, the royal gem of the Mesopotamians. A cartload of the precious stone.

Halfway down, a wooden partition divided the cart. In the front section were salt-filled urns and shallow bowls—they may have once held water or provisions. Near them lay leather-wrapped packages. I picked one up; when I unfolded it, the fragile leather disintegrated in my hands. Inside I found a statue, a cousin of the one Strauss had shown me: a priest-like figure with an elongated skull. Another held more cylinder seals of gleaming purple stone. Unlike Strauss's seals, these had been fashioned from amethyst.

The seals bore primitive drawings, clearly Sumerian, but no wedge-shaped cuneiform marks. I wondered if they'd been made in a preliterate time. If so, they'd be at least 5500 years old, just like the ones Strauss had shown me. Overwhelmed, I sat back and tried to calm my breathing. My pulse had gone into overdrive from dehydration and excitement.

Another body, resting on a long bronze spear and outfitted in a similar fashion, lay at the head of the cart. It too wore a linked necklace, except this one was broken. Someone had removed the medallion. Could it have been the medallion from my childhood treasure box? And if Helmstetter had taken it along with the other artifacts, how did Samuel end up with it?

Many questions, few answers.

A wave of dizziness hit and my vision blurred, reminding me of the precariousness of my circumstances. It seemed beyond cruel. I'd stumbled upon an enormous archaeological find but would never live to tell a soul.

My headlamp flickered ominously. I'd just about run out of time. If there was a way out, I had to find it. I stashed two of the seals and the statue in my pack. The medallion and a small bowl went into my inside jacket pocket nestled beside my phone. I drank the rest of my water, and then with grim humor left the empty plastic bottle beside the mummified man I'd first discovered. Using my aluminum crutch, the rope once more thrown over my shoulder, I limped away from the cart and its precious cargo.

The cavern seemed to stretch on and on, but by then my sense of time was so skewed I couldn't really tell. The rock walls closed in again. My headlamp dimmed and this time I knew it wasn't my vision. I got my bearings, picked out a rise on the ground to head toward, and shut off the lamp to save what juice I could. I'd stumble forward for maybe fifty feet then switch the lamp on again. The fourth time I shut it off, I thought I could see another phosphorescent glow. The cavern roof was lower here, no more than twice my height.

It wasn't phosphorescence after all but a salt seam running from roof to floor. It did look different, though; it seemed to shine.

And then it hit me: some kind of light must be coming from behind the salt crystals. *Light.* Should I pray or was I hallucinating? I plunged my knife into the crust, hacking away at it until I'd made a hole the size of a cup. I thrust my fist through, not caring that it scraped the salt and stung my hand. On the other side was precious, cool air.

I laughed like a maniac. Even gloried in my pain. Hurting meant I was alive, and now I had a way out. I attacked the salt seam with my knife again, widening the hole to the size of a large bucket. And then I had a moment of misgiving. What if it was just another cavern? I hardly dared open my eyes. When I did, the round orb of the sun blazed in a blue sky.

Forty-Two

I have no memory of forcing my way through the rest of the salt seam. When I did make it out I fell onto hard red earth and banged my knee again, sparking white-hot pain. Once the waves of nausea passed, I basked in warm sunlight. I had to close my eyes every few seconds. They weren't used to the glare, and the salt had made them dry and itchy. I felt like one of those creatures deep undersea— strange, fleshy white beings for whom the sun was an enemy.

The ground fanned out below me in a series of furrows and ledges heavily populated with boulders. Far in the distance, the terrain flattened to a dusty plain. It might as well have been Mars. I'd been thinking the cave was deep underground and forgotten we'd started out so high. Now I didn't have the slightest idea of where I was. I couldn't spot a single human being, not even a road or footpath. Still, common sense told me to make my way down to the plain. My breath came with difficulty, my throat was swelling. I had to get help from somewhere. I began the arduous process of crawling down, this time on my belly, no matter how much it hurt. When I came to a nest of boulders I had no choice but to stand on my good leg and scale them as best I could. The ledges proved to be the worst obstacles. I couldn't jump even the smallest ones, and some had thirty-foot drops. I'd knot the rope to the nearest spar of rock and lower myself down. Sometimes I was forced to cut the rope when the knot didn't come undone as it should have.

The sun had almost set when I heard the sound of water slipping over rock somewhere nearby. I searched and found a trickle spilling out of a cleft between two small boulders. I bent my head, held my mouth to it, and then spat it out. Salt. If I'd been able to generate tears, I would have cried. Night was closing in and I'd made it only two-thirds of the way down.

Another sound registered in the distance. This time a murmuring. Someone softly, insistently, calling my name. Two forms wavered in the twilight far below. I squinted to see who they were and my heart leapt. Bennet and Nick. How had they managed to find me? Overjoyed, I called out to them, feebly, but loud enough for them to hear. Bennet pointed in my direction. They stopped in their tracks, laughing together, as if sharing a secret known only to them. Yet they came no closer. Their forms turned into wispy phantoms and faded away.

Despair overwhelmed me again. I'd escaped the cave only to die on this barren, rocky land. *Keep going. Keep going. You have to find water. Have to.* Wherever that voice came from, it drove everything else out of my mind. I knew I couldn't rest. So I felt my way forward, staggering like a drunk in the dark. I don't remember how much farther I went when I fell off a ledge, hit something very hard, and passed out.

Forty-Three

March 12, 2005
Kandovan, Iran

Something soft lay beneath me. And, far away, voices. A woman and a man, talking urgently in a language I didn't understand. *Angel voices,* I thought. Alaz had told me this was the land of angels, after all. I could have been resting on a cloud.

A hand pressed gently down on my neck and moved to my jaw. Something didn't feel right. My beard was gone. Perhaps beards weren't allowed in paradise. A covering slid away from my eyes. I blinked them open and saw heavy black folds of cloth draped around a woman. I knew her face but not how I'd met her. She held a glass to my lips. "Drink it. Drink it. Water, good for you." The cool liquid had a faint herbal flavor. It tumbled down my throat, slaking my thirst. My head flopped down on the softness and I slept again.

A bright light shone on my face the next time I woke. A white rock wall rose straight ahead. For a moment I panicked, afraid I was back in the cave, until I realized I was lying in a small, white-stucco room on a single bed covered with a colorful blanket.

A chair creaked. The woman stood and came over to my bedside. I recognized her now. Alaz's sister. I was in the Nemat home.

I tried to sit up. "What am I doing here?"

She lay her hands on my shoulders and gently pressed me down again. "Very sick," she said. "Alaz he will tell you when he comes. Soon." Her lips quivered a little when she smiled. She had beautiful dark eyes and they seemed to hold my own gaze tenderly.

My leg still ached. I reached under the cover and could feel it had been swathed in bandages from the middle of my hip to my calf. The protruding lump at my knee had disappeared. Just as well they'd fixed the dislocation when I was unconscious, sparing me the cutting pain.

"How did I get here? Was I in the hospital?"

"The one who takes his mules on rides for tourists. He found you and remembered how you asked about us. He saw your yellow jacket on the rocks. Hospital not good for you. Police will find out."

Heavy footsteps echoed on a stair. My guardian angel jumped back as if she'd been stung by a hornet and stood against the wall. A tall figure blocked the doorway.

Alaz.

"You may go, Marya," he said sternly. She said a few quiet words to him and slipped out of the room. He came and stood over the bed. His face looked worn and tired. "How are you feeling?"

"Been better. What happened out there? Where are Bennet and Nick?"

Alaz rubbed his face with his hands. "You were already out of sight when we heard a crack and then what sounded like an avalanche. As soon as everything was quiet, we yelled and yelled for you. You didn't answer."

His tone carried an edge of dread. I asked the question again: "Where are Bennet and Nick, Alaz?"

His shoulders slumped as he sank into the chair. "Nick started down after you. Every second counted. He wouldn't wait for another rope to be hooked up and used the one attached to you. Bennet and I tried to brace it. Nick made it maybe sixty feet down. I could just make him out with my headlamp. Bennet leaned over on the edge and I was right behind her. Then Nick lost his footing. He screamed and tumbled out of view. That caused a powerful jolt on the rope, catapulting Bennet over the edge. It all happened in an instant. I almost went over myself. I couldn't catch her. I'm sorry."

My pulse thundered. "They're both gone?" But why hadn't I seen them lying at the bottom of the chasm? Then I remembered the rock ledge. It must have broken their fall. I turned my head away. My stomach felt as though it was filled with lead. Both of them dead because I'd insisted on going into that godforsaken cave. I swallowed painfully. "Have you recovered their bodies?"

"No. You don't need to worry. No one will ever find them."

"You can't do that! They have to be sent home—to their families. We can't leave them down there!"

"Yes we will. Do you have any idea what would happen if we went through government officials to send their bodies back to the U.S.?" He got up and paced the short length of the room. "It will be hard enough getting you out of the country. We know the back routes. When you are better we will take you to Turkey. Unless you want to spend the rest of your years in an Iranian prison."

I put my head back on the pillow and closed my eyes. Exhaustion and grief drained my will. What he said made sense. When I got back I'd see Nick's adoptive family and any relatives Bennet might have. Confess everything. They'd have a better chance of retrieving their remains than I would. I looked at Alaz. "Thank you for trying to help. My friends meant a lot to me."

He grunted and jerked his thumb toward the corner of the room. "I brought back their packs, so I got their room keys. The bags from the hotel and your climbing pack are there too. I paid for your rooms. You can leave the country as soon as you're better." He gave me a weak smile, turned, and went out.

I maneuvered to the end of the bed and stretched out my arm just enough to hook my fingers around the strap of my climbing pack. It came away easily. Too easily. I pulled it over to the side of the bed, fumbled with the zipper for the main compartment, and stuck my hand inside. It was empty.

Forty-Four

I swore. Who took the artifacts—Alaz? But maybe the donkey man had rummaged through my pack and taken them himself. I slumped back onto the bed. Who cared anyway? Nick and Bennet were gone.

Marya came in and set a little metal table beside the bed, then went back downstairs and returned with a tray bearing a steaming pot of tea and a bowl of soft, warm rice. She motioned for me to eat. I propped myself up on one elbow and dug into the rice, the first thing I'd eaten in days, bland but immensely comforting. Marya poured the tea into the cup. "Drink," she said. "Helps sleeping."

After I'd polished everything off she moved the table away and sat down. She looked at me as if she wanted to ask something but wasn't sure whether she should.

"What is it?" I tried to smile to reassure her.

She gave me a tentative nod, hesitated, then said, "Yeva. Have picture?"

I was about to say no when I remembered the photo we'd taken at the restaurant before I left for Turkey. I pointed to my yellow jacket, now torn and streaked with mud, hanging on a wall hook near my pack. Marya rose quickly and brought it over. I fumbled in one of the inside pockets, got my phone, and asked Marya to use my cable to plug it into the wall socket. The screen flashed on, overly bright in the dim light of the room. She brought the phone as close to me as she could. I clicked on the picture and passed her the phone. She took it in her hands and gazed at the image for a long time, touching the screen softly as if to reach across the thousands of miles and caress Evelyn's face. Her eyes clouded with tears. She wiped them away with a corner of her headscarf and handed the phone back. I couldn't imagine what it was like for a loved one to come back into your life after so many years.

"Thank you," she said simply. Then she turned the kerosene lamp down low and resumed her vigil in the chair.

I drifted off, but not for long. I ached for Nick and Bennet, lost forever to me now, and felt too overburdened to sleep. Only much later, when I saw Marya nod off, did I finally give in. My tears flowed freely then.

Marya straightened up and came over to me; she must not have been sleeping after all. She looked at me with a question in her eyes.

"My friends are dead," I whispered, turning away.

She stared openly now. Took in my skin, cut and battered from the caves, saw the grief written plainly on my face. She let out a little puff of breath, then bent her head and left the room. I barely heard her when she returned minutes later. She placed something in my open palm. Nick's watch. He never took it off. If he'd gone over the cliff as Alaz had said, there was no way I'd be holding it now.

I sat bolt upright. "Where …"

She pressed her fingers to my lips and shook her head. "Not dead," she whispered.

I could have wept again, this time with relief. "Where are they?"

"Alaz take them to Eden."

Forty-Five

"What do you mean? Where is it?"

The look she gave me was pained and helpless. "Not know."

Footsteps sounded downstairs. Just the old man, Mernoush, unable to sleep—or was Alaz coming up? Marya, clearly frightened, gestured to me to be silent. She extinguished the kerosene lamp and sat back down. The sound of footsteps grew less distinct. I heard her let out a sigh, and then she was silent.

Why had Alaz lied to me about Nick and Bennet? And what was he planning to do with them? Hold them for ransom? Extract information? My mind raced. *Why* he'd done it didn't matter right now. I had to find them.

I racked my brain for a clue I might have overlooked. According to David Rohl's book, if Eden really was an original name for this part of the Middle East, it denoted a vast area, hundreds of square miles surrounding Tabriz and Lake Urmia. It wasn't a dot on the map. I wondered what was worse, believing Bennet and Nick were dead or learning they were alive with no way to save them.

I pretended to sleep until Marya went downstairs. Then I dragged my jacket onto the bed, unzipped the inside pocket, and hit pay dirt. My credit cards were still tucked inside. So were the keys to Nick's Jeep—I hadn't returned them after our trip to Tabriz for equipment. The boots I'd left in my hotel room sat beside my bag. I wedged the keys and credit cards into the toe of the boot and stuffed a sock in to keep them concealed. Eventually I slept, but fitfully.

March 13, 2005

The next morning I felt well enough to walk around the room and then go downstairs to use the bathroom. I looked terrible—what a relief it was to pour warm water into the basin and have a good wash. I ran my hand over my chin, feeling naked without my beard. The birthmark on my jaw glared like an ugly red scar. I changed into some clean clothes from the bag Alaz had retrieved from the hotel.

It was mid-afternoon when Alaz came to see me. Much as I wanted to beat him to a pulp, I held myself back. I lay on the bed, pretending to be a lot weaker than I was. He went over to Nick's pack and rifled through it.

"What are you looking for?"

"His keys. I need to take his rental car back to Tabriz."

That Jeep was my lifeline. "Nick always kept the keys on him. You'd have to go back to the cave."

"No." Alaz rubbed his hand across his forehead.

"Nick used his credit card for the deposit," I continued in what I hoped was a matter-of-fact way. "You'll need it to settle the bill." None of this was true. Nick had paid cash, but Alaz wouldn't know that.

He muttered something under his breath and rushed down the stairs. I heard the front door slam when he went out.

I spent the remainder of the day planning my next moves. I wasn't sure whether I could make it to the Jeep, let alone find where Nick and Bennet were being held, but I had to try. That evening, when Marya brought my tea, I took a deep breath, explained my intentions, and asked for her help. My aim was to leave the house the moment Alaz went out again, whenever that would be. To my great relief Marya nodded solemnly in assent.

Just before dawn I heard a rustling downstairs and low voices. I looked out the window to see Alaz's tall form emerge from the front door. He greeted two shorter men. One took up position directly across from the house; the other walked off with Alaz. I prayed they'd be gone long enough.

Marya beckoned me to follow her. I stuffed our passports into my pack and then extracted the car keys and credit cards from my boot and shoved them on. She led me up a narrow staircase to the third floor.

The structure of Kandovan houses was determined by the conical stone outcrops from which they'd been hollowed out. Pockets in the stone provided natural indentations for windows and doors. Tunnels joined some residences internally; others were connected by exterior wooden slat bridges. The Nemat home had two old wooden doors, several windows, and happily, a third-story bridge spanning the space to the house next door. One of the upper doors led out onto this bridge. I made to go through it but Marya held me back. She gestured for me to leave the door open and to accompany her back down the stairs.

I followed her, matching the sound of my footsteps as best as I could to hers so as not to wake the old man. Stone steps don't creak—a big advantage. When we reached the front door, Marya hesitated and looked down at her feet. Then, as she quietly opened the door, light fell on her face. It was wet with tears. She motioned for me to stay back, pushed the door almost closed, and hurried over to the man Alaz had posted as guard. I could hear them speaking urgently, and through the crack I saw Marya gesturing to the third-story bridge with a concerned look. The guy took the bait. He ran over to the house next door, up to the bridge, and then through the narrow stone gap between the two roofs, in hot pursuit of a phantom me. I whipped out the door, and with a backward look at Marya that I hoped conveyed my gratitude, strode as fast as I could manage in the opposite direction.

Marya had given me an old black jacket that belonged to Alaz and one of his hats. I tugged the hat down to my eyes and headed for where I dimly remembered Nick's car might be. Every step hurt. Every corner I rounded I expected to come face to face with Alaz's guard. And if I hadn't spotted the donkey man's house, I might have ended up seriously lost. When I finally saw the Jeep I could barely keep from yelling for joy.

I rushed over, threw my pack in the back, and eased myself into the driver's seat. Tabriz was only an hour away. I'd find a hotel and work out my next steps. I hit the door locks, gunned the motor, and took off.

In Tabriz, I checked into the most Westernized hotel I could find. Since they required a passport, I had no choice but to register under my own name. I hoped Alaz would think I was heading straight for the Turkish border.

Once in my room, I made coffee. Fleeing through Kandovan had spent my reserves and my knee was complaining, but the caffeine did a lot to help revive me. For now I was safe. Nick and Bennet were alive. That felt like a miracle.

I plugged in my phone, sat on the bed, and let out a deep breath. Then I began sorting through everything I'd brought with me. I had Nick's sat phone and watch, his and Bennet's passports and ID, my credit cards, my books, the volume of Samuel's journal that talked about Eden, and Helmstetter's exasperating number code. If I had any chance at all of finding Nick and Bennet, that code was my only hope.

Back in Pergamon, when I'd applied the alphabet to the numbers, only some of them translated into words:

Thirty	Forty
Eight.	Six.
30 34 32 33 45	Two
Six	76 55 68 65
Zero	Seven
Five	31 34 47 30
Nine	101 80 93 90
51 30 43 40	55 59 57 58 70

What had Veronica Sills said about *The Steganographia*? That Helmstetter used it as a guide. Then it struck me: Thomas Ernst, the German professor, had deciphered Trithemius's code. Could Helmstetter have used that same code in his number columns? When I was packing my books in New York I'd stuffed in Ernst's account. I dug it out now, my heart beginning to pound.

Ernst furnished the answer. Number patterns in Trithemius's code, he explained, seemed to point to repeated messages. Ernst discovered that when these similar-seeming groups of numbers were repeated, each number in the repeated group had been increased by twenty-five. Twenty-five, Ernst said, represented how many letters there were in the alphabet during Trithemius's time. Once I went back to the original numbers and applied that logic to the rows I hadn't been able to figure out, I could fill in all the missing words. They turned out to be a six, two eights, and three zeroes. But what on earth did the columns mean anyway? I fiddled around with them and then swore in frustration.

My stomach reminded me I was starving. I ordered room service, figuring the best thing I could do was to forget the puzzle for a while and come back at it, fresh, after I'd eaten. I used the time to take stock of everything I'd gleaned up until now.

The early people who dwelled in this region, and in Anatolia, were among the first to domesticate plants and animals. They could certainly have constructed primitive walled gardens to protect their bounty from wildlife and human enemies. It was much warmer and wetter five thousand years ago, so the Bible's description of Eden—*"And the Lord God planted a garden in Eden, in the east ... and out of the ground the Lord God made to spring up every tree that is pleasant to the sight and good to eat"*—was entirely plausible. Even now, orchards abounded along the highway before you hit the industrial corridor on the outskirts of Tabriz. The notion that even a corner of the original Eden still existed somewhere on these arid plains, though, seemed laughable.

Yet Helmstetter clearly believed it did. To achieve his dream of immortality he first sought his "place of power" at Pergamon; for some reason he found the Turkish site wanting, and so went to Kandovan. His was not a quest taken lightly. He gave up a great deal in search of his Eden: his reputation, growing celebrity in America, his wife and mistress, and ultimately, his life. For I did believe Alaz's story that Helmstetter had disappeared permanently. From the description given by those who knew him best, the magician had a gigantic ego. No one like that would choose to fade into obscurity.

A polite tap on the door signaled the arrival of lunch. The server wheeled a tray into the room, acknowledged my generous tip, and left. While I ate, I thought more about Helmstetter. Like his ancestor Faust, he'd pushed the boundaries of the occult in pursuit of knowledge, believing he could unlock the path to immortality. The question was, did he find it in a place he believed to be Eden?

I turned back to the number columns and attacked them with renewed vigor, reminding myself I was looking for a physical location. And then I saw what had been staring me in the face. The period that followed the eight in the left column and the six in the right. In another minute I'd solved it.

Forty-Six

March 14, 2005
Tabriz, Iran

They were geographic coordinates.

Iran was north of the equator and east of the meridian. Coordinates showed latitude first. So 38. 8 6 0 5 9 0 would be the latitude, 46. 2 0 7 5 0 8 the longitude. I grabbed my phone, brought up Google Maps, and keyed in the coordinates. The familiar red teardrop marked a spot two-thirds the way down one of the long gorges scoring Mount Sahand. Along the thin line of dark green ran the faint blue trace of a waterway and a road that would take me close to my destination. Had Alaz and his confederates hiked overland, using mules, to reach it?

Even on a poor road, the drive would take less than an hour. I stuffed what I needed in my pack along with Alaz's black jacket and the hat Marya had given me. In the hotel tuck shop I bought a big bottle of water and some nuts and chocolate bars. The concierge directed me to a pharmacy not far away where I bought some Tylenol.

I first had to double back on the same road that led to Kandovan and worried I might meet Alaz driving in the opposite direction. To my relief, the route soon branched off to the left. This road was in much worse shape. As the Jeep steadily climbed the mountain slopes, the crumbling surface grew narrow with erosion and began bending in a series of heart-stopping switchbacks. Finally I came to a village on one side of a fast-flowing stream. Beyond it, the slopes of the gorge were heavily shrouded with trees. According to my GPS, I was closing in. At any rate, I'd gone as far as I could on the road. The area was crisscrossed with narrow tracks like the one we'd taken to the salt caves. I decided on one that ran closest to the coordinates, parked behind a grove of ironwood trees, and hoped the Jeep was sufficiently hidden. Then I got Nick's gun out from where he'd stashed it under the back seat and headed into the forest.

The buds were swelling on the trees, the branches heavily covered with green lichen. The path began to climb almost immediately. It seemed little used; I couldn't spot sheep droppings or any other signs of animal, let alone human, activity. The path veered away from the mountain stream, the sound of its clear rushing water tumbling over rocks fading into the distance.

My route led upward. Knowing only that I was nearing the coordinates but with no certainty of finding anything, I carried on this way for over two hours. It was tough going, what with all the protruding tree roots and the stones and scree carpeting the ground, and whenever my knee screamed loudly enough I was forced to stop. It was past three now. I couldn't stay out here much longer.

That's when I saw a rough series of steps cut into the side of a steep rock wall maybe forty feet high, topped with what looked to be another dense wood. It was completely silent here, as though this small corner of the world had been forgotten, somehow left behind. A bird with giant wings soared in the sky far above.

I tightened my pack around me, took a few deep breaths, and began the climb. The steps were shallow and so steep that I could grasp an upper stair with my hand and pull myself up. When I reached the top I found no pathway, just a few open spaces between the trees. But on the ground I saw an occasional broken twig. Someone had been along here recently. A deep wet blanket of last year's dead leaves covered the forest floor. I crept along as quietly as possible. After twenty minutes a clearing emerged ahead. I squeezed my way through the trees. Thankfully, they were quite mature here, the lowest branches reasonably high off the ground; I had only to duck beneath them. I snuck up to the clearing and stopped.

The tree line ended at a natural red-stone platform from which another rock wall rose, forming a cliff so high it would be impossible to scale. But I wouldn't need to. For hollowed into the rock face was a house with doors and windows, just like the ones in Kandovan. I took Nick's Glock out of my pack, knelt behind a large tree trunk, and watched.

I didn't have to wait long. Ten minutes later the door opened and a man stepped out—the same man who'd left with Alaz the previous morning. He wore no jacket, just a shirt, and carried a gun in a shoulder holster. Standing a mere twenty feet away, I had him directly in my sights. He looked rapidly to his right and left, scanning the trees. I aimed for his midriff and fired.

He screamed and went down, blood gushing from his hip then lay still as death. I ran to the house for cover, pressing my back to the facade behind the open door. From inside the house I could hear the racing of heavy boots. A second man burst through the door and screeched to a halt when he saw his comrade lying in the dirt. I shot him in the back. He toppled over the first man, writhing and kicking. I waited, counting out the seconds. No one else came to their aid. The man I'd shot in the back screamed at me in no language I understood. His eyes turned up and he fainted. His gun lay in the dirt a few feet away. I picked it up, retrieved the second gun from the other man's shoulder holster, and stuck both deep in my pockets. I kept my grip on Nick's Glock and went inside.

The place was dusty and unkempt. Like the Nemats' house, it had white plastered walls, floor cushions, and a faded, threadbare Persian carpet thrown over a rough stone floor. A flame curled up from oil in a stone basin, giving off a weak light. The room had a strange odor I somehow recognized but couldn't quite place.

Bennet lay curled up in one corner with a cushion at her back, her feet and hands bound, her mouth gagged. I rushed to her side. She looked up at me as if she'd seen a ghost.

I knelt down beside her. "It's okay," I whispered. "It's me." I brushed my lips along her cheek and held her hand while I yanked the gag from her mouth. She whimpered as I struggled with the cable used to bind her wrists and got it undone. Much as I wanted to take her in my arms I couldn't waste a minute. "Where's Nick?" I said.

"Through there," she whispered hoarsely. She lifted her hand in the direction of a curtained doorway leading into the recesses of the house.

"Shake your hands and legs to get the circulation going," I said over my shoulder.

In the next room Nick was slumped against a wall, his shirt-sleeve torn and a crude bandage wrapped around his right arm, leaking blood. Despite the injury his arms had been crossed and bound tightly to his sides. The skin around his ankles bled, too. Duct tape had been plastered over his mouth. As I reached for the tape he shook his head furiously and glared at my hands.

"What's the matter?" I ripped the tape away.

"Where's the damn gun, you fuck!" he spat, his voice barely audible.

I'd left it beside Bennet when I undid her ties.

He made a muffled sound halfway between a moan and a cry and stared at the curtained doorway behind me.

I turned to see Yersan with Nick's Glock in his hand. Behind him, Alaz pushed Bennet forward.

"Mr. Madison," Yersan said. "I have a great debt to repay to my poor friends outside."

He trained the pistol on Nick. "Make any further attempt and your friend will die." Alaz shoved Bennet toward me. Yersan motioned for us to stand facing the wall.

Alaz groped in my pockets and confiscated the other guns. "Take off that jacket. You even steal my clothes?" He pushed my face against the wall, bound my hands, and tied Bennet's again. Yersan hauled Nick to his feet and sliced the cord at his ankles. He, too, was ordered to face the wall. We were lined up execution style. Bennet began to sob.

I heard a scraping sound, something being lifted and dragged aside, something being cranked up. It reminded me of the heavy metal grates being opened on sidewalks in front of New York shops. "You first, Madison," Yersan said. "The woman last."

I turned and saw that the carpet had been pulled away to reveal an open hatch in the floor. A flight of stone steps led into a black hole. I descended in almost pitch dark, the steps slippery with mold. Nick and Bennet followed, Yersan and Alaz behind them. At the bottom I could hear one of them fumbling for something and then a snap, as if he'd locked the trapdoor shut again. A dim light came on behind us, illuminating the shadowy outline of a long hallway. I stumbled forward over the uneven floor.

We seemed to walk forever until we reached a dead end. Bennet and Nick were told to lie on their sides facing the wall on their right. Alaz moved ahead. I heard a click and then the sound of stone grating on stone. Light suddenly flooded into the corridor, so bright I had to shut my eyes. Yersan ordered me forward. I didn't want to be separated from Bennet and Nick again but had no choice. I pushed myself away from the wall and blinked in the blinding light. At first, all I could make out were two towering flames, taller than me, that seemed to burst from the ground. I took a couple of steps closer, then lurched back from the wave of heat.

"Turn to your right, Madison," Yersan ordered. A third man ducked around the corner from the source of light. The stone slid back into place, locking him in with Bennet and Nick on the other side.

Yersan kept his gun on me, Alaz not far behind. "Your friends are our insurance for your good behavior. Move."

When my eyes adjusted to the light, I gasped at what I saw before me.

Forty-Seven

Sahand Protected Area, Iran

We stood in a canyon so long I couldn't see its end. On either side gleaming red rock cliffs stretched to the sky. The canyon floor was hundreds of feet wide. I saw now that the flames weren't shooting out from the earth but rather from holes in a square of perfectly fitted stone bricks. They must have been natural gas wells, just like the fire altar we'd seen near Kandovan.

Eternal flames.

A square pool lay at the foot of these natural torches, its clear water reflecting the flames without a ripple. Electric-blue stones encircled the pool, its far side emptying into a brook that flowed on into the canyon. The surroundings were lush with plants and trees of all kinds, greener than anything I'd seen since entering Iran. Some early spring plants had even flowered, pink petals unfurled to reveal bright yellow stamens heavy with pollen. The temperature here was warmer by at least twenty degrees. A unique ecosystem, hidden from the outside world. My senses took it all in but my brain was numb. "Magnificent," I finally murmured.

"You were determined to see it," Yersan said. "You are a foolish man, but I'm happy to oblige you."

"This is what Helmstetter was searching for?" Alaz caught my eye and nodded. "How did you find this place?"

Yersan answered for him. "We are its caretakers. A tradition of service handed down by our ancestors for thousands of years. Both Alaz and I were called to serve when we were young men. It is a privilege. A sacred trust."

He motioned toward the brook. "You may explore if you wish." Like two baleful nursemaids, they trundled behind me as I walked upon a carpet of deep, rich green moss. I made my way over to the west canyon wall. The cliff face seemed to shine and I wondered why.

Alaz sensed my unspoken question. "The canyon is oriented so that it has the benefit of the sun all day long," he said. "Otherwise, this lush plant life wouldn't exist."

The rock was red quartz—vast sheets of carnelian. I'd never before seen such an expanse of precious stone, and it had neither pockmarks nor the rough, unfinished surface you'd find in natural material. Although it was awkward with my hands tied, I touched the surface. It had been polished, sanded somehow, by hand. Tens of thousands of square feet. The entire surface shimmered like a rosy mirror in the waning rays of the sun. It seemed to produce a magnifying effect, intensifying the light. I cocked my head a bit, my ears picking up a faint hum, almost as if the light were singing.

It occurred to me that the rock's satiny surface served another purpose: security. The cliff was as smooth as glass, making it virtually impossible to scale unless you had climbing equipment.

At intervals along its face, life-sized winged figures—the Apkallu of Mesopotamian art—had been carved into the rock.

"Our angels," Yersan said when he saw me admiring them. A noise startled me and I turned to see a gigantic bird take off from the crown of a small tree with a flap of its expansive wings.

Yersan raised his hand as if to trace its trajectory. "A vulture. Our ancestors believed them to be godly because they touch heaven. They fly higher than any other bird, sometimes as much as thirty thousand feet, and seem to disappear into the sky. These are the birds the ancient ones immortalized as angels."

I could hear the pride in his voice. But it cracked with sadness when he spoke again. "The man you shot in the back is dead. We will take him away to a *dakhma* to be consumed by the vultures. After three days he will enter paradise. That is our way." The image of the man writhing on the ground came back to me, yet I felt no remorse.

Yersan instructed me to head down the shiny brick pathway that followed the stream for what he said was a mile or more. I'd taken the bricks as red quartz until I saw that, through some primitive type of metallurgy, they'd been fashioned from a rudimentary pink gold.

Surely we had little time left to live—Eden's guardians wouldn't let interlopers escape with the secret to paradise—and yet I felt content to meander along the path, listening to the tinkle of brook water and wrapped in a deep, encompassing sense of peace.

The canyon walls narrowed, refracting the rosy light and creating a strange, pervasive glow that seemed to hang in the air as if it were a living presence. I had to shield my eyes against it. The hum grew louder.

We turned a bend. The light faded and I could look up again.

Ahead, the canyon ended in a low wall and a small plaza fashioned from the same bricks as those forming the path. Abutting the plaza was another building hewn into the rock of the cliff, this one boasting two huge double doors made of cedar. The stream diverged outside the wall so as to form a T-shaped moat.

Alaz undid my bonds and I flexed my hands and wrists.

"Before you enter the temple, take off your shoes and socks, Madison," Yersan ordered.

Yersan and Alaz removed their own footwear and bowed toward the strange temple. Then Alaz waded across the moat and mounted the stone wall. I followed suit and Yersan came last.

A fat vine grew around the cedar door frame, its stem as thick as a young tree, its creeping tendrils and swelling green buds spreading upward to cover a good part of the temple's lower facade. To the left of the door was a primitive stone carving of a snake, to the right a vulture. Another stone carving, this one a winged figure, was set above the lintel.

The Sacred Tree

Yersan touched the vine. "This is the tree of knowledge. It is not particularly rare. It grows in many countries, even your own. Are you surprised that it is a vine and not a tree? The art of our ancestors has always shown the truth."

Forgetting myself and the holiness of this place, I scoffed, "The tree of knowledge is only a metaphor."

"Is it not interesting that literalists take every word in Genesis as fact, except for one sentence? *'Of the Tree of Knowledge of Good and Evil thou shalt not eat of it; for in the day thou eatest thereof, thou shalt surely die.'* This is interpreted to be allegorical, that Eve was given the direst warning against temptation lest she usher sin into the world. But what if it was meant to be taken literally? What if you *could* die from ingesting the fruit of the tree? What if God, who cared deeply for his newly formed creatures, wanted to protect them like a loving parent? Warned them the same way Enki warned Adapa about eating the bread and water offered by the snake god?"

"You're saying it's poisonous?"

"This vine contains a most potent hallucinogen. Even in the hands of experts it can be deadly."

Yersan paused. "The legend of the serpent stealing the plant of immortality, first recorded in the Epic of Gilgamesh, emerged, thousands of years later, as the serpent winding around the tree of knowledge in Eden. The snake was transformed by early Christian theologians into the devil."

"Why are you telling me all this?"

Yersan smiled. "Are you not the one who wishes to taste the forbidden fruit and learn about the man who came here to seek immortality?"

Forty-Eight

Without another word, he handed his gun to Alaz and approached the cedar doors. They were so heavy it seemed to require all his strength to brace them open. Each man bowed toward the dim interior before entering. I followed them in. Despite my skepticism, I felt I'd stepped into a sacred place.

A wide stone basin sat in the center of the room. Like the Zoroaster shrine in Yersan's New York shop, it was filled with a fragrant oil. Delicate, flickering flames rippled across the oil's surface, producing a rainbow of color. I couldn't place the scent—a little like incense but not as cloying or spicy. Some kind of flower tone. Augmented by the heat, it penetrated the room. It made you want to take deep breaths as though it was a drug you craved.

Polished carnelian blocks formed the walls and floor, reflecting the light thrown by the flames. A simple room, but somehow it felt more elegant than a king's salon. I caught my breath and stopped in my tracks when the two men stepped aside to let me see what lay beyond the fire basin.

A figure was seated on a throne-like chair of wood inlaid with gold and lapis lazuli. A vulture's-head mask of hand-beaten gold, primitive but somehow all the more regal for it, covered most of the skull. That didn't disguise the skull's elongated shape, just like the statue I'd found in the salt cave and the one Strauss first showed me. The figure's white hair and beard were tightly braided, wigs perhaps, added after vultures had picked the bones clean. It wore a sleeveless wool jerkin that might once have been red but was now badly deteriorated. Gold bands embossed with rosettes circled each wrist and ankle.

Two massive wings, bent and folded, black feathers intact, jutted from the figure's back. The eyes, shell for the whites and glossy obsidian for the irises, glittered behind the mask. "Was this once a king?" I asked in amazement.

Yersan kept his tone low, reverential. "One of the seven sages, immortalized in legend as the Apkallu. A genius, a high priest from ancient times. The wings are a skillfully constructed piece of its raiment. As the myths tell us, the Apkallu and their followers, over time, bestowed many gifts on mankind: the calendar, the interpretation of the stars, the taming of plants and animals, the potter's wheel. They were worshipers of the god Enki, the giver of wisdom." He heaved a long sigh. "We will each take a place at his feet. Please sit.

"Imagine yourself," Yersan continued, "as a young acolyte. At puberty you would have been hand-picked from the community to serve as apprentice to a high priest. You would be introduced at sunset, through a prescribed ritual—the taking of the plant of immortality. Can you imagine the effect on a child's mind of seeing this gold-bedecked, winged figure when under the influence of the drug?" Yersan glanced at Alaz. "It would be like Alaz's wonderment when he first laid eyes on the sorcerer Helmstetter, only much greater. That experience, to be repeated over and over again for many centuries, gave rise to myths and, I believe, our notion of angels as messengers from heaven."

I'd have given anything to examine the priest, to take pictures. It would be a life's work just to study its meaning and cultural significance. But right now that felt like a sacrilege.

Yersan sat cross-legged to the figure's left and beckoned me to sit beside him, dead center. Then he reached under the right side of the throne and brought out a carafe and a bowl. The dishes looked similar to the bowls and urns I'd found in the cart during my sojourn in the salt caves. Utensils at least 5500 years old.

He poured some liquid from the carafe into the bowl and held it out to me. "Made from the fruit of the vine—the tree of knowledge," he said. "Thirty-five years ago Helmstetter traveled halfway across the world seeking immortality. I offer it to you— freely. And with it a promise. To reveal the true story of your birth."

"You want me to drink this?"

"It is your choice. I have partaken many times and am still here."

"Is that how Helmstetter died—from drinking it?"

Yersan shook his head. "He wanted to take the liquor. It was refused him."

He sat beside me and touched my arm. "Taste it first. And then drink the whole of it down. Do not fear. The priest will guide you."

I would die at their hands anyway. Perhaps if Yersan was lying and this was a poison, it would be a faster way to go. I said a quick prayer for Evelyn, Nick, and Bennet, then raised the rim of the plain little bowl to my lips.

Forty-Nine

Aside from a numbness in my mouth, at first I felt nothing. Neither Yersan nor Alaz spoke. My head was a little woozy, but that may have been a result of the fear coursing through my veins. Then the smooth liquor hit my bloodstream as if I'd just taken a morphine shot. My legs began to feel heavy, like waterlogged sponges. Minutes later I retched and had just enough time to turn my head to the side before I threw up. My heart hammered, the beats coming so close and loud they drummed out any other sound. My throat seized and an overpowering thirst struck me. "I need water," I heard myself croak. "Please."

Yersan loomed over me; his face seemed to have expanded to several times its natural size. His voice echoed. "Stay still," he said. "He will come to you. It will be worse if you try to move."

Torrents of fear raked my body. I could feel the poison invading every cell.

I sensed motion, was conscious of bodies nearby. I lashed out. An electric jolt tore through me; my own body felt as if it had been cleaved in two. Had Yersan gutted me with a knife? I looked down at my chest but my vision had blurred. I shook like a summer leaf spinning in a tornado. Hands held me down. It felt as though they were squeezing me flat in a giant vise. The pain was immense. I stopped resisting and lay still, which lessened the agony a little.

Someone passed a cool wet cloth over my forehead. I opened my eyes but when I focused on his fingers they appeared almost transparent; I could see glassy skin, purple-red veins, tiny capillaries.

Scent overpowered me. Cedar, the perfumed oil, the men's sweat, the garden's plants, soil, and mold. I could even smell the quartz dust drifting down from the ancient walls. Slowly the pain subsided and my heart settled down. I tried to lift my head. A cramp gripped me and I doubled in two again. I think I screamed.

"Stay still, stay still" came a disembodied voice floating through the air. When the aftershock of the second cramp lessened I lay quietly, too terrified to move.

I felt myself being lifted. The walls of the room disappeared. A flickering darkness, a soft grayness, surrounded me. A dazzle of gold flashed so brightly I had to shut my eyes. I opened my lids a fraction and looked again.

A winged figure stood before me. Tall as the tallest man I'd ever seen. His gold mask glittered. His robe was no longer in tatters. On it were painted beautiful designs in strange symbols of green, red, and blue. Jewels circled the neck of his robe. The colors shimmered and seemed to melt into the flare of rosy gold.

He held his arms crossed over his heart. The skin on his face, arms, and hands was the colour of old parchment, the hair of his long braided beard white as bleached bones. His dark eyes bored into my soul.

And then the being spoke. I couldn't understand the words but somehow knew what he was saying. As if his thoughts had the power to flow directly into mine.

An invitation.

A warmth stole over my body. I stopped trembling. Then his great wings unfolded and in the next moment I lost all awareness of time. Now I was surrounded by darkness, the indigo black of night. Far below I saw the frothy crowns of trees, the stream, the golden path. But how could everything appear so clearly in the gloom? The colors of the natural flora below me were as bright as if they'd been brushed with neon paint. The whole terrain glowed, yet each detail was crisp and clear.

I was seeing with a bird's eye.

It was cold but that didn't seem to affect me. The moon had come out, casting a silvery light, and the first stars began to appear. I sensed the winged one's presence, heard his murmurings, yet could not see him. He seemed to hold me safe in a kind of tender embrace. We flew that way for a long time. Then he left me. No, that's wrong. I was alone but at the same time my flesh had joined with the pulse at the core of the universe. My heartbeat became the rhythm of waves flowing onto the shore, the punch of thunder, the burst of a sapling pushing out of the earth, the swish of a bird's wings. I began to forget who I was and I welcomed it.

I have no idea how long that journey lasted. Only that at some point I opened my eyes and saw I was outside the temple and the great cedar doors had now closed. My head hurt yet I felt strangely energized. Voices seemed to come from far off. Yersan and Alaz leaned over me.

"Can you get up?" Alaz said. "You should have something to eat and drink now."

Yersan caught my arm and helped me to my feet. We crossed the moat, put our footwear back on, and sat on rocks beside the stream. I nibbled at some flatbread and drank a cup of strong sweet tea from a thermos Alaz handed me. By the strength and angle of the sun I could tell it was morning.

Yersan's weapon was tucked into the holster attached to his belt, but I'd lost any inclination to fight him. "Last night," I said. "Tell me what happened."

"First, I want to know: What do you think of immortality?"

"I'm not sure I would call it that. How long was I unconscious?"

"You were not unconscious, you were *more* conscious."

"How long was I out for?" I persisted. I looked at the strong morning sun again. "Must have been all night."

"You've been gone from us for two and a half days."

"No! That's impossible."

He gave me a quick look of rebuke. "Check your phone."

I was shocked when I glanced at my cell screen.

Yersan smiled. "Did time not vanish for you? Surely that is a kind of immortality. What is immortality but an absence of time, a state of being in the present? The potion helped you suspend your day-to-day perceptions and introduced you to knowledge of the world as it really is. Knowledge that the gods possess and do not part with easily. The priest chose to become your guide; you were open to him and so he put his faith in you. Even if he'd taken the drug, Helmstetter would not have been capable of that. He'd been searching for what turned out to be a simple answer but was too blinded by his perverse beliefs in magic to comprehend it."

Still feeling the afterglow of my journey, I sat quietly and thought about his explanation. "It was an incredible experience. Thank you."

"I promised to tell you about your birth but I will leave that to my friend." Yersan swept his hand toward Alaz.

"I can tell it," Alaz said, "but before I begin, are you certain you want to know?"

Fifty

"Yes."

"Very well then. Many years ago, a man came to Kandovan. A sorcerer who sought immortality. He'd learned about the beliefs of our people and wished to use them for his own benefit. He wanted fame and fortune for himself and would stop at nothing to get it. This is the man you call George Helmstetter.

"He was your father."

My breath stopped. The peacefulness I'd felt vanished like the sun suddenly blocked by a storm cloud. "I thought you said Yeva bore a child out of wedlock from an Iranian, a man who came from Tabriz."

He shrugged. "I made no mention of Iranian heritage. You assumed that. Helmstetter did come to our region by way of Tabriz."

Evelyn was my mother and Helmstetter, my father. I wished I hadn't heard it. Wished I'd left well enough alone. The man was loathsome and the thought of him putting his hands on Evelyn repulsed me. And Samuel, who I'd always known as my half brother, the person I'd looked up to most in the world, hadn't shared a drop of blood with me at all.

"What happened to Helmstetter? Why did he abandon your sister?"

"I've told you he captivated the minds of many of the villagers and that I fell under his spell when I was a young boy. Your mother did too. As Yersan said, for millennia a small circle of Kandovan men have served as caretakers for this temple sanctuary. Helmstetter managed to persuade one of the old caretakers to bring him here—the place where he believed he'd find the power to grant him immortality. Entering the temple and defiling your mother were both a great sacrilege. When his treachery was discovered he was seized, staked to the ground on a high rocky slope, cut with knives. The men let the vultures do the rest. They picked the skeleton clean. That, they burned to a crisp. The ashes were mixed with oil and burned again until nothing was left. This is an old remedy we use against sorcerers."

My astonishment upon learning I was Helmstetter's son was matched by a repugnance at how he'd died. An awful thought passed through my mind. Did I take after him? Had I inherited his casual cruelty toward people?

Yersan and Alaz led me back through the underground hallway to the house. I followed in a daze of shock mixed with an over-whelming despondency.

Nick and Bennet, along with their guard, were waiting for me in the front room.

Yersan touched my arm. "I tried in every way I could to turn you back from knowledge of this place. By the threats in America, in Turkey, in the salt cave ... and then by subterfuge. It seemed only to encourage you. Like your father, you are persistent no matter what the consequences. We have lost a dear friend, the man you shot. We wish to mourn him now and the other who has been gravely injured. We have nothing to fear from you and I want no more death. You are free to go." Yersan ordered Nick's and Bennet's bonds removed.

Bennet threw her arms around me and I buried my face in her curls. "I never thought I'd see you again," she murmured.

Nick rubbed his red and swollen wrists. "Don't look a gift horse in the mouth, Madison. Let's get the hell out of here."

I gently released myself from Bennet's embrace but kept my arm around her. I eyed Yersan. "One thing. I'd like the artifacts I found in the salt caves back. I went through pure torture to get them."

"They belong to the Iranian people."

"And you're going to give them up to the government? I doubt that."

"For God's sake, Madison," Nick interjected.

Yersan smiled. Neither he nor Alaz seemed bothered. "They'll be kept in the temple. Still on Iranian soil. And if you speak of what you have seen here, no one will believe you. You have no evidence. You were in no condition to remember where you emerged from the caves and we've blocked that opening now. All traces of it have been erased. I do have a parting gift for you, though. Something we don't wish to keep. It doesn't belong here." He rummaged in the drawer of a little table and then held out Trithemius's *Steganographia*.

I turned to Alaz. "I thought you said your father burned this."

He shrugged. "I wanted to discourage you from seeking it and go home. My father was given a fake. My sister Yeva cleverly hid the real book at the root of an ancient cypress tree when she fled the country with you." His eyes softened a little. "Please tell Yeva how glad we are to have news of her."

His words touched me. He didn't need to return the book—I'd believed his story about his father burning it—but he did anyway. I chose to think that in a corner of his heart, Alaz, my uncle, had some sympathy for me and still cared about Evelyn.

I took the book in my hands. Inside its faded, badly scarred brown leather covers the pages were held together with lead clips. "Thank you."

"You are free to go." Yersan held up his hand to indicate he had more to say. "Under good conditions, from here, it will take you eight hours to reach the Turkish border. That is all the time you have before we report the murder of my friend to the Iranian police. I wish you good speed."

Fifty-One

March 17, 2005
Turkey

Nick was in no shape to drive, so I took the wheel. After we hit the highway leading back to Turkey, I asked what had happened in the salt cave.

"We heard the crash of the salt shelf breaking off and I was pretty sure I heard you yell," Nick said. "We knew something bad had happened. I got the second length of rope to rappel down, and while Bennet and I tried to fix it around the anchor Alaz pulled a gun on us. He couldn't have planned the accident but he sure as hell took advantage of it. He marched us back to the entrance where Yersan and some other men were waiting. I almost got free after they'd taken us to the house where you found us. But there were too many of them. They beat the shit outta me."

"What I don't understand is why they didn't kill you right there."

"I don't know either, except it was you they really wanted to get rid of. And until they were sure you were dead, they didn't want to take any chances with us."

We stopped at a village to get cleaned up and change clothes before we reached the border. By the time we pulled up to the checkpoint Nick had rested up enough to take the wheel. I still had the medallion and the bowl and was sweating bricks. But Nick laid on the charm and finessed it again. We sailed through.

"Where do you want to go, my friends?" Nick asked.

"Straight to the Van airport," Bennet said wearily. "I want to get out of this godforsaken place as fast as possible."

Nick shook his head. "Still can't believe they let us go. I wouldn't have if the shoe was on the other foot."

"Maybe Alaz had trouble with the idea of killing his own nephew," I said.

Nick and Bennet gaped at me.

"I found out that Evelyn is my mother and Helmstetter was my father."

"Oh my God! Who told you that?" Bennet's voice quaked.

"Alaz. Evelyn had to flee Kandovan because she became pregnant by Helmstetter. Even if he'd been free to wed, marrying a man from outside the community would have been forbidden and having a baby out of wedlock, a grievous sin."

They listened quietly as I related the story about Helmstetter's grim fate and my experiences in the garden.

It was late afternoon by the time Nick dropped us off at the airport.

"You'll get in touch when you're back in the States?" I asked him. "I owe you a lot. I'll do whatever I can to help you get set up over there."

"Count on it." He grinned. "Always suspected you were a bad seed. That's how come we make such a good team." He gave me a pretend punch on the arm and Bennet, a quick kiss on the cheek. Then he climbed back in the Jeep and roared off.

Bennet and I headed to the booking desks to arrange our flights. We'd recovered Strauss's rare book and made an incredible archaeological find in the process. Her article would be a sensation. Yet despite all that, she seemed in uncharacteristically dark spirits.

"I've changed my mind," she said at the ticket counter. "I'm not going back to the U.S. right now. I can stay with a friend in London. After all, who knows how long it'll be before I get to see Europe again?" I heard the false note in her voice. She wouldn't look me in the eye. She'd been through a grueling experience. Maybe she just needed some time to herself, to let the bad memories fade.

"Hey, Bennet. Everything okay?"

She nodded absentmindedly. "It will be when I get to the U.K." She scored her flight to London with a quick transfer in Istanbul. I'd have to stay in Istanbul overnight before flying back to America. She slept most of the way on the plane from Van to Istanbul. I shook her awake about twenty minutes before we landed.

Bennet was quiet as we collected our baggage and walked to the gate for her connecting flight. When we reached it, she twisted off the fake wedding band and tossed it in a refuse container. "No more need for that," she said, a tinge of bitterness in her voice. "I've decided not to write the article after all. I just want to forget all this happened. There was nothing good about it. I'll email you the draft I started and all my notes and pictures. You can do whatever you want with them."

I put my arm around her. "Maybe you should give it a little more time. Leave it for a few weeks and see whether you still feel that way."

She almost cringed from my touch and backed away. "No. I won't change my mind."

"What about Strauss's advance?"

"I'll send him whatever money I have left. If he wants the rest he can sue me." There was an edge to her laugh.

"When you say you just want to forget it all, you're not referring to us, are you?"

She looked away, not willing to meet my eyes. "Yes, I do mean that. We're not a good match, John. You're a dangerous man in more ways than one. We should say our goodbyes now. Let's not prolong the inevitable."

A pang of hurt contracted my chest. I felt stunned. It must have showed.

"Take care of yourself, John." Bennet grabbed her bag and started to walk off. Then she stopped and turned, aware of how brusque her words must have seemed. "I didn't know it would turn out this way. Remember that."

I started after her but she waved me away.

Soon after Bennet's plane left the ground, I got a text message from Diane Chen. Loki was missing. She'd run through the entrance in the dog park and across the street, heavy with traffic, before Diane could stop her. Two days ago.

Fifty-Two

March 18, 2005
New York

I came home to a sad, empty apartment and stared defeat in the eye. My place felt like a tomb without Bennet and Loki. Diane had left me a long note explaining which animal rescue centers she'd canvassed but I tried them all over again. You never know. I didn't have the guts to speak to Dr. Jefferson in person, figuring he'd tear my head off for carelessly losing the dog. I sent him an email instead and got a terse reply back that no one had brought her in or contacted them. Loki, it seemed, was gone for good. I prayed she hadn't been hit by another car.

And I hoped Bennet would change her mind about me. Despite the short time she spent here, she'd filled the place with life. I missed her more than I'd thought possible.

Detective Shea sent a formal note saying I could pick up the contents of my treasure chest from FBI headquarters. I was glad for that at least.

I jumped in the shower and let hot water run over me for a long while. Then, after I'd changed into something comfortable, I poured myself a stiff bourbon. I stretched out on the couch, swirled the amber liquid around in my glass, and took a healthy swallow. Pain started to hammer at my knee again.

The mission had succeeded beyond my wildest expectations. At least Strauss would be a happy man. Yet learning the truth about my birth had plunged me into the blackest of moods. Evelyn's attempt to hide the truth had sheltered me from that dark story, and I found myself wanting those phantom, died-in-an-earthquake Turkish parents back. But it was too late for that. The price we pay for knowledge.

By rights I should go to see Evelyn right away. I told myself she'd be tired, that it was after dinner already. In truth I needed to think more carefully about how to broach the subject. I knew the news would upset her.

My night terrors had all but disappeared since entering the salt caves. I wondered if it might be the result of physical exhaustion. Whatever the reason, I hoped they were finished for good. Time would tell.

My mind went back to the first time I'd seen Strauss's artifacts, the ones taken by Helmstetter from the cart I found in the salt caves. Tricia Ross claimed they dated back 5500 years to preliterate times. It seemed to confirm that the travelers—clearly Sumerian, judging by their dress and the pottery found with them—had indeed migrated from their founding settlements in the mountains of Iran. Signs that a flourishing trade was already well established between the young Sumerian city-states in southern Iraq and their original home in Eden.

I got out the bowl I'd found in the caves and turned it in my hand. Simple geometric shapes superimposed on a grayish green background. As Rohl had pointed out, this type of pottery first appeared in northwestern Iran and Anatolia. It showed up later in the early Mesopotamian cities of southern Iraq. More evidence that the Sumerians may have originated in the mountains near Lakes Urmia and Van.

On the long plane trip home I'd read through the latter pages of Samuel's journal. The revelations they contained amazed me. In the early twentieth century a professor, George A. Barton, translated from Sumerian tablets something he called the Kharsag Epic, which recounted the earliest settlements of the Sumerian people. Samuel had transcribed some of its original words—concrete descriptions of a mountain fortress called Ed-in under the protection of a snake goddess. And that fortress encompassed a magnificent red-walled garden with granaries, a water reservoir, and a tree plantation.

> *The Serpent Lady ... spoke of creating a watered garden—with tall trees ...*
> *She spoke of the sunny, watered settlement—of the future for it; ...*
> *The mountainside with much overflowing water— all was brightness*

The inscriptions even hinted at a reason the people were driven out from this Eden—storm water, flooding, sickness. Had the original mountain settlement of Eden been damaged by floods and its people overcome by some form of plague? Did the travelers I'd found in the salt cave come from this mountain paradise? None of this could be considered hard proof of Sumerian origins or the Garden of Eden's location, but they had convinced me.

As Yersan and I had walked away from the temple I'd remarked on the oddity of there being only one cart rather than a whole caravan.

"The area around Tabriz is situated on a main artery of the Silk Road," Yersan had said. "But that's only its more recent name. These trade routes stretch far back in time. Over thousands of years, the landscape has changed dramatically. The cart may have been part of a larger company, perhaps in the lead of a caravan as it moved along the plain. The cave roof at that time was perhaps only a thin crust and the heavily laden lead cart fell through. Over thousands of years, erosion of rock from the higher elevations and sediments blown by the wind covered that section of the plain to become the series of foothills there now." He shrugged. "Who really knows? It's my guess, only."

My phone rang and broke into my thoughts.

"Madison? It's Lucas Strauss."

"I just got back. Haven't had time to call you."

"That's quite all right." His voice came through the phone like a tinny cackle. "Our mutual friend tells me you've been quite successful."

"You've been talking to Bennet?" That didn't please me; the news wasn't hers to offer. "I thought she'd washed her hands of the whole thing."

"Yes, well ..." He cleared his throat. "She's reluctant to continue with the article. Not a very reliable young lady, as it turns out."

"She had a very bad experience. I don't blame her."

"When may I expect to see you?"

I looked at the side table where *The Steganographia* sat beside Samuel's open journal, its beaten up leather covers a testament to all it had gone through. "Soon. Possibly tomorrow. If I do come then, it'll be late in the day."

"That would suit me just fine." His voice had taken on a strange ingratiating tone very much at odds with what I'd experienced before. I didn't trust it. "Hate to rush you. I'll have a bonus ready for all your good work."

"I'll call to let you know when I'm arriving."

He thanked me and hung up.

I poured myself a second bourbon. And after that, a third. There wasn't much left in the bottle so I downed that too. I struggled over to my bed and crashed for the night. Around five in the morning I woke abruptly. When I tried to sit up, I couldn't move. Minutes of dread passed by before my body came under my control again. I'd been wrong. The night terrors were back.

I got out of bed and opened a window in the living room, thinking the fresh air might help calm me down. Listening to New York wake up has always been a pleasure for me. My favorite time of the day. I'd often come rolling home from some party and instead of going to bed, sit and listen to the squeal of the trash trucks, the bang of an iron gate, cars zooming past, footsteps down the sidewalk— someone on their way to an early shift—and the reverential quiet in between. The day getting started. The great city readying itself for the deluge of millions, each one wanting something from it.

I closed my eyes, liking the feel of the cold air on my face. A stray dog yelped somewhere down below, probably in a contest for garbage with raccoons. Another yelp. A very familiar sounding one. I didn't bother tugging on a shirt, just snatched my keys and raced down the stairs in the jeans I hadn't bothered to take off.

A bedraggled black dog with a torn and dirty cast trailing from her back leg limped toward me. I scooped her up, almost crushing her to my chest. Her strange yellow eyes seemed to ask why I'd abandoned her. I was jubilant. Reuniting with Loki seemed to make a lot of things right.

Back in the apartment I gave her food and fresh water, Loki lapping it all up greedily. She'd lost weight again. I wondered whether she'd come here every night looking for me. I wound a clean bandage carefully around the torn cast, musing that now we both had bad legs. Then I carried her to the armchair in front of the window where she curled up contentedly in my lap. I put my head back. We both fell into a peaceful sleep.

Fifty-Three

March 19, 2005

When I woke up, two messages were waiting for me. I'd been holding out hope that I'd hear from Bennet, but other than sending me an email with all her pictures and notes, she hadn't spared even one personal word. Diane texted to ask whether I was home yet. It felt good to be able to tell her about Loki.

I took Loki with me when I retrieved the contents of my treasure chest from the FBI. Back home, I restored everything to the vault except the cameo. It bore a beautifully carved head of a woman whose identity had always been a mystery to me—and now I was resolved to find out who she was. I scooped up Loki again and headed out to visit Evelyn.

When I arrived she lifted her arms from the wheelchair rests for a hug, only to drop them when she spotted Loki.

"This is the black dog you told me about?" she asked. "Will it bite?"

I laughed. "Nope. Loki will be quite content to settle down with the bone I brought. She's very friendly." I took out an antler bone, all the doggy rage these days apparently. Loki snatched it from my hands and retreated with her prize. We'd never had pets at home. I realized now that growing up in the place she did, as the daughter of a sheep herder, Evelyn regarded animals as strictly utilitarian.

"You're shocking me," Evelyn said. "What happened to your beard?"

I rubbed my hand over my gristled jaw. "Just thought I'd try it for a change."

"Well, I don't like it. Please grow it back."

After I'd made us some mint tea in the alcove that served as her kitchen, I settled on the small sofa—the only seating in Evelyn's one main room—as she wheeled her chair beside me. I launched into a sanitized version of my time in Turkey, feeling the lump in my throat swell at the prospect of talking about Kandovan.

"And where is your girlfriend—that Miss Bennet?"

"She stopped off in London on our way back. Visiting with friends."

Evelyn sighed. "Easy to be any place in this world now, isn't it?"

I took her hand. "Yes, Evie. Listen, I went somewhere else too. Not just Turkey."

I drew in a deep breath. "I went to Kandovan. I met your brother, sister, and father. I know everything." Before she could react, I leaned over and folded her in my arms. I could feel a tremble run through her frail body. She cried softly for a few minutes and then sat back. She took a tissue out of her pocket and wiped her eyes.

"How did you know enough to go there?"

This time I lied, not wanting her to know I'd looked through her things. "Strangely enough I was sent there by a client to retrieve a rare book. I ran into Alaz Nemat and he saw the mark on my jaw. It reminded him of his sister's baby. So we began a conversation and one thing led to another." I avoided mentioning my experience in the salt caves or in the garden but said I'd fallen ill while in Kandovan and her sister Marya had very kindly looked after me.

I held out the beautiful cameo with a woman's face etched in profile. "I think this is a picture of my mother. It's you, isn't it?"

She'd seen it many times before and glanced at it now. "No, John. You are wrong."

"It's all right, Evie. You can tell me now. Knowing this makes me very happy."

But Evelyn wasn't listening. "You said you were sent to Kandovan for a rare book. What book?" she said sharply.

"The one George Helmstetter stole from his employer, written by a sixteenth-century scholar named Trithemius."

She turned pale. This time I worried I'd gone too far. "It's okay. We can talk about this some other time if it upsets you too much."

She sighed then looked up at me. "No. I should say it now. Keeping secrets is not good. Samuel tried to tell me that. But I insisted because … I made a promise to hide the book and … to keep another secret."

"A secret?"

Now it was her turn to give me some solace. She patted my arm. "You said that Marya cared for you when you were taken ill. Did that not strike you as strange?"

"Why would it? She was a kind woman. I think she just felt sorry for me. They were overjoyed to hear about you. Marya especially."

"John," she said sternly. "Although you are family, you're a stranger, a male, and worse, an American man from the West. Even an older married woman would not be allowed to touch you like that or be alone with you."

"They're not Muslims."

"No, their codes are even stricter that way. Yet there is an exception."

"What are you trying to say?"

Evelyn's voice trembled. "If she was your mother—that would be allowed."

I thought back to Marya's steadfast care, sitting up night after night no matter how tired she was, her glances when she thought I wasn't looking, how tender they seemed. Her sadness when she knew she was seeing me for the last time.

Loki whined and came up to me but I barely noticed her. "God, Evelyn. I had no idea. You're my aunt then?"

She turned her kind, dark eyes on me. "Not of the blood, no. I was an orphan. My parents died of influenza one very cold winter. The Nemats took me in when I was six and raised me as their own. I owe a great debt to them for that."

"Did you know about my father?"

She cast her eyes down then. "Yes. The village men killed him. In a cruel way. They were going to come after Marya, too; she had to flee from them. And they planned to end your life, you, just an innocent baby. They feared you because of that mark on your jaw. They said it was an evil mark and that it showed you were the same as your father. Marya pleaded with me to take you away and save you. I put on a heavy scarf that hid most of my head and wrapped you in a serape. Alaz rode me out on a horse. Marya would take another route. Go through one of the mountain roads and join us later. But she was not fast enough and they caught her. They beat her very badly but they did not kill her, because the baby was gone.

"After that, I knew you would not be safe even in Tabriz and we were not sure whether Marya would live. I fled to Mosul with you and met Samuel. He fell in love with you—and me. The chance to come to America seemed like a dream. And that is how it went."

Again, I reeled. The world seemed to wobble on its axis. "I am as much your son as hers, Evie," I finally managed to say. "You raised me."

She smiled then. "Yes. That is how I wanted it to be. I am so lucky compared to poor Marya."

I remembered Marya's scarred face and felt sick at the thought of what they'd done to her. "Why did you never get in touch with them again, once you were safe in New York?"

"What do you mean? I did! Every letter was sent back. They didn't want to know about me—or you."

The men in the family, she meant. They'd decided the bastard son was best forgotten. If the price was leaving Marya in the dark about my fate, so be it.

"Why not tell me this long ago? Or at least when I asked you about my parents."

"Marya made me promise. The magician beguiled her. She fell in love. After, she was ashamed. And I thought it was better you didn't know you were born into a tragedy."

"But then why go to all that trouble to hide the book?"

"Marya believed it to be magical. Helmstetter put that idea in her head. She was afraid that if she destroyed it, bad fortune would come to her."

"It did anyway."

"But you inherited one gift from your real father, so perhaps there was a little good in his soul after all."

"What was that?"

"The medallion in your treasure box. The green-colored one with the picture of a vulture on it."

So Helmstetter *had* taken the medallion from the salt caves, and it had found its way to me.

I showed Evelyn the picture I'd taken of Marya and Alaz the day before I left the Nemats. She gazed at it for a long time. I promised to frame it for her. Through her tears she told me how grateful she was that I'd given her her family back.

I got up to go soon after that. All the emotion had exhausted her. I leaned over to give her a kiss and closed the door quietly on my way out.

Fifty-Four

On the cab ride home my mind still churned over what Evelyn told me. "The sins of the father" reverberated through my brain. I felt remorseful about Marya, although she could have told me herself. Perhaps she preferred it that way. What had happened to her so long ago likely still festered in her heart. It certainly did in mine. Samuel and Evelyn had been more than good substitute parents. For that I was grateful.

I stopped off at the apartment to get some supplies for my drive to Strauss's place. I also texted Alice Jacobs to tell her I no longer needed the pages she was working on for the reproduction and would send her a check for whatever she'd already done. Then I tucked *The Steganographia* into my jacket pocket and scooped up Loki. I wanted to get away, to drive, to listen to music. The long trek to see Lucas Strauss suited perfectly.

As I approached the Porsche I called Strauss to tell him I was on my way. I spread a bath towel on the passenger seat beside me for Loki to lie on, put Coldplay on the iPod, and headed for the Thruway.

It was much colder now than my first trip out. Ice tinged the pools of water left over from the flood; the fields were white and stiff with frost. But the Thruway was clear and dry and I made very good time. I arrived at Strauss's place just as the afternoon began to slip into twilight.

This time the buzzer worked; Strauss's voice sailed over the intercom. "Glad you've arrived safely, Madison. The gate will open momentarily." His voice carried a jovial tone, although it sounded as if he had a frog in his throat. Living above that damp, dark first floor probably wasn't a great idea for an elderly man. I clipped on Loki's leash and we headed through the wood along the path to the house. She held herself tensely as we walked, hackles raised and tail down, clearly feeling more anxious the closer we got to the house. No fawns or bears this time, though; I guessed Strauss had pulled the plug.

The magician waited for me inside the gloomy, cavernous main-floor room. He had on an old fedora and a Burberry scarf wrapped around his neck. "Just got back from my walk," he said, touching the tip of his hat. Loki growled at him.

Strauss jumped back at the sound and glared at the dog. With her black fur, he hadn't noticed her in the dim light. He frowned. "I can't allow that creature in here." His voice croaked. "Apologies," he continued, "I've come down with a sore throat."

I tightened my hand on her leash. "Then we'll conclude our business outside. When I was away, I almost lost her. I'm not letting her out of my sight."

"All right," he said, "but keep the damn thing leashed and close to you; I don't want it anywhere near me."

In the living room upstairs, what had seemed an elegant, smartly appointed space felt cheerless now, despite the fire burning in the grate. Only one light was on and the blinds were shut. Strauss groaned slightly when he took his seat near the fire and put his hand to his back. "These old bones trouble me greatly in winter." Reflection from the firelight flickered over his features, distorting them. "I'm afraid it's just you and I tonight. My man Harrison is off today." He coughed a little and wiped his lips with a tissue.

I sat in the armchair nearest the door. Despite Strauss's orders, I let the leash drop. Loki parked herself at my feet, her ears perked up and her hackles still slightly raised. I gave her a pat to show her she had nothing to fear.

Then I looked up at Strauss. "This shouldn't take long."

"No, indeed not." He smiled and his cold eyes fixed on the dog again. "Have you had that animal for long? I suspect not. Am I right?"

"A few weeks, that's all. I guess you could say she strayed into my life."

"Strange," Strauss mused. "How fitting you'd choose a black dog for a companion. Faust's familiar was a dog. A black stray, too. What do you make of that?"

His dallying was getting on my nerves. I'd only just arrived but wanted to get out. Loki growled again, perhaps picking up on his hostility. I reached down to calm her with another pat. "It's all right, Loki," I said.

Strauss's teeth showed when he attempted to smile. "Loki? You named her after the Norse demon? Most apropos. Canines haven't always been regarded as a friend to man, you know. They were associated with the underworld; the superstitious believed they haunted byways and bridges to draw the unwary into danger."

"May we get on with things? It's a long drive back and already late in the day."

His gaze shifted to his desk, a contemporary design made of tempered glass with chrome drawers. A matching cabinet stood against the wall behind it. "I understand your trip proved hazardous. You almost died?"

It was my turn to frown. "Bennet told you that too?"

"Yes. We had a long phone conversation yesterday." Strauss paused. "My promise has been fulfilled, as I believe you now know your true birth story. Although it didn't sound like the warmest of family reunions."

My face reddened in irritation. Bennet had no business discussing my personal affairs with him. "That means you know about Helmstetter too? That he was my father? Bennet shouldn't have said anything."

At the mention of Helmstetter's name, his jaw tensed and his lips formed an ugly line. "Please don't blame Bennet. I knew all along he'd gotten a child off a local woman and the calamities that followed. I only discovered you were that child when Tricia Ross inadvertently let it drop."

I could feel my temper building. Loki whimpered, sensing my dismay. "How did you find out about Helmstetter and my mother?"

Strauss brought the tissue to his mouth again, coughed, and wheezed as he took a breath. Then he loosened his scarf, fumbled with the buttons on his jacket, and undid the top two. The metal buttons gleamed in the firelight. "I went to Kandovan myself on Helmstetter's trail two years after he absconded with my possessions. It was too late. By then he was long dead."

"What the hell. You didn't bother to tell me any of this? You said you'd found out only recently that Helmstetter traveled there."

"No. I eventually pried the information out of his mistress about where he'd gone."

"So the whole thing was a charade—risking my life to send me over there when you already knew Helmstetter's fate."

His gaze settled on me again. "Not at all. You returned with the book, did you not? And would you have gone over there just to retrieve the volume for me? The inducement of learning about your birth story provided a necessary incentive."

"It was all a sham." My mind went back to Bennet's cold shoulder at the Van airport.

"You knew Bennet all along, didn't you? She told me that, you know. She was aware of all this, wasn't she?"

"I was well acquainted with her parents, yes. I knew her from the day she was born." He gave me a sly smile, and waited for his words to register.

The reality began to dawn and he saw it written on my face. I barely heard his next words.

He nodded slowly. "Yes. Bennet's mother was my former assistant, the woman who married Helmstetter. Shortly after she discovered he had a mistress, he abandoned both women. He left her broken and bitter. She remarried soon after and gave birth to Bennet a year later, but never really recovered from Helmstetter's betrayal. Bennet would come home from school to find her mother half out of it from drink. Eventually the marriage broke up, and Bennet was left to cope with her mother as best she could. She grew up with Helmstetter's phantom hanging over her head. It ruined her childhood." He tapped his fingers absentmindedly on the chair arm. "I insisted that Bennet not tell you. If it's any solace, she resisted that—strongly—before she gave in."

"And Bennet knew ... about me?"

"She had no idea Helmstetter was your father, if that's what you mean. I kept that valuable piece of information from her. She would never have agreed to get involved otherwise. You seem to have gotten under her skin. When she called, she claimed she couldn't face loving the son of the man who destroyed her mother. The connection seemed too ominous. She was furious with me."

I felt the earth move under my feet. In my mind's eye, I saw Bennet's blank face at the airport, her blowing me off, wanting nothing more to do with me.

"Poor Bennet. She's quite bereft now and she really is poor, you know," Strauss said. "But don't you see? It has turned out all right in the end." He glanced at his desk again. "Forgive me for my little game. You'll find a check on my desk over there. I've rewarded you for your trouble quite liberally. You may leave the volume there too." He shifted in his chair as if he was in pain and reached around to press his hand to his back.

I welcomed putting an end to this commission and my association with Strauss. He'd been honest about one thing at least. When I picked up the check, I saw he'd paid me double what we negotiated. I took Trithemius's book out of my jacket pocket and laid it on the desk. As I did, I happened to glance at the cabinet and saw the three Mesopotamian artifacts arranged neatly on the upper shelf—the two cylinder seals and the statue.

Perhaps that's what reminded me of Tricia Ross. And then the flash of firelight I'd noticed earlier on the metal buttons of Strauss's jacket connected to a memory. The scene in Ross's kitchen flooded back. The small round thing I'd seen among the tea things. It had eluded my memory, the telltale sign of who'd tortured her. It was a bloody metal button, just like the one Strauss pulled out of his arm the night of the spiritualist séance when I first met him.

I rounded on him, ready to accuse him of killing Ross, then reeled back in shock.

He'd stood up and moved in front of the mantel, his body silhouetted by the orange glow of the fire. He had a gun in his hand.

"What the fuck are you doing?"

"Completing our transaction to my satisfaction."

"You're depraved. And far worse for murdering Ross."

He let the accusation float by him. "The good professor decided to report the three artifacts to the FBI. She'd finally concluded they must have been stolen. Graciously, she wanted to give me a chance to voluntarily hand them over first and summoned me to her house to tell me."

"So you proceeded to beat her to death?"

His lack of response was all the confirmation I needed. My stomach turned.

"So what was the deal about me? Were you taking a warped form of revenge on Helmstetter by putting his son through hell?"

Strauss's expression was full of menace. "Do you recall the Bible verse I recited at my channeling in Carroll Gardens?"

I remembered he'd stared at me after quoting that passage. At the time I didn't understand why.

"I'll refresh your memory," he continued.

> "When the unclean spirit has gone out of a person, it passes through waterless places seeking rest, and finding none it says, 'I will return to the house from which I came.' And when it comes, it finds the house swept and put in order. Then it brings seven other spirits more evil than itself, and they enter and dwell there. And the last state of that person is worse than the first.

"I meant the passage for you as much as for Gina, for that is your fate. You'll recall that Helmstetter believed himself to be a direct descendant of the real Faust?"

"You told me that."

"Faust sold his immortal soul not for fame and fortune as is commonly believed but for knowledge. It's an old story, isn't it, stretching all the way back to Adam and Eve's desire to eat of the fruit of the tree. In some respects Marlowe and Goethe recycled that myth. From Adam's time, man has not been content with his lot in life. He must rival the gods and always have more.

"The original Faust was never identified when he died. And some believe the devil made good the bargain. That he granted immortality to Faust's tortured soul."

"Do you hear yourself? That's crazy."

He smiled. "Perhaps. But Helmstetter clung to this idea. It's what prompted his own search for eternal life."

"Well, I'm sure Bennet told you all about that too. It turned out to simply be a state of mind. Time vanishes under the influence of certain hallucinogens."

"Don't be a fool. Helmstetter was brilliant. His mental capabilities totally eclipsed mine. Had he remained in America, he would have become one of the foremost magicians in history. He knew all about hallucinogens, would never have traveled halfway across the globe simply to partake of them. It is said the original Faust experienced a moment of transcendence. So too did George Helmstetter. Somehow, he discovered the secret of transformation in Trithemius's writings. He achieved his dream.

"But to close the knot he needed a suitable candidate. Someone weak. A personality barely formed. A fetus in the womb."

Thunder rolled in my head. I felt as though I was suffocating. I shook myself to get some sense back. "What are you implying?"

"Bennet told me you're experiencing nightmares. Sleep paralysis. You're losing your own identity, Madison. It's come slowly at first but it's speeding up, isn't it? Those men in Kandovan thought they'd killed Helmstetter. They were mistaken. When he died he was no more than a husk. And that's what you're becoming now. The breaks will grow stronger and much more frequent. They'll happen during the day when you're awake, not just when you're sleeping. They'll begin to merge, the personality of John Madison becoming more and more transient. George Helmstetter will be renewed. He didn't just spawn you. He possessed you."

Strauss gave me an icy smile then. "But Helmstetter did not bargain on my seeking revenge."

At that moment, Loki bared her teeth and howled. While we were talking she must have crept right up to his feet without either of us noticing. Strauss reared back in surprise, angled the gun down haphazardly, and fired.

The bullet tore through his thigh. His body jerked and he crashed into the fire grate.

Fifty-Five

The gunshot deafened me. For an instant I thought I'd been hit and terror had made me numb to the pain. I leapt over to Strauss, pulled him away from the fire, ripped off the now flaming scarf and threw it back on the coals. I used my jacket to beat out the flames in his hair and then put my hand on his neck to feel for a pulse. I couldn't find one. His skin felt slippery where I'd torn away the scarf.

One of the fire-grate pickets had punctured his temple when he fell; blood now surged around the injury. His body shuddered with convulsions. I waited. Despite my sense of horror, a new feeling welled up inside me. A manic, exuberant joy. I'd escaped what minutes ago I thought would be certain death.

Loki had retreated into a corner. I picked her up, grabbed my jacket, and plucked *The Steganographia* off the desk. As I hurried out I cast a longing gaze back at the artifacts in the cabinet, remembering Strauss had promised them to me in exchange for retrieving the book. I couldn't afford to be found with them now.

I thanked God Strauss had chosen such an out-of-the-way place. I got a plastic bag from the trunk to wrap my jacket in, charred by the flames and stained from Strauss's blood. I'd dispose of it later.

After a two-hour drive I judged it safe to stop at an all-night service station. I parked the car near a row of tractor trailers and sank my head on my arms. From the time I'd walked out of Strauss's living room I'd been on autopilot. The adrenalin had finally subsided, leaving me shaking.

Was Strauss right about Helmstetter invading my identity, slowly taking me over? *"You're a dangerous man, John, in more ways than one,"* Bennet had said. Did she sense something about me that even I wasn't aware of? Memories of my last sojourn in Iraq came back to me. Things I couldn't make sense of at the time. The two apparitions in the Kutha throne room who hadn't attacked me but instead signaled some kind of bond. My lack of compassion for the violent acts I'd carried out. How I'd felt at times. Not evil, just coldly amoral. Had those been Helmstetter's emotions coming to the surface?

No, it was impossible. Strauss was insane, his virulent hatred of Helmstetter so extreme that he'd concocted a bizarre fantasy about me. I felt utterly drained. It was all I could do to lift my head from my arms and sink back on the headrest. I stayed that way for hours, not dozing but not able to summon up the energy for much else either. When I revived, I started up the Porsche and sped off again.

April 21, 2005
New York

Weeks went by before I realized Strauss hadn't lied to me. Although I'd been feeling restless and out of sorts, I had just about persuaded myself there was nothing to fear.

Then Strauss's prediction began to come true.

A balmy day beckoned, the signs of spring just beginning to make themselves felt. I took Loki to the dog park in the square. She was no longer in a cast and had learned how to play with other dogs. A woman sat down beside me and unclasped the leash from her spaniel; he ran off suddenly and the leash fell from her grasp. I bent down to pick it up for her and something shifted, as if a plane of glass had suddenly dropped down between us.

"Thanks," the woman said. I barely heard her. The hum of traffic became a loud chorus in my ears. I felt nauseated. "Thank you," the woman said more loudly and held out her hand for the leash. I dropped it on the bench and got up without acknowledging her.

A memory had come to me. I was a young boy, perhaps twelve—no more. I wore a dirty pair of jeans that were too large for me and a man's faded shirt. I was in a farm field, all alone. A windy day and cloudy. In the distance I could see a rickety old farmhouse and dilapidated red barn. I'd flattened down the dried corn stalks to make a rough circle and looped a piece of twine around the neck of one of my mother's hens. When I tightened the loop, the hen struggled and flapped its wings in panic as its air was cut off. I passed my hand over its neck. The twine seemed to disappear. The hen scrambled up and ran away.

Not my memory. It belonged to someone else. My father. A boy raised on a dirt-poor farm who grew to become a gifted magician. A man who embraced dark knowledge and used his own son as a vehicle to renew himself. I shuddered and tried to wrench myself from the memory. To force my own personality back again. The drone of the traffic subsided. My vision cleared. Loki ran toward me. I picked her up and pressed her to my chest as if her warm body could obliterate my fears.

I was fracturing, the shell splitting just as Strauss had predicted it would, and now the new being, George Helmstetter, was emerging. I made my way home, almost unconscious of crossing the street, taking the elevator, opening my apartment door, removing Loki's leash. I collapsed onto my sofa in front of the long unused fireplace, terrified that another false memory would come to haunt me. This first schism during wakefulness had come entirely unbidden and out of my control. I now had a ringside seat to my own destruction.

Once some time had passed I calmed down a little. There had to be a way. Maybe some knowledgeable person could guide me in overcoming the process of disintegration. My mind cast about wildly. And then I remembered something Veronica Sills had said. *"There's always a way out if you know the way in."* My glance fell on *The Steganographia* sitting in the glass cabinet. Could I recognize in its pages the rituals Helmstetter had followed to achieve his transformation? I did, after all, have a perverse ally—the ability to call upon Helmstetter's own memory. He'd done the hard work by deciphering the book; my task would be to recall the steps he took and find a way to reverse them. That gave me some hope of staving off the metamorphosis. But I knew I had little time.

The next day I left New York with Loki and rented a cabin in the Catskills close to the Devil's Path where my friend and I had hiked months before. If pushing myself to physical extremes had helped ward off the sleep paralysis then, it might also delay Helmstetter's resurrection now. I rose early every morning and spent hours scaling the path, choosing the most hazardous portions of the route, concentrating on the climb as a way to force back my fears. Evenings were devoted to studying Trithemius's book. All this achieved a balance of sorts but I made no real headway.

Early spring in the Catskills often brings uncertain weather. One day it'll be fine and warm, the next brittle cold with high winds and frost, especially at higher elevations. On this morning I'd tried to free-climb a particularly difficult stretch, a high precipice of limestone off the official path. I should never have attempted it alone. If I met with an accident, no one would know. Even with a partner it would have been foolhardy. It had turned very cold and the cliff was slick with a fine patina of ice. About three-quarters of the way up I reached a brim of rock so narrow it could hardly be called a ledge. I balanced on it to get my breath and looked below me to a hundred-foot drop, jagged, slippery rock all the way down.

It had not been a good day. I'd felt especially despondent, hopeless about ever being able to reclaim my peace of mind. So easy to just slip off. And my choosing more and more perilous routes, I saw now, unconsciously pointed me in one direction. Perhaps that was the best way. Having so far failed at unearthing Helmstetter's method, I could cheat my demon father by ending it for us both.

Just then a shadow passed over me. I craned my neck and spotted a giant bird—a vulture. Its wingspan had to be at least seven feet. I'd never seen one that size anywhere in the state.

When it settled on the lip of the precipice above, a warmth stole over me. Perhaps it was just my imagination, but the bird had a strange presence. It seemed to bond with me, to give me courage. It took off suddenly with a graceful lifting of its huge wings, and as it soared upward it reminded me of that other being. The ancient priest I'd met in Eden, the vulture its emblem. The presence who had guided me into an unknown night, who I now realized was with me still, had never really left my side.

As I watched the bird grow smaller until it was only a dot in the sky, I sensed I would win the battle with the man who sired me.

Notes

Part One

5   *The only magic is really that of words:* Dr. Thomas Ernst, as
      quoted in "German Monk's 500-Year-Old Mystery Solved,"
      Pittsburgh Post-Gazette, June 29, 1998.

Chapter 6

33   *When the unclean spirit ... that person is worse than the first:*
      Luke 11:24–26 (English Standard Version Bible).

Chapter 18

98   *Aratta's battlements ... where the cypress grows:* "Lugalbanda
      and the Anzu Bird" (The ETCSL Project, Faculty of Oriental
      Studies, University of Oxford, 2003).

Chapter 20

112   *A river flowed out of Eden ... And the fourth river is the Euphrates:*
      Genesis 2:10–14 (English Standard Version Bible).

Chapter 23

131   *That man, about whom you wrote me ... the teachings of the Holy Church:* Frank Baron, *Doctor Faustus: From History to Legend* (Munich: Wilhelm Fink Verlag, 1978).

Part Two

147   *I know your works and where you dwell ... where Satan's Throne is:* Revelation 2:13 (King James 2000 Bible).

Chapter 31

183   *How art thou fallen from heaven, O Lucifer!* Isaiah 14:12 (King James Bible).

Chapter 32

192   *Genesis 2:13 describes ... the Mountain of Kush:* David Rohl, *Legend: The Genesis of Civilization* (London: Random House, 1998).

Part Three

195   *Food of death they will set ... I have spoken, hold fast:* From the Mesopotamian myth *Adapa and the South Wind* (cuneiform parallels to the Old Testament), R.W. Rogers (London: Oxford University Press, 1912).

Chapter 45

250   *And the Lord God planted a garden in Eden ... every tree that is pleasant to the sight and good to eat:* Genesis 2:8–9 (English Standard Version Bible).

Chapter 47

262   *Of the Tree of Knowledge ... thou shalt surely die:* Genesis 2:17 (King James Bible).

Chapter 52

281   *The Serpent Lady ... all was brightness:* From the Nippur tablets, "The Destruction of Kharsag," as documented by Christian O'Brien and Barbara Joy O'Brien, *The Genius of the Few: The Story of Those Who Founded the Garden of Eden* (Padukah, KY: Collector Books, 1999).

Bibliography

The following books, articles, and websites have all been valuable sources of information.

Books

Baigent, Michael, and Richard Leigh. *The Elixir and the Stone.* London: Random House, 1997.

Black, Jeremy, and Anthony Green; illustrations by Tessa Rickards. *Gods, Demons and Symbols of Ancient Mesopotamia: An Illustrated Dictionary.* Austin: University of Texas Press, 2003.

Cline, Eric H. *From Eden to Exile.* Washington, D.C.: National Geographic Society, 2007.

Collins, Andrew. *From the Ashes of Angels: The Forbidden Legacy of a Fallen Race.* Rochester, VT: Bear & Company, 2001.

Rohl, David. *Legend: The Genesis of Civilization.* London: Random House, 1998.

Walker, Reginald Arthur. *The Land of Eden.* Rhyl, U.K.: Voxov, 1987.

Wilensky-Lanford, Brook. *Paradise Lust: Searching for the Garden of Eden.* New York: Grove Press, 1980.

Articles and Websites

Atsma, Aaron J. "Asklepios," *Theoi Project,* www.theoi.com/Ouranios /Asklepios.html.

Bennet, Dina. "Border Crossing Guide: Van, Turkey to Tabriz, Iran," *Matador Network,* June 11, 2012, http://matadornetwork .com/trips/border-crossing-guide-van-turkey-to-tabriz-iran.

Bouglouan, Nicole. "Bearded Vulture," www.oiseaux-birds.com/card -bearded-vulture.html.

British Museum. "Adam and Eve Cylinder Seal," www.britishmuseum .org/explore/highlights/highlight_objects/me/a/adam_and _eve_cylinder_seal.aspx.

Brown, Peter. "Artificial Cranial Deformation: A Component in the Variation in Pleistocene Australian Aboriginal Crania," *Archeology in Oceania, 16*(3), October 1981.

Danti, Michael. "Returning to Iran," *Expedition, 47*(2), University of Pennsylvania Museum of Archaeology and Anthropology, July 2005, www.penn.museum/sites/expedition /returning-to-iran.

Eduljee, K.E. "Azerbaijan, Urmia, N. Zagros," *Heritage Institute,* www.heritageinstitute.com/zoroastrianism/urmia.

Eduljee, K.E. "Kandovan, Lake Urmia Region," *Heritage Institute,* www.heritageinstitute.com/zoroastrianism/urmia/kandovan_2 .html.

Edjulee, K.E. "Persian Gardens," *Heritage Institute,* www.heritageinstitute .com/zoroastrianism/garden.

"Faust," www.faust.com.

Gardner, Lawrence. "Kharsag Research Project," *The Golden Age Project,* www.goldenageproject.org.uk/kharsag_texts_archive.php.

Hajizan, Nizam. "Salt Lake in Urmia, Iran," *Koleski 360,* http ://koleksi360.blogspot.ca/2012/05/salt-lake-in-urmia-iran.html.

Hole, Frank. "Neolithic Age in Iran," *Encyclopedia Iranica,* July 20, 2004, www.iranicaonline.org/articles/neolithic-age-in-iran.

Kalush, Bill. "The Conjuring Arts Research Center," http ://conjuringarts.org.

Kobek, Jarett. "The Vanishing Yezidi of Iraq," *NYU Alumnae Magazine,* Spring 2010, www.nyu.edu/alumni.magazine /issue14/14_feature_yezidi.html.

Luongo, Michael. "Fighting Back with Faith: Inside the Yezidis' Iraqi Temple," *The Daily Beast,* August 21, 2014, www.thedailybeast .com/articles/2014/08/21/fighting-back-with-faith-inside-the -yazidis-iraqi-temple.html.

Mayo Clinic. "Post-traumatic stress disorder (PSTD)," www.mayoclinic .org/diseases-conditions/post-traumatic-stress-disorder /basics/treatment/con-20022540.

Morton, Ella. "Towers of Silence: The Zoroastrian Sky Burial Tradition," *Slate,* www.slate.com/blogs/atlas_obscura/2014/10 /15/towers_of_silence_in_yazd_a_zoroastrian_sky_burial_site .html.

Reinhold, Walter. "Eden's Serpent and Its Pre-Biblical Mesopotamian Prototypes," December 17, 2000, www.bibleorigins.net /ningishzida.html.

Rogge, Michael. "Paranormal Voices," http://wichm.home.xs4all.nl /dirvoic3.html.

Sansal, Burak. "Topkapi Palace," *Great Istanbul,* www.greatistanbul .com/topkapi_palace.htm.

"Southern Iraq, 4000–5500 BCE," www.newsnfo.co.uk/pages /acientfigurines.html.

Spice, Byron. "German Monk's 500-Year-Old Mystery Solved," *Pittsburgh Post-Gazette,* June 29, 1998, http://old.post-gazette .com/healthscience/19980629bspirit1.asp.

Sullivan, Meg. "What the Devil? Prince of Darkness Is Misunderstood, Says UCLA Professor," *UCLA Newsroom,* August 17, 2006, http://newsroom.ucla.edu/releases/What-the-Devil-Prince -of-Darkness-7261.

Sullivan, Robert. "J.D. Coyote: The Thrall of the Wild, in Central Park," *New York,* February 26, 2010, http://nymag.com/news /intelligencer/64322.

Tawsarn, Eric, and Dylan Shallnot. "3N Cave: The World's Largest Salt Cave," *Atlas Obscura,* www.atlasobscura.com/places/3n-cave-the -world-s-largest-salt-cave.

Thuris, Dylan. "Salt Men of Iran," *Atlas Obscura,* www.atlasobscura .com/places/salt-men-iran.

Wikipedia. "Seraph," http://en.wikipedia.org/wiki/Seraph.
Wikipedia. "Sleep Paralysis," http://en.wikipedia.org/wiki/Sleep _paralysis.

Wikipedia. "Urartu," http://en.wikipedia.org/wiki/Urartu.
Yeomans, Sarah. "Ancient Pergamon: City of Science … and Satan?" *Bible History Daily,* July 7, 2013, www.biblicalarchaeology.org /daily/biblical-sites-places/biblical-archaeology-sites/pergamon-2.

Credits

Area Surrounding Lake Urmia (Dino Pulerà, Artery Studios, Toronto)

Serpent God Icon (Dino Pulerà, Artery Studios, Toronto)

Adam and Eve Temptation Seal (Dino Pulerà, Artery Studios, Toronto)

Ubaid-Era Statue (Dino Pulerà, Artery Studios, Toronto)

Islamic Angel (public domain, Wikipedia Images)

Byzantine Seraphim (public domain, Wikipedia Images)

Apkallu, Mesopotamian Guardian Figure (public domain, Wikipedia Images)

Ningishida, Sumerian Serpent God (public domain, Wikipedia Images)

The Sacred Tree (from Thomas Inman, *Ancient Faiths and Modern: A Dissertation Upon Worships, Legends and Divinities,* illustrated by Saint-Elme Gautier. New York: J.W. Bouton, 1876)

Acknowledgments

It's always such a pleasure to work with Adrienne Kerr, whose editorial savvy, support, and advice are so valuable. My gratitude also to my publisher, Nicole Winstanley, and the sales, production, marketing, and publicity teams at Penguin Random House Canada. Many thanks to my agents, Victoria Skurnick and Elizabeth Fisher, at the Levine Greenberg Rostan Literary Agency.

I would be at a loss to write any of my books were it not for the many authors, historians, journalists, and bloggers I rely on for research. In the writing of *The Angel of Eden,* however, one author, British historian David Rohl, really stands out. His painstaking work, documented in his book *Legend: The Genesis of Civilization,* is in my view nothing short of brilliant. It has heavily influenced the ideas in this novel.

Very much appreciated also is the advice of Tanis Mallow and Sylvia Forest's help in providing expert knowledge in climbing techniques.

For their great assistance in preparing the illustrations, my sincere thanks to Dino Pulerà and Steven Mader of Artery Studios in Toronto.

SENTIMENTAL
JOURNEY

AN ORAL
TRAIN TRAVE

TED FI

with a new P

Fitzhenry & Whiteside

Sentimental Journey
Copyright © 2001 Fitzhenry & Whiteside
Previously published by Doubleday Canada, 1985

To Alex and Lisa

Fitzhenry & Whiteside acknowledges with thanks the Canada Council
for the Arts, the Government of Canada through its Book Publishing Industry
Development Program, and the Ontario Arts Council for their support of our
publishing program.

Canadian Cataloguing in Publication Data

Ferguson, Ted
  Sentimental Journey: an oral history of train travel in Canada

ISBN 1-55041-604-9

1. Railroad travel – Canada – History. 2. Railroads – Canada – Passenger traffic –
History. 3. Canada – Description and travel. I. Title.

HE2591.C3F47 2000   917.104'6   C00-932551-4

Design: Darrell McCalla

Cover image: Consolidation Type 3722, on the turntable, seen from
inside the roundhouse, Port McNicol, Ontario. *Courtesy of Robert Sandusky.*

Printed and bound in Canada

CONTENTS

PREFACE

On a hot, cloudless day two years ago, I rented a car in Edmonton and headed south to interview a farmer for a magazine article. A few miles west of Stettler, I spotted an old steel-wheel tractor rusting in a weedy field. I stopped the car and hopped out to take some photographs. As I stood at the edge of the field, camera raised and clicking, I heard a shrill whistling sound somewhere behind me. I turned and saw a steam locomotive chugging around a curve, along back-country railway tracks I had wrongly assumed were used exclusively by freight trains.

The engineer blew the whistle again as the wonderful machine, a gleaming legacy from the 1950s, rattled by. It was pulling a string of vintage passenger cars. Many of the people sitting at the windows were senior citizens but I did notice several children. Seeing the youngsters gazing intriguingly at the rolling, green landscape reminded me of my first childhood ride up Vancouver Island. I couldn't remember where I had travelled, or why I went there, but I clearly recalled the waiting room benches and pot-bellied stove and, in the wicker-seated day coach, the conductor, a god-like figure to a six-year-old boy, letting me punch my own ticket. Later trips instilled different memories: the arrivals and departures boards, the Seth Thomas wall clocks, the chattering telegraph keys, the busy porters, the conductor's vigorous, "All abooord."

Most of those things are gone now, causalities of modernization.

A few old steamers, like the Alberta Prairie Railway train I saw near Stettler, have been refurbished and put into service throughout Canada for tourist excursions. Some of the surviving locomotives are stored in privately-run museums. Morse keys and other bits and pieces of rail memorabilia rest in display cases in government institutions. Groups of school children are sometimes taken to view the aging artifacts but, as Canadian history is such a scantily-touched classroom subject, not many youngsters today fully appreciate how much the railway was once regarded as an essential – and affectionately revered – part of this country's national psyche.

In geographical terms, the train stitched over 4,800 kilometres of thinly-populated land together. Communities sprang up alongside railway tracks, many of them developing into major cities. Cattle, grain and lumber rumbled east, immigrants, furniture and dry goods rumbled west. In the late 1800s, railway builders recognized the importance of bringing train service to remote, bush-trail towns and villages. In fact, so many branch lines were laid that one city alone, Winnipeg, offered daily runs on 24 different routes.

In psychological terms, the train became one of the few things Canadians could count on remaining unchanged in a world where fashionable trends were highly valued. Everyone rode the train at one time or another, and most of them had a story to tell. How the dining car waiter served them fresh coffee and straight-from-the-oven cookies on a polished, silver tray. How they spent their wedding night in a cramped lower berth. How they sat in the observation car until dawn playing gin rummy. How they bore through a raging snowstorm en route to a troop ship and an overseas war. People always spoke of the train fondly and, as the service standards were so high, with a noticeable degree of respect.

Inevitably, change came to the railway and, sadly, it wasn't for the better. After World War II, federal and provincial governments poured enormous amounts of money into building new highways and Air Canada introduced a fleet of larger, faster and more comfortable passenger planes. With their ridership steadily dwindling, train cars turned grubby, employee morale declined and passengers staying loyal to the system often complained of mechanical breakdowns and mediocre food. The CPR and CNR merged their passenger divisions into VIA Rail in 1978 and reduced the transcontinental service to a single daily run. More cuts during the 1980s drastically shrunk passenger services on other lines.

While Canada was reducing its passenger service to a scrawny shadow of its former glory, countries like Japan and France retained their customer base by upgrading facilities. High–speed trains were put into operation. Visiting Japan last summer, I travelled to Kyoto and other major centres on clean, smooth-riding, 270-kmh 'bullet' trains that arrived and departed on time, to the exact minute. By comparison, the last train I took in my homeland, on a 40-year-old diesel between Toronto and Montreal, was more than an hour late. Experiences like that deepened my long-standing feeling that something valuable has been lost in this country.

A sense of being connected to the landscape, the feeling of being part of a tradition rooted in the nation's earliest days: when the railway dwindled and faded, it was yet another step, and a big one at that, toward a less gracious and comforting world.

In researching this book, I discovered that I am not the only person who missed the splendid, old days of Canadian rail travel. Crisscrossing the country over a six-month period in 1984, I conducted some prearranged interviews on specific topics but the overwhelming majority of stories came from people I simply walked up to and asked if they had a train story to relate. Given the abundance of rail travel in Canada, I wasn't surprised that so many of them did but I hadn't anticipated such a broad variety of stories. Looking back today, I remember a lawyer sitting on a Vancouver park bench telling me a ghost story, a retired salesman in a Toronto video store recalling railway con artists, a military veteran ensconced in a Saskatoon beer parlour weeping when he spoke of an Estevan funeral train nearly 40 years earlier.

Most of the nostalgia I encountered was for the age of the steam locomotives. I originally intended to confine this book to the steamers but, hearing so many appealing stories pertaining to diesels, I decided to include them too. Reviving personal memories of long-past rail trips I took, the researching of this book became a sentimental journey for me: when I began putting the stories on paper, I realized the book was also developing into something else, a collective lament for a way of life that will never return.

Ted Ferguson, 2000

ACKNOWLEDGEMENTS

The research and writing of an oral history is a costly and exhausting task. I would like to thank Alberta Culture for providing a grant that helped offset the travel expenses and for the encouraging words expressed by members of the literary arts branch that made the workload seem lighter. Those staff members who were particularly supportive were former director John Patrick Gillese, Ken McVey, Albi Calman, and Judy Hayman.

Most of the material was obtained from strangers in a variety of locales — on buses and trains; in offices, senior citizens' homes, parks and hotel lobbies; and at shopping centres and beaches. However, there were several prearranged interviews aimed at covering a specific subject. In that regard, I wish to thank Charles Lynch for the Diefenbaker funeral story, Syd Thompson for details of the On-to-Ottawa Trek, David Adams for the Winnipeg Ballet item, and Frank Rasky for his recollections of a journey to Hudson Bay.

Canadian Pacific historian Omer Lavallée and his Canadian National counterpart, Norman Lowe, were extremely helpful. So were Emery LeBlanc of *VIA* Rail, Tania Yakimowich of the Glenbow-Alberta Institute, Robert Turner of the B.C. provincial museum, and Donald Morris of the provincial archives at St. John's, Newfoundland.

Others deserving special mention are Gordon Pinsent, Jack Pye, Jessie Alister, Charles Templeton, W. D. Granger, T. C. Douglas, Kevin Clark, Fred Stone, Alix Stone, Jim Coleman, Douglas Fisher, the late Stephen Franklin, Gordon Copland, Pat Rose, Patrick Webb, Denise Lasalle, Laura Pitfield, the late Gordon Sinclair, Bob Johnston, Fred Kennedy, Trent Frayne, James Defelice, Dominique Clift, Peggy Holmes, Jim Kearney, L. J. Maiden, Wayne Crouse, Stu Hart, Bill Copps, Mike Duffy, Jim Taylor, Bonnie Theemes-Smith, Scotty Sandison, Bruce Smith, Don McGowan, John Venables, Alex Walinowski, Barbara Deyell, Roy Deyell, Allen Anderson, and Vince Virgo.

FIRST
IMPRESSIONS

For a few years in the 1940s, my father laid ties on a Vancouver Island railway. The job brought him many friends among the nomadic tribe of sectionhands that inhabited Boxcar Row. Failed merchants, ex-sailors, ex-cowboys, men with college degrees, men with no schooling whatsoever — all lived with their families in converted boxcars temporarily moored on a siding outside of town. Laundry hung on trees; children and dogs scampered in ravines and garbage dumps. On Saturday nights, my father led me several miles across bare fields and along the tracks to Boxcar Row. There was poker and gin rummy and tepid beer and, when someone played an accordion, the women sang "Roll Out the Barrel" and "You Are My Sunshine."

What I remember most is the impression that the children were so worldly wise. They'd been to exotic Quebec; they'd had their fortunes told at Niagara Falls. According to them, Canada was a wonderous nation populated mainly by hobos, gypsies, thieves, harlots, sectionhands, and sad wretches selling unwanted insurance policies. I also remember how cramped and strange their homes felt. Rough bunkbeds, water buckets, wood-burning stoves, a Winchester or a twelve-gauge shotgun in the corner, cleaned and ready for hunting.

I suppose I'll never know where my father's friends finally settled or what happened to their children, but when I went to do a newspaper story on a retired sports figure twenty years later, his stucco bungalow was part of a subdivision that filled the field where the siding had once been located.

The Boxcar Row visits were my first encounters with the railway and the people who worked the trains. They created the impression that, like circuses and motion pictures, trains were a source of the unusual and the romantic. Other people's first impressions were, of course, quite different.

THE BRANDON LADY

"THIS WOMAN hadn't ventured beyond the city limits of Brandon and she was going to visit her brother in New Westminster. A regular doll, she was. Five feet tall, around sixty years old. She was worried about everything. Would the air-conditioning give her a cold? Was the dining-car water safe to drink? If she rolled over in her sleep, would she fall out of her berth? I assured her that her fears were groundless. Around nine o'clock, the porter made up the berths. I went to the lounge to read a magazine and, when I returned, everyone was in bed.

"As I undressed in my bottom berth, I heard a man ask the porter for the ladder. The porter rummaged around and then I heard him say, 'I don't understand it. I can't find it anywhere.' A moment later, a woman's voice drifted down from an upper berth. The Brandon lady. 'If you can't find your ladder, porter, you can borrow mine.' The poor dear had somehow dragged the ladder into the berth. How on earth she expected to get a decent rest with the ladder on top of her I'll never know."

TERROR ON THE TRACKS

"ON HOT DAYS my friends and I would wander along the railway tracks to the open countryside outside Regina. My father was the manager at Robert Simpson's in the 1920s and our home was five miles from the bald prairie. There were four or five boys in our gang, all about ten or eleven years old. We'd step aside and watch the freights rattle past and make bets on how many boxcars they were pulling. Often, we'd stick a penny on the rails and marvel at how a train flattened it. Sometimes I'd have my dog with me. We'd leap on haystacks and scare the mice, and the dog chased them. I never considered the train a dangerous object. Not until the afternoon one almost killed me.

"My friends and I came to a bridge, a trestle, over a creek. It was long and high, and my friends dared me to cross it alone. Believe me, I didn't want to do it, but I didn't want to be branded a coward. I went out on the trestle, taking the ties two at a time. My friends had great fun prodding me. 'Templeton's scared! He wants his mommy!' 'Watch your step! It may be your last!' I tried to shut my ears to them. Looking down between the ties made my head spin. I could see big, black rocks protruding from the water.

"Suddenly, I heard a whistle. A train was whipping around a bend behind me and approaching the trestle at full throttle. I was too far out to turn back and I'd be killed if I jumped. I ran. Oh, how I ran. My heart was beating crazily. If I slipped, I was sure I'd jam a leg between the ties and the train would crush me. I ran and ran, and the engineer, spotting me, was blowing his whistle over and over.

"At the very last instant, I came to a narrow landing sticking out of the side of the trestle. It had a rain barrel on it. I lept onto the landing and hugged the barrel. This enormous juggernaut streaked by. I felt its hot wind; the engine had a thunderous roar. I stood there for a long time after it was gone. Shaking and sweating. I don't mind admitting it, those were the most chilling moments in my entire life."

A LONG, HARD WALK

"WE HAD TO WALK all night to catch the train — from our farm to the depot in Sutton, where we'd take the train to Montreal and transfer for Toronto. This was 1935. My uncle Don had sent the fare money, and we were quitting the farm. We didn't board up the house. No point. Precious little to steal, except maybe the old Commodore stove. The car had no gas and two flat tires, and the horse had died. Father would hike to the nearest store and carry food home, if he couldn't bum a ride with a neighbour. Five miles each way. He didn't want anyone driving us to the depot. He was a proud man. It would shame him to tell a neighbour the farm had beaten him and he was quitting to take work cleaning sewers in Toronto.

"The walk was painful. A warm night, thank goodness, but we had suitcases and food for the trip. I was eleven and one tired little girl. Mother and father had to stop a lot because of me. Yes, we were on time. We were actually at the depot twenty minutes early. Mother fell asleep right away on the train, but I couldn't sit still. It was so exciting. The conductor calling out the stops, the boys going through the car selling newspapers and shining shoes. You'll be surprised what really fascinated me. At the farm, we had an outhouse. On the train, I spent a lot of time in the powder room — pulling the cord and watching the water swish down the drain. I'd flush everything imaginable: an apple core, a torn-up newspaper, cigarette butts. Whatever I could lay my hands on. Say 'trains' to me today and that's the first thing I think of."

LANTERNS AT 4:00 A.M.

"THE DISCIPLINE at Upper Canada College was fairly strict. School uniforms, high standards in the classrooms, and no nonsense in the corridors. So you can appreciate how delighted I was when my dad told me I'd been accepted at Barney Hodgett's Hurontario Wilderness Camp. Fifteen years old and going away from home and I wouldn't have to read a textbook all summer! I'm a sixth-generation Torontonian. When I boarded the 5:00 p.m. train at Union Station, I discovered that the other boys were exactly like me, upper-middle-class, dyed-in-the-wool Torontonians who hadn't shaved yet. The train stopped at Sudbury for an hour and, eager for a new experience, we flocked, twenty green kids, to the first beer parlour we sighted.

"The Ledo Hotel. What a dump! A smoky, crowded basement, the kind of place where there was probably a fight every half-hour. We plunked ourselves down at tables and ordered booze. The waiter brought the beer and took our money — then said we were too young and threw us out. Back at the train, we decided we'd been had. The waiter had pocketed our money and probably sold the beer to twenty other guys. One boy said to hell with the Ledo and hauled a marijuana cigarette from his pocket. We'd never seen one. It received a thorough examination before he went up to the dome car to smoke it.

"Around 3:00 a.m. we arrived at Nicholson. The middle of nowhere. Dark as a dungeon outside, and the air was thick with black-flies. A couple of camp guides waited beside the tracks. As the train slid away, they led us to canoes, and we paddled up Windermere Lake to the camp grounds. For the next five weeks, the CPR was our main link with the life we'd left behind in Toronto. Every few days, the train slowed down and the baggageman tossed a mail sack into the ditch. That's how I received my final school marks. Tossed in a ditch.

"I'll never forget the night we went home. We paddled to the tracks and stood there, waving lanterns, at 4:00 a.m. on a lovely, cool, northern Ontario night. We saw the light, and the whistle sounded, and this magnificent machine drew closer and closer and, just when we thought it wasn't going to, it glided to a halt to pick us up. A very stir-ring scene, that. Especially the whistle. That's the sound I hope to hear the second before I die."

RUNNING AWAY FROM HOME

"FOR YEARS AND YEARS, I was scared of trains. In fact, I was almost twenty before I had the nerve to ride on one. Let me give you the rea-son. When I was ten or eleven my parents moved into a new neigh-bourhood in east Toronto. I got mad at them — I can't remember why — and decided to run away from home. It was the beginning of win-ter and really cold but that didn't seem to worry me.

"I walked for blocks until I came to a railway yard. A freight train was sitting there and no one was around so I went over and looked for a boxcar to crawl into. They were all locked tight. I climbed into the cab to look at the controls and then I went up the ladder behind the engine. The coal car was empty. I jumped down into it and waited for the train to leave. I don't know where I wanted to go, probably some-place far, far away, like Hamilton. I sat for hours. It got dark and cold-er and I got hungry. I wanted desperately to go home. I tried to climb out but the walls were too high. I was hysterical. I cried and screamed and banged the walls. Nobody heard me.

"Early the next morning, somebody came to fill the coal car and they hauled me out. I was in bad, bad shape. Scared out of my head. I still don't like trains very much. Too many terrible feelings left over from that awful night."

TEENAGE DESIRE

"CHRISTMAS, 1945. Clifford, my older brother was stationed at the RCAF base at Fort St. John, B.C., and I was spending the holiday season with him and my aunt and uncle who lived there. I was fifteen and very shy, very withdrawn. If I passed a girl on the street, my eyes scraped my boots. My idea of fun was playing hockey with neighbours' kids on the frozen pond behind our farm in Fort Saskatchewan. On really big occasions, we'd light the bonfire and roast weiners.

"So, you see, I was astounded when I saw what was happening on the train. Several young soldiers and a handful of boys a little older than me were in the coach. Before we reached the B.C. border, a bevy of young girls showed up, in groups of twos and threes. None of the girls knew any of the boys but that didn't matter. Within minutes they were all chatting away and sneaking slugs from hidden liquor bottles. I sat off by myself, gawking. The girls were overwhelmed by a handsome, bushy-haired fellow of around twenty-two. He sang cowboy songs and strummed a guitar. When night came, he went off somewhere with a girl and, all of a sudden, boys and girls were necking and petting all over the coach.

"I was sick with envy. They were having a whale of a time and there I was, a tall, fumbling, pimply creature no one looked twice at. If I slept at all that night, I'm sure I had lustful dreams.

"Clifford met the train. The rail line ended at Dawson Creek in 1945, and we had to bus it to Fort St. John. I had a wonderful holiday. My uncle's farm was near the air base. From their kitchen window, I watched Spitfires take off and land. People were proud to have a relative in uniform, and I was thrilled when Clifford arranged to let me stay overnight in the barracks. All the same, my mind was seldom far away from the wanton scene on the train. I swore I'd muster the courage to break out of my shell on the return trip.

"I didn't get the chance. The train was nearly empty. I was the only teenager. Nobody strummed a guitar, nobody necked. Praise be, the temptation had been banished. If it had been there, and if I had surrendered to it, where might I be today? Undoubtably, leading a sinful life. Fortunately, the Lord eventually laid His hand on my shoulder and, for the past thirty years, I've been a minister with the Canadian Bible Society."

STAY OFF THE THIRD FLOOR

"MY MOTHER was quite concerned. Oh, she was pleased that I had a job but, at the same time, she didn't like having me leave so late at night. Especially since it was my first trip away from Edmonton. In those days, 1928, a properly brought-up girl rarely went anywhere alone after dark. As it turned out, I wasn't travelling by myself. A girl I met at teachers' college, Mary Jackson, was going to Innisfail too. We sat together in the coach and talked about the one-room school I had been assigned to. Twelve students, grades One to Nine. Innisfail is near Vegreville, a large Ukrainian community, and I was worried that none of my students would speak English. We arrived at Innisfail at 3:00 a.m. and carried our suitcases over to the station, where we planned to camp until morning. The door was locked. A man walked past us. 'See that light over there, ladies? It's a hotel. Go in, sign the register and choose a room.' Then he said something I've never forgotten. 'Whatever you do, stay off the third floor. It's crawling with bedbugs.'"

GETTING EVEN

"THERE USED TO BE school trains in northern Ontario in the 1930s. How they operated was, a regular train would bring a special car up from the Sault, Port Arthur, or Capreol, and the car stayed put in your region for a week. When it was gone, you'd do your bloody homework, loads of the stuff, until the train came back three weeks later. The cars were old passenger coaches that the CNR and Ontario Northland had refitted. Desks, blackboards, maps, and books in one part, the teachers' living quarters partitioned off in the other.

"Was it romantic going to school on a train? You've got to be kidding. School's school, whether it's on a train or in a crummy building. My dad was a fishing guide who worked in the mills off and on at Fort Frances. After a terrific summer swimming, fishing, and catching muskrat, the last thing us kids needed was an educated asshole shoving grammar and arithmetic down our gullets.

"Once, we had this scrawny bag of bones, Miss Hanna. I was talking to a boy in class and — *whoosh* — she flung this bloody piece of chalk and hit my arm. It hurt like hell. Right then and there I said to myself, she's going to get hers. I had a pet mouse. White-coloured. My sister hated it, and she'd scream and shout for Mother if I took it into her room. I figured that if it scared Eileen shitless, it would do the same thing to old Hanna.

"I took it to school in my lunch bucket. When Hanna was in her quarters for something, I put it in her desk drawer. The kids laughed but she didn't say nothing when she came back into the room. All day I waited for the old bag to open the drawer. She didn't do it. The next morning she opened it and acted perfectly normal so I guessed she'd already found her little surprise.

"On Friday, she had us march outside for a fire drill. She didn't join us right away. At lunchtime I opened my bucket and there was a garter snake on my sandwiches. I'm terrified of snakes. I let out a funny noise, ran to the door, and chucked the bucket out. Miss Hanna said sweet-bugger-all. Didn't crack a smile. But I knew in my heart of hearts that the old bag had found out the mouse was mine and had evened the score."

A GAME CALLED JESSE OWENS

"WE DIDN'T CALL IT 'CHICKEN,' we called it 'Jesse Owens.' After the Olympic runner. What we did was follow the CNR tracks out of Stewiacke and wait for trains to come. It was a busy route in the 1940s, between Halifax and Moncton, and we didn't have to wait too long. There was Ernie Morris, Tommy Anderson, Wayne Somebody-or-Other, the Dawson brothers, and me, the only female. A tomboy. A female who thought the worst punishment for the worst sin was having to wear a dress.

"We'd run across the tracks, in front of trains. The one who got the closest was the bravest. The engine drivers went nuts. They tooted their horns and balled their fists and you'd see red, boiling-mad faces when the trains flashed by. It's a miracle nobody was run over. We'd do it the whole summer and Tommy Anderson, he got so close you'd swear he'd had it. Golly, we were dumb when we were young."

A FREE RIDE TO VANCOUVER

"MY BUDDY RALPH and I were on our summer holidays in 1952, and we decided to ride the rails to the coast. We had the money; we weren't poor. My old man was a stock broker in Calgary, Ralph's dad owned a good restaurant. It was just that Grade Eleven had been God-awful boring and we'd never been near a train and, well, it seemed like fun.

"We went to the CPR yard and climbed on the first freight pointing west. It stopped on a siding this side of Banff. We walked through town and waited to grab another ride. No problem. There's forty freights a day through that part of the country. We passed up two with brakemen on them and then ran and jumped on the third. We stood on the ladders between boxcars for a while and then went up on the roof. Terrific stuff. We lay there taking in the scenery. We saw a moose and a couple of deer. Then we came to the tunnel. The God-awful Connaught Tunnel.

"It's five miles long. We stretched out on our bellies and hung on for dear life. The smoke and the cinders were killers. I was coughing up a storm but I don't think that's what got to me. I think it was the bad ventilation. Whatever it was, I fainted. When I woke up, Ralph was bending over me and we had cleared the tunnel. He hadn't realized I'd conked out. He was amazed that I hadn't rolled off and been killed. He kept saying over and over, 'Jesus, Peter, you're a lucky guy.' I was a lucky guy, all right. But it wasn't the sort of luck you tested twice. We got off at Golden and hitchhiked the rest of the way. After our holiday in Vancouver, I took the train home to Calgary. Inside, not on the roof."

SHE FELT SPECIAL

"IN THE 1930s, folks living in southeast Saskatchewan did their important shopping in Winnipeg. They had bigger stores in Winnipeg than Regina and more movie shows. My mom would go on the morning train, shop, go to a movie, stay at my aunt's, and leave for home the next day.

"When I was seven I went with her. Didn't sleep two winks the night before. Oh, no, not just because of the shops. Because of the train, too. I'd seen it pass our farm a thousand times, and now I was going on it and I couldn't sit still.

"The conductor was a god to little tykes. Oh, yes, a god. When he came up to my mom and me in the coach, I held my breath. He talked to my mom and he took out his watch. He saw me gaping at it. 'Here, little lady,' he said. 'Would you like to look after this for me a while?'

"A gold Hamilton. With a lid that closed and a pretty gold chain. I was awestruck. Positively awestruck. I stared and stared, watching the second hand move. When the conductor came back, he took the watch and said, 'Thank you for taking care of it for me.'

"I don't remember the shops or the movies we saw. But I do remember the gold watch and how special it felt to sit on the train and take care of it for the conductor."

BATTLING THE ELEMENTS

Railwaymen used to dread taking trains through Rogers Pass in the winter. The line twisted and doubled back for five miles over dizzying grades and beneath mountain bluffs that had a despicable habit of dumping hundreds of tons of snow on the tracks. In 1899 the CPR depot at the pass was demolished by an avalanche and eight people died, the station agent's wife and children among them. Eleven years later, an enormous slide roared down the slopes while a work gang was clearing away the snow from an earlier avalanche. Sixty-two men were buried alive, still clutching picks and shovels: the force of the slide flung a hundred-ton rotary plough onto the roof of a building the snow had missed. The CPR came up with a costly but effective solution. In 1913 it began building the Connaught Tunnel straight through the base of Mount MacDonald.

The railway engineers found a way to curb nature's wrath at Rogers Pass, but there is little they can do to defeat adverse weather conditions elsewhere. Every so often, a ferocious blizzard wallops the Prairies and totally disrupts rail service. In the 1960s the CPR and CNR transcontinental passenger trains were both stranded for days in the Fraser Canyon by the same snowstorm. In the early eighties, mudslides blocked the main line west of Jasper, and flooding rivers frequently cover the rails in the Atlantic provinces. Overheated cars and alarmingly high winds have plagued the railways too, but the greatest source of misery for passengers and train crews alike has, and always will be, the cursed Canadian winter.

Like many inveterate winter travellers, I've had my plans changed by the weather. I recall getting on a train in the 1950s that arrived four hours late in Edmonton and then was halted on the open prairie for six hours by a heavy snowfall. An aging salesman took advantage of the unexpected stop to walk the aisles selling reading material out of a large, black suitcase. His sixty-odd years of living had apparently convinced him that the Canadian populace was divided equally into two categories — saints and sinners. Copies of the New Testament filled one side of the suitcase and girlie magazines the other.

IT WAS SO COLD...

"DOES THE NAME A. E. Corbett ring a bell? Back in the 1930s he was head of the extension department at the University of Alberta. He and a friend were staying overnight in a town north of Edmonton. Westlock, perhaps, or Barrhead. It was the dead of a very severe winter. Corbett's friend slept late and had to hurry to catch the train. He ran from the hotel and thundered down the platform carrying a water jug. Corbett nearly died laughing. His friend had slipped his dentures into the jug before going to bed — it was so cold in the room that the water had frozen."

WIND LIKE THE DEVIL'S DISCIPLE

"GRACIOUS ME. The weather's a fright in Newfoundland. How could you have a crackerjack railway with five hundred miles of big hills, twisting bends, and a bridge every ten miles? Terrible washouts in the spring. Simply terrible. Rivers rose and tore bridges apart. In the wintertime the storms buried the tracks under ten, twelve, fifteen feet of snow. Away back when, the Bullet was stranded at Kitty's Brook for two weeks or more. A terrible blizzard. The passengers, they burned baggage car crates and old railway ties for warmth and stretched their food by shooting wild game.

"Naw, I was never stranded. But I did have many a scary ride. John, my hubby, was stationed at Corner Brook during the war and I moved to the island to be near him. Going on the Bullet jangled the nerves. Oh, boy, was it ever so. Naw, I didn't see washouts and I don't recollect any big snowstorms. It's the wind I'm speaking of. The wind that raced in from the Gulf of St. Lawrence like the devil's disciple. Gusts eighty, ninety, a hundred miles an hour.

"You'd be rattling along on the Bullet, minding your own business, and suddenly the car was shaking and groaning and swaying and feeling like it was surely going to be blown right off the rails. Ever hear tell of Wreck House? Near Port aux Basques, it was. The McDougalls lived there. They were famous in Newfoundland. They had a wind-gauge at their house. If it was blowing hard enough to be a danger, they'd signal the railway. The Bullet halted right then and there and wouldn't budge an inch past the McDougalls' house until the gauge said it was okay. The McDougalls saved many a train from disaster. The cars were light and the track was narrow and the wind; gracious, it was unholy strong."

FROZEN CATTLE EVERYWHERE

"'DON'T YOU LOOK OUT the window, Kate.' That's what Mother kept saying to me. 'Don't you look out the window.' I couldn't stop myself. Where else was I going to look? I'd watch the scenery and everything was hunky-dory for a while and then I'd see dead cattle in the snowdrifts and, often times, they'd have to push them off the train tracks. Mile after mile was like that. All the Prairies suffered, but Alberta was the hardest hit. Storm upon storm, and temperatures away below zero.

"March 1907. I was ten. The rest of the trip is a blank to me, yet I can still remember the frozen cattle. Mother must've thought my father was crazy bringing us to such a horrible place. He repaired watches and clocks in Montreal, and he wanted to open his own store, to be independent and not work for somebody else. He picked one of the worst times in history to come out West.

"The railway yard was a genuine horror. In the countryside, you'd see cattle bunched together against barbwire fences, starved and frozen. The train was slow but it was still fast enough so you didn't have to look at the bodies too long. Somewhere in Alberta, Medicine Hat or Calgary, the train sat in this railway yard for a long, long time.

Cowboys were dragging dead cattle out of pens with ropes and horses. The ranchers had somehow driven them to the railway only to have the thermometer drop so far below zero that they froze before they could ship them out. Hundreds and hundreds. Dead beside the tracks. An awful, awful sight.

"Ten or eleven years ago, a man was in this nursing home who came West the same time I did. Mr. Hunter. Mr. Walter Hunter. He said his father had a diary. What struck him when he read it was how the trains that March had to struggle to get through the snow. Eighteen days from Winnipeg to Calgary for one train. The passengers and the train crew and the people from the tiny communities shovelled the snow from the tracks. Days and days of shovelling just to go a few miles in some places. Mr. Hunter didn't remember any of it. Too young at the time. Well, I sure can picture the frozen cattle. It's not a pretty memory to carry to my grave."

THREE GIRLS IN A PHONE BOOTH

"ANYBODY TELL YOU about the three girls in the phone booth? It isn't a big dramatic story but it might be worth listening to. It happened outside Saskatoon in the 1960s. Just when everyone thought spring was on its way a blizzard howled in from the west and crippled northern Saskatchewan. Schools were shut and the highways, and the snowploughs were barely able to keep the railway tracks clear. These three girls were en route to Saskatoon. Teenagers. It was colder than hell and the drifts were ten feet deep in spots. The train stopped for a few minutes while the snowplough cleared the line ahead of it. The girls jumped off to stretch their legs. The wind had died and they decided to walk on a country road. They went too far. The wind came up and visibility was bad. The conductor glanced about and didn't see them and figured they were aboard. The train left them there.

"The girls must've been scared silly. Nothing but blowing snow and empty fields and nobody in sight. They'd come from the coast and just had light coats on. They nearly froze walking down that road. After a few miles, they came to a country store. Only it was boarded up, deserted. They couldn't get inside. So they went into the booth, the telephone booth in front of it. Sardines in a can. Dimes in their pockets and no way to call because the phone lines were down. Shaking from the cold, they were, and worried sick. I think they were there six or seven hours. Finally, the wind stopped and, because there weren't any houses or cars in sight, they walked back to the tracks. A freight came. They saw its light and they stood on the tracks waving and yelling until it stopped to pick them up. Three girls in a telephone booth. Quite an experience."

We're Having a Heat Wave

ALL OF THE PASSENGERS trooping on at Montreal were rubbing their hands and ears and smiling and saying good-naturedly that it was bloody cold in the car but, once the engine started, the heat would flow. The engine started, the train departed Central Station — the damned heat didn't flow.

"Forty below on a January afternoon and the car was packed with trembling, teeth-chattering passengers. We bitched to the conductor, and he swore he'd take care of it. The train came to a halt two miles from the station and backed up. Praise be, I thought. They've discovered there's no heat and they're going back to the yard to fix the pipes. Wrong. The train stopped, paused, and plunged forward again, bound for Toronto. Those of us with suitcases put on what extra clothing we had, and the conductor handed out blankets. After an hour, I decided to find out if the car behind ours was any warmer.

"What a shock. Through some incredible circumstance, the car was basking in a heat wave. Like a Bermuda beach. I returned to my car, stripped off the extra clothing and, doing a Moses, led my people to the other car. We jammed the aisle, sitting and standing. Pleased as Punch. Until we realized that it wasn't a Bermuda beach anymore — it was a foundry furnace. People were drenched in sweat and becoming dizzy. Several fainted and had to be helped to my old car to recover. The whole journey was that way. People rushing back and forth between the furnace and the really frigid car where they'd cool off if they felt dizzy.

"Finally, we reached Toronto. A blizzard was pounding the city. Half the train darted over to the Royal York bar to drown their misery.

The other half hovered in doorways, squinting through swirling snow in hope of sighting a rare object, an empty taxi. I did both. The Royal York bar and a doorway. I arrived at my sister's place at 4:00 a.m. I poured myself a stiff drink and hugged the radiator until I relaxed enough to sleep."

DIFFERENT STROKES FOR DIFFERENT FOLKS

"HEAT? I'll tell you about heat. And the Germans. The ridiculous Germans. Somewhere in northern Ontario in the 1950s, in the depth of winter, the train temperature became unbearable. It hit the high 80s, I swear. I asked the porter to turn on the overhead fan in our car. There were eight or nine Germans in the same car — immigrant families. They gave us a dirty look. Apparently, they felt that the cool air from the fan would make them sick. Anyway, the porter switched it on and the Germans lept to their suitcases. Unbelievable. They put on fur-lined caps and heavy sweaters and scarfs. It was a scene from a bad comedy. My wife and I and the other Canadians were rolling up our sleeves or whatever to catch the cool breezes — and those Germans were wrapped up tight in their winter gear. We stared disapprovingly at each other all day.

"That night the heat went off. The brakes froze and we were stuck in the Manitoba bush till a section crew thawed them out. We all shivered in our beds. Then, around breakfast time, the heat came on again. Just as strongly as before. Up into the 80s once more. It was back to the fan for the Canadians and back to the winter gear for the Germans. The funny thing was, the Germans had the last laugh. They trooped off in Saskatchewan, robust and healthy. By the time we hit Edmonton, practically everyone in the car had a rotten cold that was caused by the blasted fan."

EIGHT HOURS OF DIGGING

"LATE IN THE WINTER of 1948 south Saskatchewan was clobbered by a blizzard that didn't want to quit. Three months of wind, snow, and bitter cold — 30 and 40 below. The snow drifted as high as telephone poles in open country and was hard as marble; so hard, farmers rode horses to the tops of the mounds without breaking through. No man in his right mind wanted to venture out in that weather. I know I sure as hell didn't. But I was a railroader and when I got the call, I went.

"You see, the railway was the life-line for the small towns. Should the roads be plugged and planes couldn't drop supplies, they relied upon us to help them survive. Some folks on the line south of Swift Current needed coal desperately. A train hadn't been by for twelve days. We had three engines and a plough when we left Swift Current. Eighty diggers too. The railway recruited men in beer parlours, cafés, and hotel lobbies and paid them 75 cents an hour for shovelling.

"Heavens, it was storming that day. I'd been a trainman since 1918 and an engineer since '46 and that was the most wicked weather, bar none. You couldn't see ten feet in front of you. Quick as the plough cleared a rough section, and our train moved over it, the snow started filling it in again. They were really hard-up for coal at Neville. The local citizens heard the engine whistles and rushed to the station, despite the fact that it was 40 below that day. They anxiously watched us crack through the drifts north of town. They had sacks and buckets and anything you could carry coal in.

"We didn't disappoint them. We got to Neville, all right. But what a battle. We ran smack into a 25-foot-high drift. The plough barged into it and got stuck halfway through. So the diggers went to work. Eighty men shovelled as fast as they could. Eighty hungry men, I might add. We hadn't brought any food with us, and working that hard at that temperature without eating was a terrible ordeal. Eight hours they dug. The poor souls were bone-tired.

"We unloaded coal and ran for Vanguard, forty miles down the line. The diggers could eat and rest there. My fireman, Ed Sadler, and I were terribly worried. What if we hit more big drifts like the 25-footer? The shovelling might be too much for some of the men. Travelling behind a plough wasn't very relaxing either. All you could see was a blur of flying snow, and you had to be constantly ready for the tremendous jolt when the equipment made contact. You could be pitched against the boiler head and into valves and gauges and be badly hurt.

"We were lucky. We got to Vanguard safe and sound.

"Make no mistake, that was a murderous winter for the railways.

"Chic Cane's a retired engineer. He says that in February of '48 the Broadview - Moose Jaw run, normally a three-hour trip, took sixty-eight hours. He remembers a train being held at Indian Head for two and a half days. Beside a coal shack and a water tank. The crew laboured round the clock so the engine didn't die and there'd be heat in the coaches.

"Things were worse over at Expanse. Six engines with a plough on each end were ordered to clear track and got snowed-in. Including diggers, there were ninety men aboard. The people of Expanse contributed what food they could but they had precious little themselves. The men were trapped nine days. On the tenth day, the company hired planes when the storm eased and dropped them food.

"The weather was tough on everybody. Harry Taylor, the CPR's general manager for Saskatchewan, slept on a cot in his office for months so he'd be ready for new problems. Another official, Jack Miller, rode out on a plough and came back cut and bruised. How come? The hard snow. When the plough battered it, brick-sized pieces of snow flew in the cab and struck him. Those walls of snow were as solid as the Parthenon. The arrowpoints broke on some ploughs, others were derailed, and a few had caved-in roofs.

"The only creatures that didn't mind the weather were the gophers. They hibernated and slept through it all."

A COZY LITTLE FIRE

"MY BROTHER AND ME wanted to be home for Christmas and we didn't have the train fare. So we crawled into an empty boxcar at Flanders. It was seventy or eighty miles to Fort Frances, and it was colder than a witch's heart, and we didn't think we'd live long standing on a lonely bush road trying to hitch a ride. The boxcar was like a deep-freeze. It wouldn't have surprised me if my breath had turned into icicles. We used wood chips and straw and an old newspaper to start a little fire. We fed it bits of scrap wood we'd found by the tracks. It got to be real cozy. Warm as toast, if you stayed near the fire. The train rifled along and came to the Fort Frances yard. Holy mackerel! The floor was on fire! The train stopped and me and my brother hopped out. We scooped handfuls of snow and threw it on the flames. The fire went out. Dammit, there was a hole in the floor, big enough to slip a child through. Our cousin was a CNR bull at Fort Frances and he wouldn't have arrested us. But what if somebody we didn't know was on duty that day? We lit out of there, real fast."

No Goodwill Gestures

"On New Year's Eve, I was a porter on the Ontario Northland run leaving Cochrane for Toronto. We had a full crew but only eleven or twelve passengers. People generally don't like travelling at New Year's. The train suddenly ground to a standstill. This often occurred if there was ice on the rails, and usually we'd wait for a section gang to melt it. That wasn't the case this time. The engine was acting up. The passengers muttered about the lousy service and how they had important places to be in the city. The heat went off. Just like that. One minute it was warm, the next we were shivering and miserable. The windows frosted and there were breath-clouds every time someone spoke.

"I put a sweater, an overcoat, and two blankets on over my uniform and the passengers wore every article of clothing they could lay their hands on. The train started rolling again but the heat stayed off. Most of the passengers sat in the bar car and complained until the train reached Toronto, eight hours late. I made up my mind that day that I definitely wasn't going to be a career railroader. You know what got to me? CN's attitude. CN had the dining car on the train, and the conductor wired the CN office in Toronto saying he planned to give the passengers free meals, as a goodwill gesture. A reply came zinging back. 'You want to give them free food, do you? Listen, man, we don't want you to even give them a free cup of coffee.'"

Something Dark Was Coming

"My dad was marooned in New Brunswick in the 1920s. Twenty passengers besides him. It was supposed to be a short trip, and there was no diner. The only food aboard was the two sandwiches belonging to a school kid. Everyone said they didn't want to take the kid's sandwiches and he should have them himself. That was after six hours. Six hours more, and a committee descended on the kid. He had one sandwich left, grilled cheese. The passengers tore off buttons and put them in a hat. Twenty blacks, one brown. Whoever got the brown button won the sandwich. It wasn't my dad and it wasn't the kid. An Englishman got it, a tall drink of water with no meat on his bones.

"It snowed and snowed. For two days they watched the snow blowing on the fields. The fireman used up his coal and had to burn whatever he could scrounge from the baggage car. Trunks, crates, a table and chairs, whatever he could break up with an axe. When that was gone, the passengers helped break up seats and tear out wood panels. If the fire went out, there'd be no heat and, on top of no food, they'd expire for sure. Two men tried to leave and had to come back. The snow was up to their waists.

"Soon after dawn on the third day, something dark was seen in the blowing snow. Something dark, coming towards the train. What was it? A horse pulling a sleigh. And another. Farmers in the district knew the train was stuck and they'd ridden out in a blinding blizzard to rescue the passengers and crew. They had snacks with them. Apples and preserves from their root-cellars and home-made bread. They couldn't cram many people on the sleighs so they made several trips. Taking them to their farms for hot meals and to let them sit by their kitchen stoves. That's my dad's favourite story. He's told it so often I sometimes think I was there myself."

HOORAY FOR NORRIS CRUMP!

"NORRIS CRUMP did this country a great service. When he was the big honcho at the CPR in 1960, he sent the last of the steam locomotives to the museums and scrapyards. Sure, there were people who hated him for doing it. Jerks who go around saying the old trains were romantic. Anyone who says that has a lousy memory. They've forgotten what it was like on a steamer in January. Nine out of ten trips, no problem. Trip number ten would freeze the you-know-whats on a brass monkey.

"And the summers. Oh, boy. The air was so hot and stifling in July and August you'd want to throw up. Tell the porter and he'd shove a metal ventilation screen in your window. Those crummy screens. You'd be cool, all right, but the soot and dirt from the locomotive came through them. Your pillow and sheets would be filthy every morning and, if you were in the worst spot, near the front of the train, you'd have the blasted stuff in your eyes and nose. So don't go saying the steam locomotives were romantic. With the diesels, you wake up clean in the morning."

CREATURES, GREAT AND SMALL

Back in the 1950s I lived in a boarding house where the landlady, a prim, excessively neat sort, posted a red-lettered sign inside the front door. "Rubbers and Boots Must Be Removed Here." The sign, of course, had the opposite effect. Taking offence to the rigid command, many boarders and guests deliberately stomped on the hall carpet, the wetter their footware the better. A similar situation developed on the trains. After the railways imposed a regulation stating that all non-human creatures must be transported in the baggage car, passengers defiantly smuggled pets on board in boxes, suitcases, and disguised cages. Train crews weren't above disobeying the rule. In 1924, a CPR conductor was suspended for repeatedly ignoring a company request that he cease sleeping with his Siamese cat.

Smuggled pets were a popular theme among the stories I heard involving trains and members of the animal kingdom. There were also plenty of tales about farmers whose cows were killed by speeding locomotives. Indeed, if only half of the slain-cattle stories were true, the CPR and CNR between them destroyed more cows in any given year than disease, old age, and all of the packing plants in Canada combined.

PROUD TO BE CANADIAN

"SWANSON'S HORN was the undoing of a moose. Swanson was the Vancouver inventor who created an ingenious horn for the

Confederation train in 1967. All of us on the Centennial Commission thought it was marvellous. The engineer pulled a cord and the horn played the opening notes of 'O Canada.' The Department of Transport didn't share our view. It said the horn confused railyard workers and might cause an accident. So it banned the horn in cities and at level crossings. The bad news for the moose was that it could still be used in the uninhabited wild.

"Different engineers took charge of the train in different parts of the country. The chap at the controls somewhere in the mountains of B.C. rounded a bend and saw this magnificent bull moose in the centre of the tracks. He couldn't stop in time. He yanked the cord and 'O Canada' resounded off the canyon walls. The moose was a true Canadian. He didn't run. He snapped smartly to attention, his head up, his eyes glowing with nationalistic fervour. They say he died instantly."

THE MINISTER DESPISED DOGS

"ABOUT TWICE A MONTH my folks dragged me up from North Bay to be with my uncle Warner, who worked in the mines at Cobalt. This was during the silver boom, around World War I, and the newspapers were thick with stories of ordinary men becoming millionaires overnight. All I remember about the town is slouching in my uncle's house, bored to tears. And the stock exchange. Cobalt had its own exchange in those days, and my father was always riling my mother by buying worthless shares. He could've papered Buckingham Palace and had enough left over to do Windsor Castle.

"The best part of the trip for me was the dog. His name was Cobalt, and he was a little black furball, a Heinz 57. I thought he lived on the trains but apparently he was just as familiar around town, in the taverns and barber shops, as he was on the North Bay line. A smart doggie. Smart, and friendly. He'd go from car to car. If nobody was there to push a door open, he'd sit and wait. He did tricks. People tossed him hunks of bread and cookies, and he'd walk on his hind legs or roll over and pretend to be a dead soldier.

"Everyone loved him. Except the minister. He despised dogs in general and Cobalt in particular. He was teed off by the fact that the dog tried to befriend him all the time. The minister went to the station agent in Cobalt and said, 'That dog's breaking the rules. He shouldn't be riding the coach.' The station agent said he'd fix that but he didn't sound convincing. 'Okay,' the minister said, 'if that dog's going to continue riding as a passenger, I insist that its owner be obliged to pay a passenger's fare.'

"Cobalt's owner was Arthur Slaght, the lawyer. A clever soul. He won a case for a fellow who lost his sight in a railway accident, by reading a Kipling poem, 'The Light That Failed,' to the jury as a nurse led his stumbling client into the courtroom. Slaght wasn't about to kowtow to an ill-tempered clergyman. He happened to be defending the minister's brother on a fraud accusation. He wrote the brother stating that he'd have to increase his fee in order to pay for the dog's train fares, thanks to the minister's complaining. A week later, the minister sent a note to the station agent withdrawing his complaint.

"Cobalt should've lived a long, happy life. He deserved it. But he was booted by a horse and seriously hurt. The whole town was distressed. The stock exchange posted messages on how he was doing at the vet's and, when he died, the *Nugget* ran a little story. The boom died soon after. Around 1920. My father burned his stocks. Shoved them in the kitchen stove, batch by batch, and, praise the Lord, I didn't have to visit my uncle anymore."

EUNICE GOES TRAVELLING

"EUNICE WAS OUR PET CAT. I let her out to do her business in the backyard and she didn't come back. That was in August 1983. Eunice was a black and white beauty that I got from the SPCA in Edmonton as a gift for my son, Wesley. He was eight when the cat went missing and it really upset him. I write a gossip column for *The Sun*. I began running items asking readers if they'd seen Eunice. The response was incredible — between thirty and forty calls —and I dutifully checked them all out. Boy, do some strays get around. Three times I was shown the same cat — at three different houses. A month went by, and no Eunice. Finally, I returned to the SPCA and collected another cat for Wesley.

"Two months after Eunice disappeared, the CBC phoned. Eunice had distinct markings and a cat fitting her description had been found in Churchill, Manitoba — 1,000 miles away. The cat was perched on the crossbeam in a boxcar filled with lime; the boxcar had been sealed shut in Edmonton nine days earlier and sent to the Arctic Co-op. What happened was, a girl at the Co-op, Janet Carswell, had called the Churchill CBC and they, in turn, had contacted the CBC in Edmonton. An Edmonton cop heard the lost-cat item on the air and he called the CBC and said, 'Hey, that's gotta be Wayne Crouse's cat.'

"Hard to believe, isn't it? A thousand miles in a boxcar. The CN yards are right behind my house and, I suspect, Eunice survived on mice over there until she hopped the freight. She was scrawny and frightened and half-starved when the Co-op people found her. At any rate, she's home now. Pacific Western and Air Canada let her fly free. Eunice is a happy animal. She gets along well with the other cat. I'm sure she learned her lesson. I'd be bowled over if she jumped another freight."

CROSSING THE BORDER

"YOU MUST'VE HEARD of Dick Irvin. He coached the Canadiens to three Stanley Cups, the last one in '53. How that man loved chickens. He was an old farm boy — his parents raised him at Limestone Ridge, Ontario — and when he was coaching the Habs he had a chicken pen somewhere outside Montreal. He usually bought his birds in Canada, but one time he was in New York for a game and somebody offered him a rare breed at a bargain-basement price. It was illegal to bring the birds across the border but that didn't stop Dick.

"He took them to Grand Central in a cardboard box, fifty or sixty baby chicks. He stuck them on the floor of the WC in his compartment. The chicks hated the train. They made an awful row. The closer the train got to Quebec, the more he worried about how he could sneak them past customs. Then he made a great discovery: when he used his electric razor, the birds didn't make a sound.

"So the train reached the border and a customs guy came to Dick's compartment. Dick had the box behind the WC door, which was half closed. He stood in the doorway and, when the customs guy walked in, he had the razor going. The guy was a hockey nut. He was delighted to meet the famous Dick Irvin, and he started asking hockey questions. Dick kept running the razor over the same spots. The customs guy must've stood there half an hour. When he finally left, Dick's face and neck were red and sore and the razor was so hot it practically scorched his hand.

"A ridiculous situation. Dick told me later that he got so tired of shaving his face and neck that he ran the razor over the backs of his hands — and the customs guy didn't blink an eye, he just went on jabbering."

DUCK SHOOT NEAR WATROUS

"HE DIDN'T GET his drawers in a knot too often, my dad, but he was fit to be tied that time in 1938. He had farm business in Saskatoon. The lawyer said be here at such and such an hour, and my dad was seldom late for appointments. Well, sir, the old rattler passed a bunch of sloughs near Watrous that were covered with ducks. Hundreds of them. It was behind schedule, yet the darn train slowed to a dead halt. The noise scared some ducks off but plenty stayed put. The conductor was going by, and my dad said, 'What's the matter?' and he didn't get an answer.

"Then my dad seen these two trainmen by the side of a slough. Holding twelve-gauge shotguns. Bam! Bam! Bam! Bam! They missed every shot and the ducks took wing. My dad was livid. He vowed to have the conductor rap their knuckles for causing the delay. Bam! Bam! Two more shots. A duck fell near the shore. A trainman peeled off his shoes and rolled up his trousers and waded out. He brought the duck back and the man who shot it stepped into view — the conductor. My dad didn't utter a peep. He fumed all the way to Saskatoon. At home, he wrote the CNR and named the conductor and demanded that he be fired. The letter didn't do nothing. A year passed; my dad was going up to Saskatoon, and the conductor was the same man who'd shot the duck."

YOU KILLED MY BEST MILKER

"'SITTIN' KNITTIN'.' My sister Mary Ann would say that all the time. Should anybody ask, 'What's Ruth doing today?' She'd answer, 'Sittin' knittin'.' I don't knit nowadays. Arthritis. But in the old days, I liked to be busy and when there were no chores to be done, I'd make sweaters and gloves and things for Mary Ann's children and different people in Kitchener. Even listening to the radio, I'd be knitting. So I wouldn't be wasting my time.

"Most definitely. I had my knitting bag with me on the train that day. I was probably making a sweater but I don't recall. The train wasn't speeding when it hit, but we were tossed about like ragdolls. I landed on the fellow across from me. Lucky, I didn't stick a needle through him. Nobody was injured, just shaken up a bit.

"I went outside to find out what was going on. The locomotive had struck a cow. Killed it dead. The farmer was screaming blue murder, 'You've killed my best milker! I pinched pennies for years to buy her!' The conductor calmed him. He said the cow shouldn't have been where it was, but, not to worry, the railway would pay the damages. The farmer climbed on his tractor and hauled the cow away.

"A few months later, I was on my way to Toronto again, and who should get on but the farmer. He sat next to me and we talked. I said I'd been there when his cow was killed. 'She was pretty sickly,' he said. 'Drying up real bad.' I said I thought I heard him tell the conductor it was his best milker. 'When a truck killed another cow of mine on the highway, I said that was my best milker too. Half my herd's no damn good but when somebody's paying me for them, they're all blue-ribbon prize-winners.'"

CRIBBAGE ON THE BOVINE EXPRESS

"MY FATHER RAISED CATTLE and pigs on our farm and sold them at the livestock market in Calgary. One day at the stockyards, he was told they wanted someone to babysit thirty steers on the Bovine Express, a freight train that acquired its nickname because it took seven painfully slow days to reach Montreal. I volunteered; it was a free ride and I was registered to commence classes at McGill that fall. I figured I was in for a truly rotten time. The cattle had to be led off and fed and watered at every divisional point, roughly every 150 miles. I had visions of unruly steers breaking loose and me chasing them all over hell's half-acre. Nothing of the sort. I stayed in the caboose, the crew took care of the cattle, and I didn't go near the blessed things once. I did go near a cribbage board, though. This older man, a cattle buyer who was also travelling free, enticed me into some games, and he won every time. The stakes weren't very big but it soured me on cribbage for life. Sometimes another member at the Royal Montreal Club asks me to play. I remember 1927 and the caboose and how I was fleeced, and I always say no."

AN UNCOMMON MEMENTO

"WE WERE TRAINING at Shilo and this kid joined our platoon. He was tall and broad in the shoulders and eighteen years old. His family had a farm at Dauphin. He said he was good at shooting gophers and selling their pelts and so he reckoned he'd be good at shooting Germans. One of the guys kidded him. 'Shooting German's easy, all right. But like gophers, it's skinning them afterwards that's the hard part.'

"The kid was full of pepper for a month or so. Couldn't wait to be overseas. Then the homesickness set in. He'd mope around and write long letters to his mom and dad. We got our orders in May of '42 — the train to Halifax, the boat to England. As we were boarding the train in Winnipeg, a sergeant handed the kid a letter that had been misplaced somewhere.

"We settled in our car and the kid tore the letter open. It was from his mom. He bawled like a baby. Tears streamed down his face. 'Trouble at home?' I asked. There was no trouble. The letter said good luck, we love you, that sort of thing. What made him bawl was the goat turd. He'd asked his mom for something to remind him of the farm and that's what she'd sent. A tiny brown ball from his pet goat. I'd seen guys cry but never over anything as stupid as a frigging goat turd!"

FEEDING THE BIRDS

"AUNT MAUREEN lived near McAdam in the 1960s and, on weekends, I'd bring a batch of leftovers from the bakery I had in Saint John. Stale buns and bread. No, no, not for Aunt Maureen. For the birds. They had a pond in front of the McAdam railway station and every summer there'd be forty to fifty geese camped on it. In the fall, if a fellow was careful, he could peek in the nests and see their young ones. The railway stored feed in 45-gallon drums. Between shifts, you'd have these railroaders throwing handfuls of grain around the pond. When the feed ran low, they'd phone their buddies in Saint John and they'd put the sweepings from the grain cars in old sacks and rifle them up on the next freight.

"The geese meant the world to the railroaders. Particularly to Wally Sangster. He started the sanctuary around 1955 by bringing two geese he bought to the pond. Maybe the geese meant too much to the railroaders. I can't claim it's the gospel-truth but I did hear a story that they once held a little funeral when the Atlantic Limited ran over a mother and two young ones. They say some of the boys shovelled the remains into a cardboard box, said a prayer, and buried the birds.

"I wasn't that dedicated to the geese. They were only birds, for heaven's sake. But I did like to do my bit to help them. I carried my baked goods in an old kit bag. One Saturday I was on the coach and a fellow had his lunch in a brown-paper bag on the seat next to him. Partway to McAdam he said he might skip lunch and feed the sandwiches to the geese, who likely needed them more than he did. I told him he might as well have his lunch, that when the birds saw what I had in my kit bag they'd turn up their beaks at his chintzy offering. He laughed, took out his sandwiches, and shared them with me.

"There aren't too many geese at McAdam nowadays. Three or four a summer. Hunters and chemicals down south have taken their toll. It's ironic. There isn't a great deal going on at the station either. McAdam was the CPR's liveliest junction in the Maritimes. Up to sixteen passenger trains a day stopped there, coming and going from Montreal and Boston. Since VIA ended the last of the passenger trains in 1980, there's only freights through the village. The geese and the railway station died off together."

CATTLE VERSUS SHEEP

"BLAMING THE CPR for everything used to be the sport around here. Not fair. Not fair at all. If it wasn't for the railway, southern Alberta wouldn't have the sugarbeet crops it has today. The land around some towns — Rosemary, Temple, Magrath — was so dry a man was lucky to take four bushels off an acre. That's right. Four bushels an acre. The Mormons came from Utah and built irrigation canals. Five hundred miles of canals. They teach you that in school. They don't teach you that the CPR picked up where the Mormons left off. The railway built dams and over 2,000 miles of irrigation ditches between Medicine Hat and Calgary.

"Many people blamed the range war on the CPR. You never heard of it? You should've. It's important history. Just after World War I, it dawned on the CPR that it would have more business if there were more ranchers in the Irrigation District. It paid for newspaper advertisements telling settlers it had two million acres of grassland to get rid of. Only problem was, a mild winter and a summer drought cut the water supply and newcomers wound up shooting thousands of cattle and horses.

"While the killing was going on, a lot of sheepherders rode north from Montana. With 90,000 sheep. The cowboy and the sheepherder were sworn enemies. Each reckoned there wasn't enough grass and water on the plains for the other. The CPR knew it had a dynamite situation on its hands. It told the sheepmen to stay south of its main line and to leave the north to the cattlemen. Some herders said to hell with you and crossed the line.

"Boy, oh, boy. That put the match to the fuse. A bunch of cowboys raided the herders' camp south of the line and burned them out. Set fire to their tents and shacks and scattered their sheep. Herders were beaten up on the street and, to get even, they shot at cowboys riding the back country. All summer it went on. The CPR stepped in and persuaded the sheepmen to move south and stay there.

"The range war was over. Thanks to the CPR. It did a good job of keeping the peace and building the dams and canals that made the district prosper. Try to explain that to the old-timers. They don't listen. All they want to do is rattle their tongues about how evil the CPR was."

JERRY HANNIGAN'S KITTEN

"BEFORE THE 1930s, Marysville people travelled to Fredericton on the 1:30 p.m. Suburban each and every Saturday to spend the wages they'd earned in the cotton mills. The women and children returned at four or six and the men caught the last train at ten o'clock. I was there the night Jerry Hannigan climbed on, three sheets to the wind, carrying a black kitten. The conductor says, 'Animals aren't allowed. It'll have to go.' 'Suits me,' Jerry says. 'Open the window and I'll throw it out.' The conductor shut up. Nobody's mean enough to have a kitten thrown into three feet of snow.

"Jerry soon had a peculiar habit. Nearly every Saturday he'd take the kitten with him, sometimes hiding it in his coat. At four or six, he'd take it home again, then go back to Fredericton. People asked what he was up to and he'd say nothing, just playing a little game. The kitten grew big and the conductor threatened to have Jerry banned if he persisted in trying to smuggle it on board. From then on, the cat stayed behind. I was eating lunch at the mill with Jerry and I squeezed the real story out of him. He'd walk around Fredericton and young girls would come up and say, 'What a cute kitten.' They'd chat a while and he'd say, 'Want to go to a dance with me tonight?' Lots said yes, but after a date he'd decide he didn't like them and, the following Saturday, he'd be prowling the streets with his kitten in his arms, live bait for female flesh."

HIDING A HAMSTER

"I WAS ON the last run of the old Goose Lake-to-Calgary train in 1962. I suppose it was a historic occasion but I didn't have my mind on history. I was worried about Bert's hamster. I had been visiting my parents in Saskatoon and my mother had given Bert a white hamster in a cage. He named it Snowball. Bert was ten years old and the hamster was an Easter present. The four of us were crammed into one compartment. Bert and I and my other two children, Colleen and Brian. Three kids can make plenty of noise and mine were no exception. I kept telling them to be quiet. I was terrified that the porter would stick his head in the door, spot the hamster, and toss us off the train. We took forever and a day to get to Calgary; the Goose Lake train stopped at every town along the route. Finally, we were there. We stuck a Safeway bag over the cage and smuggled Snowball safely off. After we got home, the hamster did what furry little animals always seem to do to kids. It broke Bert's heart. It up and died."

BLONDE BOMBSHELL

"YOU HAD TO BE BLIND not to notice the blonde. Leopardskin coat, black leotards, black sweater, and a face like Elaine Bédard. Who's Elaine Bédard? She was a famous model in Quebec in the 1960s. Face of an angel. As we filed through the gate and down the stairs to the train, I heard a smart alec in the crowd say to the blonde, 'Mother, I know what I want for Christmas. Don't bother wrapping it. I'll eat it here.' Oh yeah, I should mention. She had a suitcase with stickers on it. Acapulco, Paris, New York, et cetera.

"I was with Leo and Marcel. We were Laval students, and we'd been in Montreal for the weekend. Leo was very interested in the girl. To tell the truth, he was interested in every female over the age of ten. He behaved as if he was God's gift to women and, what bugged me and Marcel was, women behaved as if he was too. We were in the coach. Marcel went walking and when he came back he said he'd spotted the blonde and she was riding in compartment number this on car number that.

"Leo sprang up. He said he'd give her a nudge and see if she fell over. Not five minutes passed before he was back. He looked very disturbed. 'You guys will never guess what happened,' he said. He'd knocked on her door and she'd opened it a little. He pretended he thought she was a movie star. 'Oh no,' she said, 'I'm not from Hollywood. I'm from Verdun.' She invited Leo in. She said she was a stripteaser and she carried part of her act in the suitcase. A boa constrictor. The snake was in the toilet bowl; he liked it there because it was wet and cool. Leo looked at the snake and fled. Blonde bombshell or not, he couldn't force himself to be in that room."

BAT REMEDY

"HELL, I AIN'T AFRAID of nothing. Nothing, except Satan, airplanes, and bats. I ain't come across Satan, far as I know, and I can stay off planes, but bats I'm eternally running into. Take the time I was on the night whistler out of Medicine Hat and a bloody bat flew out of nowhereland and started dive-bombing us. Some woman shrieked and buttoned herself up behind her curtains. The porter was swinging a broom. And me, I stood like a dumb idiot, petrified, with my hands on my head, scared the bat might invade my hair.

"The conductor was no braver. He took a gander and disappeared quick. And some fool passenger, he filled a paper cup with water and threw it at the bat. What was he doing? Trying to drown it? These two farmers came in and laughed. They reckoned bats were easy to get rid of. They had the porter douse the lights. Then one farmer held the platform door open while the other stood in the doorway with a flashlight. It did the job. The bat zoomed for the light, they closed the door, and it went out the side door on the platform. Gone forever.

"A bat on a train. Who else but me, a guy who's scared of them, would find himself in such a stupid predicament?"

WE'LL SUE THEIR PANTS OFF

"PADDY NOLAN. Now there was a wit. He was a Calgary lawyer around the turn of the century and he had no use whatsoever for the CPR. He was in his office and a rancher burst in, foaming with anger. One of his horses was grazing on weeds between the ties and the midday flier to Fort MacLeod bolted down the track and killed it. 'You'll get a fat fee for this, Mister Nolan. We'll sue their pants off.' Nolan shook his had. 'I'm sorry, my friend, but I don't take cases I'm certain to lose.' The rancher was incredulous. 'How can we possibly lose? The train chased my horse half a mile before it nailed it.' 'That goes to prove my point,' Nolan replied. 'The court knows all about the railway's past performances. There isn't a judge in Alberta who doesn't think that any horse that can't outrun a CPR train deserves to live!'"

BRINGING IN THE SHEAVES

Every August and September for more than thirty years, the Harvest Excursion trains journeyed to the Prairies from eastern Canada carrying contingents of temporary labourers. The number of men travelling west to help bring in the crops was awesome — nearly 350,000 between 1920 and 1928; 45,000 in 1924 alone. The majority of the farm hands were Canadian by birth, but each year there was a large influx of foreigners. The federal government enticed them with cheap boat fares and the glamorous posters it distributed throughout the British Isles and continental Europe after the first Harvest Excursion in 1896 — posters of brawny, deliriously happy males stacking sheaves of golden wheat on glorious sunlit fields.

The posters tactfully avoided showing the less inviting realities of harvesting: the dawn-to-dusk labour for meagre wages that, at times, took place under a scorching sun. Many farm hands were treated like members of the family and slept in comfortable guest rooms. Others lived in barns, tarpaper shacks, and tents. Despite the hardships, more than half of the workers made the Harvest Excursion an annual event: some eventually married farm girls and settled permanently on the Prairies.

Bill Morris was one of them. His trips west were motivated equally by a youthful yearning for fresh experiences and the need to help his parents keep the family farm at Cobourg, Ontario, financially stable. Morris and his wife, Betty, now have their own small farm in northern Alberta, which they bought after he retired from the civil service. At eighty-one, Morris still plants twenty acres of oats every spring, just to keep his hand in. He was a neighbour of mine for many years but, as so often happens when you're doing research, I tried a dozen different sources looking for someone who had been on a harvest special before a local storekeeper said, "Why don't you talk to Bill Morris? I'm sure he was on one of those things."

"Yes, sir, I was on the Harvest Excursions, all right. Six years. From the month I became sixteen till I married and went into the post office. Come August, I'd haul myself to Union Station and climb onto the first special heading west. They had a cheap rate. In the 1920s, you could travel to Winnipeg from Ontario and Quebec for fifteen bucks, twenty-five from the Maritimes. Return fare, you'd add on another five bucks. Each train had five-, maybe six-hundred men on it.

"It's hard to say which was the worst, the sleeping or eating. You'd lie on slatted seats, without pillows, without blankets, and another guy sharing it with you. When you needed food it was the lunch counter and corned beef or the cafés near the stations. Those cafés were sure sleazy. So sleazy you'd wonder if it was chicken on your plate or alley cat. Plenty of whisky on the Excursions. Whisky, some dice, and at least one fight per trip. I heard of guys wrecking a colonist car. Smashed the windows and lights because a trainman threw a fella off for peeing wherever he felt like — on the floor, against walls, on somebody's seat. No one sided with the filthy pig, but they didn't like the trainman so they had an excuse for running wild.

"I don't recall anybody special. No faces, names. It was a long time ago. I do remember that they were from different backgrounds. Salesmen, pen-pushers, farm boys, lumberjacks, everything under the sun. Hold on. There was a painter once. He did these little drawings night and day. Of the men in the cars. The government hiring agents were in Winnipeg. You'd get a look-over and if you weren't too puny or old, you'd be assigned to a region. The painter and me were sent on to towns in southern Saskatchewan. The fare from Winnipeg was maybe a dollar. The painter got off at this one-elevator town. The farmer who was supposed to hire him saw the drawings and said he should get back on the train. He wanted a real man, used to real work. The last memory I have of them is the painter and the farmer arguing beside the track as the train moved away.

"Those farmers were the Pharaohs, we were the slaves. Take it from me, it felt like we were building the bloody pyramids. Back-busting work. Sweat running down your face and your whole body aching with pain. Oh, the farmers fed you good. You bet they did. And nobody beat you with a stick. But they expected the harvesters to be in the fields from sun-up to sun-down. Machines didn't do the stooking in those days. You'd run behind the binder, picking up sheaves, one under each arm, and stacking them in cone-shaped stooks. The binder was your enemy. It was noisy and dusty and it was cutting and spitting the sheaths out so fast you nearly died trying to keep up.

"Then there was the threshing gangs. Weeks, sometimes months, after the stooking was done, the threshers were on the fields to take the grain from the sheaves. Most farmers wouldn't hack the price of a machine and they contracted out to roaming gangs. A dozen or more men travelled with the thresher. Some gangs had their own kitchens and old railway cars on wheels for bunkhouses; others slept in tents and ate when farm wives brought their meals to the fields. Everything was hurry, hurry, hurry. The big rush was to do the crops before bad weather set in. I saw men collapse, fall right over, from exhaustion. I saw some give up; walk right over to the farmer, demand their pay, and then walk to the closest train.

"Jeez, it was rough slogging. Big money? Ha, that's a laugh. Three bucks a day was the average and, no matter how hard you laboured, five bucks a day was the most you could pull down. But, you know, we took pride in what we did. Riding the train to the East, a man could look at the levelled fields and know he did his bit to feed the country. The government was proud of its harvesters. Pictures in railway stations showed men bringing in crops. In Regina, I saw real stooks of wheat in the concourse and a banner praising the harvesters. It said, 'Thanks For A Job Well Done,' or something.

"Going home, a fella had to keep his wits sharp. Pickpockets and card sharks and floozies. The pickpockets and card sharks rode the colonist cars, dressed like us. The ones you spotted straight off were the ones with white skin. They couldn't have been harvesting if they weren't burnt brown or didn't have calloused hands. Some were really cute. They had tans and rough hands and talked farming and mixed real well. A good pickpocket could steal hundreds of dollars on a single trip. The floozies were at the city depots. Some stupid clods jumped off to buy a newspaper and ended up wasting their money in a flea-bag hotel with a degenerate woman.

"Bigger and better machines killed the Harvest Excursions. The final one rumbled west, I believe, around 1930. It got so a farmer and his family could do a crop all by themselves. Now the combines have radios and air-conditioning and fairly soon they'll be remote-controlled and the farmer won't have to leave his bed. I'm glad for them that they've got things easier but I'm sorry they're missing the companionship we had. The feeling of sharing and accomplishing you get when a gang of men work hard together."

THE DAYS OF WINE AND ROSES

The 82-year-old man sitting beside me on The Canadian last summer was not enamoured with his dinner. Poking the newly thawed salmon steak with a fork, he commented sourly, "In the old days, the Winnipeg gold-eye was so fresh it wriggled on your plate." I smiled at the exaggeration but, at the same time, I truly sympathized with him. Until the 1960s railway dining cars were well respected for their cuisine and the manner in which it was served. Superb three- and four-course meals were presented on immaculate white linen tablecloths bedecked with polished silverware, fine crystal, and floral bouquets. The desserts were fresh from the kitchen, the coffee in the tall, spotless urns constantly renewed. Broadcaster Clyde Gilmour told me that when he was a boy in Medicine Hat he became enthralled gazing through the dining-car windows of passing trains. "That was a magical world to me. The dining car symbolized the ultimate in urbane sophistication."

Although the prices were generally reasonable, not everyone could afford to eat in the dining car. Sandwiches brought from home and potato chips bought at track-side stores have always been the staples of the day-coach diet. A Nova Scotian I met in a dome car said that if it wasn't for apples and Coca-Cola half the unemployed Maritimers riding the Ocean Limited to Montreal and points west would have starved to death.

COFFEE LIKE CRANKCASE OIL

"THE RITZIEST RESTAURANT in the biggest cities couldn't beat the train coffee. In 1957 I had such a great cup that I strolled over to the kitchen and asked the cook what it was. He said a special blend, partly Mother Parker's and partly some name I can't remember. I offered him ten bucks for a pound and he said no, he'd be in hot water if he was caught selling company merchandise. In 1979 I was on the same route and ordered a coffee. The waiter brought it in a plastic cup and it tasted like crankcase oil. One sip and I wanted to barf. I called the steward over and told him about the great cup I had in '57, 'I guess it was pretty dumb of me telling the cook I loved his coffee,' I said. 'He obviously decided to stick with a winner, and he's been using the same grounds ever since.'"

BUTTER WAS A LUXURY

"THE ENGLISH GIRL sat with us from Halifax to Vancouver. She was married to a Pole and she was going to the coast to find a job and then send for him. This was in March 1953, and my husband and I had been on our honeymoon overseas. Coming from Halifax, the train had a long stop in Montreal. The railway meals were too expensive for us so we went shopping. We walked into a supermarket and the English girl's eyes widened. 'You mean, I can buy anything I want?' she exclaimed. The war had ended years earlier but the shops in England still weren't as abundantly stocked as ours. She loaded her arms with food.

"My husband and I purchased a loaf of bread, some canned goods, and an item that was a luxury for us, a pound of butter. At home I usually had margarine. To our utter dismay, the train heating gauges weren't functioning properly. We practically suffocated. I remember rolling over in my berth during the night and loudly declaring, 'What are they trying to do, bake us?' In the morning my husband grumbled to the porter. The porter said, yes, it was a trifle warm but nothing serious. When we pulled our grocery bag from under the seat, the butter had disappeared. Melted. All that remained of our expensive treat was a grease spot."

FIT FOR A LUMBERJACK

"WHO COULD FORGET the dining cars in the 1930s? Yeah, sure, the food was marvellous but the cars themselves were nothing to sneeze at. The CPR's loveliest train was the Trans Canada Limited. I rode it a lot from Toronto to B.C. It had a wonderful lounge, what they called a sunroom. Huge windows and leather chairs and sofas so comfortable you'd sink in and not want to stand up. The dining car was the Argyle. I recollect the name because my parents were from Argyle, Nova Scotia. The kitchen floor was coppered. The dining area had a thick carpet, wall to wall, and beautiful black walnut panels. The silver and china on the tables was the real McCoy, some of it dating to the turn of the century.

"The breakfasts were tremendous. They fed you like a lumberjack. Two eggs, any style, and big portions of bacon, sausage, and hash browns. Fish too, if you felt like it, and pork chops. Say you didn't feel hungry and you just ordered a grapefruit. The grapefruit arrived in a china bowl with ice around it. You couldn't rival the CPR breakfasts anywhere but, you know, there was one thing they couldn't do as well as another railway. Baked potatoes. Don't ask me why, but the Great Northern cooks had a knack for doing them on the Winnipeg - Minneapolis line that was legendary. Anyone who travelled a lot knew and praised the Great Northern's baked potatoes."

IMPROMPTU PICNIC

"DOMINION DAY in the 1920s meant riding to Steep Rock, Manitoba, from Grahamdale, Manitoba, for the July 1st fair. There'd be horse races and games of chance, and the big event for our family was having our uncles and aunts and cousins and nephews come from all over the Interlake District to meet us at the picnic ground. Mother and me wrapped salads and other perishables in damp cloths and stuffed them in big honey pails with wire handles. The desserts were raspberry preserves. We'd cart this all onto the train, along with bathing suits and blankets and cushions and, if it was boiling hot, my two brothers wouldn't wear shoes. We'd play 'Hide and Seek' and 'I Spy With My Little Eye' and 'Find the Button' and, it never failed, one of my brothers always stubbed his toe running in the aisle barefoot.

"One time, the train broke down. Hold the phone. That's not right. It didn't break down; the tracks had given way for some strange reason. We had to wait for a work gang to do repairs. We sat and sat and sat. We got hungry and Dad gave Mother permission to go ahead and put everything out for our picnic. We had it right there, in the train car. Dad played his banjo and we sang songs and shared our food with people who didn't have any. No ants, no mosquitoes, and I didn't have to put up with my cousin Lawrence, who was always pulling my hair. I wish we'd had our picnic there every July 1st."

STANDING THERE WITH ACHING ARMS

"HE WAS A HIGH POOBAH with Canadian National. A head-office manager for the sleeping- and dining-car division. He strode into the dining car and ordered soup and a sirloin steak. The train braked while he was finishing the soup, cracking the window pane beside his table from top to bottom. This was many years ago, before the stronger double glass was installed, and they had windows you could shove your fist through. I was a waiter then. The train started up again and I lunged across the table to hold the glass, which was leaning perilously towards him. I assumed he'd shift his fat rump to another table. No such luck. His steak arrived, and he sat silently devouring it, as if I was invisible. I stood there like a ruddy fool. A ruddy fool with aching arms. He ate his steak, his dessert, and he drank his cotton-picking coffee. He left the table just as the train halted in a station and I could let go of the glass without fear. He didn't leave a tip. The irony of the situation was he was well-known for his passionate commitment to railway safety and, when the window cracked, he was embarking on a tour to ensure that no harm would come to dining-car patrons from faulty equipment."

EXCITING PIES

"A TEENAGER'S BELLY is a bottomless pit. I know from experience. I used to shovel a plateful of food into my face at my dad's place, Tommy's Fish and Chips on Brock Street, and think nothing of wandering the town in search of a hamburger and milkshake an hour later. In fact, what I remember most about the trip I took west was the exciting pies. I was among four kids from Tillsonburg chosen for an army cadet camp at Banff. Me and a kid from Windsor, name of Bob, waltzed into the dining car after it was closed to shoot the breeze with the cook. He was taking cherry pies from the oven. He gave us one no charge, and Bob and me demolished it.

"We went back the next night — and the next — and the cook gave us a free pie each time. We were in Seventh Heaven. We split the pies down the middle. Cherry, blueberry, and raisin. We ate every scrap and then went off to bed. If I ate like that now, I'd be sicker than a dog half the night. At eighteen, I just crawled between the sheets and was out like a light. The third pie, the blueberry, was the best. Before I fell asleep, a very uncadet-like notion popped into my head. That pie was so good I regretted having had to share it with Bob."

AN EMBARRASSED WAITER

"I'M EMBARRASSED by the food I serve. Nine dollars for dinner. Ham, fish, roast beef; whatever you pick, it's heated-up junk. Passengers say to me, the fish was half-cooked, the beef was too stringy to chew. Last week a lady said to me, 'You've got a club car and an observation car on this train. You ought to have a hospital car.' That wasn't fair. Nobody gets sick from eating our food. It's inspected, it's healthy. But it hurts your pride to hear things like that. The desserts? Fruit cocktail one meal, apple pie the next. A hundred thousand people ask for ice cream and we don't have it. The coffee? A passenger was bitching about it and the waiter said to him, 'It's very strong, sir, because coffee's supposed to be that way. Coffee isn't any good unless you can stand on it.' The prisoners at Collins Bay get better coffee. An ex-con told me so.

"Successful people use the trains a lot. People who hate flying or aren't in any hurry. People with American Express cards and gold jewellery and wads of 50s in their wallets. And what do we feed them. Greasy spoon stuff. I take that back. I've eaten in greasy spoons that have better food. It isn't that our cooks can't cook. If they had to quit the trains and work in a café, they'd prepare terrific meals. Their wives brag about the great Sunday dinners they make at home. The reason they don't cook well for the railway is because the company doesn't encourage them to.

"There are company spies, my friend. The railway will deny it but it's a fact. Company spies ride the trains pretending to be ordinary passengers. They catch you drinking or sleeping on duty or spending too much time in a female's compartment, they report you. Fine and dandy. Guys fooling around should be reported. But the spies never say a goddamned word about the food. Or, if they do, who pays attention at head office? Talk to the cooks and they'll say they hate microwaves. They'd be overjoyed if the railway loaded fresh meat and fish and vegetables on board and said it wanted to run old-style kitchens again. The food might cost more but the passengers wouldn't mind paying an extra dollar or two for food they'd love eating and I'd be proud to serve."

A BIG CRATE OF STRAWBERRIES

"THERE WAS A BIG CRATE of strawberries on the platform at Mission that nobody was guarding. I gather it was waiting to be loaded on our train and shipped to Alberta. The year was 1927 and I was an NCO, travelling to Petawawa with four carloads of soldiers. We were Royal Canadian Artillery. A few of the boys couldn't resist stealing the berries. I didn't see them do it but after Mission I was in their car and maybe a dozen soldiers were gobbling strawberries like mad. I asked where they'd gotten them and a wiseacre said, 'On the platform, sir. They were cheap.' They ate their fill and they had a berry fight, throwing them at each other. The car was a mess.

"The railway wasn't stupid. It figured out immediately what had become of the missing berries. The station agent wired ahead. The train stopped at Revelstoke and a major ordered everyone on board to line up on the platform. 'I want the blighters who stole those strawberries to step forward and admit it.' Naturally, no one did. I was amazed that the major didn't inspect the men closer; there were stains on their hands and uniforms. That didn't seem to dawn on him. He ordered everyone back on the train. On pay day, a portion of the price of the berries was clipped from our wages and sent to Mission. Outrageous. Why should all of us been punished for what a handful of men did?"

LISTENING AND ORDERING

"'PLEASE' AND 'THANK YOU' were the extent of my grasp on the English language in 1934. I had emigrated to Canada from Poland with my wife and small daughter. We lived on bread and cheese and fruit in Halifax after we left the boat and while we waited for the train to British Columbia. We planned to stock up on grocery-store food for the trip but there was a change at the last moment and we were put on an earlier train.

"So, there we were, for four days and five nights, forced to eat in the dining car. It was winter, you understand, and we had only thin summer clothing and couldn't get off at the different towns to look for food. The first day I listened to a man order pancakes and I did the same. Pancakes for the three of us. I couldn't hear anyone order their lunch so it was pancakes once more. And again for dinner. The waiter was clearly puzzled and I imagine the chef wasn't too pleased, but they delivered the goods.

"The second morning, a young boy, twelve at the most, entered the meal car by himself and I heard what he said and ordered the very same thing. Horror of horrors. Cherry pie piled high with ice cream. It was my first example of the strange tastes North American children have. The waiter was shaking his head when he brought ours. Eating all that sweetness for breakfast, it nearly made me ill. I've never been able to face cherry pie since.

"I had two alternatives for lunch. Pancakes once more, or overcome my shyness and stand up and point at someone's meal and gesture until the waiter understood I wanted the same. Fortunately, a woman who spoke Polish appeared at lunch and the waiter introduced us and she ordered our meals for the remainder of our journey."

LEMON TARTS AND CHOCOLATE CAKE

"SIX MONTHS in Thunder Bay Correctional and when I got out back in '79, I was dying for a long, cold beer. I ordered a Blue and gulped it down. An old lady in the lounge car smiled and said, 'Young man, you sure are thirsty.' 'Yeah,' I said, 'I've been in the pen for the past six months.' Her jaw dropped to here and she finished her coffee fast. I wanted to shout at her, 'Hey, don't run away. I was only in for drunk driving.' I didn't say nothing. Screw her. I don't owe any explanations. The waiter served me a couple of more beers and I was feeling okay and then he said, 'Unless you put some grub in your stomach, I'm cutting you off. There's a limit to how stoned people can get in my car.' What was it to him? I was tipping good.

"The train stopped in some drinkwater town and I went over to a store and bought a package of lemon tarts. That's what I ate for lunch and dinner. Lemon tarts. If the waiter gave me the fish-eye, I'd gulp a tart. Get me? Okay, so I got off the train plastered. Loaded to the gills. My mum and dad and Tracy and the kids were at the station. Tracy, she's my wife. She'd baked a chocolate cake with 'Welcome Home' written on it. I sort of glanced at it and started passing out. My dad had to hold me up. I don't remember nothing after that. I woke up early in the morning and crept downstairs for a beer. The cake was in the fridge. No slices out of it. I felt so ashamed, so guilty. I knew that I'd done it again, gotten carried away with my drinking and disappointed Mum and Dad and Tracy and the kids."

INDIGENOUS FOOD

"THIS MIGHT SOUND SILLY, but for a long time I thought Kellogg's either owned the CNR or the CNR owned Kellogg's. You see, I came to this country in 1952 and, after I got on the train with a lot of other Poles in Halifax, a man and a woman from the Kellogg company came down the aisle handing out boxes of cornflakes. Kind of a welcome-to-Canada present. Naturally, I thought the railway wouldn't let them do it unless they were in business together.

"Anyhow, everyone tore open the boxes after the train pulled out and started munching cornflakes. Without milk and sugar, cornflakes aren't the most delicious thing in the world. Yet we all kept on eating them handful after silly handful, because we gathered this must be an authentic Canadian food and, if we were going to live here, we'd better get used to it."

WORTH WAITING FOR

"CAFÉS NEAR THE STATION had their specialties. One might be renowned for its roast beef, another for its great breakfasts. If you boarded a train that had no diner in the 1920s, you'd hope for a long stop near a good café. At High River, Mrs. Robinson's had raisin pies that made you drool thinking of them. The Lethbridge train would stop in the town for ten minutes and folks would rush to Mrs. Robinson's for slices of pie.

"One time about twenty people trooped into the café and Mrs. Robinson ran out of raisin pie. The conductor and the engineer came in and said they wanted some so bad they'd wait till a new batch came out of the oven. 'What about your schedule?' somebody asked. 'Don't you go having no conniption over the schedule,' the engineer said. 'We'll make her to Lethbridge okay.'

"The train was late getting away, but it was on the dot in Lethbridge. How come? Because she bore down the track like a crazy demon. The cars swayed so bad passengers banged into walls when they tried to walk. I heard a pregnant lady say all the movement was liable to bring her baby out before its time. That was a fun ride. I'm not one of those old codgers, you know, who goes around saying everything was better away back when. But the fact remains — the cafés near the railways were better. Comparing them to the places near the stations today — your McDonald's, your Kentucky Fried Chicken — is like comparing donkeys to thoroughbreds."

POLITICIANS

I n the autumn of 1965 I was driving across Saskatchewan when I came to a village that was obviously on its last legs. Most of the store fronts were boarded up and the grain elevator at the foot of the main street was being torn down. A passenger train rolled by and I had to wait at a crossing, behind a rusty pickup truck. As the train passed, a living legend appeared. John George Diefenbaker stood on the rear platform, waving stiffly. There couldn't have been more than three people on the street and yet there he was, a Canadian monarch greeting his subjects. Years later I mentioned the incident to long-time Conservative stalwart Roy Deyell. "I'm not surprised," he said. "Dief was a born actor. He had to perform, whether the audience was three or three thousand."

Diefenbaker's flare for theatrics lasted not only until his dying day, but beyond it. Before his death in August 1979, the former prime minister persuaded the Tory brass that his body should be borne across the nation on a special train to its final resting place in Saskatoon. It would, he reasoned, give his fellow countrymen an opportunity to bid an affectionate farewell to their untiring servant.

His critics called the Diefenbaker funeral train an extravagant ego trip. Perhaps it was, but the fact remains that no other modern-day politician has been so closely associated with trains. Dief loved them, particularly during whistle-stop campaign tours. He'd sit in his private car, sometimes wrapped in a bathrobe, dictating up to 300 letters a day between stops and, when the mood took him, he'd anchor himself on the car platform, usually to talk to well-wishers gathered at railway stations. "He loathed flying," said Deyell. "He said it carried him over the heads of the voters and he missed seeing their faces."

There are stories in this chapter about Pierre Trudeau, J. S. Woodsworth, and other political figures but, as he was the trains' greatest fan, the man from Prince Albert commands more space than anyone else.

QUIET, SAD, RESPECTFUL

"THE CHIEF'S BODY lay in state at the Parliament Buildings for three days. He had planned every detail of his funeral, right down to the flags on his casket, the Red Ensign and the Maple Leaf. The cortege marched from Parliament Hill to Christ Church Cathedral for the service and then proceeded to the train. The crowd lining the route was fairly large. Around 35,000 people, I'd say.

"They put the casket in the baggage car. There were specially made picture windows with wreaths in them. The inside of the car was draped in black, and an enormous wreath, from the federal government, decked in red carnations, was beside the casket. The casket was closed. That was the biggest complaint that people had, not being able to see him, but someone in the Tory hierarchy had decided that that was the way it should be.

"As the train rolled up the Ottawa Valley, a farmer stood up on his tractor, removed his hat, and held it over his heart. That was a very moving moment for me. I'll never forget it. Other than that, I guess what stands out in my mind are the crowds. So many people at Kenora that, instead of slowing down as originally planned, the train backed up and stopped. In Winnipeg, before midnight, thousands crowded the streets for blocks and blocks, waiting to file past the casket. Oh, yes, I do remember a couple of individuals. At Watrous, Saskatchewan, an 86-year-old farmer named Reeves was led into the car by his nurse. He said Dief had once visited his homestead during a campaign. And the fellow at Melville. I think his name was Bennett. He walked up the ramp, looked at the coffin, and keeled over. Died right there, a heart attack, next to the man he admired.

"On the whole, I'd say there was more fondness than grief. Only a few people brought flowers and not too many wept. At Diefenbaker's age, 83, the death wasn't a great shock to the populace. Not like John Kennedy, struck down in his prime. The crowds were quiet, sad, and respectful.

"And while all this was going on — the train rolling across the country, the mourners filing off and on — the Tories aboard the special were doing what Tories do best. They were embroiled in intrigue worthy of the Orient Express. Plotting. Whispering. Backstabbing. The whole shebang. Dief would've loved the sheer drama of it all. Personally, I was a Diefenbaker aficionado and I was looking forward to a quiet, reverent, sentimental journey. That damn Val Sears spoiled it for me. Before the train slid out of Ottawa, he wrote a piece for the *Star* saying Diefenbaker had left $150,000 in his will to the Diefenbaker Centre in Saskatoon.

"What a bombshell. The faction headed by Joel Aldred, Bob Coates, and Jimmy Johnston had different plans for the funds. Aldred, for one thing, wanted to turn the Chief's Ottawa home into a museum. John Munroe, the director of the Diefenbaker Centre, was on the train. So was Max Clement, an old crony of Diefs, who said another $150,000 was pledged to the children of Prince Albert. Aldred and his pals *versus* Munroe and his supporters. And I was cast in an unfamiliar role: Charlie Lynch, peace negotiator. I'd wander from car to car, trying to pacify both camps and, while doing it, hearing all these incredible rumours.

"The Tories had established a trust fund for the Chief. Someone told me it was supposed to contain $700,000 but had less than $500,000. It was said $200,000 had been withdrawn to help set up a trust fund for Claude Wagner. There were also claims that Diefenbaker had heard Munroe was helping Jack Homer write a book and, as he viewed Homer as a traitor to the cause, he had been considering dumping Munroe as the Centre's director.

"The will-battle raged on and on. Arguments in the club car, glowering looks in the diner, and many people rigidly refusing to talk to one another. Aldred was quite a study. Snarling on the train, then charming and good-natured when he alighted to meet the public.

Munroe was rather quiet and had a lively wit. I'll never know if my mediation influenced anyone but before we crossed into Saskatchewan the word spread. No more squabbling over the will. For decency's sake, the two camps agreed to drop the matter, at least until after the Chief was in the ground.

"With peace restored, I stepped out on the vestibule somewhere between Prince Albert and Saskatoon to play my harmonica. A warm, calm, beautiful Prairie sunset. I played the 'Red River Valley' and 'Springtime in the Rockies.' I was by myself but the Chief's step-daughter, Carolyn Weir, heard me. She sent me a note later saying it was a very emotional scene for her and that Diefenbaker would've appreciated my tribute.

"Saskatoon. Diefs last stop. He idolized Churchill and, in one respect, he outdid Old Winnie. Diefenbaker was buried near this awesome monument, the Diefenbaker Centre, on the University of Saskatchewan campus. A huge, marble building filled with Diefenbaker memorabilia. They lie out there on the prairie, almost side by side, like a pharaoh and his pyramid. By comparison, Pearson is buried in a humble little plot at Wakefield.

"On the way to Ottawa, I was struck by the notion that Diefenbaker had taken a tremendous gamble. He had hoped the multitudes would show up along the railway route, but what if they hadn't? It could have been a terribly embarrassing finale for him. And for the party — the train cost around $750,000. Well, the old showman pulled it off. People everywhere — at level crossings, on hillsides, thronging station platforms. Young and old, city dwellers, and farmers. Dief's last act was a stunning triumph."

SHEETS ON THE FLOOR

"FORTY YEARS I've been working on trains and I've never had no complaints about how I do my job. Except from Mr. Maurice Duplessis. He rode from Montreal to Quebec City all the time. He'd have a stack of newspapers in his compartment and he was forever drinking orange juice; it was like he was living on the stuff. His other big thing was not stepping on a cold floor. I'm not kidding. He wouldn't quit his bed till

I brought in clean sheets and spread them around so his feet wouldn't touch the floor. He didn't thank me. It was like I wasn't there. He was a lousy tipper; twenty-five cents. Cheap like another politician I looked after, Lester Pearson.

"Duplessis, he was the last to leave the train. We'd get to Quebec early in the day and he'd stay in his compartment. Reading newspapers and writing letters. I couldn't tell him to leave. He was the premier. One day, over half an hour went by and he still wasn't stirring so I turned off the lights and air-conditioning. He shot out of the compartment, boiling mad. 'Why'd you do that? Who do you think you are?' I said politely that I had a schedule to keep. Which was the honest truth. That, and the fact that I was starving and wanted my breakfast.

"Darned if he didn't report me. He wrote my boss saying I was a bad porter. Mr. McLean, the biscuit-maker, handed me $100 tips because he liked my service. James Dunn, the Algoma Steel man, was so happy he gave me $20 three different times. I can make beds in a whole section in three minutes flat and I've never insulted no passenger. Duplessis wasn't right. I'm a good porter and I'll be a good porter till the day I retire."

A MISTRESS, OF COURSE

"LONG BEFORE the Munsinger scandal broke in the 1960s, I was going down to Montreal with another MP, Egan Chambers. Egan and I got along well, even though he was a Tory and I was a CCFer. As we chatted in the club car, Pierre Sèvigny walked in. Sèvigny was friendly towards me but he had this slightly superior air. I'm certain he was well aware that my father, Roy Fisher, was a railway engineer and his had been a member of Borden's cabinet. In his book, *The Game of Politics*, Sèvigny had taken a couple of pokes at me. He said I had large feet and that the red sport shirt I'd worn was out of step with the dignity of the House.

"At any rate, the three of us got to talking about Sèvigny's parliamentary skills. He was associate minister for national defence. I knew he'd been a brave soldier at Normandy but I felt him somewhat of a humbug as a politician. I said all major Quebec political figures wore black overcoats with velvet lapels and black Homburgs. Egan said I was only partly accurate. He said Sèvigny once told him a successful Quebec politician had a chauffeur-driven Cadillac, a diamond tie-pin, spats, a silk scarf and, of course, a mistress. Before we parted company that day, Sèvigny reminded Egan that he'd pick him up at 9:00 p.m. They were going to a Black Watch do together.

"A few days afterwards, Egan came up to me in the House. He was grinning. 'Remember our conversation with Sèvigny on the train?' he said. 'Well, let me tell you what happened.' At nine o'clock the doorbell rang at Egan's house and a uniformed chauffeur stood there. They proceeded to a black Cadillac and the chauffeur drove to a swanky apartment block off St. Catherine Street. He told Egan he was picking Sèvigny up there, it was not the associate minister's home. Sèvigny came out, saying goodbye to a tall, good-looking blonde. He was dressed in the required form — silk scarf, tie-pin, Homburg, spats. Egan couldn't resist mentioning the talk on the train up from Ottawa. 'Yes, I was speaking about myself,' Sèvigny smiled. 'I am a very successful Quebec politician.'"

He Was Their Hero

"DIEF THE CHIEF. Railwaymen adored him. Stewards, waiters, porters, they all wanted to shake his hand when he was on their train. You know why? He defended the CNR telegrapher, Alfred Atherton. In 1950 two CNR trains collided near Canoe River in the B.C. mountains. Twenty-one men were killed — mostly soldiers en route to the Korean War. Atherton was charged with manslaughter. He was a telegraph operator, twenty-two years old, and the authorities claimed he'd sent a wrong message. Diefenbaker read of the case and realized Atherton was being made a scapegoat. He paid 1,500 bucks of his own money to join the B.C. bar and have the right to defend him. He got Atherton off.

"A great man, Diefenbaker. I shook his hand, too. Many times. Before he was prime minister he was on a lot of runs where I was steward. He slept in lower berths. I never did decide if he was doing it to watch his nickels and dimes or to be with the common folk. In the day time, the porters let him use vacant compartments. To write his speeches. Once, I was going by and he called me in. 'Listen to this and tell me what you think.' It was a speech he was delivering the following night at the Empire Club in Toronto. He was reading aloud and, when I heard things I didn't like, I tried to interrupt. He completely ignored me. Just kept on rambling. I cottoned on fast. He didn't want my advice. He just wanted an audience, albeit a small audience, to aim the words at. Which was okay with me. Great men don't have to be perfect human beings."

Trudeau's Helping Hand

"I was covering a Trudeau campaign swing through Quebec in 1974 and we made a ten-minute stop at a town in the Beauce. As usual, the radio reporters scrambled off the train in search of telephones. I zeroed in on the stationmaster's house, next to the station. A woman in her 50s, wearing a polyester pants suit, answered the door. She didn't understand my fractured French. Senator Gil Molgat wandered by. He was fluently bilingual and after he explained there wouldn't be any long-distance charges she let me in.

"The woman went off to see Trudeau and Margaret, who were standing on the observation-car platform. I called *CHUM*, did a seven-minute report, and left. A big, burly man grabbed my shoulder. The stationmaster. He demanded to know what I'd been doing in his house. Molgat had returned to the train and I tried to explain, again in broken French. Then, out of the corner of my eye, I saw the train moving down the track.

"I sprinted to the end of the platform and jumped and, thank goodness, the stationmaster didn't follow me. I ran like a maniac for half a mile. As I drew close, Trudeau clambered down the steps of the rear platform and extended a hand. 'Come on, Mr. Duffy, you can do it.' I was sweating and gulping air and I thought I'd have a heart attack. I broke my stride. 'It's okay,' I gasped. 'I'll catch up.' I walked to the station, planning to hire a cab. People were pointing behind me and saying, 'Look, look.' I turned and realized Trudeau had stopped the train for me. It was at least a mile away. Oh, no, I thought, this will kill me for sure.

"I ran again. Trudeau and Margaret applauded as I closed in on them. They were acting as though I'd won an Olympic gold medal. I was too embarrassed to climb the steps to their car. I ran past them, trying to smile through the rivers of perspiration, and hurled myself up the stairs and into the next car. Molgat was sitting inside, dictating a letter to the stationmaster's wife. Telling her how much I enjoyed visiting her town and thanking her for letting me use the phone."

FIRST-CLASS TICKET

"IF THERE WAS an important issue on which J. S. Woodsworth and the party he founded, the CCF, parted ways, it was on whether or not Canada should enter World War II. The party voted yes, despite Woodsworth's impassioned plea in the House to remain clear of the conflict. There was no animosity between Woodsworth and his colleagues over the issue. On the contrary, they respected his views and admired his courage to stand alone against the overwhelming tide of public opinion. In 1939, party officials invited Woodsworth to travel from his home in Winnipeg to Toronto for a CCF rally. Woodsworth was very ill, only months away from the stroke that ended his life.

"The officials were so concerned about his health that they purchased a first-class ticket. He regularly disdained first-class travel, preferring the extra money to go towards party expenses. He was, remember, a Methodist minister who identified strongly with ordinary Canadians. He advocated government welfare and health insurance and unemployment schemes years before they were adopted. On the appointed date, Woodsworth appeared in Toronto and delivered a good speech to the assembled party faithful. Then he returned to Winnipeg. A short while passed, and the Toronto officials received a cheque in the mail. Despite his illness, Woodsworth had exchanged the first-class ticket for a seat in the coach. He had sat up all night in both directions and the cheque was for the few dollars he had saved on the price difference."

RAFFLING A WHIPPET

"THE CCF NEEDED MONEY for Tommy Douglas's election drive in 1935 and a bright light came up with the idea of selling raffle tickets on a shiny new Whippet automobile. Party workers thrust raffle books under your nose wherever you were. Taking a train to Regina, I watched a grey-haired lady work her way down the aisle. She approached a grizzled old farmer. 'What's this for?' he wanted to know. 'T. C. Douglas's campaign,' the woman replied. Her answer dumbfounded the farmer. He dismissed her with a wave of his hand. 'I don't approve of Baptist ministers involved in gambling but maybe I'm mistaken. If God comes down from Heaven and buys a ticket, I'll buy one too.'"

PM PAYS A VISIT

"THEY HOOKED Trudeau's private car up to our train at Kenora. He'd been fishing with two of his youngsters, right after he came back east from his famous Rockies trip in 1982. The trip where our prime minister showed a pack of demonstrators at Salmon Arm what he thought of them. The middle-finger salute. The demonstrators were pissed at Trudeau because he was riding around British Columbia in a private railway car while telling other Canadians to tighten their belts. A woman at the Salmon Arm station was carrying a sign, 'Practise What You Preach.' Trudeau looked out the train window and gave her and her buddies the finger. The whole country was outraged, and when the train got to Canmore, Alberta, people threw tomatoes and eggs at it.

"Some of the dining-car crew on the Kenora train said the prime minister was an asshole for doing what he did. Others said he was a gutsy guy. No matter what we thought, we all wanted to meet him. There was a pretty waitress, named Susan, in our car. She was around twenty-one, a bright girl, full of fun. She wrote Trudeau a note and handed it to a Mountie. The note invited him to the dining car and said how we were fans of his.

"His youngsters strolled into the car after we'd served lunch. A cook took them on a tour of the kitchen, and they seemed interested in how things worked. Very polite, very self-contained boys. Very aware that they're different from you and I. That they were born to be kings.

"Around five o'clock Trudeau sent a note saying he'd be with us at eight. We finished our supper sittings and cleaned up and sat waiting for over an hour. We were dead tired and pissed off at his being late, but nobody left. It wasn't Trudeau's fault, really. His car was between the engine and the baggage car; he had to walk through the entire train and people were stopping him and shaking his hand. We stood up when he finally arrived and our service manager started making introductions. The first thing that flashed into my head was, he's smaller than he looks on TV. The second thing was, Jeez, he's so old. His face was covered with deep lines. It was hard to believe this old man was the same person who made young girls' hearts go thump, thump, thump.

"Four Americans were with us. Passengers who slipped into the car. When Trudeau shook his hand, one of them said to him, 'I've been fishing near Kenora, too, and the guide said don't eat what you catch. Why don't you do something about the acid rain that's ruining your lakes?' Trudeau was pissed off. He muttered that he was trying his best and he moved away from the guy. I didn't blame him. He was on his vacation. Why should he be pestered with the kind of questions he got in Parliament? And from an American; a guy whose country was causing the pollution.

"Susan, the waitress, presented Trudeau with a VIA pen. No big deal for a man with a limo and a mansion but it was the best gift we could muster on short notice. Trudeau kissed her cheek and she was tickled pink. I bet she had the cheek bronzed. He was with us ten minutes, talking about our home towns, stuff like that. After he was gone, the train slowed at Sudbury. I opened the kitchen door to throw the garbage bags out and saw this mob, 300 or 400 people — fans of Trudeau's, I thought — waiting at the station to greet him.

"When the train stopped, two guys ran over and tried to push past me. I shoved them back and slammed the door. The mob was hopping mad and close to tearing the train apart. We had a forty-minute stop scheduled. We cut it to a couple of minutes. The mob was racing around trying to find Trudeau's car. There was this guy selling eggs and fruit on the platform; out to make a buck from the demonstration. The mob found Trudeau's car and shouted obscenities and threw things and gave him the up-you sign. They were really going at it when the train pulled out.

"That really browned me off. They should've had more respect. Maybe Trudeau deserved to be hated and maybe he didn't. The point is, he was our prime minister. The highest position in the country. The position itself deserved to be respected. No one should be allowed to treat it like that."

HARD TO CONVINCE

"IT'S NO SECRET that John Diefenbaker wasn't the easiest person to persuade to do anything he didn't want to do. In the spring of 1963 I was his campaign manager for Alberta and I wanted him to speak at a major rally in Calgary. He refused. He had forced his popular defence minister, Doug Harkness, to resign over the nuclear-warheads issue. Harkness was a Calgary boy and Dief feared he'd be booed if he spoke in the city. I proposed a compromise. As he wouldn't set foot in Calgary, how about Strathmore, on the outskirts? Strathmore was Eldon Woolliams' home territory and Woolliams was a Diefenbaker loyalist. Dief said okay, he'd hold a meeting in Strathmore, and he came from Saskatchewan by train.

"He was prime minister and he had his own car. I boarded at Gleichen. Woolliams was there and so were Neil Crawford, Milt Harradence, and Don Johnston. It occurred to me that the gathering was a Saskatchewan version of an old boys' network; six of us were U. of S. graduates. While we were talking to the Chief, Johnston was in his compartment, banging on a portable typewriter. He was Dief's speech writer; a shrewd, intelligent fellow brimming with fresh ideas. He'd emerge now and then to show Diefenbaker what he'd written. Diefenbaker thanked him and said he liked the material, but he never used it. Throughout his campaign, he returned to the same old safe stuff that had scored points for him in the past.

"Well, Strathmore was a success. A hall packed with cheering people. Dief was so pleased that he agreed to venture into Calgary. Not to a mass meeting, to a coffee party at Henry Wise Wood School. As you know, the 1963 campaign was a disaster; the party lost the election. One wonders how things might have turned out if the Chief had only paid more attention to the great material Don Johnston produced on that train."

GETTING TO KNOW YOU

"I'LL GIVE YOU the lowdown on the numero-uno screw-up of 1972, the time the politicians of this fair province blew 150,000 big ones on a so-called familiarization tour. Eighty MPPs said they'd go but forty turned up. Brampton Billy was a no-show. He was in Europe and pledged to join them but he didn't come through. Forty MPPs off their leashes for nine days. Touring northern Ontario by train, bus, and plane. My mind boggled but the CNR's didn't. It laid on a 22-car train. That's roughly two politicos per car. The reasoning must have been that the space was needed to accommodate all those oversized egos.

"For the first four days, Ontario Northland buses trailed the train. Their purpose was to carry the MPPs and various government officials aboard the train to various local sites. Familiarization. Only the arrangements were a mess. The buses were turned away from the gates of Algoma Steel in Sault Ste. Marie because the plant was shut tight for the weekend. At Timmins, a company public relations person said that although a two-hour tour was scheduled, it was too risky for the visitors to be in the mines more than ten minutes. 'If it's that dangerous,' I heard an MPP say, 'how come the miners stay down there eight hours?' He didn't get an answer.

"Timmins is probably a beauty spot, the Paris of Ontario, but the politicians didn't have a chance to find out for themselves. The bus tour of the city was staged after a late dinner — all was dark except for a gas station, a tavern, and an *A* and *W*.

"It goes without saying that the booze eased the pain of Mission Impractical. Chambers of Commerce, private companies, and government agencies cracked open the rye and Scotch cases at the drop of a hat. The politicos stood around, glasses in hand, shaking their heads in dismay. Bad enough they'd missed the sights at Timmins and Sault

Ste. Marie; they were also denied the chance to suck up to the little people, the voters. Their hosts hustled them through old-age homes and hospital wards at a lightning clip. No doubt, in order to have them back at the train in time for the next free meal.

"Five days of that crap. Then they fished. Three chartered planes flew them at the taxpayers' expense from the last train stop at Moosonee to Hawley Lake where the trout were biting. Four days there, and then they were flown to Toronto. A terrific time was had by all. Except you and me, and we're the ones who picked up the tab."

A SIMPLE GESTURE

"WE WERE SOMEWHERE in Nova Scotia during the '58 campaign and Lester Pearson was relaxing in his car, chatting with some of his advisors. A party lackey walked over and informed him that an influential Maritimer had unexpectedly climbed aboard the Liberal bandwagon. Pearson nodded and said, Yes, that was a surprise, but he didn't seem to be overly thrilled.

"As Pearson stood up, a little old lady strode into the car, right past the Mountie guard, and handed him a white envelope. 'This is for you, Mr. Pearson. Go out and beat the pants off those wicked Tories.' After she left, Pearson opened the envelope. There was a crisp, new dollar bill inside. At this very moment, I can picture his face. Tears flooded his eyes and he turned his head away, trying not to show us how deeply he had been moved by her simple gesture."

THE
TURBULENT
TURBO

British Rail had lofty expectations for the new Pullman service it unwrapped in the autumn of 1982. Publicity releases spoke of the $250-million train's ability to achieve high speeds on the existing trackbed while offering passengers supreme comfort. On its first run from London to Glasgow, the cars swayed mercilessly: dishes jumped from tables, passengers became ill, and an aging porter declared he'd never board the train again. Twelve months passed, and the railway announced the introduction of another supertrain. "This isn't a train ride," the ads stated. "This is a total experience." The "total experience" broke down twice during its maiden trip to Manchester and the ballyhooed short-wave telephone system was such a shambles that the operators failed to connect a single call.

Reading about British Rail's troubles in the morning paper, I really felt sorry for the company's master planners. All the same, I did think they got off easy compared to the bright lights who conceived what turned out to be Canada's greatest railway fiasco — the introduction of the Turbo in the late 1960s. Billed as the "biggest leap forward in railroad technology in 100 years," the supertrain would supposedly cut more than an hour off the Toronto - Montreal run. In reality, the Turbo limped from one embarrassing disaster to another until VIA finally put it out of its misery in October 1982.

When I was living in Montreal in 1968, I saw an early sign of things to come. Several months before its official maiden trip, CN announced that the Turbo would be returning from a test run to Toronto shortly after noon on a pleasant summer day. Dozens of eager rail buffs lined the tracks along the Lakeshore, cameras ready to record the momentous event. I took the regular train into the city from Dorval. When I came back at suppertime, a few diehards were still in place, peering hopefully down the Toronto track. No one had bothered to inform them that the Turbo's wheels had jammed near Belleville and the supertrain hadn't the strength to make it past the Quebec - Ontario border.

"Oh, God. The Turbo. I've dreaded the day somebody would revive those hideous memories. It's like a *Twilight Zone* episode: 'The Train That Drove Men Crazy.' Still, if you insist…. During my first trip on the Turbo the blasted beast died twice between Montreal and Toronto. Over an hour each time. I twiddled my thumbs along with several hundred other passengers, all doubtless missing their scheduled appointments too. You may question my sanity after I admit that, in spite of that ghastly virgin voyage, I rode the Turbo approximately ten more times. I had no choice. I belonged to the CN brains trust. As much as I wanted to, I couldn't inform my superiors that I had so little confidence in our pride and joy that I preferred to book a seat on Air Canada.

"On paper, you know, the Turbo was a marvel. United Aircraft, the manufacturer, promised an average speed of eighty-four miles per hour, compared to the Rapido's sixty-seven. The Montreal - Toronto run, which took the Rapido almost five hours, would take the Turbo less than four. It could carry more customers. Each seven-car Turbo unit accommodated three hundred people while the Rapido, with its thirteen cars, hauled only six hundred altogether. I won't get technical but the reason the Turbo could go so quick was its aluminum body and its unique design. It was shaped to cut air and surface resistance to a minimum.

"Wonderful, wonderful. Our systems manager was so enthusiastic he proudly proclaimed that, and I quote, 'The Turbo is the greatest thing since the invention of peanut butter.' Miserable soul. How was he to know that the Turbo was fated to be a horror show? Although, he may have had an inkling when United said that, owing to minor problems, it couldn't have the train ready for Expo '67, as originally planned.

"Then there was the Turbo's debut outing in December 1969. A calamity. With a battalion of media types on board, the train slammed into a semi-trailer loaded with meat at a level crossing near Hawkesbury. A news photographer snapped a terrific shot of the instant the train and the truck hit, and it was splashed over front pages from coast to coast. Terrible publicity, yet our house organ, *Keeping Track*, insisted the accident was a positive event. The line I'll remember forever is, 'The company came out of the crash with flying colours, because no one was injured, and the accident proved the Turbo was tough enough to take it.' Three weeks after the crash, the Turbo was yanked from service. United said it was having teething problems. Those teething problems required a year's work and eighty modifications.

"Three times the Turbo roared back into service with great fanfare, and three times it was withdrawn again. The reason? Our hard winters. 'The Peanut Butter Express,' my unofficial name for it, was designed by Americans who surely had Botswana's climate in mind. Soon as the temperature dipped below zero, the train began falling apart. The toilets froze, the oil coolers froze, the suspension system froze, the electrical wiring short-circuited. I was on the Turbo barrelling past Oakville and the conductor, whom I knew personally, leaned over and said, 'The Turbo's a pain in the ass. The brakes are frozen solid.' My heart lept to my mouth. I had a mental picture of the train slamming into the rear of a diesel pulling propane tanks. The conductor ended my agony by explaining that he wasn't referring to the train we were on but one already in the shop.

"Summers were no hell either. The air-conditioning was always on the blink. We were outside Dorval once when the air-conditioning gave up the ghost, the engine collapsed, and there was a fire in the dining car. The staff darted about ordering everyone off the train in case the fire spread. There was a ditch next to tracks; green, stagnant, swampy water. Some passengers stepped right into it, rather than walk to the track in front or behind the train. I scarcely believed my eyes. For forty-five minutes, waiting for another train to collect them, they waded in swamp water up to their ankles. Bay Street types, three-piece suits and briefcases, just standing still, pretending everything was Jim Dandy. Even after the crew extinguished the fire, none of them questioned the puzzling fact that they still weren't permitted back on the train.

"The Turbo's mechanical demons eventually doomed it. A shame. It was a splendid-looking vehicle and, when it functioned properly, it was very cozy. The problem was Canadian National placed it in service too soon — before it was thoroughly tested. France, Germany, England, and the U.S. had similar trains in operation and the railway felt the public pressure to introduce a lightweight, high-speed train in this country. Ottawa should've been more involved. Considering our tough winters, the government should've pumped massive amounts of cash into the Turbo's development.

"Anyway, that's all in the past. Most of the Turbos died from self-inflicted wounds in the late 1970s and were buried in mothballs on a lonely track beneath Windsor Station. One set, though, did stagger on in regular service until three years ago. Now we have the LRCs. Dependable, fast, and comfortable. Not at all like the Turbo. Yet, I do recall hearing that VIA had to withdraw all fifty of its LRC passenger cars from service temporarily. Something to do with faulty wheel bearings...."

THE
SPORTING
LIFE

When the Toronto Maple Leafs travelled by train in the 1930s and 1940s, they were usually quiet and well-behaved. Former defenceman Sweeney Schriner recalled that the exhausted players crawled into the berths as swiftly as possible after a game and anyone making noise in the aisle would be devastated by a barrage of verbal grenades. If the Leafs travelled in the daytime, they read *Hockey News*, played cards, and discussed their families. That was generally the rule throughout the sporting world: even wrestlers who ranted and roared in the ring were model citizens on trains. There were exceptions — athletes who prowled the corridors in an endless hunt for mischief and, on rare occasions, entire teams that would go wild.

In the 1950s, when I was a sports writer in Calgary, I was assigned to accompany a football team on a trip to Winnipeg. The coach didn't disapprove of his players whooping it up; he joined them. As the train sped over the dark prairie, the coach and his charges drank beer, harassed waiters and porters, and poked their heads into passengers' berths, seeking the loose blonde they'd been falsely informed was in their midst. A lineman with an IQ of 30-minus was the life of the party. Until he passed out. His teammates stripped him naked, hid his clothing, and abandoned him on the smoker floor. The next morning the team assembled under the rotunda in the Winnipeg station. The lineman came running through the waiting room. He was wearing a porter's uniform.

HEY, WAITER!

"THE WILD MAN of Borneo had nothing on Ches McCance. McCance was a place kicker with the Blue Bombers in the 1930s and setting him free on a train was like letting an orangutan out of its cage. On one occasion, the Bombers were journeying to Regina for a game. Both teams were in the Western Interprovincial Football Union. McCance was roving the cars, trying to make a nuisance of himself. He was, for no apparent purpose, barefoot. A very dignified, very well-dressed matron was in the dining car, having a meal. McCance burst in and, glancing at the diners, surmised that the matron was his best bet. He jumped up on the table, stuck his foot in her soup, and stirred it with his big toe. 'Hey, waiter,' he yelled across the astonished car. 'Bring this lady another bowl of soup! This one's too cold!'"

LEAR AND MCCANCE

"IT'S TRUE, every word. McCance did leap on that poor creature's table and shove his foot in her soup. Who told you that story? Jim Kearney? He's a good sports writer, a credit to the Pacific rain forest, but I can top him. I have a better story. No, not specifically about Ches McCance. About the Bombers on a road trip to Calgary before the war. Les Lear was as zany as McCance. He buttonholed the conductor and said there was no heat in the car. The conductor said, nonsense, the car was adequately heated. Lear and McCance and some of their teammates rummaged the train for furniture that wasn't rivetted to the floor. Chairs and the like. They piled them in the smoker and somebody lit a match. When the alarmed porter ran in to investigate, Lear, McCance, and their buddies were stripped to the waist and dancing around the bonfire, whooping like Indians.

"Not a bad story, eh? I smile whenever I tell it. It must've been fun to be around those guys. Wait a minute. Don't go. I have another anecdote. McCance was involved. There used to be a football coach in the

States named Fritz Chrysler. I think he was at Notre Dame but I may be wrong. McCance heard a Fritz Chrysler was on the same train he was and he pounded on the man's door, intending to stand him to a drink. The man opening the door was Fritz Kreisler the famous violinist. When he explained that he was a violinist and not a football coach, McCance said, 'Why don't you pretend you're practising and play me a tune on your fiddle?' 'I'm sorry,' Kreisler said. 'I never practise.' McCance walked away shaking his head. 'Jesus, Fritz,' he said sincerely, 'you'd better change your ways. Take it from me, you'll never get anywhere in this world if you don't practise.'"

THE ROCKET ATE ALONE

"DICK IRVIN, THE CANADIENS' COACH, was a stickler for discipline. He'd allow the boys to play Hearts for quarters but he wouldn't allow any gambling. The team had a car to themselves and, working out of Montreal, as a dining-car waiter, I saw the boys a lot. The Rocket, he was a real serious guy. He wouldn't sit with the others; he'd eat by himself. He didn't utter more than two words to waiters. He wasn't stuck up or anything. He took hockey deadly serious, and it was like he was storing up mental energy for his next game. After he quit hockey, he was a different person. He'd get on with his wife and talk up a storm with the waiters and porters and the conductor.

"Gosh, those guys could eat. They'd have thick steaks and baked potatoes and several desserts. No wine, no beer. Irvin would've blown a gasket. Toe Blake would've too. Maybe I shouldn't be saying this but there were a half-dozen guys with the Canadiens who thought life wasn't worth living without a daily beer. They had a deal going with the porter. He'd stow a case of Molson's in an empty crew room and they'd sneak in for a quickie. Toe Blake, he suspected something was going on. If two or three boys disappeared at the same time, he'd walk through the train looking for them. The staff always covered up. They'd say they hadn't seen them and, far as I know, he never did catch them drinking. A great guy, Toe. So were Beliveau, Plante, and the Pocket Rocket. Courteous and friendly. Real gentlemen — the last of a dying breed."

FIGHTING FANS

"In my grandfather's day, lacrosse was bigger than hockey on the west coast and the company that operated the Vancouver trains, B.C. Electric, ran special excursion trains out to New Westminster for the games at Queen's Park. The trains were by no means luxurious. They weren't even comfortable. The fans had to make do with wooden benches lined up in neat rows on a half-dozen flat cars. On hot days, being in the open was a glorious experience. The fans rolled up their sleeves, got tanned, and enjoyed the cool breezes. If it rained on the return trip, if the cold winds blew, they huddled together and stared grimly ahead. It was a short trip. Less than an hour from Carrall Street through Central Park to the New Westminster depot.

"My grandfather was a Vancouver Lacrosse Club fan. The team's arch rivals were the New Westminster Salmonbellies. He used to tell the story of how he was coming home from a game and a battle broke out. A few New Westminster followers were on the train. Their team had won and they were rubbing it in. Name calling led to pushing and shoving and a man fell off the flatcar into a ditch. His unscheduled departure triggered the fight. All of the Salmonbellies were thrown off and then the Vancouver fans were punching and pushing each other. My grandfather would say he only struck another human being once in his life, and that was the once. He had to hit a fellow to avoid being grabbed and tossed overboard. The engine driver saw the battle and slowed to a crawl so no one would be badly hurt falling overboard.

"Can you imagine the reaction after the train left the wide-open spaces and entered the populated area? Traffic must have ground to a halt. People must have been rooted to the sidewalk, gawking in amazement. Fists were flying and the men who weren't defiantly standing their ground or being thrown off were jumping off and fleeing. My grandfather was among the last to go. Policemen ran out to meet the train at Carrall Street and my grandfather fled before he could be arrested."

AN OLD PRO'S ADVICE

"THIS MAY BE HOGWASH. On the other hand, it may very well be true. The story goes that a young pitcher with nothing between his ears was called up from the minors to join the Montreal Royals of the International League. A brash youngster, full of piss and vinegar, and certain God had created him to be a baseball star. He pitched a no-hitter first time out with the Royals and it seemed as though the club would be holding onto him and sending down an old pro who wasn't doing too good.

"The team was on the overnight train to Toronto. The old pro sidled up to the youngster and gave him some pointers — how to throw a meaner fastball; which Toronto batters were suckers for low-insiders. When the youngster climbed the ladder to his upper berth, the old pro pointed to the fishnet that was there for shoes and wallets and whatever. He advised him to stick his pitching arm in the net while he slept; that was the secret of giving it a good rest. The following day the youngster's arm was sore and he threw a putrid game and was yanked in the fifth inning. Still, he didn't catch on. He put his arm in the net on the return trip to Montreal. After that, it took a month to get it back in shape. He was shipped down to the minors and the old pro stayed on."

PATRICK SAT UP TILL DAWN

"BABE PRATT'S A TEETOTALLER now. He works for the Canucks as a sort of goodwill ambassador and you can't get a sip of alcohol past his lips unless you get four hulking brutes to hold him down. He wasn't always so pure. In 1936 Babe was a husky, curly haired kid from Stoney Mountain, Manitoba, who, signed by the Rangers, was happy as a clam in speakeasies, bars, and assorted nighteries. In New York, he haunted the Green Door where Helen Morgan sang. In Sudbury and Port Arthur, where the Rangers also played, he hung around places so rough that you had to be what he was, a prison guard's son, to survive.

"Lester Patrick coached the Rangers. He imposed a midnight curfew and he liked having the team travel in its own railway car because it made it easier to enforce. The Rangers were at Port Arthur one night and Babe vanished after the game. Patrick was livid. He had warned him before about ignoring the curfew. The Ranger's car was on a siding and someone had disconnected the heat hoses. The players had gone straight to bed and piled blankets on themselves to fight the cold. Patrick couldn't make himself lie down. He was hellbent not to let Babe sneak aboard. He sat near the door, a blanket pulled over him. He didn't sleep a wink. He rubbed his hands, stamped his feet, muttered, fumed, and yawned.

"At sun-up, Babe waltzed in, a bit worse from wear but happy after a night's partying. Patrick lept to his feet and declared he was fining him a thousand dollars. As Babe was earning around four hundred dollars a season, the fine was a crushing blow. He went to bed in a state of utter misery. A day or so later, en route to New York, Patrick approached him and said he'd lift the fine if Babe ceased his drinking. Babe agreed. And he did cease. The trouble was, his playing ability suffered and the Rangers dove into a terrible slump. The other players found a solution. They took up a collection to raise the thousand and pay the fine, on the condition that Babe start belting again."

GOPHER TAILS FAR TRAIN FARE

"OXBOW, CARNDUFF, MACOUN, WEYBURN. We played them all. Mostly on Saturdays. We'd take the train in the morning, play in the afternoon and be home in Estevan that night. Exciting stuff for a twelve-year-old boy. There'd be fifteen of us, our skates tied to our sticks, taking over one end of a day-coach, bragging about how fast or mean we were. Pop sold real estate in Estevan. Name of McLeod. He gave my brother, Kenny, and me two bucks once for fare and food and, in 1930s Saskatchewan, that was pretty generous. Usually, though, we earned our own fare. Trapping gophers and selling the tails to the municipal office for three cents apiece. Or collecting empty bottles around town.

"Weyburn had a tough team. They had a big guy who knew how to box so you had to be on your toes. We weren't scared, though. It's funny but the possibility that you might get hurt doesn't scare you when you're a kid. We didn't even have helmets or protective pads and only the odd guy had gloves. Yet we climbed onto the train fairly aching to be in Weyburn or wherever we were playing. Sometimes we'd sit on the train shouting, 'We're going to cream them! We're going to knock them dead!' Guess what did scare us. The conductors. If they said sit down and shut up, we sat down and shut up. It wasn't that they were so tough. It was the fact that they had the power to kick us off the train and keep us from getting to the game."

PRACTICAL JOKER

"WRESTLERS WERE LEERY of riding trains with Ray Steel. They liked him as a person, he was a nice guy, but he was an awful practical joker. Steel was a star name on the wrestling cards in the 1930s and 1940s. Ed Lewis was bigger. At one time, Lewis rated alongside Jack Dempsey and Babe Ruth as the most popular sporting figure on the continent. Steel and Lewis often fought each other and they really went at it in the ring. Steel was fighting barefoot once at Madison Square Garden and Lewis shoved him around so much he skinned the soles of his feet and left blood prints on the mat.

"On the trains, they were the best of pals, although Steel tested Lewis's patience like the Lord tested Job. Going to Toronto, Lewis got up one morning and bent over and put on his shoes. When he took a step, he couldn't move. He thought he'd been struck by polio and his feet were paralysed. Lewis was a sound sleeper. Steel had crept into his compartment at 3:00 a.m. and nailed the shoes to the floor. He got such a kick out of it that he tried the same trick again.

"This time, en route to Montreal, he nailed Lewis's fedora to the wall rack Lewis had hung it on. When Lewis grabbed the hat, he ripped the crown right out of it. Lewis yelled and threatened to break Steel in half. He could've done it. He was heavier and stronger and he was known on the circuit as 'Strangler' Lewis because of the side headlock he had; he'd squeeze you in it until you quit. His strangle hold could've done Steel in, all right. But deep down Lewis thought Steel's pranks were hilarious, even if he was the butt of some of them."

Nastiest Player in the League

"In the 1930s I played for the Edmonton Eskimos and there was a guy in Regina I hated going up against. Dean Griffing. He was from Kansas. He was six foot two, weighed 260, and was the nastiest player in the league. He'd punch your nose or slam an elbow in your gut. He stomped on my hand and the cleats broke the skin. He bit Greg Kabat's leg and there was a stink in the papers about it. Griffing was no dummy; he knew that intimidating opposing players gave him a psychological edge.

"He sure had the edge over me the time I had boils. I lay in my bed on the train going to Regina, holding hot towels to my neck all night. Walter McKenzie, the team doctor, was taking care of me. He lanced the real bad ones but this was before penicillin and sulpha drugs and there wasn't much he could do. So I lay there, soaking towels in tap water and thinking about Dean Griffing. We both played centre and if he looked across the line and spotted the boils, he'd be tempted to take a whack at them.

"In Regina, the grasshoppers had eaten every blade of grass and the stadium field had hardened. They had to bring in a tractor with harrows to break and soften the earth. Then we played. Naturally, Griffing spotted the boils right away. I tried to keep my neck from him but he got in a couple of solid thumps. Nothing serious. I didn't pass out from the pain. Although there was a thump late in the game that really smarted.

"Travelling to Edmonton, I lay with the hot towels again and I thought of that hard thump in the last half and it came to me what he'd said when I winced, 'What's the matter, kid, you got no guts?' The way he grinned. Believe me, that bothered me a helluva lot more than the boils did."

The Running Rookie

"The Maple Leafs were travelling to Chicago and the train had to go through Hamilton, which is about fifty miles south of Toronto. A veteran player, King Clancy, was in the vestibule between two cars when the train stopped at the Hamilton station. A newcomer, a rookie from the boonies, came flying down the platform and scrambled up the stairs. He was puffing hard, practically gasping. As he stepped aside to let the rookie pass, Clancy shook his head in disapproval. 'You rookies are all out of condition,' he said. 'You're not the healthy specimens we were in the old days.' The rookie managed to catch his breath and said, 'I don't like to contradict you, sir, but you're dead wrong. I missed the train in Toronto and ran all the way here.'"

HOW TO SHORTEN A LINE-UP

"A BUNCH OF US sports writers were on our way home after covering the Salmonbellies in the Mann Cup playoffs down East. This was in the 1940s; I can't recall the exact year. Anyway, the train pulled into Melville and four of us jumped off and rushed to the liquor store across from the depot. Our alcohol supply had run dry and, you'd better believe it, when Vancouverites are forced to gaze upon that miserable stubble-patch they call Saskatchewan, they desperately need to drink. It was a Saturday afternoon and every farmer for a hundred miles had chosen that precise moment to stock up on booze. A long line-up and only one clerk. We talked our way to the middle of the line and then we realized it wasn't moving. The guy at the front, a burly, bearded monster of a man, couldn't make up his mind. He was pointing at the bottles and, when the clerk brought them, he'd say that really wasn't what he wanted.

"We waited and waited, and panic set in. I turned to the *Province* writer, who shall remain nameless because he's a respected, solid citizen these days. 'We're going to miss our train,' I said. 'Oh no, we won't,' the *Province* writer said confidently. 'I'll fix this.' He stepped out of line and shouted, 'Hey, you hairy baboon, hurry up.' The guy swung on his heels. 'You talking to me, mister?' The *Province* writer took his courage in his hands. He was half the guy's size. 'Yeah, I'm talking to you, apeman. No wonder you grew those whiskers — to hide your ugly face.' The guy exploded. His eyes flared and he charged like an angry bull. The *Province* writer, of course, had expected it. He was out the door in two seconds flat. With the guy chasing him. We stepped up to the counter, past the gaping farmers, and calmly ordered our booze. We just made it to the train in time. The *Province* writer was in his compartment. The guy had chased him down the main street and through the railyard before losing him on the train. We saw the guy on the platform when the train pulled out. Glowering. The *Province* writer grinned and raised the bottle triumphantly; the guy waved his fist."

INSPIRING THE LEAFS

"PUNCH IMLACH had this problem. The Leafs had won the Stanley Cup in 1962 and 1963 and then, late in '64, they fell into a slump. Punch reached into his bag of tricks. He cajoled, he threatened, he pleaded. Regardless of what he said, he couldn't light a fire under the team. The Leafs had to go to Montreal to play the Canadiens. Punch figured a change of routine might change the team's luck. He cancelled the airline reservations and booked the team on the overnight train. He had another tactic up his sleeve too. An inspirational book. He strolled through the train passing out twenty-four brand-new copies of Norman Vincent Peale's, *The Power of Positive Thinking*.

"A sight to behold. Tim Horton, Alan Stanley, and Red Kelly were sitting in the club car reading it. Other players were walking around with it tucked under their arms; big tough guys who seldom read anything more serious then the *Hockey News* and Woody Woodpecker comics. Even Eddie Shack had one. Which was a sure sign that Punch was extremely optimistic about Peale's ability to alter people's lives. Eddie's a wonderful guy but he once said he didn't read my stories because he was illiterate. 'Trent,' he said, 'the only thing I learned to write was my signature. So I could sign hockey contracts.' How did the team do in Montreal? I don't remember. But if you look at the NHL record book for 1964, you'll find that the Leafs lifted themselves out of the slump and won the Cup. For all I know, Norman Vincent Peale may have been responsible."

ACTING LIKE A MORON

"GOING TO THE GREY CUP in 1956, we had an Alouette fan in our coach whose idea of a good time was to act like a moron. He guzzled rye from a thermos and raced up and down the aisle screaming and blowing a tin whistle. A passenger mentioned that the Molson family's private car was linked to ours. 'I paid for plenty of their beer over the years,' he said. 'Tonight the Molson's can stand me to a free drink.' He ran down the aisle, blowing his whistle. Two porters went after him. Both were feeble cases, on the wrong side of sixty. They caught up to him in the vestibule. The door to the Molson car was locked and he was kicking and banging it. One of the porters asked him to stop and he took a swing at him that, if it had connected, would've hastened his departure for the cemetery. The porters grabbed the fan but didn't have the strength to hold on. They released him, darted through the coach door and slammed and locked it. The fan went berserk — kicking and shouting and saying he'd sue the railway. They left him there. The cold night air had a sobering effect. He lost his venom and spent the rest of the trip curled up against the foot of the door, hugging himself to keep warm."

PRIDE OF THE YUKON

"THE TRAINS did in the pride of the Yukon, the Dawson City hockey team that had the raw audacity to challenge the Stanley Cup champions to a two-game series in 1904. The Ottawa Silver Seven were the champs. Real world-beaters. The Dawson team was a rag-tag pack of prospectors. Local yokels killing time waiting for spring break-up by skating on frozen ponds. The Silver Seven agreed to play them but only on their own home ice. Who'd expect a bunch of wobbly legged gold-diggers to travel 4,000 miles to get their rearends booted? Lookit, there wasn't a heck of a lot to do in Dawson City in December except hang around the saloons. The team got so excited by the idea of playing the champs that they raised their travel expenses within a week.

"The team went to Whitehorse by dogsled, a nine-day trip. It climbed on the train to Skagway where it would catch the Vancouver boat. A blizzard hit in the mountains and the train was rivetted to the same spot for three days. Having nothing else to occupy their minds, the players ate and drank too much and one guy somehow got his foot stuck in the toilet for hours on end. They missed the boat and had to wait three days in Skagway for the next one. Three days of saloon-crawling and chasing after dance-hall girls.

"They got to Vancouver safely and then it was the CPR's turn to foul them up. The train was snowed in for three days in the Rockies. A passenger went nuts and punched out the goalie's front teeth and six other players caught terrible colds. Crossing Saskatchewan, the train hit a broken rail and flew off the tracks. By the time the team made it to Ottawa — over three weeks after it left Dawson — the players were battered and exhausted and in no mood to shoot pucks. The Silver Seven crucified them 23-2 and 9-2. Needless to say, that was the first and last time a Dawson City team ever challenged a Stanley Cup winner."

No Trouble Sleeping

"THE CANADIENS had played in Boston and Toe Blake went for a stroll before the train left. He came to a fish market and saw a tank filled with live eels. He started to walk away when he thought of a great idea. He bought an eel and carried it to the station in a little bucket.

"There was this player, Bunny Dame. He wasn't a smartass or anything, but he got Toe's goat because he uttered the same words on every road trip before he climbed into his berth. 'Lucky me. I fall asleep the moment my head touches the pillow and nothing wakes me up.' Toe waited till Bunny was in the smoker, washing up. He slipped the eel under the covers, down where Bunny's feet would be. Bunny sauntered back, said good-night, and fastened the curtains.

"A minute passed. Then two minutes. Toe wondered if the eel had somehow gotten out. Suddenly there was a scream that must've awakened the whole train. Bunny bolted from the berth, white as a sheet. 'Somebody get a stick!' he yelled. 'There's a snake in my bed!'

"Everybody thought it was a hilarious stunt. Everybody except Bunny and two other players. They didn't believe Toe when he said it was only an eel. The three of them were terrified of snakes and they sat up together all night, in case Toe had more 'reptiles' he might be tempted to slip in their berths while they were sleeping."

Eating à la Carte

"Alex Shibicky had gone to the Rangers from the minor leagues and, to put it mildly, he was wet behind the ears. The Blues were on the rattler to Toronto and Shibicky strolled into the dining car, picked up the menu, and said to himself, 'Hmm, you get interesting things if you order *à la carte.*' He had a big meal and signed the bill, knowing the team would pay for it. On the trip back to New York, Lester Patrick strode through the players' car, trying not to lose his temper, spreading the word that every player — Shibicky included — had a $5 a day food allowance. Shibicky's *à la carte* order had come to $10. The players obeyed.

"A month went by and the Rangers were going to Montreal. Patrick was in the dining car and watched Shibicky consume a skimpy 75-cent dinner of sausages and mashed potatoes. 'Good grief, Shibicky,' he cried, 'You can't play professional hockey putting a crummy meal like that in your stomach. You've got to improve your eating habits.'

"Poor Shibicky, he was hopelessly confused. On the one hand, he was blasted for eating too expensively. On the other, he was blasted for not eating enough. What was he supposed to do? The Canadiens were a dynamite team and defeating them on home ice was considered a monumental feat. The Blues won 1-0 and Shibicky scored the goal. Heading down to New York, Patrick settled the food question for Alex Shibicky. 'Eat whatever you want,' he told him. 'Sausages, mashed potatoes, steaks, *à la carte.* Anything that makes you happy.' And then he added, 'As long, that is, as you keep scoring goals.'"

A Great Sense of Drama

"CALGARIANS LOVE TO PLAY the Old West role to the hilt. Cowboys and Indians. Woody Strode was a Negro from Georgia or somewhere who came up after the war to join the Stampeders. He paraded in cowboy hats and cowboy boots and, riding the train to the Grey Cup in 1948, Woody led the boys singing 'Home on the Range.' My last memory of him is very vivid. The team had whipped Ottawa and was returning to Calgary. They were living it up — champagne, steaks, the whole kit and kaboodle. At every town in the West, crowds surrounded them and got their autographs. At dusk one night the train had rumbled out of a town in Saskatchewan and was crossing the rolling fields. I looked out on the observation-car platform and there was Woody, alone, his arms raised in a victory salute. An incredible moment. All he had on was a loin cloth and an Indian headdress he'd borrowed from the Sarcee chief, Smallchild. Woody went to Hollywood and was in quite a number of motion pictures. I wasn't surprised he was good at acting. That evening on the observation car proved to me that he had a great sense of drama."

WASN'T THAT A PARTY?

"WE HAD A whale of a time going to the Grey Cup in '49. A whale of a time. The team travelled to Toronto ahead of us. Smart move. They wouldn't have gotten any sleep if they'd gone on our train. The Stampeder Special. That's what we called it. Fifteen or sixteen cars packed with happy people. And no wonder they were happy. The Stamps won the Cup in '48 and we didn't doubt for a moment that they'd do it again.

"The *CPR* lent us a party room — an old baggage car where the booze flowed like water and there were fiddlers and guitar players and lots and lots of square dancing. Nearly everybody was in western clothes. You know, white Stetsons and hand-tooled cowboy boots and belt buckles with bucking broncos on them. If a deaf man had walked into the party room, the noise was so loud he would've got his hearing back.

"Does that sound like chaos? It wasn't chaotic. People had a rare old time of it and some had to be helped to their bunks but, on the whole, it was well organized. A secretary from the Stampeders' office tacked notices up in each car imploring the fans to obey the rules and regulations. She put up the show times. When the special would stop somewhere and what show would be performed. At Brandon, the majorettes did a lasso number and at Winnipeg, the square-dancers did a routine to fiddle music. The crowds at the depots were enormous. Five and six thousand, even for a small town like Brandon.

"I did hear there was a strip-poker game. I heard it was in a certain car and I snooped around, listening at doors, but I couldn't find it. Which reminds me. The bridge players. Now there's an addiction worse than drugs. They ought to have bridge rehabilitation centres. Two young married couples nested in a compartment from Calgary to Toronto and played the silly game day and night. Oh, they probably quit for meals and to sleep but it wouldn't surprise me if they didn't. The trip home was fun. We had the same shows in the stations and the booze flowed in the party room. But we weren't as happy. Curse their souls, the Alouettes had skunked the Stamps 28-15."

THOSE WICKED COLLEGE KIDS

"ASK ANYBODY who the wildest football fans in Canadian history were and they'll say the Stampeder fans who went to the Grey Cup in '48 and '49. It's a bum rap. They were exuberant, yes, but they weren't the hell-raisers the college boys were. Years ago, the trains carrying students to Toronto for the annual championship games were nut-houses on wheels. Those kids had no respect for railway property. Especially the Queen's boys. Why Queen's? It's the elite school. The institution that rich daddies sent their spoiled brats to so they could get a piece of paper saying they're qualified to run the world. Back at the family mansion in Rosedale, those kids did everything by the book. Prim and proper. At Kingston, they'd be on their own for the first time and itching to break out of the mould, if only for a few hours.

"They'd board the train with mickeys in their pockets and whoop and holler non-stop. They'd yank the emergency cord. They'd steal silverware and blankets for souvenirs. They'd smash bottles, they'd smash windows, they'd smash one another. More than one tap was fixed so that it flooded a floor. More than one future leader tried to flush another future leader's hat or scarf or, heaven knows, his head, down a toilet. The girls on these predominantly male outings fell into two categories. They were every inch as wicked as the boys, or they had foolishly assumed they were going on an ordinary train ride. The foolish ones invariably complained of water fights that soaked their clothing and of favourite articles, such as the only shoes they had with them, being tossed off the train.

"Perhaps I shouldn't be so unkind and single out dear old Queen's. It had the worst hell-raisers but the other schools weren't that far behind. It was, after all, a Western student who was nearly killed attempting to climb on the roof. The railways finally tired of the kids' annual shenanigans and assigned policemen to the trains. The police didn't eliminate the drinking and girl-pestering entirely but they did eliminate the destruction and theft of railway property. Not many future leaders wanted to be arrested for shattering a toilet bowl or stuffing a stolen blanket beneath their coats."

The Headless Brakeman: Ghost Stories

Early in my research, an eminent historian advised me not to bother searching for material concerning mysterious occurrences on Canadian trains. "The Brits and the Americans have the monopoly in that regard. Disappearing corpses, phantom trains, strange passengers. The only unusual thing you're likely to find in Canada is a teacup reader who's made an accurate prediction." He was partially correct. A St. Catharines woman did tell me she'd met her husband after a train-travelling sage forecast that a handsome male would enter her life. And, try as I did, I couldn't pinpoint a single case of a dead body vanishing into thin air. Nevertheless, strange and unexplainable episodes have happened on our railways — or rather people allege they have.

A Chilling Experience

"You won't believe a word of this. November 22, 1973. That's the date. Ten o'clock at night. I wasn't ready to sleep and I went to the dome car. The train was in Ontario, passing a forest of trees that were pretty in the moonlight. Only two of us there — me and a man. He was up front and I was in the middle. I paid him no heed. I'm an old lady and I stopped paying attention to men a long time ago. I was looking out the window and a funny feeling came over me. Like a chill.

"I turned my head and the man was in the corridor, staring at me. It was dark except for the moon but I could see his face clear enough. He was young, maybe thirty, thirty-five. All of a sudden, his face changed. All of a sudden, he looked exactly like my dead father. My heart banged like a drum. I got up and scrambled down the steps. There were people in the lounge, laughing and talking. I went right by them without saying anything. I didn't sleep well, I tell you. I kept seeing the scene in the dome car over and over. I didn't go near the dome car again and I didn't see the young man anywhere else on the train. You don't believe me, do you? I'll swear on a stack of Bibles. That night in the dome car, I saw my father's face."

A DREAM COME TRUE

"LIKE EVERYONE ELSE on earth, I've had my share of scary dreams. Pictures so real that you wake up sweating. This wasn't one of those. I didn't sweat or scream, but it was disturbing. The night before I was leaving Winnipeg for Toronto, I dreamt a man ran down a station platform and jumped onto the side of a train and couldn't get past the closed door. He was stranded, freezing to death. The very next night at Armstrong, Ontario, a young guy who had had one beer too many realized the train was going. He ran and jumped and the doors were closed. He clung to the side, shouting, 'Help! Help!' It was below zero and the train was moving too fast for him to jump off and, if nobody heard him, the wind-chill could do him in. He shouted and shouted and, hanging on with one hand, banged the door with the other. A baggage-car worker going through the vestibule spotted him. He was pulled safely aboard. When I heard the story the next day, I didn't say a word about my dream. I was sure they'd think I'd made it up."

GHOST TRAIN

"SO YOU'RE INTERESTED in the Ghost Train, are you? Very well. I'll begin with the wreck. The date was July 8, 1908. At 8:30 on a bright sunny morning. The engine for the Spokane Flyer was whipping out of Medicine Hat on its way to Swift Current. Jim Nicholson, the engineer,

Harry Thompson, the fireman. It was scheduled to pick up a string of passenger cars and haul them to Moose Jaw. Why was it called the Spokane Flyer? Because, although it ran on CPR lines, it would dip down over the border and finish up in Spokane, Washington.

"Now, two miles east of the railyard, the Flyer came to a high embankment. It had to wind through a series of curves to climb to the flatlands above. While it was snaking along, a farmer standing at the top of the embankment saw something Nicholson and Thompson couldn't see — another train whizzing down the same line a mile away. The farmer waved and hollered. The fireman reckoned he was just being friendly and he waved back. Nicholson saw the other train when the Flyer engine reached the plateau. The passenger train from Lethbridge with Bob Twohey at the throttle. Both were travelling at a good clip and when they collided half the population of Medicine Hat heard it.

"A horrible mess, that's for sure. The Lethbridge locomotive was thrown off the tracks and the baggage car smashed to smithereens. Seven men were killed, including engineers Nicholson and Twohey. At the inquest, the CPR dispatcher testified it was Nicholson's fault. He had neglected to check with the office to learn if the Lethbridge train had left on time, which it hadn't. Easy to blame a dead man, of course, and it certainly got the dispatcher off the hook. Some of Nicholson's co-workers however, had a different explanation. Years later, they said they didn't blame the crash on any mortal being — it was fated to happen.

"This is where the Ghost Train comes in. Two months before the collision, Twohey was guiding an engine through the same cutbanks. It was eleven at night and he was under orders to link up a bunch of passenger cars at Dunmore junction for the Spokane run. A huge, blinding spotlight suddenly appeared in front of him. He shouted for the fireman, Gus Day, to jump but it was too late. Twohey fully expected to die. To his amazement, the approaching train veered to the right and flashed past his engine, it's whistle blowing. The coach windows were lit and he saw passengers looking out. Now, here's the frightening part. *There was only a single rail line running through those hills.*

"Naturally, Twohey was quite shaken by his experience. So was the fireman, Gus Day. They took the engine on to Dunmore but didn't tell anyone about the Ghost Train. They even refrained from discussing it with each other. Until a couple of weeks later when they met on a Medicine Hat street and, going into a beer parlour, finally brought the subject up. Neither had an explanation for what had happened. They hadn't been drinking and there was no way in the world that someone could've played a joke on them.

"Twohey downed a few brews and then told Day he had received another scare. A fortuneteller had said he didn't have long to live. A month at the most. As he was a superstitious man, Twohey said he intended to stay off the trains for a while. Okay? You got that?

"Now, a week or so went by and then Twohey sent a message to the head dispatcher saying he was too ill to handle a scheduled run to Dunmore junction. Nicholson drew the assignment and Day was the fireman. Late at night again. Around the same spot where Twohey and Day had seen the Ghost Train, the same thing happened. A dazzling light, a shrieking whistle, and passengers peering out of lighted windows as a train that didn't exist sped past on tracks that didn't exist.

"Enough to turn anybody's hair white. Especially Gus Day's. He'd been through it twice. I have no idea what his reaction was but I'm sure he must've fainted the day of the wreck. All he said to reporters was he was firing up an engine in the yard when he heard the news. The fortuneteller almost called the shot in Twohey's case. She said he'd die within a month. It was five weeks. Furthermore, Twohey told Day the night before the crash that he wasn't jittery any more. Whatever the Ghost Train was, he said, he had decided it wasn't a death premonition.

"Twohey and Nicholson and Day all eventually confided in their close friends at the yard, yet no one referred to the Ghost Train at the inquest. As far as we know, Day didn't tell any outsiders about the incident until the 1930s. He was retired and living in B.C. and, after reading a magazine article about a Colorado ghost train, he revealed his story to a Vancouver reporter. Other old-timers came forward to verify that Nicholson and Twohey had told them about it and that the two engineers were so honest they believed them.

"The Ghost Train hasn't been seen since 1908 but, if I had to take a train out of Medicine Hat on a dark night, I'd be good and ready to jump."

AN AWESOME MEMORY

"I WAS SITTING in the lobby of the Apasqua Hotel in The Pas. In the winter of 1944. The owner, a big, husky fellow, saw an Indian soldier come in drunk and, quickly crossing the lobby, he said he didn't want him there. The Indian left without speaking. The next morning I was on the Winnipeg train when the Indian turned up. He was still a bit drunk. He sat next to me in the coach and said he was on leave, visiting his sick mother.

"'I saw you at the hotel,' he said. 'Yes, I know,' I said. 'I saw you last night too.' 'No, no, I don't mean that,' he said, 'I mean in September, 1929. You were talking to a man in front of the hotel and I walked past you.' I was utterly flabbergasted. I had, indeed, been to The Pas in September, 1929, on a business trip, and I had stayed at the hotel. But who remembers a total stranger they saw for a few fleeting seconds on the street fifteen years earlier? Ever since then I've wondered about that Indian and the mystical way his mind functioned."

MYSTERY BOXCAR

"I HEARD THIS on George Young's talk show on *CKCK* in Regina. A man from the archives was the guest and George said, did he have any ghost stories. The man said, yes, there was the one about the mystery boxcar. It was during the Depression. A freight train came to Regina from the south and after it was in the yard a farmer telephoned the railway and said it had deposited a boxcar in his field. The railway sent people out and they were stunned. An empty boxcar was sitting all by its lonesome a hundred feet from the tracks. No markings on it and no clues as to how it travelled from the rails across a hundred feet of dirt. The railwaymen went back to town and checked the freight that had just arrived. No missing cars. An inventory was taken of every boxcar in the region and they were all accounted for. George Young was skeptical and so was the archives man. Then two listeners telephoned in and said the story was true. They'd been with the railway at the time. From what I gather, the railway never did discover where the mystery boxcar came from or how it ended up in the farmer's field."

SHE DID MORE THAN READ PALMS

"A PACK OF GYPSIES gets on at the 'Peg and as he punches their tickets the conductor says, 'No gambling, no drinking, no spitting on the floor.' Gawd. Like they were animals or something. 'Yeah, yeah, we won't do nothing bad,' one of the gypsies says, and the minute the conductor's back's turned, he pulls out a bottle and passes it around.

"I never minded the gypsies. They're people, like you and me. They used to come down our street when I was a kid, peddling pots and pans and secondhand junk. You leave them alone, they don't cause trouble. You get stupid and play cards with them and they skin you alive.

"These gypsies; there are four or five men and three women. One of the women, a cute little thing, goes to the observation car after a while. That night I'm eating supper in the diner and this old broad's giving the conductor an earful. She says the gypsy woman cheated her out of five bucks in the observation car. She was reading the old broad's palm and said her husband was a skirt-chaser. The conductor says he'll talk to the gypsy but there isn't much he can do. I had to laugh. If the gypsy said her hubby was Mr. Wonderful, she'd be happy as a pig in shit. I learnt a big lesson that day. Don't ever tell a woman bad news; it'll make her come at you with blood in her eye.

"That wasn't all I learnt. Not by a longshot. I was waiting with everyone else to get off at Edmonton and the gypsy woman, the cute one, is behind me. She says, 'You have a nice trip, Mr. Rowe?' I wasn't impressed that she knew my name. The porter could've told her. And then she says, 'Your wife's bought a new dress. It's green.' I shrugged that off, too, and went home. Wouldn't you know it? My wife did have a new dress. Sort of greenish blue with white dots on it but I'd say it was green. Explain that one to me. They should track down that gypsy woman and do research on her, for I'm sure she's got powers you and me don't have."

HUB CLARK NEEDED A HEAD

"HUB CLARK LOST HIS HEAD in the yards. I mean, he really lost it. He was a brakeman and he slipped and fell off a freight and his head hit the rails running next to the freight track and he was knocked out. A passenger train steamed down the track. It was dark and raining and the engineer took her right over Clark. Sliced his head off two inches below the Adam's apple. The CPR yards at the bottom of Granville Street is where it happened. 1928. Clark was pretty famous for a long time. The butt of the railwaymen's jokes. They'd say things like, 'Don't throw your pumpkin away after Hallowe'en, Hub Clark can use it.' By the war, though, he was forgotten. Except for the strange stories you'd hear. How somebody had seen a man in railway overalls on a rainy night and the man had no head. Me, I hold no truck with them stories. Products of overworked imaginations is what they were.

"Although I did see something strange myself. In 1942, it was. I was headed up to Vernon and there was lots of liquid sunshine when I got on the train in Vancouver. Liquid sunshine's what we call rain out here. There was no moonlight to speak of and the yard was pitch black in the plates where there were no electric lights. The train was rolling slow. Through the window, I seen a man in a yellow slicker dart from between two boxcars and go into a storage shed. Like I say, it was raining hard and the light was poor but it did seem to me that there was an empty space above his shoulders. I looked around the coach and nobody else had noticed him. Who am I to say it was Hub Clark's ghost. It might've been somebody with his head ducked really low. It did unnerve me a little. I've wished a thousand times that I'd gotten off and gone into the shed instead of spending years and years wondering what I'd really seen."

THE LIGHT FANTASTIC

"WHAT'S THIS JOKER'S NAME? Hub Clark? Never heard of him. Far as I'm concerned, there's no ghost in the Vancouver yards and never has been. Some guy's been feeding you a load of baloney. Now that isn't to say odd things haven't gone on. Maybe not in Vancouver. In Alberta, for sure. I was clerking for CN in Edmonton before I transferred to the coast. In the 1930s, we'd get these reports of mysterious lights. No kidding. Engineers barrelling at night and suddenly there's a white glow on the rails ahead. The brakes go on, the train halts, and the lights disappeared. In God's back acre, nothing for a hundred miles around, with the exception of coyotes and gophers, and they sure as hell don't light up in the dark. The engineers couldn't make heads nor tails of it. Ghosts? There's no such animal. Ghosts exist only in fairy tales. I figure the lights were caused by something real. Flying saucers. They landed and they were making maps or whatever and when the trains came along they doused their lights and took off. That's a more logical explanation than ghosts."

HANDCAR HILDA

"HANDCAR HILDA was the name they tagged on her. She lived alone in the bush outside of Edmonton. I'd pick 1918 as the year. Don't ask me how, but she came into possession of her own handcar, one of those open-air jobbies you pump the handle to operate. My father described her as a large woman. Big-boned, tall. She taught school so it's likely the railway let her use the handcar with its blessing — teachers going into the bush in those days were really appreciated.

"Saturdays, Hilda would shoot down the spur line from her cabin. To get groceries and visit friends in town. My father was walking home beside the tracks on a Saturday night and Hilda shot by. He was quite startled. That was the time of the 'flu epidemic. Fifty thousand Canadians died from it. Some prairie towns had armed guards at the train stations to discourage passengers from getting off. My father had heard Hilda was sick, so what was she doing flying past him like the wind?

"At home, my mother told him Hilda was so ill that she wasn't expected to live. My father said the neighbour who told my mother that had to be wrong. Hilda was as fit as a fiddle. My parents went to Handcar Hilda's the next day and, the neighbour had been right, she definitely had one foot in the grave. My father was so shaken that he couldn't sleep for days. He was positive he'd seen a death premonition. But Hilda surprised him. She recovered and lived to a ripe old age, and my father was forever baffled about the meaning of the scene he'd witnessed that Saturday night."

GAELIC FIRST-AID

"I SAW IT with my own eyes. These guys were on the 8:10 from Oakville to Toronto in the 1940s. Commuting to jobs in the city. They were playing bridge, like always, and one of them got a nose bleed that wouldn't stop. A stranger came over. A Scottish Highlander. He put a little bit of spit on the guys forehead and spoke a line in Gaelic. Just like that, the bleeding stopped. The Scotsman said, 'It's a talent I was born with. I'm the seventh son of a seventh son.' He said his grandfather was a seventh son too, and he had an even bigger talent. 'If he didn't like a man, he'd concentrate hard and stare at him — and he would make his nose bleed.'"

THE CRYING MAN

"DURING THE 1930s, my dad was a porter on the Montreal - Toronto run. He used to tell me a story when I was small. The story went that a weird-looking couple boarded at Central Station one night. Both dressed in black, both very pale and thin. They were like brother and sister, only they were married. Near Cornwall, the man ran into the smoker, half-hysterical, and grabbed my dad. 'My wife's had an attack,' he said. 'I think she's dead.' My dad went to the compartment and the woman was lying on the bed, stone-cold dead. The man slumped to the floor, crying and muttering, 'I love her so much. I'd give anything to have her back.'

"My dad went for the conductor. When he came back he got the shock of his life. The *man* was lying on the bed, stone-cold dead, and the *woman* was on the floor, looking dazed. My dad tried to explain to the conductor what he had seen, but he wouldn't listen. Neither would the cops. My dad was a Haitian so I guess they all thought he was caught up in voodoo. But he wasn't. Until his dying day, he swore the crying man had made some kind of pact with the devil."

HORSE ON THE RAILS

"A DREAM saved a man's life. Freeman Prevoe was the man and he was a brakeman on the Intercolonial Railway in Nova Scotia before World War I. Prevoe had second sight — the ability to look into the future. For a week he'd wake up in a cold sweat. He was having a recurring dream about a white stallion galloping on the railway tracks, a locomotive on its heels. He didn't understand the dream and he didn't understand why it scared him. One night he was on a freight train outside Egerton, and it was raining to beat the band. Prevoe was in the cab. His face paled and he shouted at the engineer, 'Stop, stop! There's a horse on the tracks!' The engineer peered into the darkness and there was nothing. The train bore on to Antigonish.

"Prevoe was beside himself with fear. First, the recurring dream; now, a vision of a horse that wasn't there. He was sure he now knew what the horse meant — death and destruction. The train swung round at Antigonish and headed back over the valley. The rain got worse. Flooding galore. Near Egerton, Prevoe begged the engineer to steer the train onto a siding and wait till morning. The engineer told him to get lost. Prevoe did just that. He crawled into a nook in a coach the train was pulling and curled into a ball, his hands over his head. The train struck a spot where the line was washedout and bolted off the rails. The engineer was crushed to death and a burst boiler scalded the fireman. Prevoe lived, and it's said he never dreamed of the white stallion after that."

The coming of the train was taken as a sign that civilization had truly reached far-flung Canadian centres. The first CN passenger train is seen arriving in Edmonton, Alberta, on October 20, 1902.

(National Archives Canada, PA-61692.)

Guiding a train through the B.C. mountains in the 1800s was not a task for the faint-hearted. Passengers and crew pose at Payne Bluff, near Sandon where there's barely enough room for the train to make it around the bend. *(Vancouver City Archives.)*

A massive snowslide derailed and partially buried this train travelling through Rogers Pass in 1886. Passengers were forced to stay at the CPR hotel nearby in Field, B.C., for almost four weeks. *(Vancouver City Archives.)*

A work gang does its bit to help build the White Pass and Yukon line that brought the CPR trains to the Klondike. The crew was excavating near the summit, over 900 metres up. *(National Archives Canada, C-5596.)*

As if to punch their way across high mountain passes wasn't bad enough, pioneer construction gangs also had to contend with wide ravines and flood-prone streams. This 1800s trestle at Mountain Creek, B.C., was a visual tribute to the grit and the skill of the workers who built it. *(O.B. Buell, CRHA Archives.)*

Above: White linen and freshly cut flowers were two of the staples on the elegant, wood panelled dining cars before the First World War. The food was something else too – marvellous three- or four-course meals served with the finest imported wines.

(Canadian Pacific Corporate Archives.)

THE CANADIAN PACIFIC RAILWAY

DINING CARS

Excel in Elegance of Design and Furniture

AND IN THE

Quality of Food and Attendance

ANYTHING HITHERTO OFFERED TO

TRANSCONTINENTAL TRAVELLERS.

The fare provided is the best procurable, and the cooking has a wide reputation for excellence. Local delicacies, such as trout, prairie hens, antelope steaks, Fraser River salmon, succeed one another as the train moves westward.

The wines are of the Company's special importation, and are of the finest quality.

These cars accompany all transcontinental trains, and are managed directly by the Railway Company, which seeks, as with its hotels and sleeping cars, to provide every comfort and luxury without regard to cost—looking to the general profit of the Railway rather than to the immediate returns from these branches of its service

The CPR once proudly advertised its superb dining facilities in magazines and on posters throughout North America and Europe.

(Glenbow Archives.)

Parlour-car riders in the 1920s could listen to the CNR's innovative radio network. Symphony concerts, lectures, and newscasts were among the live broadcasts received on board cross-Canada trains. Note the headphones on the male passenger at left. (National Archives Canada, C-26000.)

A quartet of fashionably attired and coiffured ladies enjoy a conversation in a 1920s CPR solarium car. *(National Archives Canada, C-29456.)*

The summit at Rogers Pass was a busy place in 1886. Some railway labourers lived in crude boxcar homes *(left)* and did their shopping in the stores across the tracks.
(Archives of Ontario, S-4938.)

A potbelly stove and a pot of fresh coffee helped make life more comfortable for railway workers riding the caboose. *(Glenbow Archives.)*

The velocipede was an often-used form of transportation for railway workers in the old days. *(Glenbow Archives.)*

Track inspectors toiling for the CPR's Quebec division in the 1950s rode in style. A sleek Cadillac equipped with a siren and air brakes cruised at 80 km/h and could hit a top speed of 105 km/h. *(York University,* Toronto Telegram *Collection.)*

It's the summer of 1946 and another shift has ended at Transcona shops. The railway workers are seen crossing the marble floor of the rotunda at Winnipeg's Union Station. *(National Archives Canada, C-49376.)*

The Second World War manpower shortage prompted the railways to hire record numbers of women as engine wipers, car cleaners, and shop labourers. This 1943 picture of a locomotive was taken on Vancouver Island and shows fireman, engineer and a group of women wipers. *(York University,* Toronto Telegram *Collection.)*

It was a joyful day in Edmonton when members of the 49th Battalion, C.E.F., returned from overseas service in 1918. An enormous crowd swarmed around the CPR station to welcome soldiers disembarking from an afternoon train. *(Glenbow Archives.)*

The Stampeders lost the Grey Cup in 1949 to the Montreal Alouettes, but that did not deter loyal Calgarians from staging a downtown parade. A fleet of convertibles waits at the station for the team to leave the incoming "Stampeder Special."

(Glenbow Archives.)

The poor, pitiful Turbo. Everything went wrong on the train that was supposed to set the pace for high-speed comfort and efficiency. *(Courtesy Canadian National.)*

The streamlined Aerotrain built by General Motors, that had a trial run on the Toronto-Hamilton route in 1957, never made it into passenger service. For some reason, now forgotten, the lightweight, air-cushioned passenger train failed to make the grade.

(York University, Toronto Telegram *Collection.)*

Three generations of a Saskatchewan farm family, the Jenzens, watch and wave as the special train bearing the body of former Prime Minister John Diefenbaker passes their barley field near Saskatoon, Saskatchewan. Thousands of Canadians turned up along the route between Ottawa and Saskatoon to bid the Chief a fond farewell. *(Toronto Star.)*

SENTIMENTAL JOURNEY

A small crowd of admirers was on hand at Sault Ste. Marie station to greet
Prime Minister Pierre Elliot Trudeau and his three sons during a holiday trip in 1983.
Not all of Trudeau's train excursions met with such friendly response.
After his famous Salmon Arm salute, a train carrying Trudeau was pelted with eggs at
Sudbury. (*The Sault Star.*)

On June 28, 1886, the first transcontinental passenger train rolled out of Montreal's
Dalhousie Station to begin a five-and-a-half-day journey to Port Moody, B.C.
Two weeks later, Prime Minister John A. Macdonald made the same trip on another
train. Sir John and Lady Macdonald *(right)* are seen stretching their legs during
a brief stopover at Stave River, B.C. *(Canapress Photo Service.)*

THE WAR YEARS

On a bitterly cold day in 1914, eight thousand soldiers marched 13 kilometres through the streets of Hamilton while cheering crowds packed the sidewalks. My father was one of the soldiers. The parade was a morale-boosting prelude to actual disembarkation, and he remembered the rousing sounds of the bagpipes and the bugle bands. A week later, his unit was unceremoniously trucked to the depot and placed aboard a night train to Halifax. Some of his friends were so delighted to be going overseas they could hardly stand still. The wiser ones were sullen and anxious. As the train departed, my father noticed two small boys on the platform. They wore khaki uniforms identical to those worn by the soldiers and, he told me, "They chilled my spine; their faces were like cold, pale death-masks."

Another generation of Canadian military men started boarding the trains in 1939. They had, no doubt, the same conflicting emotions as my father's friends — some delighted, some anxious. Whatever their personal feelings were, the military flow during World War II was a welcome boon for the railways. After the debilitating Depression, when more people rode freights than passenger cars, the cross-country passenger traffic soared to a stunning sixty million persons between 1939 and 1946.

SMART-ALEC YANKS

"FUNNY ABOUT THE YANKS. The ones they shipped to Wainwright had bushels of chocolate bars and cigarettes yet they were so short on solid food when they first hit the base that they'd sneak into our supply shed and rifle the shelves. The reason was, it was winter and they'd come from Alabama to Alberta with the same amount of food they'd eat in a hotter climate. Drilling in cold weather makes you hungrier and they were constantly bitching about their growling bellies. We should've felt sorry for them but we didn't. On the train, you see, they'd been real smart alecs. We travelled west together — the Yanks from Alabama and our boys from Ontario — to take part in a joint exercise. They talked down to us. As if we were dumb as doornails. As if all Americans were ruling-class and all Canadians peasants. The distance from the station to Camp Wainwright was a mile, maybe a mile and a half, over open country. We had to march it. A vicious wind was blowing. The Yanks didn't come prepared. No gloves or earmuffs or heavy coats. Maybe half of them were frostbitten. We didn't feel sorry for them then either. They were wise guys; you don't take pity on people who act superior to you."

SUPERVISION REQUIRED

"THE SERGEANT-MAJOR boarded at Moncton. We'd been in New Brunswick on special training courses and we'd had such a wild time on the trip east from Ontario that the army concluded that we needed supervision. The sergeant-major was a volunteer and we were regulars. En route to Toronto, we asked if it was all right to play cards in the smoker. He said, sure, he couldn't see any harm in it. We got a poker game going. On a cash-only basis. The porter pretended it wasn't happening and somebody kept an eye peeled for the conductor. The sergeant-major watched for a while, then joined in when somebody quit. We cleaned him out. Every nickel he had on him. Fifty dollars. He had his return ticket but no money for meals. One of the boys lent him twenty bucks. He left us at Toronto and I was positive that's the last our friend had seen of the money. I mean, who'd send back money taken from him in a poker game. The sergeant-major was a good, honest man. On his next pay day, he put a twenty-dollar bill in an envelope and mailed it to our friend."

WILY DESERTER

"EACH OUTFIT had a policy of collecting its own deserters whenever possible. I was with the Royal Canadian Army Service Corps, and, because I did commando training in Scotland, I was assigned to runaways. On this particular case, Sergeant Peterson accompanied me. A young soldier had gone *AWOL* from Borden and tried to kill his girl-friend in Manitoba. I'm not an expert on what a potential murderer looks like but he certainly didn't appear dangerous. He was tall and clean-cut and extremely dapper.

"We were on the Toronto train and several hundred yards east of the Winnipeg station the engine rammed a truck. Sergeant Peterson surveyed the accident and presumed he had sufficient time to retrieve a bottle he'd stashed in a station locker. While he was in the building, the train departed. The prisoner was cuffed to me. Sergeant Peterson had the key and our tickets. I felt no cause for alarm. I knew he'd catch up to us. The conductor walked along the aisle checking tickets.

"Suddenly, the prisoner launched into this incredible line of bull. He was telling the conductor he was the guard and I was the prisoner and, having lost the key, he'd appreciate it if the conductor located some tools and broke the cuffs. I insisted he was lying but I could see by the conductor's eyes that he was believing him. The prisoner had on a ritzy suit and tie and looked like a million. My shirt and uniform were wrinkled, I hadn't shaven, and my eyes were red from staying up late the previous night. 'Listen, you don't have to accept my word or his,' I said. 'I'm Scotty Sandison, he's so-and-so. Wire the Winnipeg station, have them page Sergeant Peterson and he'll tell you who's who.' Thank goodness, the conductor agreed. He wired Winnipeg and Sergeant Peterson sent my description and verified who I was. I took the prisoner off at Kenora and we waited for the sergeant, who was coming on a milk train. A Mountie met us at the station.

"While the three of us waited, the prisoner spilled his story. He had been mailing money to his girl from Borden and she'd promised to save it until they were married. Then this other guy came along and she'd run off with him, taking the money. The soldier was arrested in her apartment trying to do her in. I understood why he was telling me this. To win my sympathy. I suppose he hoped I'd feel he'd been shafted and let him go.

"We waited for hours and then he said he had to use the bathroom. When we walked into the washroom, it was empty. He jumped me. We had a helluva scuffle. He was two inches taller and a lot heavier but I had my commando training. I don't understand what he expected to gain. If he knocked me out, he'd have to drag my body through a window and carry it around Kenora, looking for someplace to smash the cuffs. The Mountie heard the fight and rushed in, and together we overpowered him. Sergeant Peterson finally arrived and we headed east.

"The prisoner behaved himself. Small wonder. The cuff was loose on my wrist; the one on his wrist was tight. Whenever he was lippy, I'd give him a yank. His wrist was swollen from the fight so badly you could barely see the cuff on it; when I yanked, he shut up real fast."

MILITARY DISPLAY

"THE ARMY SENT a special train across Canada in 1941. Or was it '42? The date doesn't matter. They sent the train, and me and some of my buddies trudged down to Union Station in Toronto to look it over. Make no mistake, it was a beaut. Tanks and jeeps and howitzers and Lewis machine guns on the flat cars. Spellbinding stuff for us teenagers. They had steps you went up and you could touch the guns and imagine what it was like to shoot them.

"Inside the coaches, another story. Uniforms draped on department-store dummies, and pistols, medals, and pictures of soldiers training displayed in glass cases. On the walls there were pictures of the King and Queen and Mackenzie King. Jeepers, what a show. All intended to glorify war and make you want to sign up right away.

"It was typical of us Canadians that they didn't have recruitment people on the train. And no band playing 'O Canada.' The Americans would've had a band blasting 'The Battle Hymn of the Republic,' a brigade of soldiers shoving pens under everybody's nose, and maybe a big picture of Hitler with a target painted on his chest. But us kids got the message. We couldn't wait to be old enough to join up. We were bear cubs and the military train was the honey that lured us."

WOMEN AND CHILDREN LAST

"I WAS TRAVELLING in Alberta with my mother and my two little daughters, Sheila and Heather. The train was jammed with servicemen. The four of us entered the dining car and my mother didn't like what the stewards were doing. In fact, she was furious. If two seats were available, the stewards would seat two servicemen and ignore the women and children standing by the door. Even if a serviceman had his wife with him, he'd be seated with another man and his wife would be left behind. My mother called a steward over and said it was unfair. 'Don't blame me, madam,' he said. 'I don't write the rules.' I have to admit he had a point. Rules were rules and he was obliged to obey them, even if my mother and every other woman in Canada thought they were absurd."

JARRED, JOLTED, AND BOUNCED

"I WAS WITH the RAF, a radio-navigation instructor specializing in Mosquitoes, and I moved back and forth between a half-dozen air-fields from the Maritimes to Abbotsford, B.C. The Canadian trains were a living horror compared to the ones we had in England. Certainly, the food was better here but the damn cars were always shuttering. In England, the trains glided in and out of stations and, if you were sleeping overnight, you'd be assured of an uninterrupted rest. Here, you'd be jarred and jolted and bounced and rudely awakened every time the train pulled in and out of a blessed station. I never could fathom it. What was all that shuttering in aid of?

"Then there was the Prairies. With or without shuttering, that was a ghastly experience. The first time I travelled across them I stared and stared at the wretched fields and tried to become excited if a solitary cow appeared. By the third or fourth journey, as soon as the train left the Rockies going east or Ontario going west, I'd pull my blind down and keep it down until there was something worthwhile to peer at. I'd read, play bridge, stare at the floor, and talk to other passengers. Anything to avoid what surely must be the most depressing topography on earth, this side of the Australian Outback."

SIXTY GUYS AWOL

"AT CHRISTMAS in 1943 sixty of us went AWOL at the same time and, just my luck, I was the only one punished for it. How it happened was the military powers-that-be laid on a special train to take us from Toronto to Winnipeg. Our leave-passes said we could only be away from camp five days. The trip normally took one and a half days each way, which meant three days wasted travelling. At Sudbury, they shoved our train onto a siding and removed the engine. A high mucky-muck had determined that our contingent wasn't large enough to warrant a special locomotive and we'd have to cool our heels on the siding for twenty-four hours until we hooked onto another train going west. Man, were we ticked off. The word spread it that we'd all stick together and make up for the lost twenty-four hours at Sudbury by defiantly spending an extra day at our homes.

"The locomotive that eventually pulled us to Winnipeg was late and I didn't arrive at my parents' house on Manhattan Avenue until Christmas morning. If I paid attention to my pass, I was obligated to leave for camp the same night. I had dinner, went to bed, and spent Boxing Day sitting around with my family. I was an RCAF technician at St. Thomas. When I returned there, I heard that sixty out of the seventy or eighty guys at Sudbury had shown up at the base a day late, like we all agreed to do. A group captain summoned me to his office. Before I'd gone on leave, I'd been asked to play the piano at the New Year's Eve dance. I had a hot date lined up and I'd said no. The group captain came down on me hard. 'Do you realize, Copland, that you could be shot for desertion. I don't see how I can avoid putting a black mark on your record.'

"He did see how. Undoubtedly, he saw it long before I entered his office. If I played at the dance, he said, there'd be no black mark. I said I'd do it. Then he added another punishment. A week of KP. The other fifty-nine guys got black marks, but so what? It occurred to me afterwards that a black mark means bugger-all unless you're spending your life in the military. They got New Year's off and had a wonderful time and, while they were nursing hangovers, I was chained to a sink, scrubbing dishes. Like I said earlier, sixty guys go AWOL and I'm the only one Dame Fortune gives the finger to."

EVERYONE LIKED HIM

"I RECOGNIZED HIM the instant I set eyes on him. Flanders. The sergeant who'd been kind to us at Borden in 1916. He was by himself and there was an empty sleeve in his suit. And when he turned his head like this, I caught sight of the big, red patch up one side of his face. War injuries, I thought. Flanders was walloped by a grenade or land mine. He was hunched over and hadn't shaved, and he seemed bloody miserable.

"I remembered how he was. Big, striding steps, a cock-of-the-walk manner to him. Camp Borden in 1916 was hot and desolate, a huge sandpit. Where it wasn't flat and sandy, trees were being chopped down, the stumps pulled out and burned. We slept in tents. Mosquitoes the size of walnuts. Some sergeants marched you so hard you fainted. Flanders gave you rests. He nabbed a few of us passing a bottle in a tent one night and he didn't report us. A good guy; everyone liked him.

"I hadn't seen him since 1916 and here we were, three days before Christmas, on the Kingston train. 1942 and I was an NCO. Uniforms all over the coach. I had a brown bag in my lap. A crock of gin. When the train reached Kingston, I walked over and handed it to him. 'Have a nice Christmas, Sergeant Flanders,' I said. He sure looked surprised. He obviously didn't know me from a hole in the head. Before he asked anything, I was gone. You know what? It came to me later on that Flanders was very strict religion-wise and a teetotaller. What a stupid present to have given him."

SLEEPING IN THE AISLES

"THOSE TROOP TRAINS were really something. Soldiers packed into the coaches by the hundreds and it took three engines to haul them over the Rocky Mountains. I was on one in July of '42. I left the farm to join the 22nd Heavy Artillery in Winnipeg and they sent me to Victoria for training. The trip to the west coast showed me how matters would be in the Army. The officers had berths and compartments and we were crammed in so tight in the coaches that guys had to stand up all day and then sleep in the aisles at night. Some guys who failed their medicals were on with us. You could've cut the resentment with a knife. They were headed for great jobs, three and four bucks an hour at Yarrows' shipyard. They were healthy enough to work, so why weren't they healthy enough to fight? They stayed to themselves and there wasn't any trouble. The food? First rate. Steak and potatoes. Not like the crap we were served in Victoria. The barracks were so crowded we had to sleep six to a tent for two months, and practically every night the menu was the same, spaghetti and Jello. After lights out, you'd lie in your tent and torture yourself thinking of the thick, juicy train steaks."

MUTINY AT TERRACE

"THEY HAD THREE troop trains sitting in Terrace in the summer of 1944 that soldiers refused to get on. Yes, sir. Three of them. This was during the mutiny, the rebellion the Army and the government and the newspapers covered up. Not a word anywhere outside Terrace, and I know for a fact that it took place because I was a carpenter in the town. You can take it from me, the townspeople were sick with fear that the soldiers might shoot them. There was no love lost between the soldiers and them. Due to the situation that there were thousands of soldiers, and Terrace was small and the soldiers were after their women. I seen a sign, 'No Soldiers Allowed,' at the dance hall. Which the soldiers tore down and ripped up. I knew of a grocer who hid his twelve-year-old daughter in the back when soldiers came to his store.

"That was what was behind the mutiny. The lack of women, and the lousy camp conditions. The soldiers were jammed into huts like sardines. In huts that were cold and had kerosene lamps and no electric power. Just being in northern B.C. hackled them too. The isolation. Them soldiers were from Manitoba, Quebec, Ontario, and Prince Edward Island. The Quebeckers were conscripts who didn't want to wear the King's uniform.

"So they rebelled. Three thousand soldiers. They took over the camp and held their officers hostage. The Army sent a trainload of men from Vancouver and the two groups sat on different sides of the barbwire fence, pointing machine guns and rifles at each other.

"I'm trying to think how long the mutiny lasted. Two weeks. Yes, I'm sure that's how long it was. The Army tried to talk the mutiny leaders into surrendering and when they couldn't they brought the trains in. Three big locomotives pulling empty coaches. They stood on the tracks across from the camp. An Army officer walked up to the mutiny leaders and said, 'Look, this is the last straw. If you clowns aren't on those trains in thirty minutes, we're bringing bombers from Vancouver to level this camp.'

"It worked. The mutineers laid down their arms and released the officers and marched to the trains. In formation, I haven't a clue where the trains carried them. Knowing the Army, probably straight to the boat and over to France where they shoved them in the front lines."

SIXTEEN SPARE BRIDES

"IT SURPRISED ME, all right. Why me? Why did the top brass believe I was the best man to shepherd 750 war brides from England to Canada? I didn't question the order. Even if I was an acting brigadier, as I was at the time, I didn't feel it was my place to request an explanation. I did hear a rumour. Someone told me he'd heard an officer at HQ had said, 'Give the job to ol' Eric Cormack. He's a fine father figure.' And, apparently, a general exclaimed, 'Yes, he's forty five and can't do any harm to the girls even if he tries.'

"We sailed from Southampton to Halifax at the end of January, 1946. Aboard a stripped-down Cunard liner, the *Scythia*. One hundred and fifty men sailed with us and, although the ladies were all married, I had to be alert for hanky-panky. One fellow, a sneaky corporal, was caught where he shouldn't have been, if you get my drift. I fixed his wagon. Slammed him in the brig — a tiny room near the propellers —

where he must have bounced with every wave. It was a rough crossing. Girls sick all over the boat.

"Halifax was depressing. Twenty degrees below, a raw wind, and snow. We guided the girls onto two special trains, one for Central Canada, one headed west. I was the CO of the Calgary train, 325 girls. People write stories saying how excited and happy the war brides were. That wasn't the impression I received. There was a lot of tension, a lot of worrying. To understand the reason, you have to understand where the brides were coming from and what lay ahead.

"Let's go back a few steps. In 1939 the Canadian army authorities asked me to raise an artillery regiment in Saskatchewan and Alberta — The Eighth Light Anti-Aircraft Regiment, RCA. All told 1,166 fellows enlisted and a large proportion of them were under my command in East Sussex. Our boys had plenty of time to fraternize. Their average age was twenty-two, they had money to burn and they looked glamorous in their uniforms. When they went into the villages, they met these attractive ladies in breeches, high boots, and tight sweaters. Need I say it — both sexes were impressed. I received hundreds of applications for permission to marry. I didn't approve them all. Some ladies were schemers with their eyes focused firmly on the wives' allowance of $35 a month and a $15-a-month children's cheque. I rejected a young boy who wasn't too bright, a Grade Six education and never off the farm before. He wanted to marry a very knowing widow of twenty-nine with four children.

"I'm sure you get the picture. Many of the girls married 'glamorous, fly-by-night' soldiers and now, there they were, on a train moving across a foreign country in the dark of winter. Did their husbands still want them? How would their new in-laws react? Would they be able to adapt to life in such a big, cold country? I must have heard those questions a hundred times between Halifax and Calgary.

"The trip lasted a week. The CPR kept shunting us off onto sidings to let freights and regular passenger trains go by. Damn hot in the cars. They never seem to get a decent temperature on trains, always too hot or too cold. The girls didn't grumble. They thought they were in the lap of luxury. They had their own berths and, after the rationing back home, the dining-car food was wonderful. Oranges and bananas, too.

Miraculously, they had all this fruit to eat that they rarely saw during the war. Every time you'd walk through a car, somebody was peeling an orange.

"They were good girls. They didn't cause any trouble. They sang the 'White Cliffs of Dover' and 'There'll Always Be an England' to keep their spirits up. Some played fiddles and every car had a mouth-organ or two. The smokers were off-limits. They strung up lines for their laundry and you'd be buried in dripping-wet underwear if you dared enter.

"We let them off all the way west. Sometimes at whistle-stops at 3:00 a.m. and it would take hours to locate their trunks in the baggage-car. Everything they owned was in those trunks — blankets, clothing, cutlery, wedding gifts. There'd be crowds in the larger cities, and lots of tears and some girls fainted. I couldn't release anyone unless someone in authority signed for her — a priest, a town mayor, a RCMP officer. Winnipeg was chaotic. A hundred girls got off the train and disappeared into a huge crowd. Having a custodial-care paper signed was the last thing on their minds. At first, I thought we'd fouled up on that one. Then I remembered the trunks. We set up shop near the baggage and had the papers signed when they picked up their trunks.

"The real shock was Calgary. We had sixteen spare brides. No one had shown up to claim them. Understandably, some of them were tearful and sorely in need of assurance that just because they hadn't been claimed, that didn't mean their husbands didn't love them. It just meant they hadn't been properly informed about their arrival time. The sixteen went to Currie barracks and members of the CWAC eventually helped reunite them with their husbands.

"On the whole, I'd say the war brides fit into Canadian society very well. The ones I run into seem quite happy here. One of my bombardiers married a shy, rosy-cheeked Sussex farmgirl. Ten years afterwards, I met her in Brandon. She was a poised, self-confident, fashionably dressed woman, a ladies' aid member and that sort of thing. It has been reported that some of them decided they were better off in England and returned home. What hasn't been reported is that almost all of them came back to Canada again."

PAIN AND SUFFERING

"ISN'T IT WEIRD how some folks went through the war without suffering so much as a pinprick and then returned to their homeland and, wham, they were hit by a trolley. No, I wasn't hit by a trolley but you might say my case was similar to that. Two years with the CWAC in the Midlands and the worst casualty I witnessed was a soldier who busted his leg tumbling off a horse. After V-E Day, I was posted to Camp Borden where I'd been demobbed. Riding up from Halifax, a corporal said they were short of orderlies and he'd appreciate me volunteering to lend a hand in the hospital cars. Foolish girl, I said yes.

"Long as I live I won't forget the scene. Two coaches filled with war casualties. The walking wounded in one, the total invalids in the other. Lucky me, I drew the invalids. Amputees, both legs gone, and some in pain, and boys who'd had their spines screwed up somehow and couldn't walk a step. Nobody left his berth. They just lay there, depressed and gloomy, and people brought them meals and bedpans and endless bottles of Kik-Cola.

"There was a nurse who was a surly, short-tempered bitch. The kind who makes you wonder why, if she hates sick people so much, she's in the business. I washed the boys' faces and carried bedpans and somehow managed not to try and crack the nurses' head with a good back-hander. The smell in that car was vile. Grilled cheese and urine and medicine. None of the patients stands out in my memory. They were just a massive blob of pain and suffering to me. Such a bleak scene. I was so pleased to escape that I nearly danced a jig at Union Station."

FAMILY REUNION

"The cruiser *Prince Robert* carried the fellows over from Asia in '45 and, to be perfectly honest, I had a bad case of the jitters, not knowing what shape Scotty would be in. He was a nice, lively country boy when he joined the Grenadiers and was posted to Hong Kong. After eighteen days of fighting, Hong Kong fell and he was captured. We heard about the fall on the radio at home in Manitoba and I remember saying to myself, That's it. It's all over for Scotty. Now here I was, his young, healthy sister, standing on the dock in Vancouver and praying to God that he wouldn't be a walking corpse. Four and a half years in a Jap POW camp. I won't go into the horror of it, the starvation, the torture, the beheadings.

"I was close to the gangplank. Wives, children, parents, relatives, girlfriends; they were all there. Enough tears to flood the city. Some of the fellows were carted off in stretchers. Some of the walkers didn't look too good either. Like skeletons. All bone, no meat. Men who weighed 200 pounds when they went overseas came back weighing 90, 100. Thank the Lord, Scotty looked all right. A little bloated from a rice diet but he wasn't a skeleton. 'I'm sure glad I'm home.' He said that over and over. 'I'm sure glad I'm in Canada.'

"We travelled to Manitoba by train. The CPR. All Scotty talked about during the trip was the family and our farm. How he swam in the creek as a youngster, how he chopped firewood and helped with the animals. Other Hong Kong vets were on the train. I noticed that they were doing the same as Scotty. Hardly eating and not sleeping too well and, even talking to one another, they never spoke of the war or the POW camps. A few didn't talk at all. Too depressed; too withdrawn.

"The Merritts are a big family. Eleven children. Ten brothers and me, the lone girl. After we crossed into Manitoba, our brothers began popping up along the way — climbing on at Virden and small stations. Whenever another brother appeared, there was a lot of hugging and emotion. It was like a whole series of family reunions. Mother was at the last stop, Birch Creek, where our home was. I can't find the words to describe how thrilled she was to see him; Scotty was her oldest boy. There was enough tears in Vancouver to flood the city but, by golly, the Merritts did enough bawling in Manitoba to flood the whole darn province."

ESTEVAN'S BLACKEST HOUR

"SEPTEMBER 15, 1946, was a black day for Estevan. Twenty-one boys died when a Dakota crashed at the airport south of here. Estevan was a training base for Canadian and foreign fliers and the lads on the Dakota were returning home from ferrying planes into the States. The killed boys were all Canadians but it wouldn't have made no difference if they were foreign. The town had great feelings for the fliers, foreign and Canadian. They knew them from the dances and the beer parlour and church. The pilots dated their daughters and played baseball with them and hitched rides from here to the base. My folks had many of the boys to our farm for Sunday dinner, though, thank goodness none of those who were killed.

"The CPR sent a funeral train from Winnipeg. Over a hundred RCAF were on board to go to the church service at the drill hall. After the service, the dead boys were driven to town. Their coffins were on military trucks and covered with Union Jacks. There was a procession behind the trucks, military and local people, a mile long.

"Estevan showed its respect by closing stores and schools and having flags at half-mast. The entire town was on the streets; women crying and an old soldier named Kingsley lifted his one good arm in a salute. A bugler played the 'Last Post' at the station and the coffins were loaded onto the baggage car. I can recall the locomotive number — 1248. I'll carry it to my grave. The number and how the locomotive slowly slipped from the station and how everyone watched, nobody talking, till the train was gone."

They Come From Far Away

The Cincinnati lawyer boarded the train in Winnipeg last autumn. He had a private compartment but he was seldom in it. A robust, effusive soul, he roamed the aisles and nested in the bar car, seeking companionship. Given his ebullient nature, I was surprised to find him sitting alone in the dome car, visibly depressed, as the train sped through the Fraser Valley. "Since I was a kid I've dreamed of seeing the Canadian Rockies by train," he explained. "I retired a month ago, and I've finally seen them. Now what'll I do with the rest of my life?" I replied that there was more to Canada, if not the world, than the Rocky Mountains. "I'm sure you're right," he said, half-heartedly. "But the Rockies were it with me. They were my idea of something truly romantic."

He wasn't, of course, the first foreigner to place such a high value on seeing the Rockies. Tourists began going to the mountains on a grand scale after the CPR's westward spread in the 1880s. Railway builder William Van Horne had reportedly pointed at the Rockies and remarked, "We can't export the scenery; we'll import the tourists." And import them he did. Colourful posters and brochures labelling the Rockies "The Mountain Playground of the World" swamped the United States and Europe. Plush sleeping and parlour cars were introduced, and locomotives chugging out of Banff and Jasper pulled open-air sightseeing cars. By 1900, the Rockies were an established world-class lure.

For all their drawing power, however, the mountains have never surpassed Niagara Falls as our No. 1 tourist attraction. Decades before the Rockies were a gleam in Van Horne's eye, Niagara's hotels and restaurants were jammed with foreign visitors. Tightrope artists helped promote the Falls: eight trainloads of Americans were among the 40,000 people watching the Great Blondin walk over the gorge in 1860. Magazine ads boasted that no one who had seen the wonder of Niagara had failed to be impressed. The ads didn't mention Oscar Wilde. Following his train trip to the area in 1882, he said the Falls were simply an unnecessary amount of water cascading over unnecessary rocks. "The true wonder, dear boys, would be if the water didn't fall."

ENDANGERED SPECIES

"THE CUSTOMS PEOPLE came on the train at Windsor and proceeded from car to car. The woman seated across from me was from the Deep South. Very aggressive, a person accustomed to having her own way. She had a foot-long, stuffed crocodile on her seat. The customs officer looked at the hideous thing and said he'd have to confiscate it because it was illegal to transport souvenirs of endangered species into Canada. 'This isn't a souvenir,' the woman blurted out. 'It's a pet.' The customs officer didn't blink an eye. 'In that case, lady, I'll have to put him in quarantine. Until he's well enough to travel.'"

ENERGY TO BURN

"BEING A TOUR GUIDE is an education in itself. And I don't mean because of the historic sites. It's because of the people you meet. Last summer I conducted three excursions from Toronto to Vancouver on The Canadien. Seventy percent of the clients were Americans; the others, British, South African, and German. I'm a university student and until the tours I was completely unaware of the drinking old people do. Men and women in their sixties and seventies knocking back alcohol with amazing consistency. Some had their own liquor sets in their compartments — jiggers and openers and ice-buckets. We had a man who refused to pay $2.50 for the VIA beer. If we were in the depot for more than fifteen minutes he raced to the closest tavern and drained as many glasses as he could.

"And the Texans. What a couple they were. A retired rancher and his girlfriend, both in their middle seventies, at least. They didn't just party on the train. When we stayed somewhere overnight, they carried ice cubes and mixer and bottles to their room, and I don't think there was a single café they entered without ordering a drink. One night in Banff they walked into the hotel nightclub. Faster than you can wink, they were on the stage with the band. He played the spoons and she sang 'Yellow Rose of Texas.' I didn't have their energy; I went to bed early. Somebody told me they stayed in the nightclub until 2:00 a.m.

"I trust I'm not giving you the idea that all the people on tours are heavy drinkers. Some won't touch anything stronger than tea. The really dedicated tea drinkers had their own pots and tiny stainless-steel burners and favourite brands of tea and packages of crackers and cookies. Many even had their favourite cushions, embroidered with messages like 'Home Is Where the Heart Is.'

"The biggest topics of conversation were where they'd been on other trips and their pets. Pictures. They had loads of pictures. Snapshots of dogs and cats and grandchildren and London bobbies and the streetcars in San Francisco.

"The train rides were usually fairly serene and orderly. If anything went wrong, it was during the stopovers. A General Motors executive from Detroit was canoeing on Lake Louise and when he reached for the dock he tipped the boat and dumped himself and another man in. The other man had to stay in his room the rest of the day, waiting for his shoes to dry. Several women travelled onto the Columbia Icefields in open-toed sandals and came down with rotten colds. Soon afterwards, a man got stomach 'flu on a ranch visit and passed the bug around. Thirteen of my twenty-two clients had colds or the 'flu; the washroom line-ups on The Canadien were a sight for sore eyes.

"A great experience. I'd recommend being a tour guide to anyone. Nevertheless, I was worn-out and glad to be back at university. You could say I was too young for the job; I didn't have the stamina to keep pace with those fabulous senior citizens."

PERPETUAL MOTION

"YOU HAVE NOTHING interesting to say, you keep your mouth shut. That has been my rule since I was a girl and it served me well. Not everybody goes by that rule and you only have to be saddled with a colossal bore on a Greyhound bus to know it. Or get saddled with an Ada. She was from Glasgow and she was touring on The Dominion with her husband. Bert, Bryon, something that begins with a B. They were fiftyish. My, that woman had a tongue in her head. It never stopped moving. In the diner she'd go on and on about how she decorated her 'wee' house and the 'wee' problems she was having with her 'wee' neighbours. On and on. She never asked you a question about yourself; it was all Ada, Ada, Ada. Bert, or whatever his name was, hardly spoke. If he did it was usually to correct a statement she made, and she'd ignore him.

"In the observation car she was at her worst. Hour upon hour, she'd sit beside Bert and read every sign she saw out loud. We'd pass a grain elevator and she'd go, 'Pioneer.' We'd run alongside a highway and she'd go, 'Moose Jaw 200 kilometres, Swift Current 250 kilometres.' Passing through towns she couldn't hope to read them all, but she tried. Oh, my, how she tried. 'Doug's Gas Bar;' 'Kentucky Fried Chicken;' 'Municipal Building;' 'Anti-Freeze One-Third Off This Month.' On and on. I was two rows from her and I prayed her husband would scream, 'Shut up, for heaven's sake. I see what you see.' I got fed up and left the car one day. Later on, they were still there. She was silent and, I thought, so she finally got a sore tongue.

"I read the newspaper and put it down as the train came into an interesting town. Darned woman; she switched her motor on again. 'Monarch Café'…'The Bay'…'Buy Your Snow Tires At Bell's Auto Repair'…."

GENEROUS AMERICANS, STINGY CANADIANS

"SURE THERE'S A DIFFERENCE between American and Canadian travellers. Americans are generous; Canadians are the last of the world's great cheapskates. Let me enlighten you. A Canadian eats his meal fast if there's an American at the table so he can leave first. He doesn't leave a tip because he knows the American will. An American realizes the Canadian didn't tip, thinks it's an oversight, and lays an extra dollar down to make it up for him. That's in the dining car.

"Now for the sleeping car, where I'm a porter. I was once called to a Canadian's compartment at 2:00 a.m. He awakened with an overwhelming craving for orange juice. The kitchen was closed but I managed to get him a glass. He dropped a dime in the palm of my hand. 'Thank you, sir,' I said to myself. 'I can hardly wait to reach Toronto so I can rush out and buy a package of gum.' Americans appreciate service. An American and I were talking about desserts and ice cream came up. I said they have terrific cones in the VIA station at Jasper. He had a cast on his foot and asked me to get one for him. I did. He gave me a five-dollar tip.

"One more illustration. Americans wear mile-wide smiles leaving the train. 'I had a pleasant trip. Thank you, very much, young man,' and it's paper currency dropping to your hand. Canadians leave in a sour mood. They know they ought to tip the porter and it hurts. The odd one scrapes up a dollar, the seasoned cheapskates hand you a quarter. Americans would never dream of handing you a paperback book instead of cash. There's always some Canadian at the end of the line who thrusts a copy of Sidney Sheldon's latest, or Ludlum's, or — what's the name of the girl whose sister's on *Dynasty*? — Jackie Collins'. 'This is for you, porter. You'll enjoy reading it.' Why can't it be a book I'd like. A Pierre Berton, a Walter Stewart. A book with bulk between the covers. The junk they give me goes straight to the trashcan."

NOT SO FUNNY TO HIM

"TWENTY YEARS have gone by and it's still in my head. The worst joke I ever heard. This goddamned Yank said it again and again. I heard him in the dome, I heard him in the dining car, I heard him in the corridor outside my roomette. He was a loud bugger, pushing sixty, a Montana salesman. And he was the kind of joke-teller I can't bear. The kind who never fails to laugh uproariously at his own story. He had a long, deep laugh that made you yearn to shove a fist in his mouth. Here's the joke:

'When you're past fifty, your memory falls to pieces. My wife lay down on the couch the other day and sighed and said, I've had it. My memory is so bad I didn't remember giving it to her.' What a low-grade joke. How'd you like to have that in your head for twenty years?"

CHAMPAGNE BEFORE BREAKFAST

"CHAMPAGNE, CHOCOLATES, and carnations. We had them all on the Show Trains that Sam Blyth ran across Canada in 1981. Blyth's office is in Yorkville — the trendy Toronto enclave where limos deliver mink-clad ladies to salons that charge $60 to sand their toenails. Blyth specializes in exotic tours — rides on the Orient Express, bicycling in Japan, hiking in Nepal. For over $1,000 a head, the Show Train passengers were treated like royalty on trips from Toronto to Vancouver. A glass of champagne before breakfast, a mint chocolate and a carnation on their pillows before they retired.

"Sound great? It was. Sam assigned me to be an escort on a Show Train two days after I joined his agency. I had hand-rolled cigars for the gentlemen and I poured their cognac and I got off at cities along the way to buy the best wine available. Nuit St-Georges, Chateau La Tour Mortillac, Pouilly-Fumé, Pierre Mouton. The meals were delightful. Gourmet. The chef from Winston's was in the kitchen. We had cucumber soup, Cornish game hen, rack of lamb, poached salmon, and a large selection of cheeses and desserts. The passengers adored the food but it wasn't a novelty to them. They were affluent Americans; one man said he'd traced his lineage to the *Mayflower*.

"Our theatre car was tagged onto the end of the regular passenger train. For exclusive use by our clients. It had mirrors and plants and posters and standard theatre seats bolted to the floor. The performers included Diane Stapley, Tom Kneebone, Dinah Christie, and Ricky Yorke. The entertainers on with me were Pat Rose and Tom Baxter. Baxter's a magician. Pat sang and played the guitar and wrote special songs explaining Canadian history to the Americans. Songs about Louis Riel and the men who built the CPR.

"Sam ran ten Show Trains altogether. I don't know why he stopped but there was some sort of dispute over the fact that we had our own wines and not VIA's. That's water under the bridge. Sam's got a Mystery Train going now. Eighty passengers board at Union Station and before they reach New York a dastardly crime takes place that they try to solve. Sounds like fun, doesn't it?"

SWINISH ATTITUDE

"I WAS THERE; I witnessed it. Two Americans, a man and his wife, were between Edmonton and Prince George in August 1983. There was a shrunken dining car. Six tiny tables, a buffet counter, and a take-out service in the same coach. The two Americans order a meal, the steward brings it. The steward's walking away, and the man raises his voice and says, politely, 'You've forgotten our beer. We wanted it with our meals.' The steward swung round and yelled, 'Will it kill you to wait a cottonpicking minute for it!' Unbelievable rudeness; the Americans were dumbfounded and so was I. They stood up and stomped out. The man said he was writing to the company and I hope he did. His fare was helping pay that insolent swine's wages."

OFF THE BEATEN TRACK

"THE TOURISTS belonging to the Company of Hudson Bay Explorers were a different breed. The Company of Hudson Bay Explorers was the fancy label Canadian National stuck on the passengers taking the excursion trains to Churchill. The excursions started in the 1930s and, as there were usually only two a year, you had to book your seat a year or two in advance. There were 190 people on board when I took the trip in the early 1960s. Mostly Americans and mostly world-travellers; they'd been to Acapulco, Paris, and Hong Kong, and Churchill spelled adventure with a capital 'A' to them. It was off the beaten track, like the Amazon and the Sahara. CN had movies and bingo games in the baggage car but it wasn't necessary. The passengers themselves were the best entertainment. A rolling Grand Hotel.

"The lady from Texas. She was like a parody of the tourist Texan. Plump and full of zest, wearing gold hairnets and loud slacks and scattering 'you-alls' and 'honeys' all over the place. She had an empty gin bottle with her. She was carrying it to Churchill to fill it with Hudson Bay water.

"There was a Boston man who owned a lucrative car dealership. He had a wooden leg. He claimed it didn't hinder him in business, that it was an advantage. It made him strive harder to beat out two-legged people, and potential customers always remembered him because he walked differently. He had known Admiral Byrd and would've gone with him on a polar expedition if he hadn't lost the limb. The Hudson Bay excursion was his way of fulfilling a long dream to visit a sub-arctic region.

"There was a tractor salesman. He lived in Tuscon but during the 1920s he'd been in Siberia. The Russians had bought tractors and he was over there showing them how to handle them. You know what he wore to combat the Siberian winters? Silk socks and underwear. Under his heavy caribou parka. He said the silk kept him warm as toast.

"The Chicago social worker, she was constantly needling this psychology professor, insisting that psychiatrists and Freud were fraud artists. She was seventy-four and said she was going to Churchill to find a suitable cave — one that she could crawl into and die. Like the Eskimos did when they outlived their usefulness.

"Who else? The spinster teacher. I mustn't overlook her. She had the funniest reason of all for making the trip. A friend in Iowa had dared her to. The friend said the 150 miles around Hudson Bay was the most monotonous area in creation and the teacher thought she should visit the most boring 150 miles in creation before she died. She had a magnifying glass in her purse. For studying plants.

"An extraordinary cast of characters. Most were far beyond fifty, if not sixty, and yet they reacted like excited children to the Northern Lights and the wildlife at Hudson Bay. Going back to Winnipeg, the Texan showed me her gin bottle filled with water and said she'd treasure it forever. Yes, yes. The social worker was there; she hadn't crawled into a cave and waited to die."

A SIGHT NOT TO BEHOLD

"ARE YOU FAMILIAR with the White Pass and Yukon? A miraculous railway. It goes between Whitehorse and Skagway, 110 miles, and it's got narrow-gauge tracks. It was built in the 1890s and all I know of its history is the tale that a company president once adored the railway so much that he mortgaged his home to help pay its debts. The last I heard, the White Pass and Yukon was still trying to get out of debt by taking tourists off cruise ships for day rides through the mountains.

"I was a tourist on the railway in 1965. So were the American kids. I shouldn't call them kids, I guess; they were closer to twenty than twelve. Both had on blue-jean jackets. It was hot in the coach from the sun streaming through the windows. So they removed their jackets. The boy wasn't wearing a shirt but it was the girl we all stared at. She had on a see-through blouse and no underwear, and you could see everything God had given her.

"A party of blue-haired ladies from Kansas was in the coach. They looked daggers at the girl. One of them complained to the conductor and he went over to the kids. 'You'll have to put your jacket on,' he said. 'The ladies don't like what you're showing.' The girl was furious. 'I'll do it,' she said. 'But they really don't have the right to tell me how to dress.' The conductor had a great sense of humour. 'It isn't you they're complaining about, madam,' he said quietly. 'It's your friend. They can't stand the sight of his underdeveloped chest.'"

BULLET-NOSED BETTY, A LOVE STORY

Six kilometres east of the small town of Namao, the Alberta Pioneer Railway Museum sprawls over almost three hectares of unappealing flatland. On the summer afternoon I visited the site, a group of teenage volunteers was delivering a truckload of rails they had laboriously dug out of a ravine 25 kilometres away. Dated 1911, the rails would become part of a one-kilometre-long tourist run. Other volunteers were painting and re-upholstering rolling stock scattered around the field. In a repair shed, I met ninety-year-old Carl Soneff. A retired CN foreman who had started working on Prairie railways in 1912, Soneff was lending a helping hand to a former CN mechanic toiling on a cranky locomotive engine. "We can't let these trains fall apart," Soneff told me. "They're history. People must be able to see them fifty, a hundred years from today."

With more than sixty pieces of rolling stock, the museum is Canada's second largest (the Canadian Railroad Historical Association operates the biggest museum, at St. Constant, Quebec). Its treasured possessions include an 1877 baggage car, a 1904 diner-sleeper, and a 1954 diesel-electric locomotive bearing the once-familiar CPR beaver logo. Impressive as it was, none of the equipment was quite as fascinating as the olive-green and black locomotive resting in a repair shed. This was 6060, more commonly known as "Bullet-Nosed Betty." Betty's final journey to Alberta in 1980 created a happy ending for a love story involving a 54-year-old CN engineer and the magnificent steamer. For others, the journey generated anger and disappointment.

"For ten years, Betty was on display west of the CN station at Jasper. I cared for her like I cared for my own car, maybe even better. I'd be there on my days off to oil and grease and wash her and, if the paint was faded after a hard winter, I'd slap on a few gallons. I'd handled that old steamer through the Rockies in the 1950s and she meant the world to me. My wife says that if I had the space in our living room, I'd have moved Betty in.

"So you can see why I was upset. I picked up the *Journal* and there was a story saying Betty was going on permanent display in Stratford, Ontario. The locomotive was already down East. Seven years earlier, CN transferred Betty from Jasper to use on special tourist excursions out of Toronto. Because I'd maintained it for ten years, it was in perfect running order. Don't you worry, the railway told me. We'll send Betty back to Jasper when we're finished with it in Toronto.

"I saw no reason to worry. I had a gentlemen's agreement with a former CN vice-president, Roger Graham. He didn't write it on paper but when Betty was first put on display at Jasper, he'd said to me, 'As far as the railroad's concerned, 6060 now belongs to Harry Home.'

"You see what I'm getting at. Stratford's having my train wasn't fair. No one knew and loved that locomotive like I did. CN hadn't called on anyone in Stratford to run those tourist excursions; they had called on me. I went down east time and again to take it to Montreal, Ottawa, and Portland, Maine. I was in the cab for its final trip to Niagara Falls in '79. Six hundred passengers paid thirty-seven bucks apiece for the last Niagara ride and, believe me, many of them had tears in their eyes when they said good-bye to Betty.

"After I read the *Journal* story, I jumped to the phone. I got Bob Dowling, a Jasper druggist who was Lougheed's tourism minister, on my side. Then, Dowling's colleague, Transport Minister Harry Kroeger, joined in. A week or so later, someone in the Alberta government called CN headquarters in Montreal. The railway said it wanted to dispose of Betty outright because it couldn't afford the $200,000 maintenance bill. Stratford had asked for a display train years ago and somebody at CN had said, 'Why not give them 6060?' CN and the Alberta government struck a deal. For a token sum, two bucks, the province bought Betty and stored it at the museum.

"I was happy as a lark. The Toronto paper, the *Globe and Mail*, sure didn't share my feeling. It blasted CN for reneging on the Stratford promise. What were the exact words? Oh, yeah, the story ended with two words, 'Damn CNR.' The Stratford mayor and the publisher of the town paper both told the press they were disappointed. Betty was in the Spadina shops in Toronto and hadn't been transferred to Stratford yet; I might've been pelted with vegetables or something if I went to Stratford and drove it away.

"Betty came west under her own steam. You should've seen the crowds. Everybody misses the old steamers, and Betty was the last one in service anywhere in the country. The whole town turned out at Nakina, Ontario, and half the population of Biggar, Saskatchewan. I had a ball. The most fun was hitting the whistle in the middle of the night in the northern Ontario bush. Lights blinked on in trappers' cabins and doors flew open. That whistle was a sound those old-timers never thought they'd hear again.

"Now Betty's in the repair shop. The federal Railway Act states that a steam locomotive has to have its boiler overhauled at least every ten years and Betty was near the end of her boiler-time when she arrived here. The provincial government has been wonderful. It contributed a special $250,000 grant for the shed to be built on the museum grounds.

"I'm doing much of the work myself. Don Scafe, Paul McGee, and the others haven't the time to devote exclusively to Betty. There are other trains that need restoring. Those guys are all volunteers, you know — geologists, teachers, businessmen, and retired railroaders who come out to the museum on holidays and weekends.

"Am I a mechanic? Heavens, no. But I've been around steamers since I was a pup. My dad was engineer on 6040, a model similar to Betty, between Kamloops and Blue River. In Grade Three, the teacher gave me the strap for bringing train books to school instead of proper textbooks. At thirteen, I climbed into a cab and the fireman let me fire up the boiler. When I was fifteen, I quit school to be a wiper for the CNR.

"I'm on diesels now, hauling freight. Most weekends I drive three hours from Jasper to Namao. Summer and winter. Last January, I was taking Betty apart at ten below. Honestly, it's an advantage to work when it's cold; you move faster and get more done. I'm doing the boiler but I'm also greasing and oiling and making sure Betty's in tip-top shape.

"There used to be a guy at CN in Montreal — Bob MacMillan, the president of the Historic Branch. He had a marvellous vision. Steamers hauling tourists across the country. He wanted to call the run the International Limited. He left CN and so did the idea. I have a more modest version of MacMillan's vision as my dream.

"When 6060 was built in Montreal in 1944, they built it with good steel. It's got another twenty or thirty years of service in it. My dream is a daily tourist run in the Rockies. It seems a shame to have Betty in a museum when it could be chugging up and down a line."

BOTTOMS UP!

William Van Horne couldn't bear the sight of a drunken person. Upon learning that the CPR trains sold whisky in the dining cars, the frank, cigar-smoking company president immediately banned the practice. Besides encouraging drunkenness, he said, the sale of whisky (which was primarily a working-class drink in the 1880s) was beneath the railway's dignity. Since Van Horne's day, the rail lines have had a less-dignified and more self-serving attitude towards the consumption of alcohol. It's okay to do it if you buy your booze at the company bar. It's a loathsome offence, worthy of arrest or a forced exit at the next station, if you crack open a bottle you carried on yourself.

Like the rules pertaining to pets, the alcohol restrictions have inspired defiant deeds. When railway employees aren't around, flasks and bottles have appeared from unlikely hiding places — knitting bags, children's lunchpails, and hatboxes; on a Quebec train, I saw a priest step into the vestibule and whip a bottle out from under his clerical robe. Much more ingenious methods were adopted by Prohibition bootleggers. Police raids turned up caches of illegal liquor in freight-car animal carcasses and baggage-car trunks crammed with hollowed-out books.

Whether it's in the bar car or on their own, some passengers can't imagine taking a train journey without paying throat-service to the demon brew.

An Unusual Bar

"Rusty was a wonderful dog, almost human. The baggageman on our trip from Edmonton to Montreal realized Rusty was very friendly and said he didn't have to be caged or muzzled, as long as we tied him up. Gail and I beat a steady path between the sleeper and the baggage car. To feed Rusty and take him on walks when the train stopped for a while. One day, after lunch, we took him slices of roast beef from the diner. We decided to talk to the baggageman until the next stop in an hour's time. Our sleeper was fifteen cars back and it would spare us a long walk.

"The train stopped in the bush. This was in northern Ontario. The baggageman obviously knew what was going on. He didn't blink when four men opened the door and scrambled in. Hunters. Dressed in flannel shirts and jackets and carrying rifles. 'Don't be frightened,' one of them said to Gail. 'The guns aren't loaded.' The guns weren't; the hunters were. All four were quite inebriated. The train resumed its journey. Three of the men were prosperous, middle-aged doctors. The fourth was eighteen or nineteen, a son of one of them. He was undergoing a ritual of youth — hunting and drinking with his elders.

"There was a coffin in the car. A plain wood box. The doctors used it for a bar. Honest to God. They took out a bottle of Scotch and four glasses and placed them on the coffin. The younger man was so drunk he fell down. The doctors thought it was hilarious. One thumped his fist on the coffin when he was laughing. The baggageman was appalled and said, 'Excuse me, fellas, but do you know that's a coffin? There's a dead woman inside.' The doctors weren't repulsed. Not in the least. They not only continued to use it for a bar but they made black jokes about death. When the train stopped, they grabbed their guns and stumbled off into the bush. It was an eye-opener for me. I had presumed the doctors, who deal with death regularly in their profession, would have a greater respect for it."

Two Quarts of Ale

"The town of Megantic, Quebec, is emblazoned in my memory until Doomsday. The regiment I belonged to, the 12th Manitoba Dragoons, had left Vancouver Island and was heading east to Debert. It was spring 1942. I hopped off at Megantic and dashed over to a grocery store to make a purchase that would help me endure the trip — two big quart bottles of Black Horse ale. The train began to roll as I came out of the store. I ran like hell, across a field and onto the platform. I tripped and flew and landed on my face. The bottles smashed; my hands were bleeding and I'd sprained my ankle so badly that I couldn't stand up. A pal had spotted me running and pulled the emergency cord.

"The embarrassment hurt more than the sprain. While I lay there, wishing the fall had killed me, dozens of laughing faces were pressed to train windows. Two officers came off the train. So did the conductor. He was outraged. He said I ought to be severely punished for halting a train over a couple of quarts of ale. The officers hinted that he needn't worry, that I'd be up on charges. Two guys brought a stretcher and carried me on board. I thought I was really in the soup, probably cleaning latrines for six months. As it turned out, I wasn't charged at all. Our squadron-commander was a bit of a boozer and he sympathized with my mission."

BOOTLEGGING NEWSIE

"THE CHRISTMAS RAFFLE. Boy, oh, boy. That was a time. Twelve guys wanting the last mickey of rum — and me winding up in the hay with a sexy brunette.

"Where should I start? At the beginning, I guess. I was a newsie on trains when I was ten years old. A summer job. During the 1940s, my dad was a chef for the lunch-counter on the race trains to Fort Erie, Hamilton, and Niagara. He swung it so I could be with him. I sold pop and sandwiches out of a basket and rented pillows for 25 cents a shot. We hardly ever washed the pillows. We'd turn the covers inside out between customers. At night I'd sleep on the lunchcounter and, if they shunted cars, I'd crash to the floor.

"I didn't expect to be a newsie again after I quit school. I took a course and got a job welding at Massey-Harris. Then I was laid off in 1952 and, though the wages weren't as good, I hired on at Union Station. Before long, I figured out how to make money hand over fist.

By bootlegging. In those days, Ontario had liquor rationing and if you filled out too many permits for booze they'd suspect you were selling it. My friends bought mickeys for me for $2.35 and I'd charge the passengers five dollars.

"Comes Christmas. I was on the Toronto - North Bay run and there was no bar car, and I was having a terrific trip. Six hundred bucks worth of liquor sold. Every mickey gone except one. So many people asked for it that I suggested a raffle. Twelve slips of paper for $2.00 apiece. It had to be done quietly. Some conductors turned a blind eye to bootlegging but others, like Red Storey's dad, they'd boot your ass halfway to the moon if they nailed you.

"One guy buying a raffle ticket was really obnoxious. He was so stoned that he could hardly stand and yet he insisted that he needed another drink. His wife was fed up. Fuming mad. She said repeatedly that he'd had enough and he answered her with lines like, 'Shut up or I'll shut you up.' Guess who won the draw? Of course, it was the obnoxious creep.

"His wife had a good body. She was French Canadian, twelve years older than me, and not a bad looker. Her husband stayed in the coach to yap with some people and she went with me to the baggage car. That's where I stashed my bottles. The newsies had these large steamer trunks with ice compartments to keep the pop cold. We had the only keys and nobody questioned what was inside. I'd stick my mickeys in at the station and wheel the trunks on board myself.

"On our way to the baggage car, she said her husband was a pain and a half and she wished she was travelling with a nice young man like me. I was no virgin. I knew what she was driving at. We started necking and soon as we got to the baggage car I laid her down on the mail bags and we went at it. When it was done, I unlocked the trunk and gave her the mickey. We went back to the coach, and her husband had passed out. Lucky for her, he never suspected nothing; he was the type who wouldn't have drunk the bottle; he would've clouted her with it."

TWO SELFISH PEOPLE

"SOMEWHERE BETWEEN Chatham and Toronto I wandered into the bar car to have a quiet drink. That isn't always easy for a young girl to do. Sometimes the men won't leave you alone. This time, however, no one bothered me. A couple was at the next table. They'd boarded at Chatham and were total strangers. The woman was in her late twenties, the man three or four years older. Having little else to occupy my mind, I listened to their conversation. Incredible. Simply incredible. Within twenty minutes, they were engaged in the most intimate dialogue. Discussing their past love affairs and how every one of them had failed miserably. Drink by drink, they revealed their deepest, darkest secrets. He'd say some woman was too dull and unadventurous for him; she'd say some man was too insecure and possessive for her. I thought to myself, These two are so self-centred they deserve each other. It was like a premonition. By the time the train reached the depot, they were gazing intently into one another's eyes and agreeing to find an apartment together in Toronto."

FRASER CANYON BRAWL

"THE BRAWL was in December 1962. Between Vancouver and Kamloops. On the CNR. Absolutely disgusting. Our small kiddies were with us; Heather was seven and Bonnie, nine. We were taking them to Edmonton to spend the holidays with their grandparents and they never should have been exposed to such terrible goings-on. Too much alcohol, that's what started it. Our car was split in half. One half was a passenger coach, the other half a booze-wagon. The traffic through our section from the rest of the train was practically a stampede. The noise was dreadful. Loud voices, clinking glasses, people singing carols off-key. This young married couple in our section had two kiddies under school age. They kept slipping away from them. They hadn't the willpower to stay out of the booze-car. Their kiddies were wetting and crying and other passengers had to look after them.

"They're the ones who started the fight. Not the wife, the husband. He was loaded to the gills and he found out a guy quietly sipping his drink was an ex-convict. He called him a lousy jailbird and the ex-convict jumped at him and they were hitting each other like crazed boxers. We witnessed the whole scene from our section. Nobody tried to break them up so I got to my feet. 'Forget it,' my wife said. 'It isn't worth risking your life over.' She was right. I'd had a heart attack so I sat down. Ladies were screaming and blood was flying and bottles and glasses were crashing off tables. Other men suddenly jumped into it. Not to break the fight up, but to attack each other. There were fights all over the car. Punching and kicking and wrestling and even a couple of ladies were pulling each other's hair. While the train was swinging and swaying through the Fraser Canyon.

"The man with the crying kiddies eventually clamped a full-Nelson on the ex-convict. I thought that was it. He had such a hateful expression on his face that I was positive he intended to snap his neck. Then this fantastic man appeared. The conductor. His courage was a marvel. He rushed into the booze-wagon, a stocky, little guy, and didn't hesitate. He gave the guy holding the ex-convict a sharp judo-chop on the neck. It didn't knock him out but it jarred him and he released his grip. I'd testify anywhere that the conductor prevented a man's death.

"Both fighters were exhausted. They slumped down, breathing hard and caused no more trouble. The conductor shouted and did a little pushing and shoving and the other fights ended. The Mounties got on at Kamloops and arrested seven or eight people, including the first two brawlers. One of the kiddies who had been wet and crying woke up later and asked his mother, 'Where's Daddy?' It touched my heart; the child sounded so worried and fragile. 'Daddy had to leave the train,' the mother answered. 'He won't be with us for a while.'

"I wrote to Donald Gordon, the CNR president. I described the brawl and said it was ridiculous to have children in the same coach where there was drinking. I explained that our daughter was prone to nightmares and the brawl could've scarred her mentally. He didn't reply to my letter. No one at the CNR did. I said to my wife, 'Mr. Donald Gordon's too high and mighty and he's destroyed my letter.' It wasn't so. It was simply that the wheels in a big company like CNR move slowly. Several months after the brawl, a man from the railway walked into the garage in Richmond where I was shop foreman and presented me with a cheque. The CNR had reimbursed our fares."

PASSING IT AROUND

THE BEST PARTIES are spur of the moment. Like the time I was coming to Alberta from B.C. during Prohibition. Police on the Prairies knew the dining-car cooks and waiters had a system of buying bootleg hooch in Cranbrook and Fernie and smuggling it over the border in their luggage. The MacLeod police raided the trains every so often and there were days they'd reel in quite a catch, twenty, thirty, forty bottles.

"I was coming from Cranbrook in winter and there weren't too many passengers — six or seven men, and no women, no children. This guy gets up and walks over to another guy in the coach. 'That your suitcase under the seat?' he says. 'No,' the guy says, 'I was wondering who owns it.' The guy who walked over flashes a badge — APP: Alberta Provincial Police. 'I think it belongs to So-and-So,' he says. 'He's a waiter on this train and he's hiding it out here.'

"The APP opens the suitcase and, under the clothing, there's a dozen bottles marked Burdock Bitters. That's a cold remedy. He takes a slug from a bottle and passes it to the passenger. 'Taste it. Tell me if you think it's medicine or booze?' The passenger says he can't tell. Mind you, he says this after two or three slugs. He passes the bottle to somebody and he has a pull and passes it to me. It's whisky, sure enough, but I say I can't tell either.

"The next thing I know, the APP's sucking on the bottle again. It dawns on me. He knows it's liquor and he's got a craving for it. The APP's got a genuine rubby on their force. We killed the crock and opened a second. We all got pie-eyed. Me, the APP, and the other men. We took the suitcase at MacLeod and finished the party at the stable one of the passengers owned."

FACING THE TRUTH

"MONDAY MORNING at Moosonee showed you mankind at its lowest ebb. A weekend of partying would end with a gang of men and women climbing on for Cochrane and points south. Nine a.m. and they'd be loaded from two days of solid drinking. If they were too plastered, the conductor wouldn't let them on. He knew the troublemakers by sight. If they weren't plastered to the gills and he had no excuse for not allowing them to ride, he'd put them in the same car, so he could watch them.

"I was getting on and this broad was standing there, bleary-eyed. A walrus — the shoulders and arms of a man. The conductor said the usual to her, 'Go home and sober up and catch the next train in two days' time.' The woman argued that he was wrong. She wasn't drunk; she was on medicine that made her drowsy. The conductor gave her the benefit of the doubt.

"The train was a mixed. Two passenger coaches behind four freight cars. It had a dinette. The woman sat at the counter and ordered ham and eggs. The waiter brought it, then glanced away for a second. When he looked back, her face was buried in the plate. He turned her head so she wouldn't suffocate and then he left her there. She was too heavy to move and there weren't any empty seats in the coaches any-way. She stirred in her sleep and a rum bottle fell from under her coat. She slept half an hour and the conductor tore a strip off her hide when she woke up. Then he looked at me and shook his head. 'Monday morn-ings at Moosonee will be the death of me yet,' he said."

Drowning His Sorrows

"Hey, what's this? Waiters in yellow vests, a honky-tonk piano, a bunch of people laughing and drinking. I was taking the Rapido to Toronto and I must've been the only guy in Montreal who didn't real-ize the CNR had the Bistro Car service. The car was decorated in a Gay Nineties style. Gas lamps and brass railings and one of the wait-ers had a marvellous handlebar moustache.

"I strolled in and thought — party-time. That was just what the doctor ordered for me. I'd had a thoroughly rotten week, losing two accounts and barely managing to hold onto a third. I'd stopped drink-ing three years earlier. When my wife walked out. We used to fight about my happy hours at the Eiffel Tower on Stanley Street and how I'd come home half-cut every day.

"I decided to get thoroughly, irretrievably bombed. To wash away the residue from the bad week. The piano was playing rag-time shit, the outside world was whirling by the window, and I was throwing them back, one after another. I got so stoned that I even talked to a hippie; one of those wimpy creatures with hair down to here who was, bless his soul, growing organic vegetables and taking weaving lessons. I don't know where she came from but suddenly my ex-wife's sister was standing in front of the table. 'Hello, Frank,' she said. 'Gloria will be glad to know you're still up to your old tricks.'

"Terrible, terrible. Any thoughts I had of getting back with Gloria were shot down in flames. Three years without a drink and her witch of a sister had to pick that day to take the train to Toronto."

THIRSTY THIEF

"ALBERTA AND SASKATCHEWAN were dry and Manitoba was wet. When the train crossed into Alberta from B.C. during the early days of Prohibition, the steward shut all of the liquor away inside a locked cabinet. That was the law of the land. The cabinet was in the baggage car and had a wire screen over its front. On one occasion, a line-up of thirsty patrons prompted the steward to enter the baggage car the minute the train touched Manitoba soil. He was rocked on his heels by what he found. All the little one-shot bottles were empty. Drained dry. A clever rascal had snuck into the car, stuck a tiny drill through the wire, burrowed through the caps and, presumably, syphoned the contents with a straw."

SHE HATED NEWFIE JOKES

"I WAS HEADING to the Maritimes and I met a man in the bar car who hadn't been home for thirty-two years. His mother was ninety and was going to Moncton for a family reunion before it was too late. I didn't ask why he had been away so long; none of my business. Two gals and two guys were at the table next to us and two guys directly across from them. All six were in their early twenties and well into the sauce. The foursome at one table were Newfoundlanders. The other two guys from Prince Edward Island. I had no idea there was a rivalry between the two provinces; I thought Maritimers were like one big brotherhood, united against the common foe, Ontario. They were arguing, kind of friendly yet with a good deal of pointedness. Then one of the P.E.I. boys told a joke. 'You know what a Newfie calculator is? A piece of wood with five holes for the fingers to fit through.'

"One of the gals flung a beer bottle and hit his shoulder. He jumped to his feet and she threw another bottle, just missing his head. A boy sitting with the gals jumped up and said, 'I'll take care of this for you.' She didn't need anyone fighting her battles. She had tattoos on her arms and muscles bigger than her tits. Her friends had to grab her and struggle really hard to stop her from beating up on the P.E.I. boy. After a while, they all calmed down. I turned to the guy beside me, and he was gone. In the morning he walked up to me to explain. 'When I seen the look on that gal's face, I reckoned she'd kill us all, and, by George, I didn't want to wait for our reunion till Mom joined me in Heaven.'"

SAILING TO HALIFAX

"WE WAS ON THE HMCS *Ontario*. Don, Red, and me. She was going to Australia in the winter of '51 and because she had a new laundry installed, we was sent from Naden to Halifax for a course on how to run the blasted thing. We had two 26ers when we showed up at the train in Vancouver and the goddamned shore patrol stopped us and took the booze. They were Army and we was Navy but it don't make no difference, they had the right to confiscate. It was January and colder than a bastard, and Red says we'll freeze solid if we don't get gassed up. There was a forty-minute stop in Calgary. We hopped into a cab and took it to the Ninth Avenue store. Four bottles of Jamaican rum. Soon as the train pulled out, we took over the smoker. I guess we made a bit of noise because the conductor said we'd be charged if we didn't stop drinking and pestering everybody.

"We was having breakfast in Regina when the conductor brought a CPR bull aboard and they took what's left of the rum from our berths. When we got to Winnipeg, the conductor said the bull didn't confiscate like we thought and that we could have the rum back if we swore we'd behave. The train changed crews in Winnipeg. Two minutes out of the station, we carried a bottle into the smoker. The porter came in and said we shouldn't be drinking. 'Come on, have one with us,' Don said. 'Nobody'll know the diff.' He had a shot and then another and pretty soon he was pissed like we was. Whenever the conductor showed, he'd hide in the can or pretend he was busy making a bed. We stumbled off somewhere, Christ knows where, and picked up twenty-four quarts of Molson's ale. We was stewed — me, Red, Don, and the porter — all the way to Montreal."

FAREWELL GIFT

"THE BOYS AT the *Toronto Star* had a farewell party for me before I left for the Orient. I was quite tipsy when I got to Union Station and boarded the International Limited for Chicago on the first leg of my trip. I had two crocks of champagne in my luggage, a parting gift from the boys.

"A customs agent came up to me shortly after we left the station. An American. He spotted the bottles and said he'd have to take them. This was the 1930s, and the law about taking booze over the border was strictly enforced. I said, 'Listen fella, I'm with the *Star*. Gordon Sinclair. How about giving me a break?' Deaf ears. Refused to listen. I blew up and said he hadn't the authority to take my bottles, that he was on Canadian soil. 'Okay,' he said. 'I'll cool my heels and get you at the border.'

"An arrogant you-know-what. I became determined to out-fox him. I opened a bottle and offered drinks to the other passengers, a prune-faced couple. They turned up their noses. I went into the smoker. The porter took a sip of warm champagne and said he couldn't stand the taste. I was clearly on my own. I downed a whole bottle and got truly sloshed. When we neared the border, I still had one bottle to go. I couldn't face it. I cracked it open, kissed the label, and poured all that lovely, high-priced bubbly down the sink."

THE BIG TOP: TOURING BY TRAIN

I t was an annual occurrence in Victoria. Every autumn, as the hideous prospect of returning to school loomed larger each day, the Clyde Beatty Circus train slid down the island from Nanaimo and the mainland. The *Daily Colonist* never announced its arrival time, yet somehow the news spread far and wide. Dozens of youngsters, myself included, were already there when the train reached the field outside town where the circus would camp for six sparkling days.

The lions and elephants fascinated us. Typical youngsters, we prayed for an animal to go berserk while it was being unloaded and to sow havoc on an unparalleled scale. None ever did. One afternoon, however, a white Buick convertible raced down the dirt road, spitting stones and dust, and, swerving to miss an elephant, slammed into the side of the parked train. The bumper was twisted, the grill battered, a fender crushed. The driver immediately backed up and roared over to where five or six of us youngsters stood watching.

The driver was Clyde Beatty. He had hunted in Africa and appeared in B movies and was, in our estimation, an idol of considerable stature. He was wearing a white safari outfit and he was ignoring the nasty cut on his cheek. 'You kids want free tickets? Help the men carry water to the animals.' The radiator began to steam as he sped away. He paid no attention to that either. Only Clyde Beatty could hit a train and ignore it. He was, we told each other, an even greater man than we had imagined.

PINSENT NO BULLET

"WE WERE FILMING *The Rowdyman* in Newfoundland and CN kindly took the old Bullet out of mothballs for us. We had a love scene in which I made a play for Dawn Greenhalgh while she was rolling up a ball of wool. As is so often the case in movies, we just couldn't get the scene right. For eight hours the Bullet shunted back and forth on the same nine-mile section of track outside St. John's. Dawn and I were thoroughly fed up. Apparently, so was the engineer. He was an old-timer they'd taken out of mothballs along with the train. Around suppertime, he stopped the Bullet in the yard, jumped from the cab, and walked over to our production manager, Tommy Glyn. 'What's going on back there in the train?' he asked. Tommy replied, 'Gordon Pinsent's trying to make out with a girl.' 'For eight hours?' the engineer said. 'Jeez, in my day it didn't take that long to do it!'

THE KLAN MAN WAS SO POPULAR

"FORGET THE MOVIES. Forget the dances. The biggest box-office attraction in Alberta in the 1930s was J. J. Maloney. The Ku Klux Klanner. There'd be standing room only inside Edmonton's old Memorial Hall. You'd come up McDougall Hill and there'd be six hundred people sitting on the grass and standing on the sidewalk waiting for the first meeting to end. He was so popular he had to have two meetings the same day. True believers. You should've seen the women's faces glow when he spoke. They thought he was a god.

"Who else but J. J. Maloney could pack a train? The football team couldn't, not in them days, and if a clergymen went by train, he went alone. But when Maloney rode out to the boondocks to lecture, hundreds went with him. I'm not ashamed to admit I was on one of his trains. Around 1929, 1930. He had the railway add five extra cars to its regular train solely for his people. Everyone in the country was badly off and hoping for a way out of the Depression, and Maloney acted like he had the answers. Time and again, he said the Catholics and the Jews were responsible for the economic collapse. They had bled the country. I was out of a job and desperate and, looking for somebody to boot, I was willing to think he might be right.

"The train I was on travelled to Red Deer. Just outside the south side station in Edmonton, Maloney himself walked into our car. He was a good-looker. Hair slicked down like Boston Blackie's, and he had a cool, confident way about him. He was the grand wizard, or whatever they called their bosses in the Klan, but he didn't wear a hood and bedsheet. In public, he wore black suits. The whole car cheered him, and I remember a fat woman in a huge hat giving him a bouquet of flowers. He made a little speech — about the Bishop of Edmonton and how he was sending millions of dollars every month to the Vatican. Maloney had a girl with him. A tiny thing. She said she was an escaped nun and she'd talk about the church's vices at the Red Deer meeting.

"Maloney despised Catholics, but he claimed to be a religious man. I said prayers and we all sang hymns — 'Rock Of Ages,' 'The Old Rugged Cross.' He had three bodyguards with him. He always said they were to protect him from his enemies, who wanted him dead because he exposed the truth. A boy sold newspapers on the train. Maloney's sheet, the *Liberator*. I can call it a hatemongering rag now, but in those times it was nearly as well read as the *Journal* and the *Bulletin*.

"The people going to Red Deer were from all backgrounds — labourers, wives, bus drivers, accountants, you name it. I met a lawyer who said if Maloney ran for election, he'd scoop the marbles. All those people must have been shocked when he was dragged into court. I wasn't. I expected the worst of men who set themselves up as holier-than-thou. Yet I was a little surprised. I thought he was too smart to be caught on a fraud charge. Before he was caught, Maloney could do no wrong. Afterwards, his career was finished. I remember a message written on a brick wall in Edmonton — 'Maloney's Phony.' That summed up the general feelings to a tee."

OSCAR PETERSON'S DAD

"OSCAR PETERSON'S a fine piano player. I saw him on television, and he was hitting the keys like nobody's business. He has his dad to thank for that. Yeah, Oscar has natural talent but it wouldn't have been developed if his father hadn't given him lessons. Dan Peterson was a sleeping-car porter. CPR. Over twenty years back and forth, Montreal and Toronto. He had five kids and he taught them all piano. Family recitals in the parlour. Fred, May, Chuck, Daisy, and Oscar soloing, then maybe Dan doing a four-handed number with Fred or Oscar. Long before the kids came along, Dan was in the Navy and he bought a miniature organ and taught himself how to play. Oscar's a good man but, for my money, it's his dad, the sleeping-car porter, who deserves the praise."

FIRST BALLET TOUR

"THE FACT IS, ballet wasn't exactly as popular as hockey on the Prairies. Most people thought dancers were freaks — leotard-clad weirdos belonging in circus side shows. And if you were a male dancer like I was, well you were automatically branded a raving homo. So when we set out from Winnipeg in 1945, we had no idea of what was in store for us. Would the theatres be empty? And if anybody came, would they sit on their hands and shake their heads bewilderedly?

"We were, you see, the first home-grown dance company ever to tour the country. Gweneth Lloyd ran the company, and to scrape together the train and hotel expenses we held rummage sales and put on special performances and solicited private donations. We travelled to four cities — Regina, Saskatoon, Edmonton, and Ottawa. How did we do? Fine. With the war still on and entertainment at a premium, we not only drew good houses but they were enthusiastic.

"Actually, some guys were a trifle too enthusiastic in Edmonton. We performed *An American in Paris* at the Red Cross hut. Complete with can-can girls. A batch of sailors who'd seen the performance descended upon the MacDonald Hotel looking for the girls. They came to our floor, about fifteen of them, and pounded on doors. Our manager, David Yeddeau, was a brave soul. He walked right up and ordered them to leave. He said he'd call the house detective. They trooped out, sheepishly.

"In Saskatoon there were Communists. They didn't want the girls' bodies; they wanted our minds. We were young kids, fifteen to eighteen. My dad, Charlie Adams, was foreman of the garage at Winnipeg Electric. The other kids were from ordinary, middle-class backgrounds too and, like me, not very clued in when it came to politics. The Communists invited us to a hall to watch Russian ballet films. After the screening, they turned up the lights and began politiking. The guy leading the group was real spooky — balding head and pointed beard; the spitting image of Lenin. Maybe we weren't up on politics but we knew enough to understand we wanted out of there. Someone stood up and said we had an early rehearsal next morning. We fled *en masse.*

"What with randy sailors and evangelizing Communists — not to mention the rigorous stage performances — the train was a welcome oasis. That's where we relaxed. We usually had a car to ourselves, the last one, before the caboose. The biggest hitch was the lack of space. We couldn't rehearse and we were jammed in so close that someone invariably fell asleep sitting up and tumbled over into the aisle. Meals were a main event. We'd wash up and wear our best clothes, as if we were going to a party. When the relaxation turned to boredom, we had this game. Somebody stretched his body across to the opposite bunk. Then other dancers tried to crawl across him without falling.

"Pretty innocent stuff but, then, we were innocent kids. I'm sure some parents had nightmares about their daughters losing their virginity in lower berths but Gweneth Lloyd made certain there was no carrying on. And even if she hadn't watched us like a hawk, I doubt there would have been much fooling around. We didn't see each other in a sexual way. Honestly. We'd rehearse in leotards and tights, we knew what we looked like, the nature of our art involved almost constant body contact. It bred a healthy intimacy, a familiarity that made people less inclined to go chasing after each other.

"Come to think of it, there wasn't a great deal of fooling around on the adult tours. Six years after the Winnipeg Ballet tour, I was a principal dancer with the National Ballet. We toured Canada and the States by train, primarily one-night stands. We had our share of logistical problems. Our sets wouldn't fit through the auditorium door in Red Deer and in northern Ontario they laid thin platforms on the ice in hockey rinks; your legs were fresh frozen and there was the ever-present fear of slipping onto the ice.

"The worst problem wasn't logistical, though. It was having forty adults cooped up in trains for weeks on end. As kids in Winnipeg, we loved it. As grown-ups, the lack of privacy created tremendous pressure. Every two weeks, as if a mysterious bell had sounded, the dancers drifted to the smoker for a beer party. Some pressures can't be relieved by parties. I was married to Lois Smith and, if you ask me why we broke up, I'd have to say it was the tension of being together twenty-four hours a day. Twelve years of eating, sleeping, dancing, and travelling together — positively lethal. On practically every train trip married couples were at each others' throats. Usually over minor things that became major events. Perhaps that's why my warmest memories of trains involve the Winnipeg tour. The innocence of youth. The exuberance and sense of fun that you can't recapture once you pass a certain age."

Taxi, Follow That Train!

"YOU'LL HAVE TO forgive me if I'm vague on details. After all, it was forty years ago. However, I clearly recall that it was the final year of the war and the Toronto Symphony, for which I was a violinist, had contracted to play five concerts in Michigan. A horrendous snow-storm swept southern Ontario the night we left Toronto. There was talk of postponing the tour but, as the train appeared to be quite capable of pushing its way through, the talk came to nothing.

"A young oboist — I'm sorry his name escapes me — arrived at Union Station shortly after our departure. Fearing the possible loss of his job, he hired a taxi and ordered the driver to catch up to us. The blowing snow made the highways extremely treacherous yet the driver pressed on. Our train crossed the border at Sarnia and dipped south towards our goal, the city of Detroit.

"The storm was raging in Michigan as well. The railroad tracks were blown over in spots, and we had a long delay at the station in Pontiac, north of Detroit. Finally, it was decided to transport the orchestra the remainder of the distance by bus. The young oboist had remarkable tenacity. Not realizing the train had been delayed at Pontiac, he overshot it and arrived in Detroit before we did. Two hundred miles in a taxi. He was waiting for us at the hotel and was visibly agitated. I don't recall the sum but the taxi fare was, for a beginning musician, mind-jarring. He explained that he'd expected to catch the train outside of Toronto and, failing that, had continued on, hoping to see it and flag it down every time the road came within sight of the tracks. We had great sympathy for the lad. A hat was passed and sufficient donations were collected to pay his taxi bill."

ON THE B CIRCUIT

"THE SASKATOON GIRLS' Pipe Band definitely didn't travel first class. Not in 1939 it didn't. We were B-Circuit material, meaning we weren't polished enough for the big cities and were booked into exhibition grounds in places like Yorkton, Flin Flon, Melfort, and Carman. We rode the trains from town to town but we never slept on them. Too expensive. We'd sit in the day coaches and go to hotels at night. To the hotels, not the hotel rooms. We'd sleep on camp cots in the samples rooms the hotels had off lobbies and in basements where travelling salesmen displayed their wares.

"I was all of fourteen. I'd been going to Nellie Small's dance school for years, and when she needed performers for the pipe band she culled the cream of the crop from her classes. Nellie Small suited her name. She was a tiny woman — tiny, tough, and Scottish. The band was a whiz at doing dance routines but a couple of the younger girls couldn't play a note. My friend Dorothy McCartney marched around the exhibition grounds dressed the same as the rest of us — a bright red tunic, a Buchanan-plaid kilt — and blowing a bagpipe. Her pipes were stuffed with paper and no sound came out.

"Banana splits. How I craved them that summer. I'd hope and pray that there'd be time at the next train stop to run over to the Chinese café and gulp one down. The banana splits were my method of coping with Mr. Black's atrocious food. He sang Harry Lauder songs with the band, and Mrs. Black made our costumes. Between shows, he cooked our meals, usually in a tent set up on the fair grounds. There were twenty-five girls. We'd line up like cattle and he'd feed us his specialties, hot dogs and fruit salad. Cold hot dogs and mushy fruit salad. Sometimes we'd take our food onto the trains. Once, outside Melfort, Dorothy was watching Mr. Black dole out the usual dessert from a big blue dishpan. She leaned over, alarmed, and whispered in my ear, 'For goodness sake, don't eat the fruit salad. I saw him wash his feet in that pan last night.'

"Three months we toured — Manitoba, Saskatchewan, and Alberta. Nellie Small would lead us off the train in full costume and we'd parade down the main streets, playing Scottish reels. She wore a white tunic and a black Busby. I played tenor drum and I twirled the sticks. The twirling killed my hands. My fingers were so raw they bled. At the fair grounds, we'd do our routines — sword dances, Highland flings, a soft shoe dance to 'A Pretty Girl Is Like a Melody.' There were men around the grounds — clowns, trick artists, a guy with a trained dog. I was too young to be interested in anything but banana splits but a few girls managed to avoid Nellie Small's iron grip. One girl developed a flaming passion for a concession-booth owner who was also on the circuit; her parents broke that up soon after she returned home.

"When Nellie Small organized the tour, she promised our parents fat paycheques at the end. Living as cheaply as we did, the band still failed to earn a profit, and none of the girls received a red cent. Even the promise of a Cuban tour fell by the wayside. The war made foreign travel too dangerous. No pay and no Cuban trip but, looking back, I wouldn't have missed it for the world."

TALLULAH'S TIP

"IS THERE ANYBODY on earth who doesn't have a Tallulah Bankhead story? Mine is very short. Tallulah had had a rough night after closing out the Royal Alex and, I gather, consuming more alcohol than her system wanted her to consume. She sent word to the diner the next morning that she wanted a can of ice-cold apple juice and a pot of black coffee delivered to her drawing room. I placed them on a tray and hustled along the corridors. When I knocked, her agent, a rather harried-looking man, opened the door. Tallulah was seated by the window, pale as a corpse, staring at the passing countryside. The bill was $1.90. The agent handed me two dollars and said, 'Keep the change, buddy.' Tallulah's head shot around. 'You don't have to be so goddamned cheap,' she shrieked. 'Give the silly bugger a buck.' The agent thrust the dollar tip into my hand so fast I almost dropped it."

AN EDIBLE GIFT

"THERE'S NOT A MAN, woman, or child in Saskatchewan with a nasty word to say about Edna Jaques. The best damn poet Canada's had. She's not so famous nowadays, but in the 1930s she filled halls from Vancouver Island to Newfoundland. Edna was a wonderful person; she rode the trains a lot and every railwayman in northern Saskatchewan knew and liked her. Before she was famous in the rest of Canada, she homesteaded south of Tisdale. Deep in the bush. Her hubby liked people the same way Edna did and he could talk up a storm. The trouble with him was, he had an aversion for work. He'd lie in bed half the day; Edna chopped the wood and fetched the water and fixed the fence.

"Gossip travelled like wildfire in the north. The rumour got around that Edna was expecting and her hubby wasn't earning money and their kitchen shelf was fairly bare. The Saskatoon railwaymen came to her rescue. Fellows brought what they could spare from home — tins of vegetables, sacks of flour, tins of tea, all manner of food — to the railyard. Two big boxes were shipped to Tisdale. Edna was a proud woman and wouldn't have taken charity. So they made up a tale. They wrote a note saying the railwaymen had sponsored a Best Pioneer Woman contest and she'd won the food as a prize. Edna passed on in 1977, at the age of 88 or 89, and I'll lay you odds she never was told what those railwaymen did."

CONFEDERATION TRAIN

"IT WASN'T AN EASY TASK. We had to avoid giving the public the impression that the Confederation Train was a mobile lecture hall. It couldn't be a dispensary for dull, historical facts. If the public had that impression, they'd stay away by the multitudes. At the same time, the exhibits couldn't be superficial. There had to a strong sense of the diverse elements that helped make Canada a great nation.

"As I say, it wasn't easy. But the concept we adopted was well worth the blood, sweat, and tears. The cars were an exciting mixture of sight, sound, touch, and smell. You entered a dark mine shaft. You ran wheat through your fingers. You heard the groaning boards in the steerage section of a nineteenth-century immigrant ship. We had Joseph Howe's printing press, Louis Riel's pistol, and Sitting Bull's tobacco pouch. And photos of Canadian celebrities — Bob Goulet, Marilyn Bell, Wayne and Shuster, et cetera. Canada, from the Ice Age to the Space Age.

"Nearly four years of planning was devoted to that train. I started in October 1963, and Judy LaMarsh officially unsealed the train in Victoria in January 1967. John Fisher hired me. I had been a military transport officer during the war, responsible for moving men and equipment by rail, and Mr. Fisher and Mr. Maurice Lamontagne both felt I was the person for the job. The day I accepted it, I sat in my office in Ottawa and scribbled notes on a scratch pad. What the train should attempt to reflect, who I'd like on my staff. The notes on that pad ultimately led to a situation where five hundred people were engaged in the planning and the train's actual operation. The overall budget was in the vicinity of $13 million; the six exhibition cars cost $1.5 million.

"Criticisms? Yes, we certainly had some aimed in our direction but that was to be expected in any project that large and that public. Some people in Vancouver claimed the Ice Age display — or was it the war display? — frightened their children. A history professor said the bilingual brochures were worded slightly differently, skirting around the issue of Quebec nationhood. Mr. Diefenbaker rose in the House and demanded that a portrait of the Queen be placed aboard the train. Mr. Pearson pledged to do so, and it was done.

"Justified or not, the criticisms in no way detracted from the train's impact. Nine million Canadians visited it in eighty-three locales. Thousands wrote letters to the Centennial Commission stating they thoroughly enjoyed themselves. I was very satisfied with the project. We accomplished what we set out to do. The Confederation Train was an overwhelming success."

ELEVEN TONS OF CHEESE

"LOOK HERE. It's a picture of the biggest cheese made in Canada. Eleven tons. I bet it's the biggest in history, in any country. I found the picture in my grandfather's trunk when he passed away. I think it was taken at the depot in Perth. The way those men standing beside it are smiling, they must be the cheese-makers. It's hard to tell but I think the second one on the left is my grandfather. It must be him; why would he hold onto the picture if it wasn't him? The cheese was made in Perth and shipped on a special train to the World's Fair in Chicago in 1893.

"I looked the cheese up in the library on Yonge Street. This is what I copied down. It was in the Perth newspaper in April 1893. 'The mammoth cheese was taken from its winter quarters in the CPR freight shed today and placed on a flat-car for shipment. The centre of the platform on the car settled four inches under the strain.' It says here the cheese was six feet in height and had a twenty-eight-foot circumference. The Perth band played 'The Maple Leaf Forever' as the train left to cross at Windsor. In the countryside, people streamed to the railway track by the thousands to see it go by and, in the cities, they flooded the depots. The cheese was so heavy it broke the stand in Chicago. It wasn't damaged and it won the blue ribbon. Isn't that something? The biggest cheese ever."

EXTRAORDINARY SERVICE

"EVERY THURSDAY, I'd catch the 4:06 out of Strathcona Station in south Edmonton to play with the Calgary Symphony. The attendant was a nice, old man, a Mr. King. He'd ask me how my career as a violinist was progressing and we'd talk about his daughter, who was studying law at the University of Alberta. I forgot my sweater on the seat one day. When I got back to Edmonton, it was at my house. Mr. King had looked up my address and brought it around. That sort of thing just doesn't happen on the trains, or anywhere else, anymore."

JUMBO THE ELEPHANT

"JUMBO DIED IN CANADA, you know. Jumbo was an elephant. P. T. Barnum's premier animal draw. Good grief, man, of course I didn't see him when he was alive. I'm old but I'm not that old. Barnum brought Jumbo to America in the 1800s. The reason I'm familiar with Jumbo is I was circus myself. I travelled with a rinky-dink outfit, the Thompson Brothers Circus, in the middle of the 1930s. We'd get off the train in the bush and bet the locals they couldn't wrestle our bear to the ground. The bear was muzzled and had gloved hands. A strongman in Nova Scotia spoiled the act when he clamped a bear-hug on our bear from behind and broke its spine.

"Back to Jumbo. He was huger than most elephants. Over eleven feet tall and weighing six tons. Barnum bought him from the London Zoo. He was big but gentle, and the crowds loved him. Barnum made a million with him. When Jumbo was on the road, he lived it up. His own private railway car. His trainer slept in it with him. A history professor can tell you the date he was killed. I can't. It was before the new century. His trainer was leading him to the train after a night show in St. Thomas, Ontario. A freight blasted down the track and struck him. The most famous circus animal of all time, and he died in St. Thomas, Ontario."

RAIL-RIDING RODEO

"THE ALBERTA STAMPEDE COMPANY was Pete Welsh's idea. Why not round up a bunch of cowboys and stick them on the rails as a travelling rodeo? Between 1925 and 1927, we travelled thousands of miles. We played in Winnipeg, Toronto, Montreal, Ottawa, and New Westminster in this country, and Detroit, Buffalo, and Columbus in the United States. We couldn't book into Madison Square Garden. The American rodeos had a stranglehold on the Garden and they wouldn't let us in.

"Pete's four young ones rode with us. Louis Welsh was a barreljumper, Josie did a Roman-standing routine, and the other two, the real small ones, did a jumping act with a little grey mare. Slim Watrin was with our troupe and Casey Patterson and Pete Knight and the newspaperman Fred Kennedy. Kennedy got a three-month leave of absence to be our promotion man and, when Pete Welsh learned he could ride, he had him go into the arena with a megaphone and announce the cowboys' names and home towns.

"Pete paid top dollar for his horses and he had some of the best: Midnight, Gravedigger, Tumbleweed. In the spring of '26 I rounded up a string of wild ones near Hanna and took them to Toronto by train. We took them off to water them and give them a walk every once in a while, and you should've seen the people in the railyards; they were bug-eyed watching us handle those wild horses.

"Did I mention Pete Knight? He was our star. The best bronc-buster the Lord created. He raised hell in the arenas but he was shy and quiet and didn't mix with people when we travelled. I clipped a story from the Winnipeg paper once. 'Frank Sharp wins $2,000, Pete Knight $1,500.' He was the all-round champ but I beat him in bareback and bull-riding and took top money in 1926 in Winnipeg. I sent the money to my bank in Alberta. Rodeoing was hard work and I wasn't about to blow it night clubbing and playing poker."

A SORRY SIGHT

"THE SILVER CUP was the only trophy I ever won. I had gone to a banquet in Columbus when I was promotion manager for the Alberta Stampede Company and the judges said I had on the best Western outfit. We were going to Toronto from Buffalo one night and the train was hurled into a ditch by a split rail. No damage was done to anybody or anything, except my trophy. It was terribly dented. I suppose I should've discarded it then and there but I was proud of it and just couldn't bring myself to do it. For years and years, until it finally got lost, I had the trophy around the house, even though it was such a sorry sight that I never displayed it in my living room."

MASS APPEAL

"HOW THE MIGHTY have fallen. That's what I thought when I was on the train to Toronto during the 1960s and the other passengers were playing bingo. It was part of CN's star-crossed plan to revive passenger traffic. A touch of show biz. Bingo games, special children's hours, and free cups of coffee. Their rolling stock was positively prehistoric, yet they felt they could make an old hag look younger by plastering cosmetics on her face.

"I had to laugh. I remembered travelling by train during the 1920s. The CNR was the first railway in the world to have its own radio network. Individual headphones in the parlour cars. Distinguished lecturers. Shakespearean dramas. The Toronto Symphony. Culture was a capital 'C'. The Prince of Wales crossed the country in 1924 and said the CN network was so stimulating he hoped British Rail would copy the idea. If the prince had made the same trip during the 1960s he'd have been mired in despair. Bingo, for goodness sake. The opiate of the masses. How the mighty...."

UNFORGETTABLE PEOPLE

Ask any of your friends why they don't take the train on long-distance business or pleasure trips and they'll invariably reply, "I haven't the time." What a pity. Jetliners may be the undisputed masters when it comes to speed but they are miserably deficient in the realm of human experience. Being lashed to the same seat for hours with a tie salesman pickled in rye for company can't compare to the rewards to be found on trains. Wandering the cars at will, you meet an amazing assortment of people and, should you draw a bore, you have the freedom to escape.

The conversations I prefer are generally with eccentrics. The retired mechanic describing how the Vatican and the Kremlin have a secret pact to conquer and divide the world. The bushy-haired octo-genarian explaining how he scours garbage dumps to find the bottles he requires for the glass house he's building. Great fun...as long as they don't follow you home.

Some of the individuals in this chapter qualify as full-blown eccentrics. Others simply did interesting things. If there is a common denominator, it is the fact that, for better or worse, they made a lasting impression on the people who crossed their paths.

HE THREW HIS MONEY AWAY

"HARRY MCLEAN was rolling in dough, a self-made millionaire. His construction company built the Flim Flon and Temiskaming and Northern Ontario railways and the Holland and Lincoln tunnels. The press adored Harry and so did the public. The railways, the CNR and

143

the CPR, sure as blazes didn't. To them he was a dreadful nuisance. His favourite pastime was flinging handfuls of ten-dollar bills off trains as they rumbled through small towns. Another trick of his was to run the length of a train, dumping money in passengers' laps. Tens and twenties. When Harry travelled, chaos reigned.

"His generosity wasn't confined to trains. He ran through hospital wards throwing $100 bills; he gave a cabbie a $2,000 tip; and he handed a switchboard operator a bagful of quarters worth $500. Directly across from my office is the King Edward Hotel. At the height of the Depression, Harry rented a room and tossed ten grand out the window. Another time, at the Prince Edward in Windsor, he threw fifty thousand in cash and cheques to a hysterical crowd. A cop went up to his room to order him to stop. The cop sheepishly left clutching a thousand-dollar contribution to the police burial fund.

"I remember having lunch at the Royal York with a friend on a cold winter afternoon when Harry arrived from his home in Merrickville. He was a hefty man, a six-footer with wide shoulders, dressed in a well-tailored double-breasted suit. Sitting down, he took two baked potatoes from his pockets and laid them on the table. He'd gotten them from the train cook — to warm his hands on the walk from the station.

"Asking cooks for hot potatoes didn't irritate the railways. It was his money-throwing. That and the booze-buying. Harry liked to stroll into a club car and create pandemonium by declaring that he was standing everyone in there — and everyone else on the train, too — to free drinks. A friend of mine was a CPR supervisor. He was instructed to find out when Harry was planning a trip to Toronto and to arrange a private car for him. Poor old Harry thought he was receiving the red-carpet treatment because he'd built some great branch lines but the railway was trying to keep him away from its passengers. There was a rumour that many a railway employee was under orders to stay up half the night drinking alone with Harry just to rivet him in one spot.

"Mr. X. It came to mind just now. The newspapers called Harry 'Mr. X' for years because they didn't want to embarrass his family. When they finally identified him by name, around the end of the 1930s, half the province already knew who he was by word of mouth. You know what Harry used to say? He couldn't see the point in hoarding his money unless they discovered a way he could take it to Heaven with him. He wasn't a millionaire when he died in 1961. He left his wife property worth $180,000 and a bank account with $75 in it."

MONOCLE TRICK

"The British papers dispatched fourteen reporters to cover the Royal tour in 1939. Sholto Watt was there for the *Sunday Times* and N. V. Marshall of the *Daily Telegraph*. Splendid people, all, yet the reporter who stands out in my memory is the *Daily Mail*'s Ward Price. Due to his monocle trick. Price appeared to be a typical upper-class Englishman: stiff and formal. He dressed accordingly — Saville Row suits and a bowler. And in the presence of the King and Queen he was impeccably behaved. In the presence of his fellow reporters, it was another matter. He did his monocle trick so often on the train that the reporters knew when to expect it. By the time we reached Edmonton he was anxious to have a more susceptible audience.

"He found it at the Edmonton Club. The entire press corps, over fifty reporters, myself included, were invited to dinner at the club while their majesties were wining and dining at the MacDonald Hotel. Ward was seated at a table with Alberta reporters who hadn't been on the train. Alberta reporters, and their wives. He immediately launched his tirade. 'Albertans are peasants. Their table manners are appalling.' Et cetera. He raised his voice to ensure the people at other tables heard him. When everyone was staring at him, livid with outrage, he purposely bent his head and dropped his monocle in his soup. Then he made a great show of retrieving it with his spoon. As always, his audience suddenly realized it was all a premeditated act and burst out laughing. Ward missed his calling. He was a born actor and should've been on the stage."

MAD MITCH, TRAIN BUFF

"MAD MITCH is a wonderful character. Some people might claim he's a little off-the-wall but I wouldn't say so. He's simply a guy who's crazy about trains. A genuine buff. A couple of years ago, I left Toronto to work in the Rockies for the summer. Mad Mitch was the official bagpiper at Lake Louise. He'd put on a kilt and play the pipes to welcome hotel visitors. I knew him from our days at UCC. He was such a train fanatic that he went to South America one summer and shovelled coal on a steam locomotive. I was in the Rockies about a month when he said he'd show me where the original rail line ran through the mountains. In the 1880s.

"We parked our car at a look-out point in Kicking Horse Pass and scrambled up and down the embankments around the spiral tunnels. On the side of a hill, we came to a bed of shale roughly two feet high and lined with poplars. We dug into the ground with our hands and found the unmistakable man-made road-bed made by the original workmen. No rails, no ties, only the old road-bed still visible by its small elevation above the ground.

"As we followed the road-bed back down the hillside, we came to this incredible sight. An old boiler car was sticking out of the ground. Looking at it gave me goosebumps. It must have jumped the tracks before the turn of the century and it was still lying there, half buried by eighty years of shifting earth. Mad Mitch was really excited. 'Kevin, this is terrific. I'm sure there aren't too many people who know it's here.' I was delighted but not like he was. Being close to the boiler car, a relic from the past, was a train buffs dream.

"I'm in my fifth year at Western now. Mad Mitch studied commerce at the U of T but he doesn't work on Bay Street. He's a trainman at the CPR's MacMillan yard. You might say he's wasting his education but I don't think so. His heart's in what he does. When you consider all of the people who go to jobs they hate every day, he's a very lucky man."

SHAVING ON BLIND FAITH

"COLONEL BAKER and I were early risers. We were up at 6:30 and into the smoking car to wash and shave. The porter was reclining on the seat, half asleep. Colonel Baker founded the CNIB and he was totally blind. He lost his eyes in a shooting accident. I'll never forget the expression on the porter's face when Colonel Baker took out his straight razor and started shaving. I wasn't concerned; I knew he always shaved himself. But the porter — he sat right up and stared as though he thought he'd have to rush him to the hospital for a blood transfusion."

TEASING THE SUFFRAGETTES

"THIS IS MY GRANDFATHER'S STORY. He was headed for Winnipeg and a party of suffragettes climbed aboard. He recognized Nellie McClung from newspaper pictures, but she wasn't the important one on that trip. He found out later on that Emmeline Pankhurst, the British suffragette, was touring Canada, speaking on health and sanitation. My grandfather was a quiet farmer who preferred animals to people and he said nary a word to the ladies. Other men did. They teased them whenever they had a chance and there was a nasty undercurrent to their teasing. At one point, Nellie McClung was walking in the aisle and a man made a funny remark. She whirled and said, 'Where would you men be without us women?' To which the man smartly answered, 'Still in the Garden of Eden.'"

OUT OF BED AT 3:00 A.M.

"I WAS FIFTEEN and soaking wet behind the ears when it came to dealing with adults. I had signed on with the CPR in Brandon as a callboy. Not everybody in town had a phone and what the callboy did was go around to a railwayman's house and tell him when he had to report for a shift. Most of the time you'd be dragging some guy out of bed at three in the morning so he'd be ready for a twelve-hour shift. Henry Mummery scared me. He weighed over three hundred pounds and he had played professional football before joining the railway. I recollect going to his place at 5:00 a.m. and he was already up, at the kitchen table, looking into space. 'They want you for the 6:30 run, Mr. Mummery,' I said. He turned cold eyes on me and his voice was rough as sandpaper. 'Do they now?' he said. 'Well, maybe Sunny Jim, I don't want them.' I didn't argue. I got out as fast as my legs could move.

"Old Campbell, he didn't scare me like Mummery did but he sure was a crank. If you met him on the street, he'd be nice as pie but at the yard, he'd scowl and be real testy. He had a habit that would shake the sectionmen up. He'd shove his head out of the window of the cab and give them a real ugly look. Campbell's wife, she'd crawl from bed to make him a big lunch to take to work, even if it was 3:00 A.M.. She told me he was a regular Jekyll and Hyde. 'He's one of the finest men there is,' she said, 'until he pulls on his overalls. I don't understand why, but he becomes a changed man.' Mummery and Campbell. It's funny. Back then, I was so nervous around them but when I remember them now it's with a lot of affection."

MYSTERIOUS RECLUSE

"ABOUT SEVEN OR EIGHT times a year, Willie the Recluse showed up on the Montreal-to-Toronto train. Nobody talked to him, and nobody knew much about his life, besides the fact that he lived by himself in a hovel in St. Henri. By himself, unless you count a mangy dog as a fellow tenant. Willie was an eyesore, that's for sure. Greasy, black hair that hadn't been washed for years and the same attire year-in, year-out — a rumpled flannel shirt and baggy suit pants held up by suspenders. He had an erect bearing, a proud way of carrying himself — shoulders back, spine straight — that had me wondering if he were an old military man.

"The big question among the regulars on the run was, Why was he going to Toronto? We all had business there: mine was to convince clients that, Depression or not, they should still order merchandise from my boss's factory. The rumours were rampant. Willie owned half of Rosedale and was checking up on his renters. Or he was attending corporation board meetings. Ever hear of Hettie Green? She was one of the richest women in existence and yet she lived in extreme poverty. We were certain Willie the Recluse was Montreal's Hettie Green.

"Unfortunately, I never did learn why he was going to Toronto. But I did find out a little more about him. The *Gazette* ran a story when he died, just before the war. Hoodlums tore his house apart, searching for gold bars and bundles of cash. They knocked holes in the walls and ripped up the floorboards. If they found anything, they weren't bragging in public. Anyway, Willie wasn't a military man. The *Gazette* noted that, like his father, he had dropped out of school early and, again like his father, had spent his life in St. Henri, collecting rags and bottles and assorted junk."

WORSHIPPING HIS WEALTH

"THE TRAIN WAS rolling over the Prairies and I had gone to the parlour car to read a book and have a coffee. I was thirty years old and in the ministry, on my way to preach somewhere. The car was filled with travelling salesmen. They were joking and arguing and having a good time. Then the new man entered. He was like a cartoonist's caricature of what a millionaire looked like. An expensive suit, an expansive midrift, smoking a fat cigar, and a gold chain on his vest. When he sat with the salesmen, their attitudes changed. They became first class sycophants. Agreeing with every syllable he uttered. Asking his advice and gratefully accepting his clichéd replies.

"I laid my book aside and stared in complete dismay. He wasn't about to hand them fistfuls of money. He wasn't about to steer enormous business contracts their way. Why did they sit for an hour and treat him as though he was vastly superior to them? Since that day forty years ago, I've been many places and met many people. I've hosted television programs, written novels and, for eighteen years, did the daily *Dialogue* show with Pierre Berton. Many places, many people. Yet that relatively insignificant incident has remained firmly in my mind. I cannot and will not ever be able to fathom why people bow down to others who may be morally or intellectually inferior to them, simply because they have acquired more money."

HE HEARD AN AWFUL SOUND

"EVERYONE WAS ASLEEP when I got on at North Bay. I had an upper berth and tried not to make any noise climbing into it. I removed my suit and shoes as if I was in slow motion. I had been visiting my daughter and she and her husband were forever screaming and shouting so I was glad to be on the train. I figured I'd have a lovely, quiet ride to the coast. Two minutes after my head hit the pillow, I heard this awful sound. Like somebody had a pig in the berth below me. Only it wasn't a pig. It was somebody snoring in their sleep. It went on all night. Stopping and starting every half hour. I finally got up around seven. After breakfast, I went back to the sleeper, thinking I was going to see a short, fat, bald guy with tiny eyes and a snub nose. Was I surprised. This pretty, dark-haired young girl was sitting there, reading a book. I remember thinking that some poor slob is bound to fall in love with her and spend the rest of his life sleeping with a pillow over his head."

A DOWN-TO-EARTH GUY

"BUCK CRUMP'S a pal of mine. I'm no bigshot. Before I retired, I was an ordinary guy, a locomotive engineer, and the fact that we've been friends for years speaks volumes about the kind of person he is. He started at the bottom. A labourer in the CPR yard at Revelstoke when he was sixteen. Then a machinist's apprentice, a roundhouse foreman, and eventually, between '55 and '61, company president. Some fellows would let a success story like that go to their heads but not Buck Crump. He's stayed down to earth; he never lost the common touch. He could speak to the Queen in her language one minute and a train-porter in his language the next.

"I recall leaving a train in Regina when Buck was CPR president. He was on the platform, surrounded by big-wigs. Superintendents and assistant superintendents, whatever. From all over Saskatchewan. They were fairly jittery. Laughing and talking uneasily and fingering their ties. Perfectly logical conduct. If Buck thought you were doing your job, he treated you like a fine fellow; if he thought you were lazy or incompetent, he'd tear into you like a buzzsaw.

"As I was watching, an old switcher named Smoky Wilson, a crony of Buck's from years gone by, strolled past the group. He was surprised to see Buck, who usually hung out at headquarters in Montreal. 'Crump, you old bastard, what the hell are you doing here?' Smoky yelled. Jaws dropped and faces turned milk-white. The executives were shocked. How could a lowly switcher dare to talk to the boss that way? Buck swung on his heels and looked Smoky up and down. Then his face broke into a grin. 'Smoky, you rotten son-of-a-sea-cook,' he yelled back. 'Is this railroad still stupid enough to employ a rogue like you?'

"I have a second tale. I had driven a train to Moose Jaw and I was walking alongside the cars when I glanced up and saw Buck waving through a window. He was in his business car; I knew there was a business car on my train but I didn't know it was his. He wanted me to join him and I did. We had a long chat, shop talk about the old days and where this guy or that guy was now. As I got off, the general superintendent for Saskatchewan motioned me over to where he stood beside the station. He didn't know Buck and I were pals. He seemed very worried. 'What did Mr. Crump want?' he asked me. 'Was he upset about the way you handled the train?' 'No, sir,' I answered. 'He said there was a vice-presidency opening up at head office and he wanted to know if the average worker like myself thought you had what it takes. Naturally, I recommended you for the job.'

"The last time I was with Buck was a few years ago at his home in Calgary. He invited me over the phone to visit him. He lived in Mount Royal, which is Calgary's Millionaires' Row, and I was a bit apprehensive about feeling out of my element. I went up the hill, past all these mansions, and when I arrived at his place, it was a stucco bungalow, only a bit bigger than my house in Moose Jaw. Buck greeted me at the door. He's had emphysema for years. 'When I was with the railroad,' he said, 'they called me an SOB and meant it as a curse. I'm still an SOB, only now it means Short of Breath.'"

SPEEDY FELLOW

"THE ONLY famous person I've met in my life was Howie Morenz. He was coming up from Chicago in 1934 for a game against his old team, the Canadiens. The sports writers tagged him 'the Mitchell Meteor' because he was from Mitchell, Ontario, and he was lightning fast on ice. Take my word for it, he was pretty speedy off the ice as well. His teammates had bunked down and Howie was ripping about the train.

He had a ukulele and he drove the porter in our car to distraction because he was playing and singing, even though practically the whole car was in bed.

"The porter quietened him down by letting some of us play poker in the smoker. Howie loved the game and settled in for the night. One of the players had three or four bottles of booze in his satchel. We took our drinks with water, but Howie took his straight from the bottle. What amazed me was what he did in the morning. He slept on the smoker seat for a couple of hours. I was washing when he got up and said he'd better freshen up, he had a hockey practice. He then did something I've never seen another man do — he raised a bottle to his mouth and gargled with whisky."

UNDER THE FREIGHT

"I WAS ON the day shift at Red Deer General when they brought little Randy Gulliford in. You know who he is? Well, he was the talk of Alberta for a while in 1984. Randy was a seven-year-old boy who fell under a freight train and lived to tell the tale. I'd better correct that. He didn't fall, he threw himself under it.

"Randy was collecting rocks on the tracks near his house and sticking them on the rails. He liked to watch passing trains demolish them to powder. He was preoccupied by what he was doing and he didn't notice the freight until it was nearly on top of him. The engineer blew the horn and the child panicked; instead of jumping off the tracks, he threw himself face down onto the ties and gravel. The train went right over him. Eighty cars of a CP freight heading north to Edmonton. Going forty miles an hour. The poor child lay there for five or ten minutes, pushing his little body down. The ground was shaking and the noise terrified him.

"The miracle was, he wasn't hurt. Not a bruise, not a scratch. But he was trembling like a leaf and they brought him to the hospital to make sure he was okay. His mother ran into the room crying. Randy looked up at her with big eyes and promised never to play on the tracks again. After the scare he got, I'd wager that's a promise he'll keep."

HOMEBRED INVENTOR

"EVERYBODY'S INTERESTING. Everybody. Doctors are supposed to be dull because all they do is work but that's not so. They read the *Reader's Digest* and they know facts. The same goes for accountants. I don't moan and groan if I'm seated next to an accountant in a dining car. It was an accountant who explained J. W. Elliott to me.

"Who's J. W. Elliott? A godsend to railroaders. He invented the rotary plough. That's the dandy machine that clears the tracks in winter. Elliott was a Toronto dentist around the middle of the last century. I like to visualize him getting the idea while drilling some miserable sod's teeth. How the plough works is, a big wheel powered by a rotary motor grabs the snow and tosses it through a hole at the top of the machine. Very simple, very effective.

"And I wouldn't know about J. W. Elliott if it wasn't for the accountant. Everybody's got interesting facts stored in them."

TOO BLAND FOR MOVIES

"THIS HAPPENED in the 1950s. The Dominion was crossing the Prairies and the steward seated me with another chap who was travelling alone. He was very average-looking. A grey suit, tall, neat hair, and a bland face. He was drinking milk. He produced a flask from his pocket and poured something into the milk glass. He said it was medicine but it smelled like alcohol to me. I inquired as to what he did for a living and he said he was an actor. He named several motion pictures he'd been in, and I had to confess I hadn't seen any of them. He finished his meal before I finished mine. As he prepared to leave, I wished him luck in his chosen profession, although I suspected that such a bland-looking person didn't have much of a career in motion pictures. I also asked his name, so that I could watch for it in the future. The name stuck in my mind. Ronald Reagan."

GETTING THE BREMEN SCOOP

"Remember the *Bremen*? It was the German plane that made the first east - west crossing of the Atlantic in 1928, and then crashed in the wilds of Labrador. The three crewmen were alive. A bush pilot named Schiller snapped pictures of the wreck with a Brownie and radioed home saying he planned to land at Murray Bay at such and such a time. Murray Bay was a cottage and beach haven on the St. Lawrence, at the end of the train line from Quebec City.

"The newspapers were frantic. This was front-page stuff, the biggest aviation story since Lindberg flew the Atlantic by himself. Pathé News and reporters from New York, Montreal, Toronto, everywhere, rushed to Quebec. *The Toronto Star* was horrified by the prospect that it might be beaten on the story. It wanted Schiller's film so desperately that an editor phoned Quebec City and hired a special train.

"The *Star* had this fabulous character, Fred Griffin, on its payroll. He'd do anything for a story. He led the *Star* team that flew to Quebec City. A pack of American reporters and photographers were at Palais Station waiting for the regular passenger train to Murray Bay. They're gazing out the station window and what do they see but Griffin and his gang getting on a special train. They added two and two and pursued the *Star* boys. Some of them clambered aboard as the train pulled away. Griffin and the others literally threw them off. They punched and shoved and actually lifted one fellow up and flung him out the door. He was so mad he tossed a mickey at Griffin. It hit the side and shattered.

"Schiller didn't land at Murray Bay. He landed fifteen miles away. The roads were snow-bound. Griffin and the *Star* men hired a horse-drawn sleigh. When they got to the airport, some Americans were there. A Hearst reporter grabbed Schiller's film and Griffin grabbed it from him. He handed it to a local pilot who swore he'd fly to Toronto. The weather got worse and the pilot landed in Quebec City. Another *Star* man, Roy Greenaway, was there. He hired another train and took the film to Montreal. From there, he carried it to

Toronto by cab. The *Star* scooped the world on that one. When I was at the *Star* in the 1950s, the old-timers were still talking about the *Bremen* story."

NOBODY KNEW HIS NAME

"RUTH CUSHING and I were at the station in Edmonton. The spring of 1929. We were travelling up to Peace River to teach summer school. The station was crowded and busy — freight and passengers coming and going. As I sat on a bench waiting for my train, I spotted a tall, aristocratic man with a long, well-trimmed beard and a swarthy complexion. He wore a fawn-coloured, big-brimmed hat. Not a Stetson, some other kind of hat. I asked someone who he was. She said he was a remittance man whose father was British and mother East Indian. He owned a lodge at Berwyn. No one seemed to know or use his name. Hardly anyone wore long beards like that so they referred to him as Jesus Berwyn. That's what most people called him. Jesus Berwyn."

WAS IT TRUE OR FALSE?

"I WAS INTRODUCED to Sir Edward Beatty at a banquet in 1930. He was well on in his years — he had run the CPR since 1918 — and he remained an impressive figure. Shorter of stature than I had antici-pated but a handsome man with a strong voice, a virile stride, and remarkably rivetting eyes. He had many achievements behind him, and can you guess what I longed to ask him? About the gloves. The story in CPR offices was that he had gone on inspection tours in the early days with a pair of pearl-grey gloves. The engineers cared for their locomotives and polished the brass until it gleamed. However, there were porters and chefs and others who weren't as fussy. They say Sir Edward would climb on a train unannounced, pull on his gloves, and walk though the cars, running his hands over metal and wood. A speck of dirt or dust resulted in a severe chastizing. A spot-less car would bring a hearty congratulation. I spoke with Sir Edward for twenty minutes prior to the banquet and I was seated near him during it. I never inquired. Somehow I felt intimidated. I'm still curious and I'd dearly like to know whether the story was true or not."

THE CONDUCTORS DIDN'T SPEAK FRENCH

"I'LL BE CAREFUL here. Marc Brière's a lawyer and, with lawyers, it's best to stay with the facts and to leave your own opinions out of it. The facts are, Brière left his suburban home on the Lakeshore and caught the morning train to Montreal in January 1967. The conductor said, 'Can I have your ticket, please,' and he said it in English. He was from Ontario and didn't speak French. Brière refused to give him the ticket unless he asked in French. The conductor messaged ahead and two policemen boarded at Beaconsfield and made a grand show of taking Brière off. The trouble was, they didn't know what to do with him. So they bought him a coffee and drove him to his office in Montreal.

"A few months afterwards, Brière was on another train to the city and the same thing happened. The conductor didn't speak French and Brière wouldn't surrender his ticket. This time they let him stay on but the CPR police questioned him at Windsor station. Questioned him, and let him go. Separatism was a potent force in Quebec in 1967 and, no doubt, they didn't want to enrage the French populace. So a few weeks pass and a reporter calls Brière up and asks what the outcome of his dispute with the railway is. The outcome, Brière says, isn't too hard to swallow. The railway's so leery of riling the French Canadians the conductors are avoiding him and he's been riding free of charge back and forth to his office every day."

BURNING UP THE TRACK

"BEYOND A DOUBT, the last place fifth columnists planned to attack in the Dominion of Canada was a CNR railway bridge north of Lake Nipigon, near Jacobs, Ontario. There was nothing for miles in any direction except bush. Yet the Army, in all its wisdom, feared saboteurs might drop from the sky and blow the bridge up. In November

1939, myself and two other kids were dispatched north to guard it. What a boring job. You were either sitting watching the river flow down the gorge or you were in the woods, hunting game.

"One afternoon I heard a distant whistle off to the east and, looking along the track, I saw this big freight locomotive, a 4,000, whipping down the mile-long straightaway towards the bridge. It was going like the wind. It whisked past me, hauling a dozen boxcars, at eighty, eighty-five, miles an hour. The average speed on that section was sixty. I remember standing there with my mouth half-open and wondering, Who the hell is driving that locomotive? The next time I was in Jacobs the section foreman told me the engineer was Crazy Fred Lindstrom. From Sioux Lookout. I knew him well from growing up there. He was a legend. He had been warned several times about speeding but he obviously couldn't help himself. When he had a chance, he'd throw the throttle wide open. The CNR had surmised he'd made the trip too fast and suspended him.

"The weather turned really cold in December. The two boys I shared the patrols with were transferred out. I was twenty-one and lonely and frustrated and, because I was alone, I had to be at the bridge from midnight to dawn. I slept in an old construction boxcar beside the track. It had a bed and a kitchen and a large, cast-iron coal heater. It was 25 below when I crawled in the sack one morning at 4:30. I was asleep a few minutes and a sectionhand knocked on the door. I let him in. He warmed his hands and told me about Lindstrom. Crazy Fred had gone so fast that the wheel-drivers had burned the rails every thirty or forty feet for seventy miles. It cost the railway millions. The iron had a tendency to break once it was burned and the weather was cold.

"The sectionhand opened the stove draught when he came in. He forgot to close it as he went out. I quickly fell asleep. Several hours later, I suddenly woke up. The roof was in flames. I was sleeping in the buff. I lept out of bed and grabbed what I could — a parka, ski pants, and moccasins. I threw my camera and two rifles out the window. The fire had spread down the walls and was between me and the door. I ducked my head and plunged through the flames and burst outside into the freezing cold. I yanked on the moccasins and the clothing and left the fire to burn itself out. I walked the four miles to Jacobs. Roy Fisher, my father, happened to be bringing a freight to the water tower. I climbed aboard and explained about the fire and we talked about Lindstrom's incredible fast run.

"Months later, my father said Lindstrom was on Vancouver Island. My father was a union 'griever' as well as an engineer and his job was to help men get reinstated. He said there was nothing he could do for Lindstrom. So Lindstrom had taken work engineering on a logging-camp line. A dangerous, rotten job, but I imagine he was happy because he was still driving a train for a living. Crazy Fred. He's dead now but that fast run of his in '39 is still remembered by railwaymen all along the line between Armstrong and Sioux Lookout."

A PRIVATE
WORLD

J. K. L. Ross liked to travel in style. A Montreal millionaire whose main purpose in life was to spend his inheritance, he owned six Rolls-Royces, a 23-metre yacht, and a bicycle with an ermine-covered seat. His favourite possession was a private railway car. Built to his own design, the car contained seven staterooms with satin-sheeted beds and bathrooms with gold-plated fixtures. In the 1920s Ross enjoyed taking friends to Blue Bonnets race track. The guests eating succulent meals in the chandeliered dining room were a stimulating mix of politicians, sports writers, chorus girls, and clergymen.

Most of Ross's money was gone by 1940 and, fittingly, so was the era of the private car. The opulence that had made the cars a must-have item for the wealthy elite since the 1800s led to their demise. Few people dared to flaunt their riches in such a highly visible manner during the Depression. Even the CPR fretted over the public image presented by its relatively inexpensive executive cars. An edict instructed company brass to leave the blinds down entering stations. A second edict said, No, leave them up: the great unwashed were gazing at the covered windows and imagining all sorts of wild and extravagant goings-on.

In the last quarter of the twentieth century, there were about fifty privately owned railway cars in North America. The Department of Transport maintained two for the occasional use of the prime minister and governor-general. Paul Higgins, president of Mother Parker's

159

Foods, has a private car. James Conklin, chairman of Conklin Shows, once owned a car too. Until recently, one of the best-known private cars in this country, *The Métis*, belonged to a Montreal-based advertising agency, Grenier Harries MacLean. When I interviewed the company chairman, Michael Harries, at his office, I noticed a scale-model of the car on a table opposite his desk. Its presence gave silent testimony to how strongly he missed the car.

"Money. To put it succinctly, that's what it took to have our own private car. Lots of money. The yearly maintenance and repair bills approached the $20,000 mark and a return trip, Montreal-Toronto, cost roughly $3,000. It was well worth it, though. The car helped create business for the agency at a time when we needed it.

"We bought it in the mid-1970s. More and more companies were leaving Quebec and, in order to survive and grow, we had to grab a slice of the Toronto market. Easier said than done. There were at least 120 ad agencies in Toronto. Unless we dreamed up a novel way to attract attention, we'd be totally ignored.

"I don't know where the idea came from. I'm not a rail buff; perhaps it was seeing the old Westmount station down the street from my office every day that planted the seed. Anyhow, I couldn't just go out and buy a car. It took two years to find one large enough and in good enough condition. In April 1978, I received a letter from CN informing me that *The Métis* was up for tenders. To be sold 'as is.' *The Métis* had an interesting past — built in 1928, used primarily on the Gaspé line, and part of many Royal Visit trains. The train to the Gaspé *The Métis* was on was called the St. Lawrence Special — a weekend run to deluxe summer resorts. From the 1950s on, it was a business car for CN executives.

"I trotted down to the Point St. Charles yard to look it over. It looked great to me but I was no expert. Eighty-five feet long and all but three or four inches of that eighty-five feet crammed with mechanism. And there were no tires to kick. I submitted the lowest bid I dared, $10,500. A few weeks passed and then CN called and said I was the new owner. I returned to the Point with mixed feelings. Excited over the purchase, and worried that our agency might have an expensive lemon on its hands. I was lucky. The car was in splendid mechanical shape. All it required was a couple of new wheels and a little fiddling with the plumbing in the CN shop.

"The interior was something else. Too plain and dingy. I had a friend who was a designer. He must have doubted my sanity in buying *The Métis* but nevertheless he designed the interior for me. We didn't alter the basic layout. We added fabrics, glass, and furnishings and, of course, a paint job. There were four bedrooms with bathrooms, and showers, a beautiful mirrored dining room, a kitchen, and a very smart lounge at the rear. It was all done in '1940s New York.' Dark and light greys, beiges, and browns. My wife selected the materials for the curtains and bedspreads and sewed them herself.

"Everything was flawless. Not a single scratch or dent. I didn't want the car to be a musty shrine to railroad memorabilia. I wanted a sophisticated, luxury setting that could impress potential clients. Far, far better than telephoning someone from a dreary hotel room and making an appointment at a crowded restaurant.

"I changed the name from *The Métis* to our agency's initials, *GHM I*, and began taking it to Toronto. The media coverage was fabulous. The *Toronto Star*, *Homemaker's*, and *Canadian Business* did stories and *Good Morning America* carried a six-minute item. You can't buy that kind of publicity. When I phoned a prospective client, he had usually heard about our car and was delighted to be invited to have lunch aboard it. Marvellous meals. Prepared by a chef I'd bring from Montreal. A leisurely lunch, served on Wedgwood china, and featuring tiny quiche lorraines, Beef Wellington, fruit flan, and French wines.

"Needless to say, I felt like a king. I'd roll to Toronto overnight and wake up at 7:30 parked beneath the CN Tower. At times, alighting in the railyard, I'd ask myself, 'Is this for real? How in heaven's name did you wind up with this enormous, beautiful object?'

"The monthly bills always brought me down to earth. With a thud. Parking overnight at the CN Tower cost $150. Tagging behind the regular VIA train was $1,000 per trip and the switching charge — that's for moving your car off and on a siding — was at least an extra $1,000. Plus the chef, the food, and so on. The switching charges hurt the most. A fifteen minute procedure and, in the States, the maximum charge is a mere $150. I know of an elderly German businessman who dreamed all of his life of crossing Canada in a private car. He was wealthy, but he wasn't keen on throwing his money away. He cancelled the trip when he found out the railway might charge him as much as $40,000 for going from Halifax to Vancouver.

"It's a crying shame. Our agency may well have held on to its car if it wasn't so expensive, and I'm certain other people would be buying and refurbishing them. After we opened an office in Toronto in 1981, the *GHM I* was no longer needed for business trips. I sold it to a rich Texan. I wish it had remained in Canada but no one came forward to buy it. Will I ever buy another private car? I'm not a wealthy man. If, however, I won a million dollars in a lottery, I'd be tempted to get another one. Tempted, mind you. I'm not absolutely certain I'd be willing to face those maintenance and repair bills again."

"THE PRINCE GEORGE EVENTUALLY:" BEST LOVED TRAINS

T he populace of several central and northern B.C. communities flocked to the tracks in full force on August 29, 1956, to welcome the first train to run over the newly finished line between Squamish and the Peace River district. Can-can girls danced in the streets of Prince George, a posse removed Premier W. A. C. Bennett from the train at Williams Lake and pretended to hang him for 'cluttering the countryside with trains and making it unsafe for cowboys to sleep there.'

The citizenry had good cause to be jubilant. The Pacific Great Eastern railway had been under construction since 1912. Moreover, Premier Bennett had purchased five modern diesels for the 1170-kilometre route. For decades, the PGE's partially completed line had been a laughing stock. The antique locomotives, rickety cars, and the trains' habitual slowness earned the PGE many derisive nicknames — the Please Go Easy; the Prince George Eventually; Past God's Endurance. My favourite was the line I heard a conductor shout to boarding passengers at the Vancouver terminal in the early 1960s: "Welcome to the Puff, Grunt and Expire!"

On the other side of the country, the narrow-gauge railway spanning Newfoundland was also the butt of local humour. Owing to its aversion to speed, the regular passenger train between St. John's and Port aux Basques was labelled the Newfie Bullet. Not that the Bullet didn't have excuses for its conduct. The line was pummelled by rain, snow, and wind; ocean-born storms splashed salt water on the rails, the salt froze and the trains lost their traction. The scorn and curses notwithstanding, the Bullet's final run on July 2, 1969, was a sad day. Track-side spectators waved and wept and wore black armbands.

The PGE steamers and the Bullet held memberships in the same fraternity. A brotherhood of spunky, ridiculed, and much-loved trains that pioneered railroading in this nation.

SHIRLEY WOULDN'T WAIT

"'CONDUCTOR, my daughter's going to have a baby. Right here. On your train.' Those were the words she said to me. I was walking through a coach on the Kettle Valley run and this older woman ran up to me and said her daughter was travelling to the hospital in Nelson and she wasn't going to make it. She looked mighty anxious to me, and after I realized that I might have to deliver the baby, I wasn't the calmest person alive.

"I left her and hurried to the sleeper where Frank Collins was the porter. He laughed when I said, 'Can you make up a berth so a lady can lie down and have a baby?' He thought I was joking. While I was trying to convince him that I wasn't, the pregnant young lady and her mother came up to us. The young lady could hardly walk and she looked more anxious than her mother and me combined.

"Frank made up a lower berth in record time. His hands practically flew. When I said I'd be right back, he grabbed my lapel and said, 'Perley McPherson, don't you dare leave me. I can't handle this by myself.' I promised I wouldn't be long. I walked through the cars, asking if there was a doctor on board, and in the very last car, the very last person turned out to be a registered nurse.

"Frank had hot water and towels ready. He said he'd seen a baby born in a cowboy movie and knew what was needed. Just then, we reached Farron. I jumped off and wired the station agent at Castlegar, telling him to have a doctor meet the train. By now, the young woman was in pain and sweating badly. Frank made sure nobody entered the car so she wouldn't begawked at by strangers. We got to Castlegar all right and a doctor joined the registered nurse. He said the woman might be able to hold on till he could get her to the hospital in Nelson. Well, the baby had other plans. It started coming out.

"And that's where it was born. On a Kettle Valley train in the rail-yard at Castlegar. The crew and the passengers whooped and applauded when I announced it. She'd had a girl. The mother, a Mrs. Munch, said she wanted 'Shirley' for a name. The crew had something different in mind. In the dining car, they posted a notice christening the baby, 'Miss CPR Castlegar Collins McPherson Shirley Munch.' For the child's sake, I hope her mother didn't take a fancy to that name and decide to officially keep it."

Slow Going

"CALL IT what you may. The PGE, Wacky Bennett's Folly, or the new name the government put on it a while back, the BCR. Whatever you call it, the railway's still got the same problem. It will never get into the *Guinness Book of World Records* for being on time more than any other railway. I'm speaking from experience. Sixteen years with the PGE and I'm an authority on late trains. You can't blame the crews. They try, they really try. It's the country that defeats them. Mountains and valleys. They tool around a bend and a rock slide's dumped eight tons on the tracks. They come to a bridge and the sucker's been swept away by a flood.

"There was a train that went to Prince George in the 1960s. A local merchant was waiting on the platform with his brother at Quesnel. They were going hunting north of Prince George. The train pulled in and the merchant glanced at his watch and beamed. He saw the engineer coming towards him, and he said, 'Good job, fella. You're right on time. Two o'clock exactly.' The engineer could've kept his mouth shut but he didn't. 'Don't congratulate me, mister,' he said. 'This is yesterday's train. We're twenty-four hours late.'"

THOSE TRUNKS WERE HEAVY

"WHEN I THINK of trains, I think of Flin Flon in the late 1920s. I was an insurance inspector for Employer's Assurance Corporation. Twice a year, I'd travel up from Winnipeg — in gas-lit coaches where the heat sometimes failed and you had to wear all the clothing you had with you. I didn't mind, really. It was nice to get out of the city. There wasn't enough business to have a full-time agent in Flin Flon, and lawyers and local businessmen sold insurance on the side. My job was to help them fix the rates. Most of the people on the train were miners. They'd bring alcohol on board but they kept to themselves and you'd never know they were drinking unless you saw them in the washroom using tap water for mixer.

"Miners — and salesmen. I'd nearly forgotten about them. The forlorn wretches from Toronto and Montreal. They'd have these huge steamer trunks jammed with samples — bolts of cloth, tools, men's suits, and the like. They hated being in northern Manitoba, especially in the depths of winter. Their biggest complaint was having to drag those trunks. Some weighed one hundred pounds. You'd see these fellows pulling their trunks down a street towards a train depot in some tiny hamlet at two o'clock in the morning. Pulling, shivering, and cursing. Looking in vain for a horse and buggy to hire, hoping beyond hope that somebody would drive along and give them a lift. What a terrible way to earn a living. A 20 percent commission — 25 in the winter — and forced to drag those cumbersome trunks as though they were a ball and chain."

HITTING THE WRONG KEYS

"You had to be a dwarf to be comfortable on the Newfie Bullet. I'm not tall — five foot seven — and I had to curl up in my berth. The corridors were so narrow that if you had an inclination you could hold hands with the person in the berth across from you. And the swaying — Oh, boy, did the Bullet ever sway. I was covering a Diefenbaker campaign for the *Globe and Mail* and, for some reason, I left my car in St. John's and rode the Bullet to Port aux Basques. I had a deadline. I sat in a roomette and banged my story out on a portable typewriter. The blasted train rocked back and forth so much that I kept hitting the wrong keys. Every few words had a wrong letter somewhere. The train stopped and I ran to the telegraph office with the story. The telegrapher vowed he'd make the corrections but he didn't. He sent the story exactly as it was typed. The guys on the news desk in Toronto had a good laugh at my expense. They thought I was smashed to the gills."

Destructive Dog

"Jim Walsh was a baggageman on the 'Muskeg Mixed.' The Muskeg Mixed is the title we had for the old NAR run from Edmonton to Fort McMurray. It hauled passengers, freight, and mailbags to Conklin and Cheecham and Margie and other whistle stops along the way. Bush country. Every fall and spring there'd be a half dozen dogteams in the baggage car. They'd be tied to the railings and they'd howl and bark and snarl at each other for 250 miles. It could drive you nuts. One time Jim went out for a smoke and when he came back, a big husky had broken loose and torn into a pile of furs some trapper had spent all winter getting. The bloody dog must've chewed five hundred bucks' worth of coyote pelts. The trapper was hopping mad when he found out, but the dog just kept wagging his tail and looking like he was the honoured guest at a real nice party."

My Grandfather's Diary

"It's too bad you can't read my grandfather's diary. I don't have it any more; it's in the St. John's archives. My grandfather came from Scotland in 1890 and got work with the railway. He helped build it; Placentia to Notre Dame Bay — about 250 miles and most of it through hard rock. He didn't write much in his diary; he was too tired at the end of the day. Still and all, some of it was interesting.

"The boys cooked their own meals in iron pots and took to frying bacon and eggs on their shovels. The company was cheap. Run by a cheap Scot and his three cheap sons. The boys had to put up their own tents or shacks or sleep on the ground. Six dollars a week for six days' labour, sun-up to sun-down. The company sold them their food, and on Sundays a preacher came round. My grandfather put nothing in the collection plate because he figured the company would take its share of that too.

"You'd think he'd hated it, but he didn't hate it at all. He liked being with the boys, doing tough work, and when it was finished, he wrote in his diary that he'd had a real good time."

THEY TRUSTED CONDUCTORS

"FOLKS TRUSTED conductors in the old days. On the NAR, a man would hike ten miles through the bush, flag the train, and give the conductor a note. 'This is a message for my wife in the city. Will you phone her for me?' He did, of course. I recall the day a trapper whose name was Wilson or Winslow signed a cheque and had a friend give it to the conductor. The friend said, 'He wants you to cash it in Edmonton and leave the money at Olson's store. He wants so many hundred-dollar bills, so many fifties, and the rest in twenties and tens.' The cheque was for a thousand. It's a different planet we're living on now. Nobody trusts nobody with a dime."

A TALE OF VENGEANCE

"MOUNT CURRIE'S a big reserve, one of the biggest in Canada. The Indians go up to Lillooet to buy provisions, and they usually travel light — a shirt, a pair of pants, and a bottle of Kelowna Red. When the BCR was the PGE, an Indian tried to bring something on the coach that couldn't be drunk. His flea-bitten dog. The conductor said no, that it had to go in the baggage car.

"This Indian was well-spoken and dressed fairly good, and you had the impression that his mission in life was not to take any crap from a white man. He said to the conductor, 'Where I stay, my dog stays. And I'm not staying in no baggage car.' 'Suit yourself, chief,' the conductor said. 'You and your dog can stay at the reserve together because you're not getting on my train.' The Indian's last words were, 'Your railroad's going to pay for this.'

"A week went by, and a freight was hauling lumber from Quesnel to Vancouver. It came to a standstill near the bottom of a hill south of the reserve. The engineer poured on the juice and the wheels spun and spun and spun. The tracks were coated with grease. A section gang brought sand on a flatcar, but even with the sand it couldn't get enough traction. The train was delayed for hours; solvents were brought from Lillooet, and the guys on the section gang removed the grease, inch by blessed inch.

"I can't prove it was the Indian with the dog who did it. The railway never did find out who greased the tracks. But I have a feeling it was him. While the wheels were spinning, while the crew was busting its ass applying solvents, he was hiding in the woods, laughing and saying to his dog, 'Maybe next time, Rover, they'll let you ride in the coach.'"

Unsung Heroes

"THE MEN who built the White Pass and Yukon Railway were genuine unsung heroes. They had mile upon mile of sheer cliffs and deep gorges to lay track over. Keep in mind there were no back-hoes, no bulldozers, in the 1890s. Only horses, shovels, picks, and hammers and, of course, Mr. Nobel's stupendous invention, dynamite. Some cliffs were over one hundred feet high and eighty feet wide; they had to hang on ropes to blast and cut. They built a 250-foot-long tunnel through a mountain and a cantilevered bridge over Dead Horse Gulch.

"Thirty-five men perished building the White Pass and Yukon. And unlike the CPR, not a solitary Oriental coolie was used. The labourers were local prospectors who needed the money for grubstakes. When the news hit camp of a gold strike at Atlin, 1,500 men ran off, taking their shovels and picks. The contractor, Big Mike Heney, was mad, but not for long. Another 1,500 men replaced them within a week or two.

"The railway was finished in 1900. It had been built for the Gold Rush, but by the time it reached Whitehorse the rush was nearly over. Still, it served a fine purpose. The train brought in minks and sables for the dance-hall girls who had rich boyfriends, and the hotels stocked up on expensive French wines. Big Mike Heney celebrated the railway's finish in true Yukon fashion. He hauled a case of champagne off a train, cracked the bottles open at the station, and offered everybody in sight free drinks."

CRUMBS AND DEAD FISH

"SLEEPING-CAR PORTERS on the bush lines were the worst. Their customers had filthy habits, and the porters got sick and tired of tidying up after them and they became sloppy and lazy. It was easy to spot a bush-liner's tracks. The beds were improperly made; there was no soap or clean linen in the washrooms; the 'Silence' sign wasn't posted at night in the sleeper. Crumbs on the floor and seats — little kiddies ate crackers and cookies and the porter didn't bend down to clean the mess. In Saskatchewan, the farmers wore their dirty boots on board and deposited clumps of mud. In north Ontario, you'd find a dead fish under a seat. The Invisible Man. I'd come on at Winnipeg and had passengers tell me they didn't see their porter for hours on end. They shouldn't have allowed bush-line porters on The Dominion. That was main-line, pride of the fleet. Whenever one got on, he set the railway's standards back a hundred years."

FIVE FRIGHTENING DAYS

"WE HAD to sign blood-chits before they let us leave. A blood-chit's a piece of paper that says your family won't sue for compensation if you're killed. I wondered why the PGE wanted us to sign it. What was so dangerous about a train ride from Vancouver to Prince George? Then they showed us the transportation they'd laid on for us. My God! A 1938 Ford mounted on train wheels! They said surveyors, engineers, and PGE executives used it, and I thought, Sure and a lot of other people with enemies in the department that handled the transportation assignments.

"Nuts. Completely bonkers. A single track from Vancouver and it had a million blind curves and somebody had already told me that the engineers didn't bother tooting their whistles on the remote stretches where they didn't expect anyone to be. This happened in 1958. I was doing a story for *Weekend* magazine on the wonderful and wacky railway built by the wonderful and wacky Bennett. Harry Filion was the photographer; he was the racetrack photographer in Vancouver when he died two years ago, but back then he was a freelancer. Harry hit the scales at 330 and did he ever have the jitters. The driver the PGE assigned us and I were both reasonably light and limber. Coming up to blind curves, I was constantly primed, ready to leap out. Harry was stuck in the back with his equipment. And his prayers. He had a helluva task climbing in and out when the Ford was standing still. Harry knew that if a train shot around the bend, he was a goner.

"Five days. Five hair-raising, nerve-twitching days. Watching and listening and hurrying onto a siding when a train appeared in the distance. God, those dreadful curves! We were going through a string of them on a high mountain pass and the driver chose that very moment to offer the opinion that the railway wasn't worried about us. After all, he said, we'd signed the blood-chits. 'The only thing that worries the PGE', he said, 'is the damage that might be done to the locomotive if we strike one head-on.'

"I said we really shouldn't be so nervous. The railway's head office had promised to inform the engineers that we were out there. 'That means sweet bugger-all,' the driver said. 'There are men on this crazy railway who hate head office so passionately that they might be tempted to hit us, just to give the executives a bad case of heartburn.'

"He was pulling my leg. At least, I think he was. At the time, Harry and I weren't too sure. The car stopped beyond the curves moments after he said it, and Harry picked up his camera to shoot a river valley far below. He was shooting through an open window. I turned to watch. His hands were shaking, and he had to use a tripod.

"There was a happy finale to all this. After we were safely in Prince George, the PGE presented Harry and me with its version of the Red Badge of Courage. We returned to Vancouver on the regular passenger train, and three bottles of Seagram's VO were stashed in each of our berths, compliments of the railway's P.R. department."

BEAVERS ATE THE LINES

"THE IDIOT who hired me in Montreal had a glint in his eye. I didn't see it then; I see it now, when I remember his face and our conversation. I asked him how I was to get to the camp, and he said it was no problem, I'd catch the Bourlemaque Central Railroad. The year was 1944, and I told him I didn't know they had a railway in that part of northern Quebec. 'Oh, sure,' he said. 'And it's first-class service, better than the CPR.' A joker, that guy. The 'train' turned out to be a Chevy half-ton on train wheels. That was the whole shooting match, the whole operation of the Bourlemaque Central. A half-ton that went to East Sullivan and Aumaque mining camps and other places along a ten-mile route. The muskeg was like soup and real trains would've sunk, so they built a rinkydink line using logs instead of regular rails.

"The passengers were in the truck box — with any freight that had to be delivered. On my first trip, I was by myself. Only me and a crate of drilling equipment. I sat and peered at the trees through the slats; they had a rack made of slats around the box so you wouldn't topple out. Other trips, I wasn't as lucky. Standing-room only. On Friday nights, the box was packed with miners and prospectors and oddballs who lived alone in the bush, going to Val D'Or for the weekend. Sundays, the Lord's Day, the miners coming from town had hangovers and were surly and, if you stepped on a foot, they threatened to knock your block off.

"The beavers, the rotten beavers. They ate the lines. Chewed the bejesus out of logs, and if the truck was going fast and hit a chewed log on a sharp curve, it turned over and spilled you out. If it was a bad break, we'd chop down a tree and repair the line before we continued on. The deer and moose were okay. They'd run. But sometimes a black bear stood on the track and wouldn't budge and you had to get off and throw rocks at it.

"The loveliest sight was the day the Chevy arrived with the girl. The camp boss said she was the new cook and she'd been in a convent and we mustn't touch her. We all agreed. All but a couple of jerks who didn't care if they lost their jobs. They teased her for two days. Telling dirty jokes, crap like that. Then one of them left a note in her shack saying he'd give her money if she'd you-know-what. The saddest sight was the day of the note. The girl carrying her little suitcase and leaving on the Bourlemaque Central."

Too Dedicated

"Those old-timers were dedicated to the railway. Too dedicated, if you ask me. Look at Alex Ball. He was a brakeman for Algoma Eastern in the 1930s. Algoma Eastern took ore to the smelter at Sudbury, and you'd think it was the most important job in the universe the way the old-timers went at it. Once there was a rock slide at the height of winter, thirty below zero. Alex Ball lept off the train and started moving the rocks. He didn't want to wait for help to come because it would put them behind schedule. He froze the tip of his nose and lost part of an ear. Worst yet, there were holes in his gloves. He froze his fingertips and the doctors had to pull off the nails."

Forgotten Railway

"It seems to me that the Kettle Valley Railway's pretty well forgotten. The railway, and the mess of trouble we had getting over the Coquihalla Pass. The KVR connected Penticton to Hope — part of the CPR's southern route through B.C. Take my word for it, the whole blamed route was cursed from the very start. As though somebody cast an evil spell on it. Trains only began going over the Crowsnest around 1900, and in 1903 half of Turtle Mountain fell onto the town of Frank, killing seventy or eighty folks and burying the rail line. Besides that, it was all slides and derailments for decade after decade, and then the confounded Doukhobours had fun dynamiting the tracks about twenty years back.

"The KVR section of the Crowsnest route was the biggest bitch. Summer rock slides. I remember a freight coming around a curve, hitting rocks, and toppling the engine. Charlie Carnie, the engineer, had his ear cut off. They had to get him to Merritt on a hand-car where the doctors sewed it back on. Up in the Coquihalla in the winter, the snow piled seventy feet deep in places. And I'm not talking avalanches, I'm talking normal snowfall. Some winters the white stuff was too thick, and they'd shut the whole pass down for a month or so.

"What burned me was the dumb story about the Coquihalla. Some newspaperman who never left his desk in Vancouver wrote that the reason the KVR took most trains through the canyon at night was so as not to frighten the wits out of the passengers. It's true the trains seemed to hang over the cliffs and the grades were fairly fearful. Going east, you'd climb 3,400 feet in forty miles and there was a section where, going into Penticton, you'd drop 3,000 feet in fifty-five miles. It jangled the nerves, I won't deny it. But it was ridiculous to say the railway travelled at night to avoid scaring people; that was the way it was owing to what were the best departure times in Vancouver and elsewhere.

"The KVR started up in 1901 or thereabouts and the CPR signed a 999-year lease for it around 1915. The KVR pretty well operated as a separate railway until the CPR made it part and parcel of its operations in the 1950s. No, they don't go over the Coquihalla no more. In the winter of '61 –'62 avalanches wiped out three bridges in one day, and the CPR said, 'That's it. We're closing that bitch for good.' Know what springs to mind first when I recollect the KVR? Strangely enough, not the Coquihalla. What I remember most are the points along the line. The construction engineer was crazy about William Shakespeare. He named the points Romeo, Juliet, Jessica, Lear, Portia, Iago, and Othello."

HE NEEDED A JOB

"I WAS SIXTEEN years old in the summer of 1928 and I needed a job. So I took myself down to the rail office in Penticton and said I was willing to be anything, a wiper or a callboy. Those were lowly jobs but they got your foot in the door. The super didn't seem too interested so I mentioned that my father and grandfather were railroaders in Manitoba. That was a big plus in them days. Generations of the same families worked for the CPR and their kids got the first nod when jobs opened up.

"The super said he'd take me on if I was willing to be an apprentice fireman on the run over the Coquihalla Pass. I didn't know zero about the pass so the super filled me in. He said it was up in the mountains and the grades were so steep that it got real hairy at times. He leaned forward like this, across his desk, and looked me square on the eye. 'The fact is, son, it's so hairy on the express runs that we tie the crew inside the cab. So they won't get thrown out on the curves.

"I lit out of his office fast. A couple of weeks later I found the courage to write to my father and tell him why I hadn't taken the job. I was worried that he'd say I was chicken. He wrote back that he'd laughed himself silly when he read my letter. Then he wrote the words that convinced me I'd been right in not taking the job. 'The railway would never rope its crews in on that run. There's so many wrecks and injuries up there, the crews need every chance they can get to escape.'"

Affairs of the Heart

Before World War I a trainload of joyous newlyweds, members of a religious sect, supposedly embarked from Toronto to Niagara Falls for a mass honeymoon. I say "supposedly" because the man who told me the story couldn't provide details nor is it recorded in railway archives. It was one of numerous instances where someone I interviewed referred vaguely to a story they'd once read somewhere. There were also several references to mail-order brides — seamstresses, and shop girls who journeyed west in response to farmers' urgent pleas in lonely hearts' ads. No mail-order brides crossed my path.

Neither did anyone who could lend credence to the hippy wedding story. A woman in Kamloops, B.C., said a couple were married on a train en route to Jasper in the 1960s: the bride's dress was covered, neck to toe, in flowers and the groom, a draft dodger, thought he looked his best draped in a Viet Cong flag. A man in Montreal related a similar tale: in his version, the ceremony took place en route to the Gaspé and both parties were bedecked in floral arrangements.

In all likelihood the bizarre hippy wedding never did take place, en route to Jasper or anywhere else. Still, the trains have had their share of incidents involving love, marriage, and assorted affairs of the heart.

A SISTER'S PRACTICAL JOKE

"TAKE A gander at this. Our wedding picture. Me and Marg and people belonging to our two families. My brother Hugh's the one in the dark suit. He came from Fredericton for the wedding. On the right, the chubby girl, that's Marg's sister, Betty. The practical joker. When they were kids in Regina, Betty put Dodd's Laxatives in her aunt's aspirins. She was always tying tin cans to the tails of her neighbours' dogs. She'd phone up the corner grocer and say, 'You got Robin Hood in a box?' He'd say, 'Yes, I have.' Then she'd say, 'Well, let him out. He's suffocating.'

"On our wedding day, June 11, 1937, Marg and me kept an eye on Betty. We didn't think she'd do a joke at the ceremony, but with Betty, you couldn't be sure. No, no. She didn't do nothing. Everyone threw rice and Marg's dad drove us to the station. We were going to Vancouver, the Sylvia Hotel. We had a drawing room on the Transcontinental and, mark my words, I planned to make that drawing room our honeymoon suite. Marg was nervous, all right. Like a cat on a hotplate. S-E-X was a no-no before we married. She was a good Christian girl who'd blush scarlet if she even heard a dirty word. Marg asked me to step outside while she washed up and changed. She had this romantic picture in her head. Her lying in bed in a frilly outfit and me slipping into the dark room and joining her.

"I sat in the smoker, finishing a pack of Player's. I wasn't as nervous as her but I had the jitters. Me and Marg were engaged three years and on one hand I could count the number of times we kissed. Suddenly, the porter sticks his head in. He says Marg's bawling and is there anything he can do to help. I hurried back to the drawing room.

"Marg was on the edge of the bed. She wasn't crying anymore but her eyes were red. Her blessed sister — Betty, the practical joker — had snuck into her suitcase the day before the wedding and sewn the clothes together with a needle and thread. A blouse was sewed to a skirt, stockings to a sweater. Her frilly outfit was sewed to a collection of underthings.

"Too cruel to be funny. Marg was really upset and could've throttled her blamed sister. I got scissors and a razor blade from the porter and she sat there, cutting the threads. Yeah, sure, we had our honeymoon night but that joke of Betty's spoiled the mood."

THE DETERMINED NURSE

"LOVE OR desperation. I can't say for sure what made her do it. All I can say is she was one stubborn lady. She'd been with the Red Cross overseas and when I ran into her in 1943, she was crossing Canada in the middle of January, completely unfazed by the blizzards and freezing weather. Bodywise, I'd say she was bony and tall. I have no recollection of her face but I remember she wasn't too pretty. Not ugly, not a clock-stopper, but no candy-box model.

"Her boyfriend was a teacher at Lac la Biche, north of Edmonton. Some idiot had mixed up his Army papers and he'd been written off as a reject. Now the mistake had been found and he was expecting to be called up any day. The plough was clearing the track ahead and we were crawling from town to town. Then the plough busted down ten miles south of Lac la Biche. We twiddled our thumbs. The nurse said she was pushing forty and her younger sisters were married and living in the Maritimes. She said her parents were happy because, at long last, the teacher was marrying her and she was hurrying to Lac la Biche so they could tie the knot before he was shipped Heaven knows where.

"We were gazing out the window and saw a couple of Indians clamber down and start putting on snowshoes. The nurse jumped up. She tapped on the window and gestured for them to wait. The next thing I knew, she was out there. They talked and smiled, and one of the Indians climbed back on the train. She'd paid him to rent his snowshoes and look after her luggage. The last I saw of her, she was stumbling off towards the town, a couple of feet behind the other Indian. Love or desperation. It beats me which it was."

THE NB SPECIAL TO CHATHAM

"FOR A YEAR and a half, every weekend, I rode the NB Special to Chatham when I was courting Bonnie. What's the 'NB' stand for? Numb Bum. We called it that because the railway, no matter what shiny, high-powered diesels they used, persisted in tagging these hideous, antique coaches on behind them. No padding on the seats. You shifted and shifted your rump and, after the first hour, it still felt like the wood was driving right through your flesh.

"Every agonizing weekend. I was a visual arts teacher in Toronto, Bonnie a health-planning consultant. I'd leave work early on Fridays and fortify myself physically and intellectually for the trip: I'd buy two packages of wintergreen Life-Savers and a copy of *Maclean's* at Union Station.

"The railway schedule promised a three-hour journey. It lied. The train was never less than thirty minutes late, sometimes up to an hour. Bonnie said that in twenty years of living in Chatham she never heard of the train being precisely on time or, God forbid, ahead of schedule. Another frustration. The railway seemed to have a strong commitment to not telling people over its PA when the darn thing was going to be late. On one hair-freezing cold night Bonnie stood waiting for me for an hour before a voice meekly announced over the PA that the train had been cancelled and hadn't even departed Toronto.

"Weekend after weekend, Toronto to Chatham. You had to be love-sick to stand the trip. Or, for that matter, to stand Chatham. A great town for fruit farmers but not much action for a visual arts teacher. I'd take Bonnie to a movie Saturday night or to Momma Rossini's Italian restaurant. And the Bluebird Café. Sylvia Tyson wrote a song about the Bluebird. She's a Chatham native and, judging by the fact that she hasn't resettled there, she must feel it's as invigorating as I feel it is.

"I wish I could use the old joke and say the best thing about Chatham was the train to Toronto. Were it only so. For all the escape it offered, it took every fibre of discipline I possessed to drag my bones to the station Sunday night and deliberately subject myself to another Numb-Bumming ride."

A School Outing

"I was in Grade Eleven at Govan High School in 1946. Govan's in southern Saskatchewan, a farm town. The kids from Nokomis invited us up for a day and everyone in our school went, sixty kids. It was only thirteen miles to Nokomis but that was a big deal, going so far by train. The gals wore their nicest saddle shoes and bobbysox and the fellows drowned their hair in Wildroot Cream Oil. We were a pretty tame lot. One brave guy smoked a cigarette and two other brave guys sipped a beer in the washroom. The girls huddled and giggled and whispered about which nifty guys from Nokomis they'd seen at the last track meet. When we got to Nokomis, we had a skating party and a dance in the school gymnasium and then we trundled down to the station. Going home, the talk was of new Nokomis romances started and old Govan romances ended. The following summer, the Nokomis kids came by train to Govan. For a treasure hunt. I don't doubt they did and said the same things that we did and said coming and going on the railway. Just like our mothers and fathers had and, maybe, some of our grandmothers and grandfathers, too."

MOTHER WAS A SKINFLINT

"THE REVEREND Andrew Rodden married Joe and I at First United Church. In April 1939. My parents didn't give us a wedding present and they didn't send flowers. Two months after we married, they said they'd treat me to a holiday weekend in Penticton, as sort of a late wedding gift. Joe had to deliver sawdust on the Saturday so I went without him. Father had a steady job as a CPR gardener and they could've afforded a better present. But Mother held the purse strings in our family and, the truth is, she was a skinflint. The original frugal Scot. The hill up Fraser Street in South Van was quite steep and we had to climb it to shop or go to school. Wasting five cents on streetcar fare was considered a terrible sin. Mother dragged herself up the hill to make deposits. A quarter, fifty cents, whatever she saved went in the bank and never came out.

"I should've realized what the Penticton holiday would be like. For starters, Father had a CPR pass and he got the three of us on the train free. We sat up all night because his pass didn't cover the berths. A man carried a tray up and down the aisle, selling chocolate bars and pop. When he came near, Mother pretended he didn't exist. The trip lasted twelve hours and we didn't have a speck of food. By the time we reached Penticton, I could've eaten a horse, dead or alive. But Mother was appalled by the restaurant prices. We had tea and toast for breakfast and that's all.

"Penticton in June was a lively spot. Movies and dances and picnics and boating. We didn't do any of that. It cost money. We window-shopped and, when our feet got sore, we sat on a bench and stared at the lake. No lunch. Mother bought each of us an apple for dinner. I had a $2 bill on me. Saturday night I tossed and turned and dreamed of food. I couldn't get away to spend the $2. I was eighteen and married but, to save money, Mother had the hotel put a cot beside my parents' bed for me to sleep on. I didn't dare buy food in front of her. I'd never have heard the end of it if I had.

"Sunday morning, more tea and toast. No lunch, more walking and sitting, and apples for dinner again. It's a wonder I had the strength to walk to the train depot. Father went into the smoking car and lit up a cigar. An Arabella. That was the only fun he allowed himself. Two five-cent Arabellas a week. We stayed up all night in the coach again and Monday morning we were in Vancouver. When I got to my place, I rushed into the kitchen and started cooking a meal. I couldn't wait for it to be ready. I ripped open a box of shredded wheat and devoured nearly the whole package.

"Mother passed away five years ago. Ninety-seven years old. She had $30,000 in the bank. I often think of the fun she denied herself, just to leave $30,000 for somebody else to spend."

SHE LOVED TRAINS WITH A PASSION

"When I was young, I had a girlfriend who was crazy for trains. Audrey was her name. I was earning fair wages as a plumber's helper but that girl nearly bankrupted me. She'd have this craving every Friday to board a train and go off somewhere for the weekend. Grand Forks, Nelson, Trail, it didn't matter to her where. It was the train ride that was important to her. And, by God, she'd be in a stew if I didn't get a private compartment. I was a slow learner. It was a while before I cottoned on to how strange she was. Audrey loved trains with a passion.

Literally. On those trips, when we were in the private compartment, she couldn't get enough of me. The minute the train left the station, it was into the sack.

"Now here's the strange part. When we were at different towns, staying in hotels, nothing happened. She made excuses. Headaches, upset stomach, an aching back. I couldn't lay a finger on her. Same in Vancouver. Even at the drive-in I couldn't get to first base. But on the trains...the sky's the limit. This carried on for a year. I'd skip meals and work extra hours so I could pay the train and hotel bills. I really liked Audrey, even if she was strange. Why we broke up, I don't remember. I do remember that she dated a friend of mine for a few months. No, sir, I never did ask him if he took her on train rides. But, you know, I didn't see them around the usual places on the weekend."

BROOMS DIPPED IN OIL

"TOM WAS the first man I saw in Moncton. I walked down the platform and he was by the station door, dressed to the nines. He wasn't movie-star handsome and he didn't notice me, so I don't understand why he made such a big hit. But he did. That was sixty years ago and I still recall his watch-chain and vest and how his shoes glowed. I walked through the station and caught a bus to my aunt's boarding house. She and her husband rented strictly to bachelors. Eight men in a big, old Victorian house. They were a decent bunch but she was worried that with a young lady on the premises they might not stay decent.

"At suppertime the first day, Tom came in. He was downcast and I bet he didn't say two words during the meal. His parents had promised to be on the train and they hadn't shown up. The dirty buggers always did that to him. Promised to visit and didn't bother to send a message saying they wouldn't be there. Selfish, mean people. Thank the Lord, Tom wasn't like them. He was a quiet, generous man who never hurt a living soul. After I got my job in a store, I moved in with a family down the street. Tom dropped by now and then and took me out for walks and pretty soon we'd decided to marry.

"Tom was a railroader. A fireman. The men he worked with wanted to do our wedding up good. They had a banner over the church door. I can't recollect the exact wording but it was something like, 'Love Keeps Us On The Right Track.' They hung lanterns and there was a huge wreath shaped like a locomotive. The church was near the railyard. The trains all blew their whistles at the same time when the ceremony began. And the arch, oh, it was wonderful. The men had brooms dipped in oil. When we came out the church door, they lit them and we walked under.

"Tom was sore at his parents for not coming to the wedding. They sent him a letter full of excuses and a present. A bedspread he shoved in a drawer and never used. Right after the wedding, we took the train to Niagara Falls. We had a lovely time. The Falls were beautiful. Lots of water. On the way home, we stopped at a small town in Quebec. Tom spotted this steam engine on a siding. A relic from the last century. He clamoured over it as though he had discovered a gold mine. I pretty near had to get a team of horses to pull him onto our train. For years and years, I teased him about it. He always grinned and teased me back. He'd say he liked that old steam engine better than Niagara Falls and our honeymoon."

Family Feud

"There's a flagstop at Hixon, south of Prince George, and the Dayliner stops to pick up this old man. The car's full of tourists — Germans, Limeys, Yanks, some languages I can't make heads nor tails of. The Dayliner climbs the Thompson River canyon and follows the Fraser beyond Lillooet, and the scenery's out of this world. Anyhow, the old man sits with me and says he's a trapper. He sure looks it. Red flannel shirt and Kodiak boots and a white beard and there's a gouge under his eye where a chain-saw brushed his face. He's got sandwiches with him. Because the BCR charged him seven bucks for eggs and sausages the last time he went to Vancouver. He was telling me about his lake, and how some hippies were stealing from his traps.

"Then a guy in a green leisure suit gets on at Quesnel. As he passes us, he says to the old man, 'How you doing?' and the old man answers, 'Okay.' After the guy's gone, the old man says, 'That's my son.' 'Oh, yeah,' I say. 'I'll change places if he wants to sit here with you.' His face goes stiff. 'Forget it. I ain't sat with him for twenty years and I ain't about to start now.' He tells me his son married against his advice and he won't forgive him.

"The two of them, father and son, ignore one another till we're at the BCR terminal in North Van. We're getting off and the son comes up and says, 'Where you off to, Dad? Visiting your pal Bill?' He says it in a friendly voice. The father says nothing. Just stares into space and walks to the parking lot. As he gets a taxi, he turns to me and says, 'Don't go feeling sorry for him. I'm not as bad as you think. He ran off with his step-sister. He was thirty-two and she was seventeen and till God punishes them in the next world, I'll punish them in this one.'"

AN UNHAPPY JOURNEY

"MY FATHER and mother were married in Vancouver in 1942. They spent their wedding night in an apartment above the grocery store my father owned on the North Shore. The next morning a government man banged on the door. He said that just because you don't live with the other Japs across the inlet in Jap Town, you shouldn't think you're immune to the evacuation. He insisted that they go to Hastings Park that very day.

"Hastings Park was where they usually kept horses and cows — for the race track and agricultural shows. Hundreds of Japanese families slept and ate in the barns until they were assigned to trains taking them into the Interior or further east. As you know, the Canadian government declared 25,000 Japanese Canadians security risks, even if they were born here.

"Four days after they were married, my parents were sent to a sugar-beet farm in southern Alberta. My mother was very self-contained. She prided herself on not showing her feelings. Yet my father surprised me a while back when he described the trip. He said she broke down the minute she got on the train, and she cried practically all the way to Lethbridge."

The biggest event of the year for many youngsters was
the arrival of the circus train in their community.
(York University, Toronto Telegram *Collection.)*

When Klu Klux Klan leader J.J. Maloney journeyed outside Edmonton in the late 1920s and early 1930s, he was usually accompanied by hundreds of devoted followers. The "Free Speech Specials" went to small Alberta communities where the black-suited Maloney gave hate-mongering speeches and led the crowds in hymn singing and prayer.
(Glenbow Archives.)

Prairie settlers were often in need of extra dollars. Many earned money collecting and shipping buffalo bones to fertilizer factories in eastern Canada. These homesteaders are loading bones at Moose Jaw, Saskatchewan, in the late 1800s.
(Glenbow Archives.)

The ad campaign the federal government and the CPR mounted to lure potential settlers to western Canada was so effective that many trainloads of Americans migrated north. These Colorado families arrived at Bassano, Alberta, in 1914.
(Glenbow Archives.)

The promise of free land and escape from religious persecution brought Doukhobour settlers to western Canada. These members of the Russian sect landed at the CPR station in Winnipeg, Manitoba, in 1899.
(Glenbow Archives.)

It wasn't very fancy but it got the job done. Passengers on a northern Ontario spur line travelled to the main line in a horse-drawn wooden shack.
(Archives of Ontario, S-15927.)

Opposite page, top: ▶
This photo taken of first-class compartments shows that it was possible to travel in comfort and style. *(Canapress Photo Service.)*

Opposite page, bottom: ▶
On the other hand, most early-day immigrants found themselves travelling aboard the bargain-rate colonist cars, which were cramped and agonizingly uncomfortable. Passengers are shown reclining in upper berths during an 1885 trip to the West.
(Canapress Photo Service.)

Tying the knot in bygone times often meant spending your wedding night on a train. This bridal couple received a rousing send-off after they drove to the station in Vulcan, Alberta, circa 1919. *(Glenbow Archives.)*

Going to school in many isolated northern Ontario communities
used to mean learning the three R's in converted railway cars.
Every year the rolling schoolhouses would be spruced up
before taking bush-dwellers' children aboard. On the right
is Fred Sloman, the founder of "School on Wheels."

(Courtesy Canadian National.)

◀ *Opposite page, bottom:*
Eager to entice more tourists to the Rockies, the CPR added open-air observation
cars to its mountain runs in the late 1800s. This photo was taken during the 1920s,
before the Depression all but dried up the flow of tourists.

(Canadian Pacific Corporate Archives.)

The Duke and Duchess of York joined members of their Royal party
seated on the front of the CPR locomotive that bore them across Canada in 1901.
The Duke and Duchess later became King George V and Queen Mary.
(National Archives Canada, PA-11848.)

The Prince of Wales *(centre)* catches a breath of fresh air outside Ottawa
during a 1924 Canadian visit. The prince was en route to the ranch he owned
near High River, Alberta. *(National Archives Canada, PA-138861.)*

The train bearing King George VI and Queen Elizabeth passes through the Rockies
on the Royal Visit of 1939. A telephone system on board allowed their majesties
to make daily calls to their little daughters at Buckingham Palace.
(Canadian Pacific Corporate Archives.)

Oh, what a lovely flap this train caused. When the CNR promised locomotive 6060, a.k.a. Bullet-nosed Betty, to the city of Stratford, an angry Alberta railwayman protested, and succeeded in having it transferred out West instead.
(Courtesy Canadian National.)

Bullet-nosed Betty travelled under her own steam back across the country in 1979, after a seven-year stint as an excursion train from Toronto to Niagara Falls. The determined ex-railwayman who lobbied for her return to her original home, still dreams of a tourist run for the old locomotive in the Rockies. Many would agree with his comment: "It seems a shame to have Betty in a museum when it could be chugging up and down a line." *(Courtesy Canadian National.)*

No one would have believed it happened if someone hadn't snapped a picture.
A Grand Trunk locomotive travelling along an Ontario line in the 1890s shot up
the nose of an idle snow plough and came to rest on top of the plough extra.
(Public Archives Canada, C-24682.)

Construction crews often had to make their own entertainment deep in the bush.
These off-duty workers had a bit of fun faking a hand-cart accident at a Fort Frances,
Ontario, railway camp. *(Archives of Ontario, S-11408.)*

Nobody mentioned it at the inquest, but some railwaymen believed the sighting of a Ghost Train preceded this head-on collision. Seven men died in this wreck outside Medicine Hat, Alberta, in 1903. *(Glenbow Archives.)*

A large group of curious on-lookers turns up at the site of a McKellar, Ontario, train wreck. *(National Archives Canada, PA-25114.)*

The star-crossed Turbo slams into a meat truck at a level crossing near
Hawkesbury, Ontario, on its maiden Montreal-Toronto run in 1969.
London Free Press photographer Ernie Lee won a
National Newspaper Award for this picture.
(London Free Press.)

It was a miracle that no one was killed. That's what everyone said after a CP freight carrying thirty-nine tankers filled with hazardous materials derailed at Mississauga, Ontario, in November 1979. *(Toronto Star.)*

THREE EXTRA MALES

"WHEN BARB and I got married, I went to great lengths to ensure that the fellows I'd gone to law school with at the University of Saskatchewan didn't play any tricks on our wedding night. Before the ceremony, I hid our luggage in a locker at the train station. After the wedding, I steered Barb into the day coach and we sat near the window and waved to the wedding party on the platform. I had booked a compartment and I figured that if they saw us in the day coach they wouldn't find the compartment and do anything wild. The train pulled out and Barb and I went to the compartment. 'We really fooled them,' I said as I opened the door. Well, of course, we hadn't.

"The room was decorated with toilet-paper streamers and balloons and three of my best friends were sitting there, grinning from ear to ear. Mel Shannon, Ted Hughes, and Bob Nesbitt. They said we were all such good buddies that they'd decided to go on our honeymoon with us and had bought tickets through to Banff. I didn't believe them but Barb did. As the train left Saskatoon behind, and our friends settled in, she became quite apprehensive. Then we came to Delisle, about twenty miles west of Saskatoon. All three jumped up and departed. Another friend, Bob Fraser, had followed the train in his car to pick them up. Barb was so happy when she realized she wouldn't have three extra males hanging around our honeymoon cottage in Banff."

BORN LOSER LOSES HIS WATCH

"I REMEMBER the night my father-in-law drove me to the station. He's been in his grave fifteen years, God Rot His Soul. It wouldn't surprise me to learn that my conduct that night hastened his departure. Excuse me. I shouldn't be so flippant but, oh, that man loathed me. His daughter, my first wife, was his pride and joy. He was the classic case of the father who was positive his princess had married a born loser. He may have had a point. I lost my job a week before the wedding and Pam and I were in Kamloops to borrow some money. I was young and frightened of him, and I stayed half-cut all weekend. On Sunday night, leaving for the train, he could barely conceal his loathing for me.

"Five feet of packed snow and black ice everywhere. I slipped on the steps and flew into a snowbank. I said jokingly that I'd sue him and make more money than I did collecting UIC. He was not amused. At the station, I raised my arm like this — to check the time — and my watch wasn't there. Pam was fit to be tied. It was her birthday gift to me, an expensive Bulova with a romantic message inscribed on the back. She was sure the strap broke when I fell, and she begged her father to search for it. He promised he would. Not for my sake. For hers.

"He drove home and froze his knackers digging in the snow. Couldn't find it. He froze them again the next day. He cleared half the yard and nearly wrecked his back. When Pam phoned from Vancouver and mentioned I'd found the watch, he cursed a blue streak. Where was it? When I was on the train, I took off my coat and jacket and saw this bulge on my arm, way above my wrist. Before supper, feeling no pain, I'd gone into the bathroom at my father-in-law's to wash up and I must have pushed it there."

PETE AND THE WIDOW

"PETE WAS our hired man and we were sorry to have him go. He was strong as a bull. Never had a sick day and didn't trouble us at night. He kept to himself in the shack over by the coulee. He was with us from November 12, 1936, to November 22, 1939. Three years. Boys from all around Red Deer were joining the military and Pete felt he had to go too. I took him to the station in the pick-up. Five minutes before the train pulled out, the widow came galloping down the platform. I couldn't believe my eyes. I didn't know they even knew one another. She lived on a quarter-section down the road from us. If people had known she and Pete were linked up, there would've been a scandal. He was ten years younger, and her husband wasn't in the ground but six months. In front of my eyes, they had a big scene. Kissing and crying and promising letters. Anyway, Pete went to the war and was killed. The widow sold the farm and moved to Edmonton. A year or so ago, there was a story in a farming paper — the *Western Producer*, I think. It said she was well-known for her kindness to soldiers during the war. It said she'd go to the train station and bring them to her house for home-cooked meals. No hanky-panky, nothing like that. It didn't say nothing about Pete. I'd lay bets, though, that whenever she'd go to the trains, she'd see him in the young boys she talked to."

BLUSHING BRIDE

"RUSSELL AND I were married in Victoria on May 23, 1944. We had tickets for the train to Edmonton, or rather we thought we did. At the CNR office in Victoria, the ticket man said, 'Yes, yes, I know May 24th's a holiday but I can still guarantee you a berth.' We took the midnight boat to Vancouver on our wedding day, and the next night at 7:30 we boarded the Transcontinental at the Main Street station. The train was packed. Every seat, every berth, booked solid. The conductor strode up to us in a crowded car and inspected our tickets. He got really, mad. 'What are you two trying to pull? This says May 25th, not May 24th.' We'd been so busy with the wedding plans that we hadn't checked the date. While Russell was explaining, the conductor spotted my corsage. He turned his head and raised his voice for the benefit of the men in the car. 'Oh, you're honeymooners. Well, we'll find a place for you to sleep!' He got a big laugh. I was a shy girl, and I turned beet-red. He did find us a lower berth; to this day, I don't know how. We were awfully grateful to have it. But those words of his — 'Oh, you're honeymooners. Well, we'll find a place for you to sleep.' I must've blushed down to my toes."

TWO LONELY PEOPLE

"CLAIRE WALLACE wrote a gossip column for *The Toronto Star* in the 1930s — 'Over the Tea Cups.' The name sounds silly today but back then it suited the times perfectly. I had this mental picture of little old ladies in Rosedale sipping tea and munching watercress sandwiches, oblivious to the Depression swirling around them. My brother Donald read the column religiously. Why, baffles me. We lived in Lancaster,

Glengarry County, and our life, on the farm, was a million miles removed from Claire Wallace's house parties and horse shows.

"One January day, Donald read that a young English girl was spending several months in residence at the Lord Simcoe Hotel. She said she'd like to live in the country. Donald was lonely and sensed that she was too. He wrote her and she wrote back. They spoke over the telephone and they exchanged little gifts. In the spring, he hinted in a letter that they might make a good married couple and he invited her out to the farm.

"A date was arranged. Donald was to meet her at the station in Lancaster. The day before she was to arrive, he was overcome with the idea that he had to see her before she saw him. He travelled to Toronto and got on the same train she was taking. An English girl caught his eye. A blonde beauty, I gather. That's her, he thought. That's the girl I'm going to marry. The blonde left the train at Brockville. When the train was approaching Lancaster, he spied another English girl. Nice-looking, yes, but what a horrid personality. She was pushy and loud; very rude to the coloured porter. Her manner of dress astonished Donald. Mannish pants, boots and shirt, and she surely must have believed she was plunging into the wilderness for she had a Boy Scout knife on her belt. Poor Donald — she was the only woman who alighted at Lancaster.

"Donald stayed glued to his seat. At the next stop, he telephoned a friend in Lancaster and had him go tell the girl he had been called away to Montreal. She wrote him once or twice, but he didn't answer. He still feels guilty about being such a coward and avoiding her. Nonetheless, he's glad he hadn't bowed to temptation and done more than merely hint at the possibility of marriage in his letter."

THE END OF
THE GOLDEN AGE:
THE GREAT
DEPRESSION

I f there was a barometer that could be used to gauge the economic prosperity in the 1920s, it was the state of the nation's railways. Crack express trains — the Continental Limited, the Trans-Canada Limited, the International Limited — drew elegant new coaches around the country. Both the CPR and the CNR reported record passenger and freight traffic and, inspired by the boom, they upgraded the colonist cars by installing lunch-counters.

Then came the stock market plunge of 1929. The Golden Age of Canadian railroading was abruptly terminated. Locomotives began hauling lines of empty boxcars, and the passengers were largely of the non-paying variety, freight-hopping hobos raking the land in search of work. Faced with declining profits, the railways cut branch-line services and tried vainly to clear the hobos from the trains.

My uncle was one of those hobos. Long after the Depression ended, he would sit beside our kitchen stove, rolling his own cigarettes and describing the hard times he'd had. "Riding the rods sure rattled your bones," he'd say. "You'd be down 'neath a boxcar, hanging on for dear life, while the train acted like she wanted to throw you

189

off." I remember him saying that he'd travelled with a youth who lost both legs when, trying to climb onto a rolling freight, he'd slipped under the wheels.

My uncle's term on the road lasted two or three years; the Depression itself endured for an intolerable ten years.

BAKING FOR THE KIDS

"I LOST my Jenny in 1952. She was a fine woman. She felt so sorry for folks worse off than we were. In the 1930s, we'd take little trips out of Winnipeg, just to look at the countryside. Jenny would bake cookies and cakes and wrap them in wax paper. When the train slowed down, she'd throw them to kids at the side of the tracks. They were badly off. Mostly Indian kids but some whites too. The kids knew when the trains came by and they'd be waiting. Jenny wasn't the only one, you see. Other passengers would throw candies and magazines out, and once, I remember, a man threw a handful of nickels and dimes."

A GREAT COUPLE

"YOU MET the greatest people on the road. People you planned to meet again so you could repay their kindness but you never did. Like the Slomans. Fred and Cela. They were the very first to run a railway school in Canada. Pioneers. They started in the 1920s and, all through the Depression, they stayed at it. What the Slomans did was take their schoolhouse, an old CN boxcar, from town to town in north Ontario. Out in the wilds, where there were no regular schools.

"The Slomans didn't turn up their noses at anybody. Not even a filthy bum like I was in them days. I was walking on the tracks at Stackpool in '34, and their boxcar was on a siding. The missus was standing beside it, washing clothes in a copper tub. She asked where I was off to and I said Toronto. Her husband poked his head out the door and said why didn't I stay for lunch. I hadn't eaten for a while; I was in no position to say no.

"The school part of the boxcar had wooden desks and a Union Jack. A car battery was on the floor. They used it to operate a beat-up projector and show movies about beavers and birds. Not just to kids. Not by a longshot. The Sloman's were such good people that they showed movies to trappers and railroaders and whoever else was around at night. They taught grown-ups how to read and write. Night classes with kerosene lamps burning and a potbelly stove blazing in the winter. The part of the car the Slomans lived in was small. But it was clean and done-up okay — lace curtains, flowers in clay pots, a big bearskin rug on the floor.

"I recollect Fred Sloman saying that on a school day the kids would come from all over the map. In the winter, some walked miles on snowshoes. In the summertime, some paddled canoes to school or hitched rides on handcars. One mother brought her three kiddies six miles on foot to be in a class. The four of them sat at the back, asking questions now and then. At three, they left with the others. As they got to the door, the mother turned to Fred Sloman and said, 'My kids were nagging me to give them an education. I'm so glad they finally got one. Thank you, very much.' The family tramped off into the bush and never came back.

"I was reading in the paper that the Canadian government gave Anne Murray a medal for her contribution to Canada. I've got nothing against Anne Murray but, I ask you, what did she do for this country except pay big taxes because she's filthy rich? The government ought to track down the Slomans, if they're alive, and give them a medal. I wasn't the only Depression bum they took in for a meal. And all those years of roughing it in the boxcar, educating people at twenty below, should mean more than singing love songs for money in Las Vegas."

RIDING THE RODS

"THE ONLY men who rode the rods — I mean the actual rods under the boxcars — were men with no sense. Your uncle did it all the time? Sorry, I don't mean to insult your family but those rods are no place for a human being. I'm speaking from experience. I tried them once coming out of Halifax. The rods are these steel bars, fourteen, could be fifteen, feet in length. They're arranged close together and a man can stretch out on them. A man, that is, who doesn't mind having his fillings shook from his mouth or eating dust and cinders all the way to where he's going. One time was enough for me. If your uncle did it regularly, well, all I can say is he was a braver man than Gunga Din."

STARING AT SIX SLEEPING MEN

"IN 1934 I had a free ride from Montreal to Vancouver. No pay, just meals and a ticket in exchange for guarding six Chinese businessmen from Boston. I haven't a clue why the government felt they needed guarding. They were well dressed and respectable-looking and they obviously had no intention to jumping off and beginning life over again in a Prairie hamlet. There were three guards — myself, another McGill student, and the head guard, a CPR employee who was older than us and extremely conscientious.

"He insisted that we stay up all night watching the Chinese, then take turns napping during the day. After a couple of nights of staring at six sleeping men, the other student and I were thoroughly fed up. The other student was studying medicine at McGill. Somewhere west of Regina, he decided to do something about the absurd night-shifts. The head guard made a pot of coffee every night on the potbelly stove at the end of the car. The medical student strolled over to the stove and dropped a sleeping pill in the pot. We both had a good night's rest, and the head guard didn't wake up until very late the next morning in the Rockies."

OFF TO OTTAWA TO TELL BENNETT

"ALL I OWNED was in my dufflebag — a clean shirt, a blanket, a change of underwear, a razor, and a bar of soap. Notice, I said all that I owned and not all that I needed. I didn't have food or money. Like the others on the On-To-Ottawa Trek, I counted on the government or ordinary people's generosity to keep me from starving. Yeah, that does sound chancey, but what choice did I have? I couldn't stand the relief camp another minute. The Almighty R. B. Bennett had determined that the best place for a single unemployed man was a tarpaper shack. With a straw-filled mattress, no windows, and it was so cramped you bumped into each other. The food was fifth rate. And for sweating your butt off clearing brush, you were paid the grand sum of twenty cents a day.

"So we blew our corks. Fifteen hundred men turned up at the CPR yard at the foot of Gore when Slim Evans and the camp reps spread the word that we should go to Ottawa and tell Bennett what he could do with his camps. April 9, 1935. That's the date we gathered. The CPR didn't want us there but they didn't want a riot so the railway cops moved aside and let us on the first east-bound freight. The lucky ducks crawled into vacant boxcars. I was on the roof. With a few hundred other guys. I knew plenty of them by sight; I was the strike committee rep at the Boston Bar camp. The train we were on only went to Kamloops. We had to sleep in a park there overnight and grab a freight through the mountains in the morning.

"The tunnels were a nightmare. Hot as Hades and cinders blowing in your eyes and nose and mouth and dirtying your clothes. Up front, close to the engine, they damn near choked to death. Their faces were black. Yet we weren't discouraged. The general feeling was anger and frustration, and yet we had this camaraderie, the sense of all being in the same fix. In the parks, or wherever we slept, there'd be guys playing accordions and mouth-organs and sometimes a chorus, hundreds of men, sang our unofficial anthem, 'Hold the Fort.'

"We hadn't eaten much in Kamloops — mostly coffee and sandwiches the strike committee rounded up from local citizens. Golden was amazing. It's a wonderful little town on the B.C. side of the Rockies. When the train pulled into Golden, dozens of people were in a field next to the tracks — cooking dinner for us in old bathtubs and washpans. Beef stew with dumplings. Well, maybe it wasn't beef; some said it tasted like moose but we were famished and grateful and it didn't matter.

"We were an eyesore when we hit Calgary. I had a suit, but many of the men had on khaki fatigues, the camp uniforms we despised. The fatigues were filthy from the cinders and the men were unshaven and dog-tired. We paraded down the main streets and people on the sidewalks cheered. There wasn't any cheering when we got to our destination, the Exhibition Grounds. They made us sleep on the floor in a Stampede display building. With loose straw for bedding. Like cattle.

The Alberta relief office wouldn't give us food money so we picketed it. Smack in the centre of Calgary, kitty-corner to the Hudson's Bay. They gave in and provided food vouchers for 25-cent meals.

"The ride to Medicine Hat was pure misery. Pouring rain all night and those of us on the roof were drenched and cold. At Medicine Hat, a tough police sergeant who usually chased rail-riders off trains nearly broke down when we arrived. He looked at the massive line of strikers leaving the train and said to one of our leaders, 'This isn't fair. They're all so young. What's happening to this country?' The relief office handed out groceries, and we waited at a picnic ground, in the hot sun, for our clothes to dry. Then we swarmed onto a freight headed for Regina.

"And that's where the On-To-Ottawa Trek finished. Bennett messaged the Mounties and the police at Regina — Don't let those bastards reach Ottawa — and they obeyed his command. Anyone with half an eye and an arsehole could see the riot coming. We were bucking the system and gaining strength. Every town and city we passed through, more men joined us. On the day of the riot, I was at an exhibition baseball game; the park had let the Trekkers in free. After the game, I returned to the old building at the Exhibition Grounds where we were staying. I was in charge of making sure my group behaved themselves. We had strict discipline on the trek; no drinking and no hooliganism.

"The riot was downtown, a couple of miles away, and most of the Trekkers were at the Exhibition Grounds when it occurred. Evans tried to stage a meeting in Market Square and, the way I heard it, the Mounties and the local police tried to break it up. They pulled Evans off the platform and went at the strikers with clubs and boots and charging horses. A policeman was killed and several Trekkers injured. We woke up the next morning surrounded by Mounties in steel helmets, aiming guns at our building. I'm not stupid and I'm not insane and I didn't go outside and neither did anyone else. The temperature climbed to 90 above, and the Mounties were hugging the hedges for shade.

"We negotiated with government men for three days and we finally agreed to halt the trek if we were fed and given passage home. We travelled to the west coast in day coaches and with enough sandwiches to supply a small army. So many that we donated the leftovers to striking longshoremen in Vancouver.

194

"Evans was in the Regina jail for a while. He was a labour organizer in Alberta after that and he was hit and killed by a streetcar in the 1950s. Evans was a left-wing radical. I wouldn't call him a Communist, although Bennett believed he was. Myself, I did belong to the Communist Party. I quit in the 1950s when I realized the party had become too narrow-minded. As for the other Trekkers, most didn't have a political ideology. They were, plain and simple, a bunch of good-hearted, honest young men who hopped those trains hoping like hell to do something that might improve their lives."

A HOBO'S FAVOURITE SHELTERS

"WE HAD our favourite shelters. Mine in Toronto was an abandoned warehouse off Spadina with a broken padlock. Outside the city, my favourite was the milk-stop at Emily. I'll explain. Mornings they'd load forty or fifty cans of cows' milk onto the 8:40 to Toronto and, twelve hours later, the railway sent the empties back. There was this platform, next to the tracks, made of big, thick cedars. The local farmers built it in the early 1930s. Before they built it, the trains went all over the place, picking up cans at level crossings. With the platform, farmers trucked their milk to one stop.

"The platform was about ten feet long and maybe ten or twelve feet wide. Enclosed on three sides. I'd have to share it sometimes. I only minded if one of the guys smelled bad. I said to this guy who smelled bad that he needed a dip in a river. He took a little bottle of women's perfume from his pocket and sprayed himself. Then he really stank. Like a two-bit whore. He must've stolen it because perfume wasn't on a hobo's must-buy list. I wonder if the platform's still there. If it is, I bet nobody sleeps under it. Not with UIC and welfare and all the hand-outs the government gives people these days."

MOONLIGHT MAGIC

"THE FARE on the Moonlight was sixty cents, to Winnipeg Beach and back. Leave the city early on a Saturday afternoon and come back around midnight. Unless I missed the train home. Then I'd sleep on the beach or, if I had dough, chip in a dime to rent a crummy cabin with some other guys. No need to tell you what I did at the beach. I was fifteen. I chased girls. I'd cruise the dance pavilions and the roller-rink they had out there in the 1930s and try to cozy up to girls who probably knew as little about sex and were just as scared as I was.

"The Moonlight had a kind of magic to it. I was a North End kid and, like everywhere else, the North End was suffering hard. Two hundred men lined up all night if a single job came open. Families existed on food vouchers and some begged in the streets. Suicide, alcohol, and broken homes. My dad was a beat cop, and he heard a hundred sad stories a day. I'd ride the Moonlight and all the bad things somehow evaporated. I recall trips where the train was filled almost entirely with teenagers — boys and girls, laughing and horsing around. Some couples practised jitterbug steps; some guy might sit like he was hypnotized, memorizing the words from a Sinatra song sheet. The conductor ran himself ragged, trying to keep us quiet.

"At times, there were Jewish families on board. They had cottages at the lake. We had a saying that made them laugh: 'Give Us Back Winnipeg Beach, We'll Give You Back Jerusalem.' Jewish families, but no Dew-Drops. I never saw one of them on the Moonlight. The Dew-Drops were Winnipeg's toughest street gang. Double-breasted suits and they blocked their fedoras in a certain way, sort of Western-style. They hung around poolrooms and their idea of fun was to beat people to a pulp. I don't know why the Dew-Drops stayed in town. Maybe it was because there were no pool tables on the Moonlight."

NOBODY BOTHERED THE WOMEN

"I CROSSED the country nine times in the summer of 1933. Riding the freights, Halifax to Vancouver, Vancouver to Halifax. I picked berries in the Okanagan, shovelled grain in Brandon, and carried eighty-pound bags of cement for five bucks a day in Calgary. My dad rode the rods too. In 1908. He quit a strip-mine in Kansas and stayed on the freights until he homesteaded north of Red Deer.

"Naw, the rod-riders weren't rough guys. The odd one was but most were nice, ordinary fellows. The young punks today, they're rough. If you got in a boxcar with one of them he'd rip your head off for drug money. In the Depression, men helped each other. They'd tell you where the best soup kitchens were or who might have a bit of work for you. The Catholic priests were great. Go to church and you'd be sure of some bread and a piece of cheese.

"The women — nobody laid a finger of them. There were a few winos or whores, but most were on the trains because they were hoping a new city meant new luck. There was a water tower on the main line at Fort Macleod. Me and two buddies were resting under it, waiting for a freight, when this young woman came along with three tykes. She was scared to death. She'd never ridden the freights. She was heading for Vancouver, where her husband was working on the docks.

"I spotted a passenger train stopping at the depot. I walked over to it and asked the conductor if he could spare a little food for the woman and the tykes. They hadn't eaten all day. 'I can't do that,' he said. 'I'd lose my job.' I went back to the water tower. Ten minutes later, the passenger train crept by. The conductor was on the platform between two cars. He threw us a chunk of roast beef and half a loaf of bread. You hear tales of railway thugs beating the daylights out of railriders but I never seen it. All I seen was guys like the conductor, doing whatever they could."

FURNITURE MIX-UP

"IT WAS LIKE the Wallace family train. Mom and Dad and me and my two sisters were in the coach, and everything we had was in boxcars behind us — five cows, three horses, twenty chickens, four sows, and a rooster in one boxcar; our dishes, furniture, and toys in another. When the train rounded a bend, we'd look back and see the boxcars and hope the animals were okay. At Minnedosa, a hobo tried to sneak into the animals' boxcar and the railway men chased him off. Dad said he was hungry and likely would've stolen a hen. To make a long story short, we got where we were going and the railway switched our boxcars to a siding. Our new farm was empty; the man who'd sold it to us even stripped the doors from the frames. We slept on the bare floor and went into town the next day to have our things trucked out.

"While we were with the animals, Dad had a railwayman open the other boxcar. He looked inside and then came over to us. 'Pretend everything's hunky-dory,' he said. 'Don't let on it's the wrong stuff.' What happened was, they'd loaded somebody's furniture in Regina that wasn't ours. Dad couldn't face having us all spend another night on the bare floor so he brought it all home. A day or so later, after cursing the CPR day and night, he told the station master about the stupid mistake. The station master discovered our stuff had gone to a second-hand dealer in Weyburn and we had a shipment he'd bought sight unseen. By the time the CPR traced it to him, he'd sold ours. So he said, keep what you got. Which was fine with us. It was newer and better and there was a terrific CCM bike that us youngsters really enjoyed having."

THE TWO COMMANDMENTS

"VIC AND I rode the freights from Timmins to Vancouver. Vic's my brother; he was the mayor of Hamilton for fourteen years. In 1936 we were restless kids who wanted to see the country. We hadn't much money but the hobos made certain we didn't starve. We'd go into a jungle and they'd share their beans. We stooked hay for money and did temporary factory jobs. The emphasis should be on the word 'temporary.' A boss would pick Vic and me out of a crowd and hire us because he could pay kids fifty cents less than he paid adults. At noon, he'd go back to the crowd at the gate and say, 'Any of you fellas willing to work for a boy's wages?' Two guys would say yes and he'd sack us on the spot.

"There were two Commandments I heard many times on the road — 'Thou shalt not go into Field' and 'Thou shalt not mess with Capreol Red.'

"Field is the first town west of the Horseshoe Tunnel in the Rockies. It had a reputation of being a company town and the company was the CPR. If a hobo was caught by the Mounties on the streets, he was nailed for trespassing on CPR property and jailed for thirty days. You had to leave the freight after the tunnel and walk miles through the bush to catch another train on the far side of town.

"Capreol Red — he was a sweetheart. They don't make them like that anymore, thank goodness. He acquired his nickname because he had red hair and he patrolled the railyards at Capreol, Ontario. The rail-riders hated him. If he nabbed you on a freight, he'd belt you with a two-by-four. They used to have iceboxes in some of the old boxcars. To keep fruit and things in. The boxes had clasp-locks on them. The story goes that a band of hobos lay in wait for Capreol Red and stuffed him in an icebox. He was found dead weeks later. What's the name of the TV show? 'Believe It Or Not.' I'm inclined to believe it. He had enough enemies."

HIDING BEHIND THE BUREAU

"LISTEN TO THIS. In hard times, you do what it takes to survive. My old man was forced to sell the farm at Yorkton and buy a smaller place at Biggar. We didn't like to move but we didn't sit and mope. We packed our belongings and loaded what we could in boxcars. I'll skip the details. The nub of it is, when we were at the depot, watching them load our stuff, my old man boosted me up into the boxcar. We were low on cash and every penny counted and he figured he could save paying my fare.

"I crouched behind a bureau. I had jelly sandwiches and a milk bottle full of water. I hid until the CPR slid the door shut. Twelve years old, and scared shitless. It took hours for the train to quit Yorkton. I had a pile of *Star Weeklies* and *Family Heralds* stashed in a drawer. I read the comic pages and glanced at the pictures and ate my sandwiches. The heat was roasting and I drank the water long before we got to Saskatoon.

"Anyway, the CPR opened the boxcar with the animals at Saskatoon to water them. Somebody's pigs ran out. Not ours, somebody else's. Four or five of them broke through the flimsy crates. The yard gang darted around, pulling pigs from beneath trucks and trains and wherever and, for the fun of it, some passengers hunted them too. I remember one porker never was found. Somebody probably put it in a safe place until he could claim it later for Sunday dinner.

"Now hear this. While the pig-chase was on, a rail man decided to inspect the inside of the car I was in. Why he did was beyond me. He couldn't have guessed I was there. But he came in and caught me hiding behind the bureau. He took me to his foreman, who took me to the conductor, who took me to my parents. The conductor and my dad had a long chat and after it was done, I finished the trip next to my parents. I thought my old man had paid my fare. Guess again. Years later, Mom told me he'd said I was his brother's orphaned kid, a regular juvenile delinquent, who'd stowed away because I was yearning to be on a farm. The conductor had agreed that a healthy farm life might be just what the doctor ordered for me. He passed a hat and collected my fare from other passengers."

MONEY ON THE SIDEWALK

"How I stumbled upon the money was incredible. I had hitched a freight ride to Owen Sound, hoping for farm work. There wasn't any. I was downtown and wondering where my next meal was coming from and, all of a sudden, there it was. An envelope filled with money lying on the sidewalk outside the Bank of Nova Scotia. Three hundred and forty dollars. It never entered my head to go into the bank and ask who'd lost it. I'd been up against it too long. Finders keepers. The sun was shining on me at last.

"I had lunch and bought a suit and took the train to Toronto. I had a purpose for the money. I'd go home to B.C. and live off it as long as I could. I had this image in my head: me walking into my mother's house in Salmon Arm carrying a bag of groceries — steaks and roasts and biscuits and Ceylon tea.

"Did I have a time going to B.C. Three sheets to the wind when I got on at Toronto and the same when I got off at Salmon Arm. Everybody was my pal. I bought drinks and slipped them twenty bucks if they had a hard-luck story. I bought stocks in a useless mine and I tipped waiters and porters till their eyes popped. I was off the train twice. Winnipeg and Regina. Shacking up with women. Footing the bill for food. By the time I got to Salmon Arm I wasn't flat busted but I was close. I didn't take Mom the steaks and roasts but I did take her the biscuits and tea."

PUNK WITH A KNIFE

"I CLIMBED into this boxcar at the CPR yard in Ottawa and a young punk was crouching in the corner. 'I don't want company,' he said. 'Bugger off.' I said, 'Want it or not, sonny, you're stuck with it.' He sprang to his feet and flashed a knife. About six inches long. I didn't argue. I jumped down and walked along a line of cars looking for another open door. A railway cop lunged at me from between two cars. Before he could tell me to clear out, I told him there was a maniac with a knife who needed his attention. He went to the boxcar and climbed right in.

"I expected the punk to come flying out and land on his ass. Either that, or the cop would be bleeding like a stuck pig. Five minutes went by and I was beginning to think the punk killed the cop. Then the cop jumped out and walked my way. 'It's all right,' he said. 'He's my nephew.' Well, wasn't that lovely? The punk with the knife could've been Jack the Ripper but it was all right to let him be there because he was his blessed nephew. Gawd, no wonder I have such a lousy opinion of men in uniforms."

CLOTHING FROM ONTARIO

"IT WAS a Sunday and soon as church was over we drove to the station and waited on our sleigh for the relief train. It seemed like all of Biggar was there. Friends and neighbours, farmers and townsfolk, and strangers from Unity and Wilkie and other places. Two hours we waited, sleighs, Bennett buggies, and half-ton trucks stretching two miles. It was February and bitter cold, and everyone was gaping down the track and up at the sky, worrying about which might come first, the train or the blizzard that was predicted.

"The train was first. The trainmen opened the Biggar boxcar and the volunteers distributed the clothing. Out of cardboard boxes. Mother got a dress, brand-new, and father a suit that was chewed at the cuffs and had a cigarette burn. I got a shirt and gum boots. I hated that shirt. It was a bright green you could see a mile off, and I'd only wear it doing chores or in the house. Never to school, no matter how my mother tried to make me.

"My folks had mixed feelings about the relief train. They were glad to have the clothes but, at the same time, they resented the Easterners who donated them. 'How come we're suffering and there's folks in Ontario so rich they can afford to throw things away?' That's what my dad said. And, the fact is, a lot of people on the Prairies in those years agreed with him."

NEW FACES
ACROSS THE
LAND

They arrived by the tens of thousands — the English, the Ukrainians, the Germans, the Scots, the Chinese. People from different backgrounds, bringing different values and customs with them. The bulk of the two million newcomers to this country arriving between 1881 and 1911 journeyed west on torturously crude colonist cars. The Canadian government not only offered them free land but it sweetened the pot with an unusual proposition: one shilling off the boat and train fare if they supplied their own mattresses. World War I and the Dirty Thirties restricted the immigrant flow (only 158,500 people came here between 1931 and 1940) and, after World War II, even tighter regulations made it more difficult to gain entry.

The immigrants' initial experiences in Canada weren't always happy. To be sure, acts of generosity were frequent. A Swiss woman told me a Canadian family on the train cared for her three children splendidly when she suffered from a near-paralysing depression. A Polish man said an elderly couple he met en route to Winnipeg drove him 80 kilometres to a homestead south of the city. Yet there were incidents of coldness and bigotry. A transplanted Jamaican told me he was given a jolting reception when he arrived in Halifax. As he sat on the Ocean Limited, a passing stranger said angrily, "We've got our quota of jungle bunnies in this country. Go back to where you came from."

COOKED THEIR OWN MEALS

"I'M EIGHTY-SIX years old and I came to Vancouver from Montreal on a colonist train in 1911. There was a big, wood stove at the front of the car and we had to cook our own meals. My mother had fruit and vegetables in a wicker basket and we had other things in old biscuit tins. People would climb aboard with food for sale — hard-boiled eggs and mince pies and fresh bread. And milk. Yes, there was small bottles of milk that mothers bought for their babies.

"There were four of us — my mother and father and me and my older sister, Florence. My father had farmed in England and we were going to Salmon Arm in the B.C. Interior. My brother had written and said the land there was good. Nearly everyone in our car was from the Old Country so we got along perfectly, despite the hard seats and the cramped space and the noise from the babies crying. Nobody argued over whose turn it was at the stove. We did it all very orderly, and at times some families pooled their food and cooked it all at once.

"There were no berths. I remember that the clearest. How hard it was to sleep. The porter pulled down this rack and two men crawled up there for the night. The women and children slept on the hard benches under them — the same unpadded seats we'd sat on all day. We'd just curl up and lie there and suffer through until the dawn.

"The ringing bells on the locomotive. They had bells on trains then and Florence and I thought Canada must be a very religious place because we kept on passing churches. Florence got in trouble once. My father didn't permit secular reading on a Sunday. He caught her with a novel — it wasn't very spicy by today's standards — but he was mad and he made her wash our dishes for the rest of the trip."

THEY WEREN'T STUPID

"I'LL TELL YOU a story but I don't want you to get the wrong idea. My parents weren't stupid. If you gave Father a hammer and nails and a stack of lumber, he could build you a house as beautiful as any in Saskatoon. All the measurements exact. He can add and subtract in his head, without touching a pencil. Mother could size up strangers the same way. She'd listen for two minutes and know straight off if they were no-goodniks. Right on the button, every time.

"So don't say they were dumb Ukrainians. Ukrainians are no dumber than anyone else. Now here's my story. They migrated to Saskatchewan in 1927. Born and raised on farms near an isolated village, and they never read a newspaper or heard the radio. An Indian got on at the 'Peg. They couldn't take their eyes off him. They'd never seen a brown-skinned man. The Indian shoved a piece of chewing gum in his mouth. What kind of strange food was he eating? My father was astonished. He turned to my mother and said, 'Indians don't swallow their food like white people do. Their stomachs must be different. They chew their food like cows chewing their cud....'"

AND ONE WAS MISSING

"THE Chink Trains are what they were known as. They had Chinamen on them who'd been building roads and dams in Quebec and the Maritimes. Fifty, maybe sixty on each train to Vancouver, where they'd be plunked aboard boats for China. These were the ones who the government said couldn't stay in Canada. They'd been on temporary contracts. I was a guard. A buck a day and meals, which was okay for the 1930s. I boarded at Windsor station on this particular trip and it was smooth sailing up to the Manitoba border. Our head guard, Carruthers, had said we didn't have to worry none because they didn't want to escape. They had money in their pockets and they were going home to buy wives and land.

"I'm not sure exactly where it happened. A station west of Winnipeg; maybe it was Souris. Anyhow, Carruthers comes into the smoker and says there's supposed to be fifty-four Chinamen and we've got fifty-three. One of the bastards slipped off at Winnipeg. Just then this other guard comes in and says the problem's been solved. Guess what he did? He got off at Souris or wherever it was with two other guys and went down the main street and grabbed the first Chinaman they saw. He was screaming and kicking and jabbering so much that they had to give him a few slaps in the mug to shut him up. I often speculate on whether he had a wife, and if she ever did find out that he didn't come home for supper that night because he'd been shipped off to China."

PEOPLE LIKE US

"THE POLITICIANS never looked upon the Chinese as real people. They were like emotionless machines to them, good for hard labour, and if you killed a few hundred, like they did building the CPR, so what? I guess I wasn't much better myself. I didn't look at them as machines, but I didn't think they were exactly like you and me. Not until 1928 and the trip from Toronto to Vancouver.

"Gordie Harris and I were hired to guard fifty Chinese coolies returning from construction jobs in Bermuda and Barbados. They had plenty of cash on them but I gather they preferred to go back to China rather than pay the government its blood money, the $500 head tax every Asian who wanted to settle in Canada had to pay.

"Gordie and I got bored somewhere on the Prairies and decided to play a trick. The Chinese slept on bedrolls in a colonist car and every man-jack of them wore the same black cloth slippers. When they were sleeping, we snuck around the car, taking one slipper from each coolie and switching it with someone else's. In the morning, sheer chaos. Everyone was yelling and running around trying to match up the slippers. They weren't mad. They were laughing and having a good time, like you and I would. If the politicians who thought they were unfeeling machines could've been there, I know they would've changed their minds about the Chinese."

MUMPS AND A LOST RING

"THIRTEEN SLEEPERS filled with Hungarian refugees left Montreal for Chilliwack on January 9, 1957. Most of the passengers didn't speak English and I felt a real sympathy for them. I knew what it was like to be in a strange country. The year before, I'd moved from Jamaica and had to fumble about the streets of Montreal asking policemen for directions and feeling like a fish out of water. These folks, the

Hungarians, were worse off than I was. I'd only emigrated to take a job as a porter so I could earn more money. They were running from violence and death and the Russian tanks. I could go home when I wanted; they couldn't. I wouldn't say they were depressed but they weren't dancing. On this train, there were mostly young women and two or three had babies.

"Which reminds me. One lady with a three-year-old had the mumps. The conductor put her and the child in a bedroom and I was instructed to give her special service; meals in the room and make sure the utensils were washed separately. A doctor boarded at Winnipeg and said mumps were contagious. Son of a gun; I didn't know that. When we reached Chilliwack, an ambulance took her to the hospital. The other passengers were going to an old army base. As she was getting off, the mumps lady suddenly grabbed and hugged me. For being so kind to her. I nearly died. For days afterwards, I was feeling my throat and peering in mirrors. Luckily, I didn't get the mumps.

"Funny, you're asking me about that trip. A little while ago, it came up in a conversation at my doctor's office. On that same train, a girl dropped a ring down a sink while washing her hands. She was almost hysterical. Tears in her eyes and wringing her hands. I got a wrench and unscrewed the gooseneck. As I was doing it, the government translator said why the girl was so distressed. It was the school ring her boyfriend gave her before the Russian invasion and now the boyfriend was missing and maybe killed or jailed. The ring was in the pipe. I yanked it out and she was the happiest woman on earth. She swore she'd never take it off her finger again.

"I was at my doctor's office on Lasalle Avenue. I'd been his patient eighteen years and he had a red-haired receptionist for nine of those years. I was early for my appointment and the receptionist and I got to talking. She mentioned she was a Hungarian refugee and I said I was on a train in January 1957 with Hungarian refugees. Her eyes lit up. She was on the same train. We didn't remember each other but we both remembered the girl and the ring. She was the receptionist's friend. She said the girl's boyfriend hadn't been killed or jailed. He escaped through Austria and joined her in Canada. They got married and had two babies and they still live out West somewhere."

LIKE A NAZI CAMP

"THE GOOD Lord was mad at me. Otherwise, he wouldn't have punished an Irishman by putting him in with a bunch of Ukrainians and Poles. An awful trip, it was. From Montreal, where the ship docked, to Winnipeg, where half the Uks in the universe planted roots. They packed us in the car cheek by jowl. Big, broad-shouldered men who'd knock your block off if you glanced at their women.

"It baffles me why they weren't skinny-minnies. They didn't eat full meals. They ate hunks of bread and bites from thick sausages. Garlic. The stink would've killed a weaker man. I'd lie in my bed (if you can call a slab of hardwood a bed) and hear them farting and snoring. How I'd wish the trip was over so I wouldn't have to smell garlic and I could hear the sound of English once more.

"At Winnipeg, they herded us into the immigration hall on Water Street. 1928, and I'm telling you, this set-up could've been a blueprint for a Nazi camp. The immigrant car was moved from the main line to a siding behind the hall. We were led right into the building by government guards. There was a high, wire fence a mountain goat couldn't scale and the doors were locked so none of us could go into the streets. The staff ordered us about as though they were SS trainees. 'You, over here!' 'You, sign this!'

"The building was brick and three floors high. Cafeteria and toilets on the ground floor, men's and women's dormitories on the second and third. The bunks were three tiers high and each had a thin mattress and a grey flannel blanket. The dormitories throbbed with the stench of disinfectant. Trust me, you get a very peculiar odour when you mix disinfectant and garlic in a hot room. I slept near an open window.

"The idea was to hold those of us travelling to various parts of Manitoba until we caught connecting trains. It also gave the officials another chance to check us over. There were about fifty men on our floor, including some who were in trouble with immigration. An interpreter said to me that the chap on the bunk below mine had claimed to be born on such-and-such a day and his papers had a different date on them. He'd been in the hall two weeks. It was either Dauphin for him, where he wanted to farm, or back to Poland.

"After one night, I left for Swan River. The coach was half empty and not a whiff of garlic. In fact, I recall a woman seated by me smelling of flowery perfume. Half an hour out of Winnipeg, a man left the washroom and sat by himself. The Pole from the bunk beneath me. How he snuck out of the hall was a mystery. But there he was, big as day, travelling to God knows where, for he didn't get off at Dauphin. I just smiled to myself. I didn't think of reporting him. No skin off my nose. Besides, he looked like a halfway decent fellow, and Canada needed all of those it could get."

STUMP-FARMERS

"DEEP COVE to Victoria isn't very far, twenty miles as the crow flies. But in the early days the Interurban Railway was very important. We travelled to school on it. One hour every morning from my family's farm to downtown Victoria. The Interurban began before World War I. Premier McBride drove the last spike. The coaches were painted dark green and had bright red tops. The line went broke in the 1920s when people started using their own automobiles and public buses.

"Twenty or so youngsters rode to school on it. Immigrants' children. The conductors kidded us about our homework and our farms. They called the immigrants 'stump-farmers,' because they cut down the huge Douglas firs and, if the stumps were too big to pull out, they planted their crops around them.

"The kidding didn't upset me. There was one girl it sure did upset. She hated being in the sticks. She thought people in town looked down on her. One conductor was very cruel. He would tease her until she almost cried and then he'd walk away laughing. Her mother got on the train and gave the conductor a piece of her tongue and he never spoke to that girl again.

"Life was hard for the immigrant families. The wives sometimes were on the Interurban with us. They'd have baskets and baskets crammed with homemade butter and vegetables that they'd sell at the Victoria market for a few extra dollars. Another thing. Scott and Peden's store would send salesmen out to Deep Cove on Fridays to take orders for groceries. The following Monday, the groceries would be delivered on the afternoon train. Don't you wish stores still did that today?"

LOOKING FOR LAKE LOUISE

"I'M NOT a violent person but there's a man in Jasper I'd love to punch. It's been twenty years and his face is clear in my memory. He resembled Vince Edwards, the TV star. Tall and very dark. I was an immigrant, new from Hungary, and going to Kelowna to be with my brother. When the train stopped at Jasper, the 'Vince Edwards' man was on the platform, wearing hiking boots and a Mackinaw. I told him it was a dream of mine to see Lake Louise. He pointed across the street and said the lake was four or five blocks behind the post office.

"'Do not let the train concern you,' he said. 'They have to load fuel and will be here well over an hour.' I was young and naive and I foolishly believed him. I wandered the streets searching for a glimpse of the lake. I stopped a couple for directions but their English was worse than mine and they didn't understand. I think they were German. After twenty minutes, I heard the train bell and ignored it. I went into a store that sold tourist trinkets and the clerk burst out laughing when I asked which street the lake was on. He said I couldn't see Lake Louise from Jasper even on a cloudless day; it was over one hundred miles south, beyond the mountains. It goes without saying, the train was gone when I got to the station, and so was the Vince Edwards look-alike who set me up."

BELLYACHE REMEDY

"THE OLD woman in the berth above me came down with a bellyache west of Regina. A German immigrant pulled his suitcase from under his seat and said he had some tea that would fix her up. The suitcase was fascinating — jammed with herbs and spices and teas and whatnot, wrapped in brown packages. The old woman said for him not to bother but he persisted and she took a handful of dried leaves from him. She said she'd have the steward make her a cup of tea from them.

She didn't tell him but she told me later what she did. She flushed the leaves down the crapper. She didn't trust foreigners. She was frightened that he might have given her some sort of addictive drug."

FASCISM IN CANADA

"NOVA SCOTIA. A beautiful name for a beautiful province. I remember gazing at the green landscape and the pretty towns flashing by and remarking to my wife that I was certain we'd made the right move coming to Canada. 'This country's not like Germany,' I said. 'This country's at peace with itself.' We were fleeing Hitler's Germany. The Brownshirts and the Jew-baiting of the 1930s; we were Jewish and we didn't want our children to grow up in that atmosphere.

"I fell into a conversation with a salesman in the dining car. A gentile. He lived in Toronto and, he said, because I was a Jew I should steer a clear path around the Balmy Beach district. Young people without work were roving the lakefront in gangs, beating up Jews. There was the Swastika Club, whose members broke up Jewish family picnics and scared Jewish bathers from the water. Young Jews were patrolling the boardwalk armed with pick-handles and lacrosse sticks and fighting the Canadian fascists.

"Canadian fascists. I left the dining car depressed. It hadn't occurred to me that a sickness like fascism could be transmitted to North America. It seemed a peculiarly European disease. I only went to Balmy Beach once before the war and I felt uncomfortable. Always looking over my shoulder for Brownshirts. It's strange. I was at the beach last summer and I still didn't feel right. It's as though the ghosts of the 1930s are lingering around the boardwalk."

THE SALESMAN WAS CLEVER

"THE IMMIGRATION agent in Halifax informed me that the railway was very obliging and allowed a new Canadian to take his goods on the train free — furniture, tools, farm machinery, livestock, everything and anything. My wife and I were walking the streets and we saw, in a store window, a kitchen cabinet precisely like the one she had and adored in Prague. Glass doors and made of walnut. Why not buy it? We had just enough money and the railway would ship it free. I paid the money and arranged to have it delivered to the railway.

"I was at the immigration office and happened to read a leaflet. Holy cow. The free freight for new Canadians only applied to second-hand or used goods. The agent hadn't said that. I telephoned the furniture store and said I couldn't afford the shipping charges, I had to have my money back. The salesman said he'd take care of it so I could have the cabinet shipped free. A clever fellow. He painted it a loathsome colour, a bluish green, and made a terrible job of it. The railroad looked at the cabinet and figured no one would do such a thing unless it was ugly and old underneath the paint. They shipped it, no charges, and my first month in Winnipeg, in our tiny apartment, I scraped the paint and applied a lovely new coat of varnish."

WHAT WILL BECOME OF ME?

"I WAS well-off compared to other immigrants going west. I spoke some English, I had a little money, I owned a shirt and tie. Some of them were so shabby and broke. Nevertheless, I was as concerned as they were about the future. Mile after mile, gazing at the mountains and trees and plains, I pondered, What will become of me? Whatever did, I knew it would be a far cry from pre-war China. We were German and my father managed German-Asiatic Bank branches. Seven-bedroom houses, five or six servants and, as a child, I had my own stables of Mongolian ponies.

"I had been to Germany before I migrated to Canada. I'd seen people climb out of the rubble in Hamburg — from cellars beneath destroyed buildings — and go off to work. I was eighteen and I wanted a better life than that. I borrowed a little money and went to Toronto. When I decided to go on to Vancouver, friends said, 'Don't go there; it's the wild frontier, an uncivilized backwater. There's no jobs, you'll starve.'

"I sat on the train and thought, What if they're right? What if there are no jobs? There were plenty of DPS — Displaced Persons — aboard and I recall looking at them and thinking some of us would do all right, but which ones? Still, I knew that regardless of how bad it was in Vancouver, at least I wouldn't be climbing out of rubble.

"I stayed in a boarding house in New Westminster and found work in a sawmill. All the immigrants were in the mills — Poles, Germans, Chinese, Hungarians. The wages were good and I saved my money and went to school. I eventually got a white-collar job. When I retired two years ago, I was the manager of the Bank of Montreal branch at English Bay."

AGAINST
THE LAW

We called him "Fearless Frank," after a character in the Dick Tracy comic strip. He wasn't exactly a hero to the youngsters in my neighbourhood but we did make admiring jokes about his peculiar passion. Around 1950 Fearless Frank was arrested in Victoria for trying to steal a locomotive. It was revealed in court that he'd committed the same offence before in other Canadian cities. Wearing a railway uniform, he'd climb into the cab of an unattended locomotive and head for the main line, defying the potential danger posed by any oncoming trains.

Since their inception, the railways have had to contend with a broad variety of criminal activities. There have been armed holdups and shootings but, like Fearless Frank's odd inclination, most illegal acts have been of a far less serious nature. Around 1900 the appropriately named Will Steele was caught several kilometres from the Charlottetown yard with his two adolescent sons carrying a potbelly stove from a colonist car. In the mid-1930s a vigorous gang wandered the Prairies dismantling flatcars on isolated sidings and selling the parts to scrap-metal dealers. Bootleggers, prostitutes, and conmen have all done business on trains — and so did light-fingered conductors.

ALI BABA'S CAVE

"MY UNCLE was the worst thief I ever met. Fifty years with the CNR and, Holy Hanna, it's a wonder he didn't bankrupt the company. I'm ashamed to admit he was a conductor. I was a railwayman myself and, to me, the conductors are the salt of the earth — intelligent, honest, dependable. They're like ship's captains. Riding herd over the crew and taking the passengers' problems into account. My uncle — oh, how that man disgusted me. He'd stuff his pockets with silverware and candies and anything that would fit. Far as I know, he never took the passengers' things. Always the railway's. Once, I was laying ties a mile west of the station and I saw him throw a pail of lard off the caboose. Two of his kids scampered from the bush and retrieved it. His crews knew he stole. They didn't report him because he was popular. He drank with the boys and he had lots of off-colour jokes for them. If a guy's popular, they think it's okay if he steals. If he's a miserable creep, they say it's awful and blow the whistle.

"My uncle's house was Ali Baba's cave. Loot, loot, and more loot — CNR blankets, CNR sheets, CNR ashtrays, even bloody CNR toilet-paper. He had a framed picture of the Rocky Mountains in his parlour. Stripped from some station wall. It grated me every time I went over to his place to pick up my dad. Especially the time he bitched about the wreck. A passenger train and a freight hit head-on outside town. He'd gone out with his truck late at night, thinking the clean-up crew might let him haul something off. They didn't. They told him to get lost. What a ghoul he was. People killed and injured and all he thought of was there might be something worth stealing. I thought for sure the railway would get his number before he cashed his first pension cheque. No, sir. They gave him a dinner and ran his photograph in the newspaper. And when he passed away, his obituary praised him to the skies.

"All I've got to say is if they run trains down below, they'd better keep him off them. That man would steal the devil blind."

BAD APPLES

"SOME branch-line conductors in the old days were bad apples. Get on in the bush at night and they'd tell you there's no empty berths. Slip them coin of the realm and they'd find you one faster than you could say 'crap and corruption.'

"Another trick was to pull you aside and offer you a special deal. They'd sell you the stub from the ticket somebody else paid for on another trip. Half price. Though hard cash wasn't always what they were after. I saw a farmer get on with a big basket full of eggs. The conductor ended up with half of them.

"Then there was the chappy in Saskatchewan. He was a beaut. I won't tell you his name or the line he was on. He's dead, but why shame his children? People said he used to have this game going with some of his regulars. He'd toss their fare up towards the ceiling. The money that landed to the left of him went to the company, the money to the right to himself. If money landed in front of him, he'd give it back to you."

PURLOINED CHURCH

"Is THE little Anglican church still in Windermere? The white wooden building? There's quite a tale behind how it got there. Donald was the CPR divisional headquarters in the B.C. mountains in the 1880s. The rail workers who lived there liked their minister so they built him a church. Then the railway decided to move the divisional centre to Revelstoke. There was no church in Revelstoke; the people went to a local school for Sunday services.

"The CPR figured that Donald would become a ghost town. It agreed to move the citizens' houses and belongings on flatcars to Revelstoke. The Anglican poobahs in New Westminster said they didn't see any reason why the church shouldn't be shipped out too. Well, there was a storekeeper in Donald who did see a reason. His name eludes me. I believe it was Carson but I'm probably wrong. Anyway, the storekeeper had done most of the labour and he figured that, when it came right down to it, the church belonged to him. Some of the locals supported his claim. So when the CPR sent a work gang to dismantle the building they were shocked to discover it wasn't there. When the foreman asked a local yokel what had happened, the man said a tornado had carried it away.

"It was no tornado. It was the storekeeper and his supporters. They had taken the building apart, board by board, and shipped it a hundred miles by train and barge, claiming it was only a stack of used lumber. The storekeeper had opened a new place at Windermere, you understand, and some of the Donald people had moved there.

"It didn't take the CPR long to solve the mystery of the vanishing church. The Anglican poobahs said the building was stolen and we want it shipped to Revelstoke forthwith. They ranted and raved for some time but in the end they agreed to let the church stay in Windermere. You know what? The bell disappeared. The storekeeper was out-foxed by another thief. The bell eventually turned up in Golden. The little church there had no bell so a bunch of loyal parishioners raided the Windermere church and made off with theirs. The purloined bell is still at Golden and, unless they've hauled it off to a historical museum, the little white church must still be in Windermere."

LAST TRAIN ROBBERY

"CANADA'S LAST train robbery happened in August 1957. It was no big deal. What I mean is, the robbers didn't make off with a bundle the size of the Brink's job or anything. They'd been fed wrong information. Someone had told them there'd be a huge pile of cash aboard that a Toronto bank was sending to a Windsor factory for its Friday-night pay packet.

"Three robbers in all. They walked into the railyard at Woodstock wearing railway overalls and peaked caps. When they burst into the mailcar, they had revolvers and their faces were covered by bandanas. They tied up the mail-car employees and rifled the bags. No factory payroll. They had to settle for five grand pieced together from packages and letters. Five grand isn't bad, but, like I said, no big deal. Not the kind of haul guaranteed to steep Canada's last train robbery in everlasting glory."

KIDS WITH RIFLES

"OH, SURE, there have been shootings on trains. During the Roaring Twenties, a bootlegger out West pulled a gun on a rival and, I do believe, wounded the man. And in the 1950s an ex-soldier turned strange in northern Quebec and fired a few shots into a passenger car, wounding one or two people.

"I don't recall any murders. Nothing premeditated, like an Agatha Christie novel. The biggest peril was an accidental death caused by kids. Before the railways improved their windows, a .22 bullet could pass through them. Could, and did. The kids didn't mean any harm. They would be hunting rabbits and they'd take a potshot at a passing train. Trying to hit the engine, I suppose.

"I remember a woman eating lunch in the dining car when a bullet came through the window. It took a bit of skin off her nose. What could the railway do about it? Stop the train, chase the kid who fired the rifle, and give him a good licking? I'm afraid not. All it could do was cross its fingers and pray nobody got killed the next time."

THE MAGISTRATE UNDERSTOOD

"MY MOTHER was a court reporter in Timmins and she often came home after a day of working in Magistrate Atkinson's courtroom shaking her head and muttering, 'It's happened again. He falls for it every time.' Atkinson was a circuit-court judge who travelled the north country from his home in Haileybury. He was a balding fellow with a distinct English accent and, I gather, a German mother or a parent enthralled by Wagner, for his first name was Siegfried. He was a rigid teetotaller. During Prohibition he was riding a train and someone slipped a bottle of whisky in his suitcase. Atkinson opened the suitcase in the presence of other people and exclaimed, 'You've got to believe me, I don't know where it came from.'

"Gossip travelled far and fast in the north and everyone soon knew about the magistrate's surprise bottle. For years and years, every once and a while, a man nailed in possession of illegal liquor and dragged into Atkinson's court would assume a puzzled expression and vow, 'With God as my witness, I don't know where the bottle came from.' Inevitably, Atkinson would say, 'I understand how that can happen, my dear fellow. Charge dismissed.'"

HE DEFIED THE BLACK HAND

"BEFORE the Mafia, there was the Black Hand. It turned up in Canada in the 1890s. It was an extortion ring for the most part, and it made life unbearable for many Italian immigrants in Montreal and Toronto. Fort William was also infested. Italians worked on the docks there and the Black Hand sold them illegal goods and ran a violent protection racket. It would send letters demanding protection money and sign the letters with a handprint dipped in black ink.

"About 1932 I was on my way to Fort William to article in a law office. An old man boarded at Marathon. He was dressed in a ragged suit and an open-neck shirt and his shoes were scruffy. As he passed by me, I saw the scar on his cheek. Shaped like a cross. The man beside me said the old man was well-known around the Lakehead. He lived in a shanty and he had been in and out of mental hospitals. His past was intriguing. Apparently, he had refused to pay a Black Hand extortionist and thugs carved the cross on his cheek. He still refused. So they sent a message to Italy and his father was murdered. The man beside me said the old man hadn't been right in the head since. Guilt and remorse. By holding onto a handful of dollars, he'd caused his father's death."

BUSINESS AS USUAL

"SHE WAS a smart girl, I'll say that much for her. Attractive too. Her name was Brenda and when we met in the drinking car, where I was having a ginger ale, she referred to my vocation as 'the reverend trade.' She said things like, 'How's the reverend business?' and 'Wouldn't you be shocked if you ascended to Heaven and the devil was running the place?' We were both travelling from Montreal to Vancouver and, as it turned out, were in the same sleeping section.

"For two nights, she didn't sleep in her assigned berth. The porter said she must have found a boyfriend. In the dome car on day three, I overheard a man and woman talking about her. They said she'd slept with two different men in two different compartments and they were considering informing the conductor. The railway had strict rules against immoral conduct. During the war, you know, porters would literally pull couples from berths if there was hanky-panky going on.

"As fate would have it, Brenda appeared in the dome car shortly afterwards. I sat down and repeated what the couple had said. 'To blazes with them,' she said. 'I have to making a living.' Brenda told me she was a prostitute. A college girl who'd gone wrong and earned money entertaining men in her apartment.

"Her family resided on the west coast and, because she was saving her money to get married, she made up the train fare by selling her services. 'The railroad sells meals and alcoholic beverages, there was a man in the lounge last night selling insurance, and you're doing your darndest, reverend, to sell me religion. If everyone else can do business as usual on this train, why can't I?' She wasn't caught on that trip and I presume no one reported her. Business as usual. A great pity that such a smart and attractive girl would chose to conduct her life in that manner."

She Couldn't Care Less

"SOME FOLKS have got more money than they know what to do with. This lady was around fifty and had good clothes and was travelling to Vancouver. It was in the 1960s and I was a conductor on The Canadian. She said her diamond ring was missing and I thought, Oh, yeah, I bet I know who took it. A bunch of dirty hippies were in the car next to hers. Who else would sneak into her room and steal it? I asked if it was valuable; I mean, really valuable. 'Fifteen hundred dollars,' she said. 'Well,' I said, 'I'll get the police at the next station.' You'd never guess what she said. 'Forget it. It's not worth the trouble.' She hiked off to stretch her legs when the train stopped at the station. The car foreman and I went through her compartment. We found the ring in the sink. It had fallen down the drain. You'd think she'd be overjoyed to have it back. She just murmured, 'Thanks', and put it on. No big deal to her. It was only a $1,500 ring."

ALL THAT GLITTERS

"THE OLDEST confidence trick in the book is the phony gold brick. Right? It's been done so often that no one would ever fall for it. Right? Uh uh. Not right at all. A guy who owned a café in a small town in southern Alberta was going home from Calgary and he met two sharpies. They convinced him they'd been goldminers in Yellowknife and they'd smuggled out enough dust in their lunch pails to make a brick. One of them took him in the train can and showed him the brick in a satchel. He said it was worth $25,000 but they needed cash for a business venture and might let it go for less. Fifteen grand, maybe. The café owner was a cautious soul. He had skimped and scrounged for years so he could afford his dream, a retirement cottage in the Okanagan. He had $13,500 saved.

"Confronted by the sharpies, greed conquered caution. Would they accept $13,500? They hemmed and hawed but said, as he had them over a barrel, they'd take his offer. They departed the train with him. Slept overnight at his house. His wife was as excited about buying the brick as he was. The next morning he withdrew his savings from the bank and the sharpies vanished. Five years passed. The café owner read in the *Albertan* that gold prices were soaring. He dug the brick up in his basement and took the train to Calgary. The assayist gave him the bad news. The brick was solid lead, coated with a thin layer of gold. The café owner couldn't call the Mounties. Buying under-the-counter gold was itself an illegal act.

"His cousin, who told me this story, says the brick's on display in the café owner's TV room — a constant reminder of the follies of greed. In the meantime, the man's skimping and saving for a retirement cottage in the Okanagan."

BLOOD AND DRAMA

"THE PEOPLE who write history in this country have a herd mentality. Like sheep. Like cattle. Or maybe I should say, like pigs running to the same trough at feeding time. These days, Bill Miner's hot stuff. There's been the Grey Fox movie, a CBC documentary, and a spate of articles and a paperback book. Certainly, he does deserve the publicity. I'm not disputing that. What I'm saying, my friend, is the writers all zoom in on the same story and hack it to death and neglect other stories in the same general area that might even be better.

"Let's examine Bill Miner first. When I taught school in the Fraser Valley the kids enjoyed hearing about him. He was a Yankee who spent twenty or thirty years in San Quentin for robbing stagecoaches. He was chased into B.C. after he robbed an Oregon train; a posse on his tail. In 1904 Miner and his gang pulled Canada's first train hold-up. At Mission. They took $7,000 from a CPR express car. Two years later, they hit a mail car at Ducks. They rode off with $15.50 and missed $40,000 that was also in the car. Miner was eventually caught and he died in a prison hospital. So much for Bill Miner. Now I defy you to tell me if this isn't a better story.

"August 2, 1920. I've committed the date to memory because I researched this in the old *Calgary Herald*. August 2, 1920, and three Russian-born ranch-hands get on a CPR train headed from Lethbridge to Cranbrook. They intend to rob the Emperor Pic; he was the King of the Bootleggers and he always had a fat roll of bills on him. The Pic didn't show up, so the Russians — Basoff, Akoff, and Auloff — robbed the passengers instead. Basoff fired a shot at the conductor when he tried to pull the emergency cord and barely missed him. The train stopped at Sentinel, on the B.C. - Alberta border. Before jumping off, Auloff made a fatal mistake — he grabbed the conductor's gold watch, an Elgin.

"The Russians scored only three hundred dollars. Nonetheless, the fact that they hit a train caused the biggest manhunt the West ever had. Hundreds of police and armed farmers. A week after the hold-up, Basoff and Akoff walked into a Chinese restaurant in Blairmore. Thirty miles from the robbery. A squad of lawmen rushed in, guns blazing, real Wild-West style. Akoff and two cops were killed, and Basoff escaped. The Mounties brought in bloodhounds and the fool dogs ran off in three different directions. A CPR engineer spotted Basoff walking on the tracks the next day and the railway cops caught him at the Pincher Creek stockyards, quietly eating a can of bullybeef.

"Okay. Akoff and Basoff got theirs. That left Auloff. He had split from his pals and crossed the American border. In those days the mining and logging camps were full of Russian immigrants. The Mounties assigned a Russian-speaking undercover man to try and find him. He wandered through Washington and Oregon, off and on, for four years and Auloff always eluded him. At long last, he got his break and arrested him in Montana. The fatal mistake tripped Auloff up. The gold watch belonging to the conductor. Auloff pawned it and the Mountie came across it in the pawn shop. Basoff was hung, Auloff got seven years in jail, and the conductor got his watch back.

"How's that for a good tale? Blood and drama. It sure beats the Bill Miner legend all to hell."

THE LADY VANISHES

"IT WAS EASY as pie for me to tell the Toronto woman was a lulu. She had booked an upper roomette and, when she boarded, she decided she'd rather have the lower so she changed the number on her ticket. Took out a pen when nobody was looking and made the seven into a nine. Another woman got on at Winnipeg and said, 'Hey, porter, there's somebody in my space.' I checked the two tickets and, realizing the Toronto woman had changed hers, steered her into No. 7. Then came Regina. I saw the Toronto woman leave the train and I didn't see her return. I figured she was in another car. Lo and behold, when we got to Calgary, I realized she hadn't slept in her bed. She was booked through to Vancouver. Everything she owned was in the roomette — her suitcases, clothing, her purse and wallet.

"We searched the train. Zip. Zero. She was nowhere to be found. So we contacted the RCMP and the Regina police. Had she been murdered walking around Regina? Had she decided to do herself in? I thought I'd never know the answer. I'm only a porter and, unless it was a murder that made the front pages, nobody would tell me anything. My superintendent called me into his office a couple of weeks later. He wanted me to make a statement about her disappearance. She had been found, he said. She was a wealthy lady who simply was fed up with her marriage and wanted to start a new life with a new identity in a place nobody would expect her to be. The Mounties got her when she needed money and went down to the welfare office."

GOLD BARS ON THE PLATFORM

"THE COPS came barging into the pub at Kirkland Lake where I was having a brew. They didn't have their weapons out but they looked pretty upset. 'What's going on?' I asked. They didn't answer. Just gave everyone the once-over and ran out again. What was going on was the Larder Lake robbery. Kerr-Addison shipped its gold to the Ottawa mint by train in 1964. Guards delivered the bars in a truck to the railway depot and the local agent heaped it on the floor in his office. Sometimes, the bars didn't go in the office; they sat out on the platform, in plain view of the guys waiting for the regular train.

"The night of the robbery that's where the gold was. Six bars, worth half a million or so. The agent kept an eye on it but he thought it was safe; the bars were too heavy for anyone to pick up and run with. Two guys in masks jumped the agent and tied him up and lugged the bars to their car. Kirkland Lake's up the road from Larder. The cops went crazy — looking everywhere. What did they think they'd see in the pub I was in? Two guys in masks paying for their booze with gold bars?

"So, anyhow, the Mounties found the robbers' car in the bush, beside a lake. The robbers had flown the coop in a Cessna, a float plane. A clean getaway. The plane was last seen winging over the border into Michigan."

HOW BRANDON GOT ITS BELL

"HOMER LOGAN'S my name and I was a fireman for the city of Brandon in the 1920s. That should explain why I'm familiar with the bell the railway bought for the Brandon fire hall. Well, that isn't exactly right. The railway didn't contribute the money up front. No fat cheque from the CPR or anything. Long before I was with the department, some merchants gathered donations for a bell, a 1,500-pounder, to commemorate Edward the VIII's Coronation. The bell was ordered from New York City before they had the proper amount of money raised. The merchants ran to the city council for help. The city council couldn't come up with the money but the police chief had an idea.

"There was a whorehouse on 17th; Dolly's, I think it was. The railroaders blew their wages there. And so did the train passengers. On hot August nights, they say there was a steady line of males from the 8:30 train to the bawdyhouse. The merchants were pleased to have the police chief's help. Once a week, for months and months, the police raided Dolly's and the girls were fined. The fines were turned over to the bell fund. I won't suggest that the Almighty took a dim view of raising money from an illicit activity. The fact of the matter is, when the bell arrived from New York City it had a very mysterious crack."

RISKY BUSINESS

"THE CRIMINALS are the same, but the nature of the crimes they commit has changed in the past ten years. When I was with the CP police in Quebec in the mid-1970s, cigarettes were a hot item. I remember this gang that hopped on a freight at Three Rivers and hung from the roof to break the boxcar door open. They tossed the cartons out. Hundreds of them. The highway was beside the tracks and a truck kept pace with the train, scooping up the cigarettes like an old-fashioned threshing machine picking up a crop.

"Now the thieves are into electronics. And do they ever take risks to get them. Know those tri-level trailers? The ones loaded with new automobiles? The thieves go on them. Between stops, they go after the radios and stereo cassette players. They've got to have nerves of ice. There's strong winds and the trains belt along at fifty and sixty miles an hour and there's hardly any space between the automobiles.

"Fussy. They don't take just any car radio. Your Escorts, your Chevettes, have radios costing maybe eighty to a hundred bucks — not worth bothering about. You get fifteen big cars on a tri-level, fifteen Lincolns, Fords, Chryslers, and the radios cost maybe a thousand bucks apiece. Good money for a few hours work; worth risking breaking your neck over.

"We had a case recently where some guys hopped on a freight in northern Ontario. They broke the car windows and filled burlap bags with loot. Trains slow down going through Sudbury. They jumped off, and we caught one of them red-handed. The brakeman on that train was surprised. He hadn't seen a thing but, then, the train was almost two miles long so it's no wonder he didn't.

"Ninty-nine percent of railway police work these days is patrolling the yards and investigating freight thefts. Besides radios and cassette machines, they like to break into boxcars on sidings and cart off computers and VCRs. It's the electronic age and, like any businessman who wants to succeed, a good thief has to keep up with what his customers want."

A Class Act:
The Royal
Tour of 1939

As world records go, the standard set by CPR locomotive No. 2850 was unlikely to excite the masses. The stainless-steel-clad engine bore King George VI and Queen Elizabeth across the nation in 1939 and, in the process, became the first train in history to pull a string of cars that far without a substitute locomotive filling in. The record may not have been too impressive but the train itself certainly was. The engine and twelve cars were adapted and fitted specifically for the Royal Visit. The cars were finely, though not luxuriously, decorated. Their majesties' quarters, two spacious cars at the rear, contained full-sized bedrooms, bathrooms, and lounges. A telephone system was installed so they could make daily calls to the little princesses at Buckingham Palace.

The 1939 Royal Visit was probably the most complicated of all Royal tours in Canada. It was conducted almost entirely by train and, as it marked the first visit to our country by a reigning monarch, the organizers tried to ensure that every region had an ample chance to view the King and Queen. Following the tour, locomotive 2850 was placed on exhibit at New York's World Fair. Says CP historian Omen Lavallée: "The train crew and everyone associated with the visit deserved to feel proud. The Royal tour of 1939 was a class act."

The man largely responsible for the tour's success was career diplomat and civil servant Hugh Keenleyside. When I visited his home in Victoria, the first thing he did was show me the inscribed photographs of the King and Queen that their majesties had given him in 1939. The photos hung on a living room wall; more than forty years afterwards, the tour remained a valued part of his daily life.

"I thoroughly enjoyed organizing the tour but, believe me, I wouldn't have wanted to do it again. The planning took eight months. Eight months of late hours and going over every tiny detail, right down to the designs on the cutlery the King and Queen used. Every person in Canada wanted to meet them. Perhaps not everyone, but it seemed that way. Letters reached my office in Ottawa by the hundreds. 'The King and Queen will be tired of official functions so why not have them drop over to our farm for Sunday dinner with our family.' Gifts. The most popular articles were, for some reason, two-gallon tins of maple syrup. We received dozens and dozens. A fellow said in one note, 'Dear King and Queen. If you like this syrup, mail me five bucks and I'll mail you another can.' Dresses. Women from across the country offered to make the Queen a dress if she'd send them her measurements or, better yet, if she could drop by the house.

"Those requests were readily dealt with. We wrote letters saying the Royal couple were unable to accept their kind invitations. If we had any qualms about anything that might not be so readily dealt with, it was Quebec. There were rumours that French Canadians opposed to the visit might cause a fuss. Perhaps a nasty demonstration. As it turned out, the Quebec response was marvellous. *The Empress of Australia* docked at Wolfe's Cove May 17. Every foot of space that could be occupied by a human being was occupied. Thousands upon thousands of loyal subjects were waving flags and cheering and shouting, *'Vive le Roi!'* The din was thunderous. Particularly when the King walked down the gangplank and stepped ashore. A luncheon with Prime Minister King and Premier Duplessis was arranged at the Chateau Frontenac. Along the route, the crowds were enormous and enthusiastic. To my knowledge, not a single negative incident occurred.

"We actually had two trains. The blue and silver Royal train for the King and Queen and their entourage and a green and maroon train for the press and security people. Have you heard about the buzzer?

The engineer of the Royal train had a buzzer in his cab. If he saw a large crowd at a rural depot where the train wasn't stopping, he pressed the buzzer and the Royal couple hurried to the observation-car platform to wave.

"The Royal train left Quebec City on the morning of the 18th. In Montreal, 100,000 people gave the Royal couple a roaring welcome. Mayor Houde opposed conscription and he went to jail during the war but he was a perfect gentleman and host at a civic dinner. Their majesties unveiled the National War Memorial in Ottawa and attended Parliament. In Toronto, they met the Quints. The Dionne quintuplets. A special train — the Quintland — carried the little girls from Callender to Toronto. They sat by the window, blowing kisses to on-lookers. When they arrived at the Parliament Buildings, they ignored the rules of decorum. All five ran across the crowded room and began hugging and kissing the King and Queen. A wonderfully spontaneous moment and the King and Queen loved it.

"Journeying to the West, I often joined the Royal couple in their dining car. The table was beautifully set, of course, with gleaming silverware and crystal and the meals were superb. Generally, there were around ten people at the table, including local dignitaries. The conversations were — how shall I put it? — pleasant. All small talk. How many people live in your town? Have you travelled to any foreign lands? Nothing to stimulate the brain.

"Observing their majesties at close range, I had an insight into their relationship. He ruled the Empire; she ruled the roost. The Queen was an exceptionally strong woman. I don't mean to imply that she was unbearable. She didn't nag and she didn't contradict him. Yet I received the distinct impression that she was aggressive and domineering and, in spite of her famous warm smile, she had a will cast in iron. The King, on the other hand, was quieter and less zealous about his role in the world. He had a speech impediment and I suspect that contributed to his reticence. Whenever I see the Queen Mother on television, I say to myself, Yes, she is a charming and gracious woman but she's cut from a stronger cloth than the press ever gave her credit for.

"Speaking of the Queen, I should mention her hairdresser, Frank Powell. He was a nice fellow, red-headed and large of girth.

Somewhere on the Prairies he had to share his compartment with a slender Ottawa official. The official said he'd take the top berth because he didn't want the bed breaking under Powell's weight and falling down on him. He was only joking. During the night, the top berth collapsed, dropping the official on top of Powell and practically crushing him. Powell had an ugly gouge on his forehead that didn't clear up until after the tour.

"Frank Powell may not agree, but I felt the western portion of the tour went swimmingly. My fondest memory is of Melville, Saskatchewan. Thousands of farmers and their families travelled hundreds of miles in Bennett buggies or using precious gas. They were thin and ragged from the ravishes of the Depression, yet they had tremendous spirit. When the King and Queen stepped onto the flood-lit platform at the railway station, they cheered and sang 'God Save the King.'

"I heard 'God Save the King' many, many times. The Melville version was the most touching but the Calgary version was the most unusual. An Indian band played tom-toms and sang it in Cree. What else do I remember? In Winnipeg, the Royal couple received a gift I had difficulty picturing on the walls of Buckingham Palace — two stuffed elks' heads. Then there was the Vancouver mayor, Telford. He disliked dressing up and he said he wouldn't wear his official robes for the visit. When he heard the crowd roar as the King and Queen approached, he was overcome with emotion. He ran back into his office and put the robes on.

"On May 31, their majesties boarded the Royal train at New Westminster to return to the east. How well I remember Edmonton. Twenty-six trainloads of loyal subjects descended upon the city from the Yukon and Northwest Territories. The usual type of events took place in Ontario. A visit to a Sudbury nickel mine, the grand tour of Niagara Falls. A famous singer, Ann Jamison, met the train at Guelph. She wanted to perform for the Royal couple but her union wouldn't allow it. From Ontario, their majesties went to New York and Washington. President Roosevelt served hot dogs at Hyde Park and the press was outraged. It felt the monarchy had been slighted. Slighted or not, the King and Queen survived the tempest and toured the Maritimes and Newfoundland before leaving for England on June 17.

"Fortunately, there were no major foul ups during the tour. Millions of Canadians saw the King and Queen and strengthened their feeling for the monarchy because of it. See this booklet? It's the official program for the visit. Queen Elizabeth visited Victoria a few years ago and I showed it to her. She was absolutely fascinated. Like every other member of the English aristocracy, she had grown up hearing how splendid the tour had been."

Wrecks and Runaways: Train Disasters

Back in the 1960s I had a neighbour in Montreal who was a retired railway engineer. He said the railwaymen used to call him "Brasso Bob" because, in the days when engineers took personal charge of their own locomotive's maintenance, he polished the brass fittings twice a day. He had such a tidy apartment that I was inclined to believe him. What I had difficulty accepting were the tales of horrific accidents he was forever dispensing — accidents involving head-on collisions, shorn body parts, and washedout bridges. He even insisted that a speeding passenger train had smashed through two walls at Windsor Station in the 1920s and killed several passersby on the sidewalk.

Doing research for this book, I found numerous reports of major rail mishaps in newspaper and railway archive files. Ninety-nine Polish immigrants drowned in 1864 when a Grand Trunk train bolted into a canal near Montreal and, in 1907, seven passengers died and 114 were injured after a crowded train streaking to the Toronto exhibition derailed at Orangeville. Exploding boilers and wooden cars that crumbled easily caused many deaths before improved equipment and higher safety standards reduced rail-travel risks. Reduced, but didn't eliminate them. As recently as 1983, a VIA passenger train was in a dire accident. Five people were killed when a Dayliner approaching Calgary switched onto a siding and smashed into a row of parked tank cars.

While I was digging some of those facts out of the files at the CP archives in Montreal, I discovered that Brasso Bob had been right about the Windsor Station crash, although he did have the details wrong. On March 17, 1909, a locomotive went out of control as it sped towards the Montreal depot: it hit a downgrade at 80 kilometres an hour, destroyed a stop-block, crossed the platform, and crashed through the waiting-room wall. Several cars telescoped over a nearby street and the locomotive sank part way into the station basement. None of the train riders were seriously injured but a passenger's wife and two children were crushed to death in the waiting room.

Bad Luck Louis

"SOME PEOPLE have no luck whatsoever. Louis Hémon, he was a puny little runt who couldn't hear too good and was very shy around women. He was perpetually broke. Somehow he managed to get to Canada from France. He lived on a farm in Quebec and wrote a book about one of his neighbours. After he mailed the book to a publisher in Paris, he borrowed some money and got on a train. His burning desire was to see the Canadian West.

"The train had a stop-over at Chapleau. Louis alighted to stretch his legs. A locomotive roared down the track towards him. He didn't hear the whistle. At the last second, he looked up, saw the train, and lept backwards onto the next track. Like I was saying, some guys have no luck. Louis jumped right in front of a speeding freight. He was buried at Chapleau, in the town cemetery. The year after he died, 1914, the book he wrote, *Maria Chapdelaine*, was a big sensation. Pitiful Louis, he wasn't around to enjoy the fame and fortune."

Did a Foreign Agent Do It?

"A TROOP TRAIN shot off the rails at Arnaud in the spring of 1943. Two hundred soldiers aboard, and it could've been a horrible disaster but nobody was hurt. Not severely, anyway. One guy was asleep and opened his eyes to see wheels spinning six inches from his nose; the underside of the coach slammed through the roof and into his berth.

Another guy saw a chunk of steel rail shatter a window and slice his rifle down the middle. Somebody else was thrown from one end of a car to the other, and another guy's head went right through a window.

"The accident was a popular sight for folks around Arnaud, Emerson, and Altona. Only people who didn't come to look at it were the blind and the retarded. Seven coaches and the engine left the rails and the roadbed was chewed up for 125 yards. Two and three feet deep in places. The CPR police and the army guards wouldn't allow anyone up too close to the scene — to stop looting, and to be sure no local yokels walked away with important evidence. The train hadn't hit anything and the rail line hadn't caved in on its own, so right off the bat the CPR suspected somebody in Arnaud had done something wrong. Maybe on purpose.

"A foreign agent. That was the talk that was around the district. A foreign agent, privy to information that the special troop train was coming through Arnaud, had sneaked into town just before the accident, a little past midnight on a Saturday night. We heard gossip that an open switch was to blame. The troop train raced onto a siding and when the engineer slammed the brakes it derailed. Nobody with the CPR said they opened the switch so the foreign agent idea seemed a good guess.

"For a week the Mounties and CPR police were thick as fleas — stopping cars and talking to people on the street and going out to farms; visiting schools and beer parlours. Always the same questions, 'How and when did you hear of the accident? Who exactly told you?' There was a reward, $500, and scent-dogs came from Winnipeg to try and trace a trail from the switch to whoever opened it. A Mountie phoned his boss from a farm and heard a lot of party-line clicks. He wondered if the neighbours were trying to find out if he had any information on the accident. 'Hell no, that isn't the reason they're listening in,' the farm wife said to him. 'They just want to know if my husband's boozing and beating me again and I'm phoning my mother to complain.'

"I could be mistaken but I don't think they ever arrested anyone. The Mounties asked questions every now and then and the reward poster stayed up for long enough. The foreign agent, if there was one, didn't come back to Arnaud. Unless he was to blame for the wheel falling off my truck when I took grain to the elevator four months after the accident."

FLYING FIREBALL

"I LIVE in Mississauga, where the tankers exploded in 1979. I was close to the accident. Too close for comfort. The CPR tracks are behind my house. Around midnight I was in the bathroom, swallowing aspirins for a headache, and I heard a terrific bang. Actually, several bangs. Bang! Bang! Bang! I looked out the window and a fireball was flying through the air. Over my neighbour's fence and onto his lawn. In his backyard. It was bright red and round, and I thought it was part of a falling star or something.

"My wife and I ran outside. In our pyjamas. Our neighbour and his wife ran out too. The sky was lit up like it was noon; the smoke and flames were half a mile away, over the roofs of other houses. 'What do you think it is?' my neighbour said. 'A bomb?' I told him I hadn't the vaguest. The fireball had bounced and come to rest about four feet from my neighbour's kitchen. It was a red-hot train wheel. The grass around it was smouldering. His wife went in and out of the kitchen with dishpans of water; she poured them on it until it cooled.

"We climbed in my car and tried to drive to the accident. I had my Nikon with me. The police blocked the road and we couldn't get through. Too bad, because I'm a good photographer and could've taken some good shots. Early the next day the police knocked on my door and said we should clear out. The freight that derailed was loaded with chlorine and propane. Some of the propane cars had blown when a busted axle pitched the train off the tracks. Now they were scared that the rest of the propane might go up or, worse, the chlorine might leak out. Chlorine wrecks your lungs; you get enough of it, it'll kill you dead. Some say it has no smell but they're completely off-base. They put small doses of chlorine in public swimming pools and that's the smell you get, only stronger.

"Everyone in Canada knows what happened next. They evacuated the whole of Mississauga. Two hundred and fifty thousand people. I stayed with my in-laws in Hamilton. The propane didn't ignite and the chlorine didn't leak out. That was the amazing thing about the Mississauga derailment. The potential for a tremendous disaster was there, yet not a solitary soul was killed."

VALUABLE ANTIQUES

"WE FOUND the Rockingham cup and saucer in a little antique shop in Winchester. They had griffins on them. A griffin's a mythical animal with an eagle's head and a lion's body. When Lord Rockingham made a dinner service at his pottery, he'd only put the griffin on one out of twelve pieces. So the ones we had were valuable. We paid four pounds, a fair amount in 1946, but considerably less than their true value.

"Harry packed the Rockinghams in a cabin trunk. We had other valuable chinaware as well. Royal Doulton, Wedgwood, some beautiful wine decanters. We had so much, Harry packed it in two trunks and had to carry some Dresden figurines with him in a suitcase. Some of it we bought at antique stores; some pieces were family heirlooms. We had been visiting my father in Yorkshire and he wanted us to have Grandmother's china for our home in Edmonton.

"The boat voyage was all right. The train certainly wasn't. First, we struck a farm truck at a level crossing in northern Ontario. Then we stopped to remove a cow from the cow-catcher. And then, just outside Melville, we had a terrible jolt. The train halted so fast I was thrown in the aisle. The tender had jumped the tracks. No other cars, just the tender behind the locomotive. The first thing I said to Harry was, 'Oh, dear, the antiques.' 'Never worry, Peggy,' he said. 'They're insured.' They were smashed. The Rockingham, everything; except for the Dresden.

"When we went to the insurance office in Edmonton, the man said our policy covered the boat and not the train. 'And, besides, Mrs. Holmes, there's a small clause in your policy that says we don't pay if the packing wasn't done by a professional packer.' Fancy that. We had handed over good money for a contract that they knew they could easily get out of."

$6 MILLION WRECK

"THE WEATHER was lousy. Eighteen to twenty inches of fresh powder and it wouldn't quit coming down. If memory serves me, there was more snow in the four days before the wreck than there was for all of November for the previous ten years. Not that I'm blaming it on the snow. Speed was the cause, but the weather was a factor and a big one at that. And let's face it, that area's jinxed. Three hundred railway people have died in those mountains in the last hundred years.

"Railwaymen call the place where the wreck happened 'The Hill.' Now that shouldn't be confused with the Big Hill. The Bill Hill's the stretch up near Field. The Hill's up from Revelstoke and it's about ten miles long and comes at the end of forty miles of the most treacherous track in the country — steep grades, hairpin curves, and that awful winter icing.

"I was on the derailed train. I'll describe it but you'll have to hide my identity. It's only been eight years and the railway's still sensitive and I'm not supposed to talk to outsiders about it. It was, you must know, the biggest wreck dollarwise in Canadian history. Six million bucks.

"Okay, here's the dope on it. The unvarnished facts. Going down The Hill in winter, ten miles per hour is considered a safe speed. When we went out of control, we were hitting eighty-five. That was at 12:30 a.m. on November 22, 1977. The train was CPR Extra 5820 West; seven 3,000-horse diesels hauling coal cars to Vancouver. Tim Hamm was the engineer. Clarence Thacker, the trainee engineer, and trainman Greg Tirrell were in the cab with him. When we started down and the speedometer nudged past ten, Clarence pushed the bottom to brake. The shoes gripped but didn't hold. Too much weight — 14,000 tons of coal were pushing us from the rear. Clarence hit the button a couple more times and the speed kept increasing. In less than thirty seconds, we were doing thirty-five.

"Bill Belton, the conductor, was in the caboose with a brakeman, Jim Gullickson. Bill got on the radio-phone and said, 'Tim, what's going on? Aren't you guys using the emergency brakes?' 'Hold onto your hat,'

Tim told him. 'We just did use them and we still can't slow her.' Bill knew what that meant. He was on a runaway plunging down a dark mountainside and, unless a miracle happened, a crash was inevitable.

"The speedometer went to sixty and the train was lurching from side to side so wildly that we thought we'd derail any second. Some of us thought of jumping and taking the chance we wouldn't slam into a cliff, but not Tim. He was a brave bugger. He had made up his mind to stay with the train until the very last.

"That's about when the signal lights appeared. Telling us an east-bound freight was on the same track, three or four miles away. Tim took the radio-phone and warned the engineer on the eastbound to find a siding real quick. Our speed went up. Seventy, seventy-five, eighty. Christ, I was scared. Sweating bricks and my heart drumming. I was sure I was racing to the graveyard.

"At eighty-five, it derailed. A steel bar behind the third diesel snapped as we rounded a bad curve below Flat Creek and barrelled onto a bridge. The cars and engines beyond the third diesel jack-knifed and broke loose. They went flying down an embankment to the Illecillewaet River. Diesel fuel ignited and, oh, what a sight; the sky lit up with explosion after explosion. Five engines and seventy-eight coal cars were wrecked. Telephone poles snapped, track tore up and two railway bridges, solid steel, were destroyed. It took six days to clear the wreckage. A hundred men worked twenty-four-hour shifts. About 1,000 feet of track had to be repaired.

"Without the 14,000 tons forcing it down the slope, Tim and Clarence and Greg were able to brake their engine and bring what was left of the train to a halt. Bill and Jim had detached the caboose from the other cars and used its brakes to stop it before the wreck. I guess a miracle did happen in a way. No one was killed or hurt. That was good news for us but the CPR wasn't very happy. It's hard to be happy when you've gone six million into the hole."

SILVER IN THE LAKE

"THIS IS a map of B.C. Here's Trail. Slocan Lake's north of it. Right here. About twenty-eight miles long and a mile wide. There's a fortune in silver in that lake. A fortune. The CPR operated train barges between Slocan, the town, and Rosebery further up the lake. Up to the 1950s, they operated. The country was rough and there were no roads and the mines and smelters used to float everything on barges. They lost a barge loaded with freight cars in the 1940s. The barge sprung a leak, tilted sideways, and dumped the cars in the water. No, no, the silver wasn't on that one. The silver went into the lake around the turn of the century. The reason escapes me. But the train car fell off a barge and took the silver bars with it. Slocan Lake's 800 to 1,000 feet deep in spots. Nobody knows where the silver went down, and it's still there."

An Ungodly Scream

"I was almost cooked alive once. I was the engineer on a passenger train coming in from Saskatoon and, at Creecy Junction, outside Regina, I suddenly saw a high-octane gas car straddling the track. I was doing sixty and couldn't stop in time. The fireman shouted 'Plug her!' which meant emergency, and then I heard this ungodly scream. A CPR official, new to his job, was riding in the cab with us. He thought he was going to eternity and, in my eighty-three years on this planet, I've never heard such a harrowing scream.

"The gas car wasn't completely sideways on the track. It was at an odd angle. The oil refinery train had just hit a truck and the gas car had jumped the rails on one line and was lying on ours. I braked and prayed and then we hit it with a sickening screech of metal. My side of the engine lifted four feet off the tracks and rolled. It nearly flipped over. The gas car didn't explode. It was knocked off the tracks and rolled. Our train righted itself and kept on going.

"A switcher was clinging to the side of the gas car. The accident happened so fast he just held on tight. When we knocked the car off the tracks, he was heaved onto his belly. He scrambled to his feet and ran like blue blazes. The gas car ruptured and lost 12,000 gallons, but it didn't blow up. That was twenty years ago and I thank my lucky stars whenever I think of it."

QUIET NIGHT AT HOME

"I WAS with the CPR in the Kootenays in the early 1960s. One day this welfare case, a real no-goodnik, comes up to me on the street in Nelson and says to me, 'I thought you'd like to know there's going to be an accident if you don't fix the bridge.' I says to him, 'What bridge?' and he says, 'The bridge near my house. Part of it fell down last night.' 'Listen, mister,' I says to him, 'bridges don't just fall down.' But he dug in his heels and insisted that it did.

"I drove out to his place. A dump that pigs wouldn't live in. There was a small trestle not far from the house and, sure as hell, part of the rails were ripped up and pieces of wood were scattered all over the gully below. I didn't have to be psychic to know what happened. Doukhobours. Russian religious nuts. They were blowing up railway lines because the B.C. government was forcing their kids into public schools.

"The no-goodnik waltzed over while I was inspecting the damage. 'Didn't you hear the explosion?' I says. 'What explosion?' he says. 'I had some friends over last night to try my home brew and we didn't hear nothing.' I had to laugh. Whatever it was he and his friends had been drinking, it had to be the most powerful stuff ever brewed in the Kootenays."

SOMEBODY MADE A MISTAKE

"IT WAS unnerving, to say the least. I was sitting on the Dayliner to Calgary, reading a client's file. I heard the brakes squeal and I felt a hard thud and when I looked out the window, a truck tire flew past. A pick-up carrying hay had taken too long crossing the tracks at Olds and the train had banged its rear end, sending hay and a back tire flying. The truck spun in a circle five or six times and when it stopped the driver climbed out, looking petrified. The Dayliner engineer talked to him for fifteen minutes and then we continued on.

"I gathered that was it. I mean, one accident during a short, three-hour run should be the limit, shouldn't it? I settled back into the files.

I'm a computer consultant and I was meeting a client in Calgary. This happened in March 1983. I had boarded the train at eight in the morning in Edmonton. Dayliners are lightweight diesels. They can go up to ninety-five miles per hour and need only two men, a conductor and an engineer, to run them. The problem is, the Edmonton-to-Calgary corridor has so many unsignalled crossings that the trains are known for hitting vehicles. *Alberta Report*, in fact, quoted a Dayliner engineer as saying he has a near-miss every trip. 'In one year,' he said, 'I hit four cars and a cow. It shows you the cows are smarter than humans.'

"So be it. About ten minutes south of Olds, it got foggy. I was staring out the window and wondering if it might rain or snow, and then it happened. The train lurched so abruptly that my head slammed the glass. There was a terrible screeching and grinding and, before I had time to react, it lurched again and my head hit the back of the seat. Blood gushed from my cheek and nose. All around me there was an awful, awful scene. Seats pulled from their rivets, windows shattered, people crying and moaning, the car filling with steam from the broken heating system. I stumbled to my feet. The front of the train was caved in; metal and suitcases and seats were twisted together.

"The conductor had been flung from one end to the other. He was lying on the floor, both legs broken. The engineer's name was Stewart. The conductor was calling to him, 'Stewart, you all right? Can you answer me, Stewart?' There was a young girl, a waitress at Chi-Chi's. She was looking for a first-aid kit and she saw a hand protruding from beneath a pile of seats. She squeezed the fingers and the hand squeezed back so she knew he was alive.

"I staggered out the door. I went to an AGT booth to phone for help but, wouldn't you know it, the phone was out of order. A woman went by me and flagged a car on the highway and they got help from the town of Didsbury. Five people died, including the engineer, Stewart. The train had been switched onto a siding by mistake and crashed into a line of tankers filled with sulphur. I had a broken jaw and that's healed now but I doubt I'll ever get over the crash. I'm still shaking."

PAYING THEIR RESPECTS

"A TRAIN full of us soldiers went from Shilo to Chilliwack in 1957. When we were in the B.C. mountains, the train stopped and we were lined up beside the track. An officer pointed to a small cairn and said this was where the Canoe River wreck killed all those soldiers going to Korea. The CO said a few words and we bowed our heads in silence. It was, I thought, a splendid gesture. Apparently, for years after the wreck, every troop train that travelled through the canyon would stop near the cairn and the soldiers would pay their respects."

JOURNEY'S END

My last train ride was nearly over. In the soft morning light, The Canadian was rushing through yellow grasslands east of Calgary. An American behind me was becoming excited at his first glimpse of the Rockies. Mr. Brown joined me. He asked where I was going and I said to the place where all of my travels eventually finished, a farmhouse in northern Alberta.

Mr. Brown had spoken to me the previous day. About his globe-trotting ventures since he retired from the civil service. Now he began to talk about his wife. She had died in 1976 after thirty-five years of a good marriage. Every year or so, he returned to Vancouver to visit friends. While he was there, he never failed to walk past the house he and his wife had occupied for more than twenty years, a stucco bungalow in Burnaby. He never spoke to the new owners. He studied the flowerbeds, the crabapple tree, and the fence he'd put up and then he walked to the bus stop. The house where he had been happy was, I realized, the place where all his journeys ended.

WHAT HAVE I DONE?

"I'LL NEVER forget my reaction when I got off the train at Pikwitonei. I looked at the two grubby, little stores, the cemetery, the Anglican church, and the decrepit schoolhouse and I thought, Is this all there is to this burg? What have I done to myself? What I'd done was sign a one-year contract. I was twenty-three and fresh from the University of Manitoba, and in 1947 $89 a month for teaching in a Cree settlement was better than starving.

"Or was it? A big, old Cree woman married to an Irishman followed me off the train. She was drunk, and travelling up from the 'Peg she swore and yelled and was a general, all-round nuisance. I had sat looking at her and praying, Please, Lord, don't make her the mother of one of my students. When she got off at the same stop I did, I breathed a deep sigh, and dragged my trunk over to the school. The building had been constructed in 1887. Hand-hewn logs chinked with moss. Inside, it was unbelievably dirty. Nothing had been washed for years and the schoolroom had an old oildrum you put logs in. Over and over, I kicked myself for signing the contract and jumping into what was obviously about to be the worst winter of my life.

"It wasn't the worst, after all. It was wonderful. The conditions were deplorable — forty-eight students in one room, grades One to Eleven — and the woman from the train did have a daughter in my class: a hellion who delighted in beating up the younger kids until they bled. But the Cree were marvellous — warm, gentle, and kind-hearted. I'd sneak over to the railway coal dock at night and fill my bucket for the stove. The Indians found out and started leaving firewood at my door. And food. In the morning, there'd be moose meat or fish. The first day of school, one of them scared the hell out of me. He pounded on the door at 4:00 a.m. He had brought his grandson. They had walked miles and miles and wanted to be sure they were at school in time.

"The train was Pikwitonei's connection to the outside world. It was the only entertainment I had, and I'd watch them unload some utterly mundane object, like a carton of canned fruit, just for diversion. The Anglican minister came by train once a month and, oh, yes, the school superintendent came too — Mr. McDonald, a short, severe Scot in a dark suit. He belonged to the same Masonic lodge in Winnipeg as my father but that didn't help me none. He reported me for teaching in improper clothing — a sports shirt and no jacket. Hundreds of miles into the bush, teaching poverty-stricken Cree kids, and he wanted me to dress up.

"I often think of Pikwitonei. I'm a geological consultant with Golden Eagle now and living a totally different lifestyle. Those Indians were so kind. When I left the settlement in the spring, they made me one of the most endearing gifts I've ever had — a pair of moosehide moccasins and gauntlets."

SHORT-TERM GUESTS

"LET'S SAY it was the late 1930s. I won't say where I was coming from or why I was heading to Calgary. My wife would scream blue murder if she read this and recognized me. On the train, I met another young, struggling businessman like myself and when I commented that I hated paying the Palliser's healthy rates, he wrote down the address of a boarding house that he said accepted short-term guests. Breakfast, dinner, and a clean room, at a fraction of what the Palliser charged.

"The address was on Ninth Street West. The number's inscribed in my brain for eternity: 1813. I hired a taxi at the CPR station. The driver peered at my suitcases oddly but didn't utter a word. As we crossed Eighth Street, I remarked that I hoped the boarding house I was going to wasn't filled with gloomy, unemployed men. He burst out laughing. The stranger had played a joke on me. He had presented me with the address of a notorious brothel, Pearl Miller's.

"I said I was shocked and told the driver to take me to the York Hotel. Two nights afterwards, a client and I were having beers in the dingy tavern and he said he felt like having some fun. I pulled out the slip of paper with Pearl Miller's address. And that's as far as I'll proceed with this story. Although, I might add that Pearl Miller's became my destination every time I was in the city. The Ninth Street house and the one she had on Ninth Avenue during the war.

"She's gone now. To her heavenly reward. She was a notorious madam but, in her old age, Pearl turned to religion and convinced many a girl to desert the brothel for the Bible. The house on Ninth Street's gone too. The last time I went past the spot there was an apartment block on the site."

SATURDAY NIGHT AT PORT STANLEY

"WHAT WAS the name of the pavilion? I wish I could remember but it was forty years ago and I'd have to sit and think a while to get it right.

I do remember everything else about the place. A large, wood building with a gabled roof. The town was Port Stanley, and on Saturdays the train from St. Thomas was jammed with servicemen. All from the training school the Air Force was operating in, appropriately, a former mental institution. The train ride wasn't long, perhaps an hour, even though we had to change trains at London.

"The Saturday night dance at Port Stanley. Wow, that sure does bring back memories. A big, revolving, mirrored ball; 400 people crammed in; so hot and stuffy the management opened the windows to catch the breezes from the lake. Mart Kenny played there and, I think, the Casa Loma Orchestra. The girls were from Port Stanley, Alymer, Dutton, all along the lakeshore, and there were never enough to go around.

"The washrooms were the pits. You'd line up outside, gritting your teeth, especially after downing half a mickey, and it was a filthy stink-hole inside. My pals and I started going outside the pavilion. A guy would be strolling on the beach with a girl, hoping for an easy score, and suddenly he'd come across three drunken airmen pissing in Lake Ontario. That killed all notions of romance really fast.

"I'd do sambas and waltzes and foxtrots until my legs were wobbly and sore and then I'd head for the station. If I didn't make it to London by 2:00 A.M., I'd miss the last train to St. Thomas and have to walk five miles. Under normal circumstances, five miles isn't a lot but when you've danced all night, it's positively painful. God, how I remember those nights when I'd be dragging myself up the road at 4:00 A.M., cursing the train, the pavilion, and everything else in the world."

A MECCA FOR TRAVELLERS

"CUTE AS a bug. Tiny hands and feet. Red hair, cut short. And great, big eyes. I can still picture her, standing in the dining room, writing down orders. Paying no mind to the men looking her over. I honestly can't tell you what the biggest attraction was, the redheaded waitress or the hotel itself, but whenever the train took me to Darlingford, I stopped at the Empire.

"If I'm not mistaken, an English couple owned the hotel. The Whites. She played the piano and Mr. White the violin. Tunes like 'Daisy' and 'Pack Up Your Troubles.' You'd be in a wonderful dining room, the walls decorated with paintings of Manitoba outdoors scenes, and the Whites were in there with you, playing while you ate. It was the place in Darlingford the train travellers zoomed right to. The regular boarders had their own tables, and the train people sat by themselves. A one-armed man once played a harmonica, and a French girl sang songs for the boys lost overseas in the Great War.

"A poolroom was next door. With a barber chair in it. I'd go from the train, have a ten-cent shave and a two-bit haircut, and shoot a game of billiards before having a meal at the Empire. Poolrooms were off-limits to females. Any woman who dared to step over the threshold into the poolroom was peddling her wares, if you catch my meaning. One time the cute waitress stuck her head inside the door and made a saucy face at me. She was a devil. Lots of fun. I should put an ad in the *Free Press*. Remember me? Bill Bowen? I was at the Empire in 1920 and I'd like to see you again. I may do that some day. The notion comes across me now and then."

FAVOURITE BAR

"WHEN I MOVED from Edmonton to Montreal in 1948, I stored my bags in the luggage room at Windsor Station and phoned a friend who had said he'd pick me up. He was delayed for some reason and I had two hours to kill. I walked out of the station and turned right. Boy, was I excited. This was it, the big city! I was going to live in the middle of all this marvellous action! I crossed the street and came to a sign on an old building — Alberta Lounge. This was a great surprise. Imagine, a touch of my home province here in downtown Montreal. I don't know what I expected. Probably waiters in cowboy outfits, bar stools made of saddles, and a singer trying to sound like Wilf Carter.

"I went in and it was nothing of the sort. Just a big, dark room full of people drinking; the only difference was, they were drinking in two languages. I was nineteen but I looked older and when I ordered a beer, I was served it. A piano player came out. A Negro. He was great.

His fingers danced on the keys. I had my beer and I eventually met my friend. After that night, the Alberta Lounge was a haunt for me. I was transferred to Toronto in the 1950s and when I took the train up I'd nearly always check into the hotel and then wander over to the lounge. It was a kind of home away from home. The piano player went on to bigger things and I always like to say, I saw Oscar Peterson when he wasn't a star."

OYSTERS AND ICE

"THE OTHER NIGHT I was at the Fort Garry for a meeting and I saw the damnedest thing. Possibly it's a regular service at the hotel and possibly it isn't. The front page of the *Free Press* had been carefully pinned to the wall above the urinal in the men's room off the main lobby. At eye-level so you could catch up on world affairs while you were doing your business. A nifty idea but Granny wouldn't have approved. She lived at the Fort Garry in the 1920s. She swore that newspapers were the devil's instruments because they carried Stanfield underwear ads.

"She was a terrific person, despite her puritanical streak. She could've given you some train stories. Could she ever. She cooked at the Regina station restaurant before World War I. Exquisite menus — oysters and Chateau Lafite-Rothschild for $1.50. Some waiters deliberately served slow if they realized you had to catch a certain train. You'd be rushed and wouldn't want to wait in line for your change and they'd pocket it.

"Another job she had was cooking for work gangs at Smithers, B.C. Before they were refrigerated, the boxcars used blocks of ice to keep food fresh. The trains parked beside the lake at Smithers and the gangs cut the ice when it was two feet thick. Some days, they'd load a hundred boxcars.

"No matter why I was in Winnipeg, visiting Granny was the most important reason for my being there. My parents died when I was young and she was all the family I had. She had old photographs on her walls, a red velvet settee, and a gramophone she never listened to. She asked me the same questions when I came up from Steinbach.

How was the train trip, and did I meet anyone interesting? I almost wished I was in a wreck and then I'd have a good story for Granny but, alas, nothing ever happened."

A PARK IN CHAPLEAU

"PEOPLE RIDING trains don't pay much attention to the park at Chapleau. It's smack-dab behind the depot, at the corner of Elm and Monk, but all they do is run over to Houde's store and stock up on ice cream and grapes and cigarettes. VIA should have a loudspeaker on its trains and the conductor's voice would come over it and say, 'Here's Chapleau, Ontario. There's a park you mustn't miss.' I go through the park every time the train brings me home. Nope, I'm not a railway man. I'm a carpenter. My grandfather was on the trains. He was a 'Outlaw' at Dunvegan. They named them the Outlaws because they'd be canned elsewhere and the Dunvegan line in northern Alberta was one of the few that hired them. The conditions were rough. Fourteen- and fifteen-hour days and rotten food and they never changed the sheets in the bunkhouse; you'd lie in dirt and old sweat all night. He was a good man, my grandfather. I guess that's why I go through the park. Out of respect for him and the others.

"What others? Well, there's a black marble slab in the park with names on it. The names of one hundred railwaymen who died in accidents in the district in the last hundred years. Rae and Turcott are two I remember off-hand. And Desbais. He's the most recent, 1980. There's an old steam locomotive in the park too. I don't know where it used to run but it's got a CPR beaver on it. The train doesn't mean much to me. It's the marble slab and all those names. Like my grandfather did, they put their lives into building the railway into something worthwhile in this country. I like to think that when I walk by, they look down from above and say to each other, 'There's old Tom taking his hat off to us again. It's good to know somebody cares.'"

SENTIMENTAL JOURNEY

INDEX

INDEX